WHITE CHRYSANTHEMUM

WHITE CHRYSANTHEMUM

MARY LYNN BRACHT

Chatto & Windus

LONDON

1 3 5 7 9 10 8 6 4 2

Chatto & Windus, an imprint of Vintage,
20 Vauxhall Bridge Road,
London SW1V 2SA

Chatto & Windus is part of the Penguin Random House group of companies
whose addresses can be found at global.penguinrandomhouse.com

Penguin
Random House
UK

Copyright © Mary Lynn Bracht 2018

Mary Lynn Bracht has asserted her right to be identified as the author of this
Work in accordance with the Copyright, Designs and Patents Act 1988

First published in the UK by Chatto & Windus in 2018
First published in the US by G. P. Putnam's Sons in 2018

penguin.co.uk/vintage

A CIP catalogue record for this book is available from the British Library

HB ISBN 9781784741440
TPB ISBN 9781784741457

Printed and bound by Clays Ltd, St Ives plc

For Nico

It is nearly dawn, and the semi-darkness casts strange shadows along the footpath. Hana distracts her mind so that she doesn't imagine creatures reaching for her ankles. She is following her mother down to the sea. Her nightdress streams behind her in the soft wind. Quiet footsteps pad behind them, and she knows without looking back that her father is following with her little sister still asleep in his arms. On the shore, a handful of women are already waiting for them. She recognises their faces in the rising dawn light, but the shaman is a stranger. The holy woman wears a red and royal blue traditional hanbok dress, and as soon as they descend upon the sand, the shaman begins to dance.

The huddling figures step away from her twirling motions and form into a small group, mesmerised by the shaman's grace. She chants a greeting to the Dragon Sea God, welcoming him to their island, beckoning him to travel through the bamboo gates towards Jeju's tranquil shores. The sun sparkles on *the horizon, a pinpoint of iridescent gold, and Hana blinks at the newness of the coming day. It is a forbidden ceremony, outlawed by the occupying Japanese government, but her mother is insistent upon holding a traditional gut ritual before her first dive as a fully-fledged* haenyeo. *The shaman is asking for safety and a bountiful catch. As the shaman repeats the words over and over, Hana's mother nudges her shoulder and together they bow, foreheads touching the wet sand, to honour the Dragon Sea God's imminent arrival. As she stands, her sister's sleepy voice whispers, 'I want to dive, too,' and the yearning in her voice tugs on Hana's heart. 'You will be standing here one day soon, Little Sister, and I will be right beside you to welcome you,' she whispers back, confident of the future that lies ahead of them.*

Salty seawater drips down her temple, and she wipes it away with the back of her hand. I am a haenyeo *now, Hana thinks, watching the shaman twirl white ribbons in circles along the shore. She reaches for her sister's small hand. Side by side they stand, listening to the waves tumbling onto the beach. The ocean is the only sound as the small group silently acknowledges her acceptance into their order. When the sun rises fully above the ocean waves, she will dive with the* haenyeo *in deeper waters and take her place among the women of the sea. But first they must return to their homes in secret, hidden from prying eyes.*

》-《

Hana, come home. Her sister's voice is loud in her ears, jolting her back to the present, to the room and the soldier still asleep on the floor beside her. The ceremony fades into the darkness. Desperate not to let it go, Hana squeezes her eyes shut.

She has been held captive for nearly two months, but time moves painfully slowly in this place. She tries not to look back on what she has endured, what they force her to do, what they command her to be. At home, she was someone else, something else.

Ages seem to have passed since then, and Hana feels nearer to the grave than to memories of home. Her mother's face swimming up to meet her in the waters. The salt water on her lips. Fragments of memories of a happier place.

The ceremony was one of power and strength, just like the women of the sea, just like Hana. The soldier lying next to her stirs. He will not defeat her, she promises herself. She lies awake all night imagining how she will escape.

Hana

Hana is sixteen and knows nothing but a life lived under occupation. Japan annexed Korea in 1910, and Hana speaks fluent Japanese, is educated in Japanese history and culture, and is prohibited from speaking, reading or writing in her native Korean. She is a second-class citizen with second-class rights in her own country, but that does not diminish her Korean pride. Hana and her mother are *haenyeo*, women of the sea, and they work for themselves. They live in a tiny village on Jeju Island's southern coast and dive in a cove hidden from the main road that leads into town. Hana's father is a fisherman. He navigates the South Sea with the other village men, evading imperial fishing boats that loot Korea's coastal waters for produce to repatriate back to Japan. Hana and her mother only interact with Japanese soldiers when they go to market to sell their day's catch. It creates a sense of freedom not many on the other side of the island, or even on mainland Korea, a hundred miles to the north, enjoy. The occupation is a taboo topic, especially at market; only the brave dare to broach it, and even then only in whispers and behind cupped hands. The villagers are tired of the heavy taxes, the forced *donations* to the war effort, and the taking of men to fight on the front lines and children to work in factories in Japan.

On Hana's island, diving is women's work. Their bodies suit the cold depths of the ocean better than men's. They can hold their breath longer, swim deeper, and keep their body temperature warmer, so for centuries, Jeju women have enjoyed a rare independence. Hana followed her mother into the sea at an early age. Learning to swim began the moment she could lift her head on her own, though she was nearly eleven the first time her mother took her into the deeper waters and showed her how to cut an abalone from a rock on the sea floor. In her excitement, Hana lost her breath sooner than expected and had to race upwards for air. Her lungs burned. When she finally broke the surface, she breathed in more water than oxygen. Sputtering with her chin barely above the waves, she was disorientated and began to panic. A sudden swell rolled over her, submerging her in an instant. She swallowed more water as her head dipped beneath the surface.

With one hand, her mother lifted Hana's face above the water. Hana gulped in air between racking coughs. Her nose and throat burned. Her mother's hand, secured at the nape of her neck, reassured her until she recovered.

'Always look to the shore when you rise, or you can lose your way,' her mother said, and turned Hana to face the land. There on the sand, her younger sister sat protecting the buckets containing the day's catch. 'Look for your sister after each dive. Never forget. If you see her, you are safe.'

When Hana's breaths had returned to normal, her mother released her and commenced diving with a slow forward somersault down into the ocean's depths. Hana watched her sister a few moments longer, taking in the serene sight of her resting on the beach, waiting for her family to return from the sea. Fully recovered, Hana swam to the buoy and added her abalone to her mother's catch, which was stowed safely in a net. Then she performed her own somersault, down into the ocean's thrumming interior, in search of another sea creature to add to their harvest.

Her sister was too young to dive with them when they were that far from the shore. Sometimes, when Hana surfaced, she would look first to the shore to find her sister chasing after seagulls, waving sticks wildly in the air. She was like a butterfly dancing across Hana's sightline.

Hana was already seven years old when her sister was finally born. She had worried she would be an only child her whole life. She had wished for a younger sibling for so long – all of her friends had two, three, or sometimes even four brothers and sisters to play with each day and to share the burden of household chores, while she had to suffer everything alone. But then her mother became pregnant, and Hana swelled with such hope that she beamed each time she caught a glimpse of her mother's growing stomach.

'You're much fatter today, aren't you, Mother?' she asked the morning of her sister's birth.

'Very, very fat and uncomfortable!' her mother replied, and tickled Hana's taut stomach.

She tumbled onto her back and giggled with delight. Once she had caught her breath, Hana sat beside her mother and placed a hand on the outermost curve of her bulging stomach.

'My sister or brother must be nearly done, right, Mother?'

'Nearly done? You speak as though I'm boiling rice inside my belly, silly girl!'

'Not rice, my new sister . . . or brother,' Hana added quickly, and felt a timid kick against her hand. 'When will she, or he, come out?'

'Such an impatient daughter sits before me.' Her mother shook her head in resignation. 'Which would you prefer, a sister or a brother?'

Hana knew the correct answer was a brother, so that her father would have a son to share his fishing knowledge with, but in her head she answered differently. *I hope you have a daughter, so that one day, she can swim in the sea with me.*

Her mother went into labour that evening, and when they showed Hana her baby sister, she couldn't contain her happiness. She smiled the widest smile her face had ever known, yet tried with all her might to speak as though she was disappointed.

'I'm sorry that she is not a son, Mother, truly sorry,' Hana said, shaking her head in mock sorrow.

Then Hana turned to her father and pulled his shirtsleeve. He leaned down, and she cupped her hands around his ear.

'Father, I must confess something to you. I'm very sorry for you, that she is not a son to learn your fishing skills, but . . .' She took a deep breath before finishing. 'But I'm so happy I have a sister to swim with.'

'Is that so?' he asked.

'Yes, but don't tell Mother.'

At seven years old, Hana was not skilled in the art of whispering, and gentle laughter rippled through the group of her parents' closest friends. Hana grew quiet. Her ears burned. She hid behind her father and peeked at her mother from underneath his arm to see if she had also heard. Her mother gazed at her eldest daughter and then looked down at the hungry infant suckling her breast and whispered to her newest daughter, just loud enough for Hana to hear.

'You are the most loved little sister in the whole of Jeju Island. Do you know that? No one will ever love you more than your big sister.'

When she looked up at Hana, she motioned for her to come to her side. The adults in the room grew quiet as Hana knelt beside her mother.

'You are her protector now, Hana,' her mother said in a serious tone.

Hana gazed at her tiny baby sister. She reached out to caress the black tuft of hair sprouting from her scalp.

'She's so soft,' Hana said with wonder.

'Did you hear what I said? You are a big sister now, and with that comes responsibilities, and the first one is that of protector. I won't always be around; diving in the sea and selling at the market keeps us fed, and it will be left up to you to watch over your little sister from now on when I can't. Can I rely on you?' her mother asked, her voice stern.

Hana's hand shot back to her side. She bowed her head and dutifully answered.

'Yes, Mother, I will keep her safe. I promise.'

'A promise is forever, Hana. Never forget.'

'I will remember, Mother, always,' Hana said, her eyes glued onto her little sister's peacefully dozing face. Milk dripped from the side of the baby's open mouth, and her mother wiped it with a swipe of her thumb.

As the years passed, and Hana began to dive with her mother in the deeper waters, she grew accustomed to seeing her sister in the distance, the girl who shared her blankets at night and whispered silly stories into the darkness, until she finally succumbed to sleep. The girl who laughed at everything and anything, a sound that made everyone nearby join in. She became Hana's anchor, to the shore and to life.

〉〈

Hana knows that protecting her sister means keeping her away from Japanese soldiers. Her mother has drilled the lesson into her: *Never let them see you! And most of all, do not let yourself be caught alone with one!* Her mother's words of warning are filled with an ominous fear, and at sixteen Hana feels lucky this has never happened. But that changes on a hot summer day.

It is late in the afternoon, long after the other divers have gone to the market, when Hana first sees Corporal Morimoto. Her mother wanted to fill an extra net for a friend who was ill and couldn't dive that day. Her mother is always the first to offer help. Hana comes up for air and looks to the shore. Her sister is squatting on the sand, shading her eyes to look out towards Hana and their mother. At nine years of age, her sister is now old enough to stay on the shore alone but still too young to swim in the deeper waters with Hana and her mother. She is small for her age and not yet a strong swimmer.

Hana has just found a large conch and is ready to shout at her sister to express her joy, when she notices a man heading towards the beach. Treading water so that she can lift herself higher to see him more clearly, Hana realises the man is a Japanese soldier. Her stomach knots into a sudden cramp. Why is he here? They never come this far from the villages. She scans the beach within the cove to see if there are more, but he's the only one. He is heading straight for her sister.

A ridge of rocks shields her sister from his view, but it won't do so for long. If he stays on his current path, he will stumble upon her, and then he will take her away – ship her off to a factory in Japan like the other young girls who disappear from the villages. Her sister isn't strong enough to survive factory work or the brutal conditions they are subjected to. She is too young, and too loved, to be taken away.

Searching the horizon for her mother, Hana realises she is down below, oblivious to the Japanese soldier heading towards the water's edge. She has no time to wait for her mother to resurface, and even if she did, her mother is too far away, hunting near the edge of the reef where it drops into a cavernous void with no sea floor in sight for miles. It is Hana's job to protect her little sister. She made a promise to her mother, and she intends to keep it.

Hana dives beneath the waves, swimming at full speed towards the beach. She can only hope to reach her sister before the soldier does. If she can distract him long enough, perhaps her sister can slip away and hide in the nearby cove, and then Hana can escape back into the ocean. Surely he wouldn't follow her into the water?

The current crushes against her as though desperate to push her back out to sea, towards safety. Panicking, she breaches the water's surface and takes in a deep breath, catching a glimpse of the soldier's progress. He is still headed for the rocky ledge.

She starts to swim above the waves, aware she is exposing herself but unable to bear staying too long beneath the water for fear of missing the soldier's advance. Hana is halfway to her sister when she sees him stop. He digs in his pocket for something. Plunging her head back into the water, she swims even faster. In her next breath, she sees him light a cigarette. With every subsequent breath, he moves just a little more. He blows out a puff of smoke, takes a drag, breathes it out, again and again with each lift of her head, until the last breath, when he looks out at the sea and notices Hana's race towards him.

Only ten metres away from the shore, she hopes he can't see her little sister from where he stands. She is still hidden by the rocks, but not for long. Her small hands are on the stony sand, and she is beginning to push herself up to standing. Hana can't shout at her to stay down. She swims faster.

Hana pitches beneath the surface, pulling the water out of her way with each stroke, until her hands touch the sandy ground. Then she shoots to her feet and runs through the last few metres of shallow water. If he has called out to her as she runs to the ledge, she can't hear him. Her heart thunders in her ears, blocking out all sound. It feels like she has travelled across half the earth in that sprint to the shore, but she can't stop yet. Her feet fly across the sand towards her sister, who is smiling at her in ignorance and preparing to greet Hana. Before her sister can speak, Hana lunges at her, seizing her shoulders and knocking her to the ground.

She covers her sister's mouth with her hand to keep her from crying out. When she sees Hana's face hovering above her, she knows better than to cry. Hana gives her a look only a little sister would understand. She pushes her sister into the sand, wishing she could bury her to hide her from the soldier's sight, but she has no time.

'Where did you go?' the soldier calls down to Hana. He is standing on a low rock ledge overlooking the beach. If he stands on the edge he could look down and see them both lying beneath him. 'Has the mermaid transformed into a girl?'

His boots crunch on the stones above them. Her sister's trembling body feels fragile in Hana's hands. Her fear is contagious, and Hana, too, begins to tremble. She realises there is nowhere for her sister to run. From his vantage point, he can see in every direction. They will both have to escape into the ocean, but her sister can't swim for very long. Hana can remain in the deep water for hours, but her little sister will drown if the soldier decides to wait them out. She has no plan. No escape. The realisation sits heavy in her gut.

Slowly, she releases her sister's mouth and takes one last look into her frightened face before standing. His eyes are sharp, and she feels their piercing touch as they creep over her body.

'Not a girl, but a grown woman,' he says, and lets out a low, grumbling laugh.

He is wearing a beige uniform and field boots, with a cap that shades his face. His eyes are black like the rocky ledge beneath his feet. Hana is still recovering from her swim to shore, and each time she gasps for breath, he glances at her chest. Her white cotton diving shirt is thin and she hurriedly covers her breasts with her hair. Her cotton shorts drip water down her shivering legs.

'What are you hiding from me?' he asks, trying to peer over the ledge.

'Nothing,' Hana quickly answers. She steps away from her sister, willing his gaze to follow her. 'It's just . . . a special catch. I didn't want you to think it was not claimed. It's mine, you see.' She hauls one of the buckets onto the ledge, leading him further away from where her sister lies.

His attention remains on Hana. After a pause, he glances out to sea and up and down the beach.

'Why are you still here? All the other divers have gone off to the market.'

'My friend is ill, so I'm catching her share so she won't go hungry.' It is a partial truth and comes easily.

He keeps looking around as though searching for witnesses. Hana looks out to her mother's buoy, but she is not there. She still hasn't seen the soldier or even noticed Hana's absence. Hana begins to worry her mother is in trouble beneath the surface. Too many thoughts flood her mind. He starts to inspect the edge of the rock ledge once more, as though he senses her sister's presence beneath him. Hana thinks quickly.

'I can sell them to you, if you're hungry. Perhaps you can take some back to your friends.'

He doesn't seem convinced, so she tries to push the bucket closer to him. Seawater spills over the rim, and he quickly sidesteps to avoid its drenching his boots.

'I'm so sorry,' she says quickly, steadying the bucket.

'Where is your family?' he suddenly asks.

His question catches Hana off guard. She looks over the water and sees her mother's head duck beneath a wave. Her father's boat is far out to sea. She and her sister are alone with this soldier. She turns back to him in time to see two more soldiers. They are heading towards her.

Her mother's words echo in her mind: *Most of all, do not let yourself be caught alone with one.* Nothing Hana says will save her now. She has no power or autonomy against imperial soldiers. They may do with her as they wish, she knows this, but she is not the only one at risk. She tears her eyes away from the rolling waves that beckon her to dive back in, to escape.

'They're dead.' The words sound true even to her own ears. If she is an orphan, then there is no one to silence for her abduction. Her family will be safe.

'A tragic mermaid,' he says, and smiles. 'There *are* treasures to be found at sea.'

'What have you got there, Corporal Morimoto?' one of the approaching soldiers calls out.

Morimoto doesn't look back at them, his eyes remaining on Hana. The two men flank her, one on either side. Morimoto nods at them, a curt tip of his head, before trudging back up the sand the way he came. The soldiers grab her arms and drag her behind him.

Hana doesn't scream. If her sister tried to help, they would just take her, too. Hana will not break her promise to keep her sister safe. So she goes without saying a word, but her legs defend her in wordless opposition by refusing to work. They hang from her body like useless logs, weighing her down, but it doesn't deter the soldiers. They grip her harder and raise her off the ground so that her toes drag thin trails in the sand.

Emi

A thin orange line streaks across the horizon, illuminating the grey December sky above the dark waters of the South Sea. Emi's knees protest in the cold predawn hours. Her left leg feels heavy. It drags slightly behind her as she shuffles down to the shore. The other women are already there, donning wetsuits and masks. Only a handful of the usual divers stand beside the water's edge, shivering in various stages of undress. Emi blames the wintry morning for the scant attendance. In her younger days, she too would have thought twice about leaving her warm bed to dive beneath icy waters, but age has toughened her.

Halfway across the rocky beach, Emi can hear JinHee telling the women a story. It's one of Emi's favourites. She and JinHee grew up together. Their friendship has spanned nearly seven decades, surviving two wars. JinHee's arms swing wildly like a broken windmill, and Emi listens for the dramatic pause that always comes before the laughter. A gust of wind lifts a blue tarp into the air, revealing an old fishing boat, its white paint peeled into curls. A cackle of laughter chases the wind, and the boat disappears beneath the blue plastic sheet. Her friends' weather-roughened voices bring pleasure to her ears. JinHee sees Emi hobbling towards them at her turtle's pace and raises her hand in her faithful *hello* salute. The other ladies turn and wave in welcome.

'We're waiting for you,' JinHee shouts. 'Late riser today?'

Emi doesn't waste her energy responding. She is carefully scanning the sharp stones on the beach to avoid slipping. Her knees have loosened up, making her limp less prominent. Her left leg nearly steps in time with her right. The other divers wait for her to reach them before they trail into the water. Emi is already wearing her wetsuit. Living in a house steps from the beach has its perks, even if it is only a tiny shack. Her children are both grown and living in Seoul, so all she needs is a place to sleep and cook her meals, and a shack is nothing more and nothing less than that. JinHee hands Emi a mask when she arrives.

'What's this?' Emi asks. 'I have my own.' She lifts her mask from her styrofoam cooler and shows it to JinHee.

'That old thing? It's cracked and the strap has broken a hundred times.' JinHee spits onto the beach. 'This one's new. My son brought me two from Taejon.' She taps the glass of an identical mask already strapped to her face.

Emi gives the new mask a good looking over. It's bright red and has *TEMPERED* printed on the glass. It's pretty, and she feels tired when she looks back at her old one. The rubber strap is tied in double knots in three places, and there's a chip on the left side of the glass that obscures her view underwater. It hasn't leaked yet, but it will one of these days.

'Go ahead, put it on, you'll see,' JinHee urges.

Emi hesitates. She fingers the shiny plate glass. In the sea, the other ladies have already released their buoys to mark their spots. Their heads bobble next to the floating orange buoys, and one after the other they dive beneath the gentle morning waves. Emi watches them for a moment before handing the mask back to JinHee.

'I brought it for you,' JinHee says, and pushes it away. 'I don't want it. I only need one new one.'

JinHee mutters to herself as she waddles towards the water, her fins slapping the surface with each step. Emi knows she can say nothing to change JinHee's mind. Her stubbornness is second to none. Looking down at the two masks, Emi holds them in front of her, side by side. Her black mask looks ancient next to the red one, but it would be a shame for her to accept JinHee's gift. She wouldn't be able to put it to good use for very long.

'Yours is cracked, and you know you go too deep. It'll explode one of these days, and then you'll be blind!' JinHee shouts over her shoulder before she dives beneath the water to swim out to her favourite spot.

Emi places the red mask inside JinHee's cooler and stoops to put on her fins. Then she follows her old friend into the sea. The cold sends a shock wave through her bones.

JinHee waits for Emi to come up beside her, the water lapping at her chest.

'What was it today?' JinHee asks.

Somehow JinHee always knows when Emi has had the nightmare. Perhaps her old friend can see the evidence in Emi's expression, or maybe another silver hair has grown overnight. Without fail JinHee will demand to know which demon has swallowed the faceless girl.

This morning, Emi doesn't want to recall the creature that awoke her in such a fright, but she knows her friend will never let it rest. Emi stares at the calm waters and lets herself remember.

There's the voice she only hears in her dreams. It is a girl's voice, at once familiar but also strange, so that Emi does not recognise the speaker. The girl calls Emi's name; her voice wafts towards Emi in waves, as though travelling from across a thousand leagues of empty sea.

She wishes she could call to the girl, but as is often the case in dreams, she cannot speak. She can only stand on the rocky cliff and listen to the girl's cries upon the whirling wind, as Emi clings to the razor-sharp rock with her bare toes, straining to see the small figure through her wild hurricane hair, which lashes against her face.

A tiny boat rides the choppy waves towards the cliff where Emi stands, and a young girl sits in the boat calling her name. Her face is a white featureless dot amidst the dark sea. Emi lets out a silent scream as the girl tumbles overboard, swallowed by a great blue whale that is sometimes a grey squid and at other times a terrifying shark, but last night, it was a whale, midnight blue with razor-sharp teeth like a monster. Then she awoke, clutching her throat, parched and sweating, and the dream faded from her waking memory, leaving her with an image of a girl lost to a war long ago.

'The squid, I think,' Emi tells JinHee, though she is not certain why she lied. Perhaps it is easier to listen to JinHee harp on about a false dream rather than a true one. 'Yes, it was the squid.' She nods her head determinedly, as though that is the end of the conversation, but JinHee won't let her off so easily.

'Was it grey again? Or white this time?' She prods Emi. 'Come on, I'm trying to help you.'

'What does the colour matter?' Emi shakes her head, wiping a lock of hair from her eyes. 'It swallows her just the same.'

'Grey is sickly and white is unnatural, ghostly. A healthy squid is red or brownish-red, sometimes bright orange. What is haunting you may be a ghost squid, a phantom from your past.'

Emi hisses through her teeth. JinHee has always been fantastical but is even more so this morning. She wades deeper into the sea, moving just as slowly as she did on the shore, but once the waves reach her shoulders, she dives and is suddenly transformed. Emi is a fish, at one with the sea, weightless, and beautiful. The vacuumed silence beneath the waves soothes her as she searches the seabed for the day's haul.

Diving is a gift. That's what her mother told her when it was her turn to learn the trade. At seventy-seven years of age, Emi thinks she finally understands what her mother meant. Her body has not aged well. It aches on these cold winter mornings, rebels in the summer heat, and threatens to quit each waking day, but she knows that she just has to manage the pain until she can get into the water; then she can be free from the shackles of age. Weightlessness calms her ailing body. Holding her breath for up to two minutes at a time as she dives in search of the ocean's bounty is like meditation.

It's dark eighty to a hundred feet beneath the waves. It feels like falling into a deep womb, the only sound the throbbing in her ears from the slow, steady beat of her pumping heart. Slivers of sunlight pierce through the gloom in shards, and her old eyes quickly acclimatise to the dim haze. She dives head first, her body held firm, searching for the familiar reef of her hunting ground. Her mind relaxes, thinking only of what she will find when she reaches it. Seconds pass, slowly, and a voice intrudes upon her solitude.

Sleep now, the voice urges, calm and serene, like a hand gently caressing her face. *Let go of this life.* Emi stops her descent before she crashes into the rocky floor. Her years of experience aid her. She pushes the voice from her thoughts, forcing her eyes to focus.

After scouring through a few bunches of swaying seaweed, she spies the red octopus stalking a blue crab. The crab skitters sideways, sensing danger, but the octopus is sly and hides inside a crevice. The crab halts and resumes its scavenging. The octopus slides two legs along the sand, stretching until its bulbous body emerges, surrounded by its radial tentacles. It becomes an underwater blur, snatching the crab and disappearing back into the crevice. Emi has witnessed this tragic play many times over the last year. Emi feels a kinship with the octopus and its battle-scarred skin. One of its tentacles is shorter than the others, probably from a lucky escape. Unlike Emi's lame leg, the tentacle will repair itself, and it will be as though nothing ever happened.

Near the crevice is a crop of sea urchins, and Emi plucks them from the sea floor. The octopus senses her and ejects an inky-black cloud, shrouding the crevice in underwater smoke. She waves it away and feels, for an instant, spongy flesh, soft against her fingers. She yanks her hand to her chest and then shoots upwards, swimming towards the surface, while watching the fleeing octopus disappear into the murky horizon.

As Emi catches her breath, ChoSun chides her. 'Next time why don't you stab it with your blade? Mr Lee will pay a good price for that octopus, yet you always let it get away. Such a waste.'

The women keep eyes on one another as they dive. They have trained themselves to watch out for those diving nearest them, in case one of them gets into difficulty. *Mulsum*, water-breath, means death for *haenyeo*, and two have already lost their lives this year. Still, Emi wishes they wouldn't watch her so closely. She has no desire to stay below longer than her breath allows. Perhaps ChoSun is waiting to take Emi's spot in the order of things, to take over her diving territory and finally have a chance to cut the life from the old octopus.

'Let her be,' JinHee says, her voice stern.

ChoSun shrugs and dives in an elegant forward somersault with hardly any splash, like a sea lion.

'She's just jealous you can hold your breath longer than she can, you know that,' JinHee says, blowing water from her nostrils.

'You agree with her,' Emi says.

'Of course I don't,' JinHee retorts, turning her nose up. She adjusts her green net, and the mollusc shells clatter.

'It's all right. I know it doesn't make sense. It just seems a shame to capture that octopus. She's like an old friend.'

'Old friend indeed!' JinHee laughs, choking on seawater. She splashes Emi and shakes her head. They dive together and resume their scouring.

When her net is a quarter full, Emi surfaces to rest her lungs. They feel tight today, and she's not swimming as well as usual. Her mind is foggy. JinHee surfaces next to her.

'You OK?'

Emi searches the sky and gazes towards the rising sun. It hovers over the horizon. Soon it will launch upwards into the sky and the sea will awaken and the fishermen will invade the waters with their motorboats and nets. The voice in her head is silent. The only sounds are the lapping of the waves against her buoy, the high-pitched fragmented chorus of *sumbi* by her friends as they expel the remaining air from their lungs each time they surface, and the seabirds cawing overhead in the morning sky. Emi turns to JinHee and catches her eye.

'You off so soon?' JinHee asks.

'Yes, it's time. Will you take my catch to market?'

'Of course. I wish you luck,' she says, and gives a curt goodbye salute.

Emi nods and swims back towards the beach. She glides through the water, enjoying the gift her mother gave her. It feels like a thousand years have come and gone since she first learned to dive. It hurts too much to remember the past, and Emi pushes the memory away. She reaches the shore and commences the arduous journey back up to her shack. On land, the heavy meat of her flesh hangs on her slender bones. She trips on a stone and pauses to regain her balance.

A thin cloud cover is blowing in, turning everything grey once again. Emi suddenly feels her age plus ten more years thrust upon her. A slight pause follows each careful step forward, as her left leg takes its time catching up. Picking her way along the beach, she likens herself to the blue crab scuttling along the seabed. One step at a time, she finds her footing among the rocks, slowly, carefully, for she knows all too well anything can happen in the blink of an eye. Unlike the crab, the old octopus won't get her today. There is somewhere she needs to be, and time is not on her side.

Hana

Jeju Island, Summer 1943

The Japanese soldiers force Hana into the back of a truck with four other girls. A couple of them bear marks on their faces. They must have resisted. The girls ride in silence, from shock and fear. Hana glances at their faces, wondering if she recognises them, perhaps from the market. Two of the girls are a few years older than her and one much older, while the fourth girl is much younger than them all. She reminds Hana of her little sister, and she holds on to the thought. That girl is in this truck because she doesn't have an older sister to save her. Hana tries to send the girl comforting thoughts, but tears continue to trail down the girl's cheeks. Crying is the furthest thing from Hana's mind. She doesn't want the soldiers to see her fear.

The truck arrives at the police station as the sun dips beneath the roof. A few of the girls' eyes light up at the sight of the station. Hana gazes at the small building, her eyes narrowing into slits. There is nothing in there that will save them.

Four years ago, her uncle was sent to fight the Chinese in the Japanese emperor's name. He was instructed to report to this police station. Few Koreans held official positions, and if they did, they were sympathisers, loyalists to the Japanese government, traitors to their own countrymen. They made her uncle enlist and fight for a country he despised.

'If they can't starve us to death, they'll kill us on the battlefield. They're sending him to die. Do you hear me? They're going to murder your little brother,' her mother shouted at her father when she found out they were ordering him to fight in China.

'Don't worry, I can take care of myself,' her uncle said, ruffling Hana's hair. He pinched her sister's cheek and smiled.

Her mother shook her head, anger rising from her shoulders like steam from a boiling kettle.

'You can't take care of yourself. You're barely even a man. You haven't married. You have no children. They're exterminating us with this war. There will be no Koreans left in this country.'

'That's enough,' Hana's father said in a voice so quiet that it demanded attention.

He looked pointedly at Hana and her sister. Their mother faced him, squaring off as though about to lash out at him with more words, but then she followed his gaze. Her mother's face crumpled, and she sank to the floor, hugging herself, rocking back and forth on her knees.

Hana had never seen her mother behave like that before. She was always so strong and sure of herself. Hana would even have described her mother as *hard*, like a rock is hard against the deepest pressures of the ocean, smooth to the touch, yet unbreakable. But on that day, she became as vulnerable as a little girl. It alarmed Hana, and she reached for her sister's hand.

Her father went to her mother's side and held her. They rocked together until her mother finally looked at him and said something Hana would never forget.

'When he is gone, who is left for them to take?'

Her uncle walked assuredly to the police station, carrying his spare clothes and food, carefully prepared by her mother's hands, in a bag slung over one shoulder. He left for the war with a brave face, and he died on the front line, six months later.

Hana conjures up his youthful face. He was nineteen when he died. He seemed so old to her twelve-year-old self. She thought of him as a grown man because he towered over her and had a deep voice. Now she understands that he was too young to die. He must have been terrified, just like she is now. The fear a tangible pain pulsing through her limbs like electric shocks. Fear of the unknown future. Fear she may never see her parents again. Fear her sister will be left alone in the sea. Fear of dying in a foreign land. The Japanese army sent her uncle's sword home, a Japanese sword that her father tossed into the sea.

Sitting in the truck outside the same police station, Hana understands why her uncle's departure left her mother so bereft. She doesn't want to think of her mother helplessly rocking on the floor again now that she is next to be shipped off for the emperor's war.

'Out,' a soldier commands, letting down the truck's tailgate.

He leads the girls single file into the station. Hana makes sure to be neither the first nor the last in line. Like in a school of fish, she hopes the middle is safest from predators. The station is quiet. She can't stop shivering. Her hair is still damp with seawater and her diving clothes don't cover very much of her body. She hugs her arms and does her best to keep her teeth from chattering. Silence, that is what she strives for, so that she can become invisible.

At the reception desk, a police sergeant looks the girls over and nods to the reporting soldier. He is Korean, a sympathiser, a traitor. He will not help them. The last flickers of hope leave the girls' eyes, and they all stare at the streaks in the newly waxed floor. The desk sergeant tells the girls to write their names and family names into a ledger, along with their ages and parents' occupations. Hana already lied on the beach, telling Morimoto that her family is dead, and she hesitates, not knowing how to keep the lie going.

The officer behind the desk doesn't know her but probably knows her parents, at least by their Japanese name, Hamasaki. Her mother's Korean surname is Kim, her father's is Jang; married women always keep their surnames. The two girls before her want to please the soldiers and act like dutiful subjects by writing their colonised Japanese names, but Hana suspects it is too late for such manoeuvres. Instead, she combines her parents' names into one, *Kim, JangHa*. She hopes this false name will keep them from finding out her family is still alive and perhaps returning for her sister, while a small part of her hopes that her parents will read the name in the ledger and know that she passed this way. This last hope keeps her from faltering.

After they write their names, the girls are led into a small office. The dingy beige walls are plastered with propaganda posters proclaiming the benefits of volunteering for Japan's war effort. Similar posters decorate the market where the *haenyeo* and fishermen sell their daily catch to villagers and Japanese soldiers alike. The people on the posters are drawn with smiling faces and bright Japanese eyes. Hana never liked these images. They remind her of the false expressions everyone wears when the soldiers come near their stalls.

Her father is the only grown-up Hana knows who cannot put on this false expression. Instead, anger from the injustice of his brother's death radiates from his face, plain and unyielding. Whenever a soldier approached her family's stall, picking through the seafood with the tip of his rifle, he would catch sight of her father and suddenly lose focus. The soldier's hands would begin to tremble, and he would simply walk away, wordless and confused.

Hana has witnessed this peculiar transaction on many occasions, and each time she wondered if it was the pain in her father's eyes that the Japanese soldier saw, or something more sinister. Did the soldiers see their own deaths foretold in their reflection? It always pleased Hana to watch the soldier scurry away as though singed by magic.

As she stands with the other girls, surrounded by posters of loyal subjects with false expressions, she does her best to arrange her features so she exudes wrath, so that any soldier who gazes upon her face will scurry away from the flames within her eyes. Perhaps she, too, possesses her father's magic. The idea gives her a small amount of hope.

'Put these on, hurry up,' a soldier shouts at them. He gives each girl a beige dress, nylons, white knickers and a cotton bra. The dresses vary slightly in style, but they are cut from the same cloth.

'What are these for?' one of the girls whispers, careful to only speak Japanese in the presence of the soldiers.

'It must be a uniform,' a second girl answers.

'Where are they taking us?' comes a terrified voice from the girl Hana thinks is barely older than her own sister.

'It's for the Women's Patriotic Service Corps. My teacher mentioned they were recruiting volunteers,' says the girl beside Hana. She sounds confident but still quivers with nerves.

'Volunteers for what?' Hana finally manages to ask. Her throat is parched and her voice raspy.

'No talking,' a soldier shouts, and pounds on the door. 'Two minutes left.'

They hurriedly dress and stand in a line on the far side of the room. When the door opens, they shrink away. Morimoto enters and eyes Hana up and down before commencing his visual inspection of the other girls. He brought her here. He is sending her away. She memorises his face so that she will know who to blame when she returns home.

'Good. Very good. Now, go and find shoes that fit. Then get back into the truck.' He waves them out the door but grabs Hana's arm before she can pass. 'You look much younger in these clothes. How old are you?'

'Sixteen,' she answers, trying to yank her arm out of his hand, but he digs his fingers into her flesh. Her knees nearly buckle from the sudden pain, though she doesn't make a sound.

He seems to think about her answer as he watches her struggle to keep silent. She lowers her eyes, but he lifts her chin and makes her look at him. He drinks her in as though his thirst will never be satisfied.

'She'll ride next to me.' He releases her.

A soldier standing outside the office salutes him and then takes Hana to find a pair of shapeless shoes. An old man leans against the wall, and as she passes him, he turns his face away from her. She despises his cowardice in that moment, but then she forgives him for his fear. They are all afraid. A soldier can crush a Korean man's skull with the heel of his boot, and if the family demands punishment for the crime, they may find their home burned to the ground or they might simply disappear, never to be seen again.

Outside, cold wind unfurls around them. It is as though the gods have confused the seasons and decided to send a lonely chill into the approaching summer night to accompany them. The idling engine drowns out the girls' sobs as they realise they really are being taken away from their homes. Hana doesn't want to leave the security of the group. When a soldier pushes her towards the front of the truck, she resists and tries to stay behind the last girl and climb into the back, too.

'Hey, not you. You're in there,' he says, pointing to the passenger door.

The other girls clamp their eyes onto Hana, their expressions a mixture of fear and desperation. Starting towards the open door, she thinks she also sees relief in a few of their eyes, relief that it is not them.

Hana climbs in next to the driver. It is no warmer inside the truck. He glances at her and returns his attention to the windscreen as Morimoto slides in after her. He smells of tobacco and liquor.

They drive through the night in silence. Hana is too afraid to look at the soldiers on either side of her, so she sits still as a rock, trying to avoid notice. The soldiers don't talk to one another or to her, preferring to stare blank-faced out the windscreen. As the seaside slips away, Mount Halla grows into a looming darkness in the sky, before falling away as they reach the other side of the island. The driver rolls down his window and lights a cigarette. The scent of the ocean rushes in, and Hana drinks in the comforting aroma as the truck winds down narrow roads leading to the coast and the channel between Jeju and the southernmost tip of mainland Korea. Nausea roils in Hana's stomach, and she clutches it, willing it to settle.

Far beneath them along a rocky shore, Hana spies the awaiting ferry docked in the port. The truck's engine grumbles over the empty road, but Morimoto's silence permeates even that noisy space, and Hana senses the power of his rank.

The driver drops them near the docks and salutes Morimoto before racing away. New soldiers armed with clipboards process them and mix them in with other girls huddling inside a makeshift corral beside the docks. Seabirds soar overhead, oblivious to the scene below. Hana yearns to sprout wings and join them in their flight. A soldier shouts orders to the growing group of young women and girls, and they are led towards the ferry. No one utters a word.

As Hana climbs the stairs leading up to the gangway she stares at her feet. Each step takes her further away from her home. She has never left the island before. The realisation that she is being taken to another country terrifies her, and her feet freeze, refusing to take another step. She might never see her family again if she boards this vessel.

'Keep moving!' a soldier shouts.

The girl behind her nudges her forward. There is no choice. Hana steps forward, while saying her silent goodbyes. To her sister, she will miss her the most, but Hana is thankful to have saved her from this fate, wherever it leads. To her mother she wishes safety in her dives. To her father she wishes courage on the sea, but secretly she also wishes he will find her. She imagines his small fishing boat trailing after the ferry, determined to bring her home. It is a hopeless sight, even in her mind, but she wishes for it nonetheless.

The ferry has small cabins below deck, and Hana and the girls from the truck are placed in one packed with at least thirty others. They are dressed in similar uniforms and their faces wear the same frightened expressions. A few of the girls share what little food they have tucked into pockets. Some of the soldiers felt sorry for them and gave them tokens of sustenance during the journey: a few rice balls, a scrap of dried squid, one girl even received a pear. Most are too distraught to eat, and sharing the food gives them some relief. Hana accepts a rice ball offered by a young woman who looks at least twenty.

'Thank you,' she says, and nibbles at the hardened rice.

'Where are you from?' the woman asks.

Hana doesn't answer; she isn't sure she should talk to anyone yet. She doesn't know whom to trust.

'I'm from south of Halla Mountain. I don't know why I'm here,' the woman says when Hana doesn't answer. 'I told them I'm married. My husband, he's fighting the Chinese. I have to return home, for his letters. Who else will receive them if I am not there? I told them I am married, but . . .' Her eyes plead for understanding, but Hana can't help her. She understands nothing.

A voice joins in. 'Why did they take you if you're married? Is your husband in debt?' A small group gathers around the married woman.

'No, he's not in debt.'

'That you know of,' another woman says.

'She said he's not in debt. He's at war.'

Others voice their opinions and soon the questions grow into a debate. The younger girls refrain from joining in, and Hana edges away from the women, seeking solace with the quiet ones. Their eyes are large with fear, while the older girls and women fill the small room with anger and incomprehension.

'Then why are *they* here, if this is a debtors' ferry? They're just children.'

'Their parents are in debt,' comes one answer.

'Yes, they've been sold, just like us.'

'That's not true,' Hana says, her voice shaking with resentment. 'My mother and I are *haenyeo*. We owe no man a debt. Only the sea can claim a debt from us.'

The room grows quiet. A few of the women are surprised to hear a girl so young speak with such authority, and they say as much to her. The younger girls shift closer to Hana, as though hoping to soak up some of her strength. She sits against the back wall and hugs her arms. A few of the girls follow her and do the same. They sit in silence, and Hana wonders what their fate will be when they reach the mainland. Will the soldiers ship them to Japan or somewhere deep in China among the fighting?

Hana replays the moments in the truck sitting between the two soldiers. The driver never acknowledged her presence, even once, but Morimoto seemed to notice her every movement. If she shifted, he shifted; if she coughed, his arm moved against hers. His body, even his breaths, synchronised with her own. It took every ounce of restraint to keep from looking at him, and she failed only once.

He had lit a cigarette, and the heat from the flame warmed her cheek. She had turned in fear that he would burn her, and their eyes met. He had been watching her, seeing if she would look at him. She stared back at him, examining his face, until he exhaled a lungful of smoke into her eyes. Coughing, she quickly turned away and resumed staring out of the windscreen.

The ferry slides slowly into the channel and the choppy sea turns Hana's stomach. She wishes she was diving beneath the ocean's surface, swimming back home. Her sister's terrified eyes flash in her mind. Hana closes her eyes. She saved her sister from this uncertain journey. At least her sister is safe.

'Do you think they'll take us to Japan?' a girl asks her.

Hana opens her eyes, and she feels the gaze of the others on her. She sees their expectant faces and wonders why they are asking her.

'I don't know,' she answers apologetically.

They seem to shrink into themselves, swaying with the movement of the ferry. She feels powerless to console them. Stories from the villagers surface in her mind. Once taken, girls never make it back home. There are no swords with notices of appreciation sent to the grieving parents of girls. Girls disappear. Only rumours reach home, rumours that can never be shared with the remaining children.

Not long after Hana became a fully-fledged *haenyeo*, she overheard two women in the market speaking in hushed tones about a village girl who was found on the north side of the island.

'She's riddled with illness and driven mad by *rape*,' one of the women said, catching Hana's ear. She didn't know what the word meant. She leaned in, hoping the woman would explain.

'The father had to hide her in the house. She's wild now . . . like an animal.'

The other woman shook her head sadly. She lowered her eyes. 'No one will have her now, even if she manages to get well. Poor girl.'

'Yes, poor girl, and her poor father. The shame will follow him to an early grave.'

'Such a heavy burden for him.'

The women continued consoling the girl's father as though he were there to hear them, and Hana was left wondering what could make a girl turn wild and drive a father to an early death. Later that night, Hana questioned her mother.

'Where did you hear that word?' her mother asked, agitated, as though Hana had committed a grave offence.

'In the market, these women were talking about a girl who was taken by the soldiers.'

Her mother sighed and turned away from Hana to resume her stitching. They sat in silence, Hana watching her repair a tear in her swimming shorts. Her needle dipped in and out of the shorts at speed, mesmerising Hana. Everything her mother put her hands to she performed with absolute precision. Diving, sewing, cooking, cleaning, repairing, gardening – her mother was flawless in them all.

'Perhaps you don't know what it means?' Hana shrugged, knowing this would get a rise out of her mother and force her to answer the question.

'Once I tell you, I can never un-tell you. You're certain you are ready to know?' Her mother didn't take her eyes off the task at hand, leaving the question hanging between them like a thundercloud.

Hana did want to know. She deserved to know. After all, she was now a member of the diving women, and as such, she faced the same dangers they did each day in the sea against storms, sharks and drowning. Risking her life made her practically a grown-up. She had matured both in mind and body so much that a few boys who lived nearby had mentioned the topic of marriage within earshot whenever she passed them on the beach.

One of them she even found slightly more interesting than the others. He was the tallest of the group, with the darkest skin but the lightest eyes and sunniest grin. She thought he also seemed the most intelligent, as he knew better than to shout at her like his friends did. Instead, he would appear at her mother's stall and chat to them both as he purchased goods. His father was a schoolteacher but had to work as a fisherman now because the schools had Japanese teachers. He had two younger sisters and would need a good wife who enjoyed being around younger girls. She didn't know his name, but that would come much later. Perhaps when her father was there to ask it of him, and perhaps they would be promised to one another.

'Yes,' Hana answered her mother. 'I want to know.'

'Fine, I will tell you, then,' her mother said, and her voice was void of emotion. 'Rape is when a man forces a woman to lie with him.'

Hana blushed as her mother continued.

'But rape by the soldiers is more than just one act. The girl the soldiers took was forced by many, many soldiers to lie with them.'

'Why would they do that?' Hana managed to ask even though her face had flushed to a deep red.

'The Japanese believe it will aid them in battle. Help them be victorious in the war. They think it is their right to release their energy and receive pleasure, even when they are so far from home, because they risk their lives for the emperor on the front lines. They believe this so much that they take our girls and ship them all over the world for this purpose. This girl sent home, she is a lucky one.'

She looked at Hana then, gauging her response, and when Hana said nothing, she stood and handed her the swimming shorts. Hana stared at the perfect stitching. She knew what it meant to lie with a man, or at least she had an idea what it was. She had never seen the act, but she heard it sometimes at night when her parents thought she was asleep. Quiet whisperings, her mother's hushed laughter, her father's muffled groans. She couldn't make herself understand what it meant to be forced to do this, for many, many soldiers to force themselves on a woman at one time. Her mother had said the girl was lucky to come home. Hana didn't mention what the women had said about the girl's father going to an early grave.

)) ((

The door to the ferry's cabin opens, and two soldiers enter. They scan the group and then reach for a girl, seemingly at random. A small cry escapes her, and the soldier smacks her. She quietens, shocked by the sudden blow. The other soldier continues scanning the girls.

'*Haenyeo* girl, come out,' he says. 'Corporal Morimoto requests your presence.'

Hana recognises the driver of the truck now that she hears his voice, but she remains where she is.

'Hurry up, come on, you have been summoned.'

A heaviness hangs in the air. The other girls' eyes are surely moving to her location, giving her away. Afraid the slightest movement will betray her identity, she is desperate to keep still – yet small tremors shake her whole body. Surely he will single her out as she vibrates under his gaze.

'There are no *haenyeo* here. You must have the wrong room,' a voice across the cabin pipes up.

A murmur of agreement rises among the other girls, but then the driver looks Hana's way.

'No, you, you there, girl, come here. I remember you. You're the *haenyeo*. Come with me now.' He rests one hand on the pistol holstered at his hip. 'Don't waste any more of my time.'

There is nothing for her to do but obey him. She rises to her feet and steps out of the safety of the other girls and goes to him. He takes her by the wrist and leads her away like she is a prisoner marching towards a firing squad. The ferry's narrow hallways sway with each undulating wave coursing beneath the vessel. Hana holds her free hand out to steady herself against the wall.

'In here,' he says, and opens a metal door.

Hana steps inside. The door slams shut behind her. The metallic clang echoes as she stands face-to-face with Corporal Morimoto. He doesn't speak, but his eyes send shivers down her arms. She steps backwards.

'Lie on the bed,' he says in a commanding voice. He motions towards a cot hinged onto the wall.

Hana backs into the door. Her hand blindly searches for the doorknob.

'There are two guards standing outside that door,' Morimoto says. He speaks calmly, as though this is not a novel situation but merely a part of his daily routine, though his expression betrays his hunger. Beads of sweat glisten on his forehead.

Hana turns and peers out of the porthole. He isn't lying. Two guards stand on either side of the door, their shoulders barely visible in her peripheral vision. She turns back to face Morimoto.

'Lie on the bed,' he says again, and takes a step sideways, making space for her to pass by him. She hesitates. He wipes the sweat from his forehead with a handkerchief and impatiently shoves it back into his trousers.

'If I have to say it again, I will invite those soldiers in to join us, and this will be much more unpleasant for you than it has to be, when I'd rather keep you for myself.'

He retains an air of calm authority, but Hana senses something more behind his demeanour. He is like a shark before it seizes its prey from the dark ocean's depths, prowling beneath before the strike.

The thought of two more soldiers cramming into the small cabin frightens her into action, and she does as he commands. He laughs when she curls into a foetal position on the cot, and he starts to unbuckle his belt. Hana closes her eyes. The leather strap slowly slides out of his belt loops. The hairs on her neck stiffen as he nears the cot. She fights the urge to open her eyes, instead squeezing them tightly shut. His hand startles her. His fingers lift the hair out of her face and caress her cheek. She can smell his breath now. He is kneeling beside her. His hand trails down her neck, her shoulder and over her hips, and comes to rest on her knee. She opens her eyes.

He is staring at her face. She can't read his expression. He appears flushed. She stares back at him, waiting for something terrible to happen. He grins at her, but his eyes are vacant. She flinches even before he lifts the hem of her dress.

'Please, don't,' Hana manages to whisper. The words sound weak even to her ears, but he doesn't stop.

'Don't worry. I came to know you quite well on our trip to the coast. I grew to like you, very much.'

She squirms away from his touch but he grabs her thigh and squeezes so tight, she cries out.

'You mustn't make me tear your dress, or you'll have to travel to Manchuria stark naked. Is that what you want, travelling for days and days on a train full of soldiers without a single piece of clothing to cover your beautiful body?'

His eyes dare her to speak. She stops squirming but can't keep from shaking. He's taking her to Manchuria. Manchuria is the end of the world, much further from home than she imagined.

'Good.' His grip eases, and slowly, he lifts her dress up over her waist and pulls down her new nylons and cotton knickers. He folds them, taking the time to place them neatly on the edge of the cot. He stands, and she watches as he slips his trousers down to his ankles. She can't take her eyes off his erect penis.

'I'm doing you a favour; breaking you in like this is a consideration most girls like you won't get. It's usually a terrible surprise. At least this way, you will know what to expect.'

He climbs on top of her, and she shuts her eyes. His breath in her face, his weight on her chest, these things she feels in the darkness behind her eyelids. Then he forces himself inside her, tearing her youth to shreds with each thrust. The pain is like a knife stabbed into the tender space between her toes, except it's not happening there, it's happening somewhere closer to her heart and to her mind.

He pants through the exertion, grunting like a boar. She imagines that's what he is, a black Jeju pig that lives beneath the latrine behind her house and eats human excrement. She holds this image in her mind so that she won't picture what he is actually doing, even as she feels each thrust as a searing pain at her very centre. His grunts increase in frequency, until he shudders against her body, seizing as though in shock. Then he goes limp, lying upon her, pressing against her chest, pushing her body deep into the hard mattress until she can barely draw breath.

When Morimoto finally rises to his feet, Hana turns away from him, curling back into a ball around her pain. She listens to the sounds of him getting dressed, the rustle of his trousers, the slide of his leather belt, the shuffle of his boots on the floor.

'You're bleeding,' he says.

Hana turns to look at him. He points between her legs. She rolls onto her other side and peers at a small bloodstain on the sheet. Prickles run down her neck. The thought that she might die flashes through her mind. She keeps her knees tightly closed. He smiles at her.

'It was everything I hoped it would be. Now you're a woman,' he says, and looks genuinely pleased. 'Clean yourself up. Then you can rejoin the others.'

He tosses a handkerchief at her and exits the room. It briefly floats through the air and lands like a soft petal on her stomach.

Emi

The taxicab is late. Emi sits atop her suitcase next to the road with a steaming mug of ginseng tea warming her hands. She scrutinises each approaching vehicle, but only passenger cars drive by with people going to work or taking children to school. A few of the drivers wave at her as they pass, and one of them honks the car horn, startling her. Hot tea spills onto her pink trousers. She wipes at the spreading stain with her mitten-covered hand, ignoring the burning sensation on her thigh.

Emi only manages to visit her children once a year. When she was younger she would visit twice a year, but never more than that. Her relationship with her children is distant. It's easier to see them in her mind than in person. They never come back to the island, except when they returned for their father's burial. They were already grown up when he died, but returning to their childhood home seemed to revert them back into children. They stood awkwardly by her side and wept openly, her daughter more so than her son. They only stayed three days and then they flew back to Seoul. They had stood at the airport, no longer childlike, both wearing black work attire, and neither had looked her in the eyes when they said goodbye. Perhaps, as she had with them, they had decided she was better seen in their minds than in person.

Emi usually takes the ferry. There's a bus stop down the road that's not too far for her to walk to on her own. It goes to a port on the other side of the island, closer to the mainland, where a daily ferry sails to Busan. It's an overnight and arrives early the next morning when there's a free bus to Seoul, but the journey is too tiresome for her now. She no longer has the energy to cross her country at eye level and watch the trees and mountains slide by. Her bones ache, and sometimes she forgets things, so this time she must fly and hope the clouds will not block her view of the land.

The tightness in her chest returns, and she closes her eyes. *Don't remember*, she tells herself silently. *It's just an airport. One time. There and back. And then never again.* She can let herself remember on the way back home. Her hand touches her chest, willing the pain to release, and she wonders all the while if she really will make it back this time. A car crests the slight rise in the road, and Emi opens her eyes. A horn sounds, announcing the taxicab's arrival, and she stands to wave it down.

'Sorry I'm late, Grandmother,' the driver says as he hurries to help her with her suitcase. 'The roads are slippery and there was an accident back there. We'll have to pass by it on the way to the airport.'

Emi looks at her watch.

'Don't worry. We have plenty of time,' he says, stowing her suitcase in the trunk.

Emi doesn't respond. She tucks her empty mug into her handbag.

The driver helps her into the back seat and slams the door shut before scurrying to the front of the car and into the driver's seat. In his hurry, he turns the car round too quickly, and it narrowly misses sliding sideways into the ditch. Emi grabs hold of the car door and prepares to crash, but the tyres regain traction, lurching back onto the road. Emi doesn't comment on his driving. It's not sensible to encourage conversation with a poor driver.

When they reach the accident it's still in the clean-up stages. The cars on the road are backed up, with drivers craning their necks to get a glimpse of the damage. A man stands on the shoulder, sobbing. He shudders, making the hem of the powder-blue blanket wrapped around him dance in jerky waves. The burned-out shell of a Hyundai lies on its side. A tow truck backs slowly towards it. Emi notices a Mickey Mouse doll lying in the grass. She spies red shorts through the brittle brown blades and looks away.

'I told you there was a bad accident. I'm never late,' the taxi driver says.

His eyes don't leave the man in the blue blanket. He stares at him in the rear-view mirror long after they pass him by. Emi wishes he'd keep his attention on the road ahead; she doesn't want to miss her plane.

The driver sees her watching him in the mirror and clears his throat before finally looking back at the road. He manoeuvres around two slower cars, and soon they're out in front of the traffic, driving at a good pace. Emi can't stop thinking about the doll lying lifeless in the grass, the man's shoulders as he wept, the bloody red of those shorts. She feels in her bones that something precious was lost.

》《

At Jeju International Airport, Emi lifts her suitcase onto a luggage trolley and follows the signs to Korean Air. She doesn't let her mind wander. She keeps it in check by reading the signs that guide the way to the ticket counter, the security checkpoint, the departure gate, and finally the gangway that leads to the aircraft that will take her to Seoul.

Once the plane lifts into the sky, Emi can rest. She lets herself think about seeing her children in Seoul. Her son is meeting her at Gimpo International Airport even though she said she was happy to take the subway to her daughter's house. He's bullheaded and wouldn't hear of it. He would rent a car and meet her at arrivals.

'You're too old to ride the subway on your own,' he said on the telephone when she protested.

'I'm too old to sit on a train for thirty minutes?'

'You could get confused and lose your way,' he answered, and she knew the matter was settled.

The stewardess announces the flight to Seoul is a little over an hour, so in-flight purchases will be available straight away.

A few days before her flight, Emi had asked JinHee to drive her into the town so she could go shopping, but JinHee had better advice.

'They have very good gifts in the aeroplane catalogue. You shouldn't go into town to shop. Just buy them on board the plane. That way you only need to take one carry-on. Your leg,' JinHee said, motioning towards Emi's errant leg.

'I want good gifts, not junk,' Emi protested.

'It's not junk. You can buy Chanel No. 5 perfume! You call that junk?' JinHee shook her head.

Emi pushes the call button and waits for the attendant to arrive and take her order.

Her son is partial to whiskey, so she buys him a bottle of Jack Daniel's. Her daughter-in-law and grandson like chocolates, so she picks out two boxes of assorted truffles. For her daughter, she chooses a large bottle of Chanel No. 5 perfume and thinks she will not tell Jin-Hee. Her daughter is not married and has no children, but she has a dog. Emi selects a stuffed cat from the children's section of the in-flight magazine, the closest thing to a dog toy she can find.

The captain lands the plane with a cathartic bang. The passengers shriek with surprise and fear, and then embarrassed laughter fills the cabin. Emi waits until most of the passengers exit before standing to retrieve her purchases from the overhead compartment. A young woman rushes past her at the last minute, and the bag slips from Emi's grip, hitting her on the forehead.

'Sorry, Grandmother,' the young lady calls behind her, but doesn't stop.

Emi rubs her forehead. The bottle of whiskey is heavier than she thought. She worries it might bruise. A male flight attendant comes to her aid.

'Are you OK? Can I get you an ice pack?' he asks.

'No, thank you,' Emi says, and laughs. 'I should move faster, perhaps.'

'Are you sure? It looked like it hit you very hard.'

He peers down into her face as though searching for blood. Emi shies away from his gaze, gathering her handbag and bag of gifts.

'Don't worry, it's probably just a little bruise. I've had worse,' she says, and hobbles away from him, down the aisle.

There are many things in Emi's memory worse than getting hit in the head with a bottle of whiskey. A soldier's boot. The image appears to her so suddenly that she flinches. She pauses to steady herself and catch her breath. Worrying someone might notice her distress, she straightens up and heads for the exit.

'Thank you for flying Korean Air,' the captain of the plane says to her with a bow as she passes him at the exit. He's standing next to the pretty flight attendant who took her gift order. The buttons on the captain's coat shine as though they are brand new, and Emi wonders if this was the young captain's first solo landing.

At arrivals, she spots her son standing a head taller than the ladies crowded around him. Emi is struck by how many women are waiting. She wonders if there's something special happening in Seoul, but then she remembers and feels embarrassed for forgetting about her own purpose for being there. Her son's concern is apparent when she comes near.

'What happened? Did you hit your head?' her son asks, gazing down into her face.

He looks older than his sixty-one years when he crinkles his forehead like that. When he was a boy, Emi would smooth the wrinkles away with her hand and tell him he'd get old too fast if he kept worrying. She fights the urge to touch his face with her wrinkled palm now.

'It was an accident. A girl in a rush, that's all. Nothing to worry over. You look tired,' she says.

'I am. I had to go to work at four this morning so that I could extend my lunch to get you at the airport.'

He turns to one side and ushers her in front of him towards an awkward-looking boy standing slightly behind the crowd. Emi smiles and rushes towards her grandson with arms extended.

'How you've grown, you're taller than me!'

He blushes as she hugs him, pinning his arms by his sides in a long embrace. When she finally releases him, she has to look up slightly to see into his face.

'I brought something for you.' Emi reaches into her shopping bag to retrieve the box of chocolates.

'Not now, Mother. Let's get to the car first. I'm in one-hour parking.'

Her son leads her away, and her grandson follows without protest. Emi marvels at her grandson's new-found self-control. A year ago, he would have thrown a tantrum if his father had interrupted his chance of receiving a gift. He was a miracle child, as her daughter-in-law was over forty when she finally conceived, and they spoiled him rotten. Emi had spent many sleepless nights worrying over how he would turn out, but looking at him now, her heart is content. He's shy, obedient and kind. He's carrying her suitcase for her, but also for his ageing father. He's only twelve. What a difference just one year has made.

Emi follows her son to the car park, looking back at her grandson, marvelling at his maturity. She remembers her son at that age. He wasn't as tall as her grandson. Perhaps it's all the Western food he's eating. She wonders if she shouldn't have bought him sweets, but then decides a little chocolate never hurt a growing boy.

Emi remembers the first time she had chocolate. It was after her daughter was born. Her husband brought home a bar of chocolate and broke it into little squares for her and her son to eat. It was like eating the food of the gods. She never forgot that first bite. How it melted on her tongue. How she reached for a second square, and a third, before her husband could change his mind and take them away. But he didn't. He just sat and watched her eat the chocolate. It was the first time she thought that perhaps he did care for her after all. It seemed as though it pleased him to see her enjoy the chocolates so much. She couldn't understand how he didn't eat a piece, when he clearly knew how delicious it tasted, but she didn't comment. She never spoke to him if she could help it. That's how their marriage lasted so long. It was loveless but survived because she always held her tongue.

'Here we are,' her son says, opening the door for her to get into the car.

She climbs into the passenger seat and, remembering the chocolates, reaches into her shopping bag to hand the box to her grandson. He grins when he sees it, tears off the cellophane wrapping, and opens the box as eagerly as she hoped. He pops one of the chocolate truffles into his mouth before blushing and shyly offering one to her.

'No, no, they are all for you. I enjoy watching you eat them. Go on, have another one.'

Hana

At first Hana doesn't move. Her groin sears with a burning pain. She fears the wetness between her legs. Is she bleeding to death? Slowly, she sits up, but she is too afraid to look down to see what he did to her. She breathes through the pain, slowly letting air out through her nostrils.

When she has steadied her breath she looks down. First she sees the blood, but then she sees it is mixed with a thick fluid dripping out of her. It is this she feels, not blood. She isn't dying.

She dabs between her legs with the handkerchief. Each touch against her skin awakens a new pain sensor in her mind. This is rape, just as her mother described it. Hana shuts her eyes, wishing she didn't know, that this was a nightmare she would soon wake up from.

The door's metal handle squeaks as it turns, and she quickly pulls up her cotton knickers and nylons. She forces her knees closed even though it hurts to do so and stands warily, waiting for another soldier to attack her.

'Hurry up, we need this room,' the soldier says, leading her back to the small cabin containing the rest of the girls and women.

Hana pushes through the inquisitive stares and makes her way to the very back of the cabin. She sinks to the floor, facing the wall so she won't have to look at them. She feels the girls watching her, but she doesn't care. The soldiers take two more girls with them when they leave, locking the door behind them.

Soon a murmur of concerned voices rises up among the women questioning what the soldiers are doing. Some of the voices are aimed directly at Hana, demanding to know what happened to her, but others are simply laments from the women who know what is happening and fear they are all destined for the same fate. A fist pounds on the door. The room falls silent.

Hana covers her face with her hands. She's afraid the women will know what happened to her just by looking at her. She suddenly wants to cry. She holds her breath for as long as she can, focusing on nothing but the need to breathe and her will not to give in. When the urge to cry passes, she lets herself breathe again, gasping gulps of air.

The tender skin between her legs still burns from the assault. She does her best to move past the pain, but images of Morimoto's naked legs and other parts of him she doesn't want to recall invade her thoughts. She squeezes her eyes tightly shut, pressing against her eyelids until white light flashes behind her fingers, blocking the images out. When her eyeballs feel near to exploding underneath the pressure of her fingertips, a girl whispers into Hana's ear.

'Where did they take you?'

Hana jerks and looks up. Her vision is at first blurry, and it takes a moment before she recognises the young girl from Jeju Island. She's so slight, her dress falls loosely around her shoulders and waist. It hurts Hana's head to imagine Morimoto, or any of the soldiers, doing to this young girl what he did to her.

'Stay near the back,' Hana warns. 'Maybe if they don't notice you, you'll be safe.'

'Won't you tell me?'

'It's better if you never find out.'

The door opens before the girl can speak again. The two girls are returned to the cabin and the door shuts without the removal of any more. The overhead lights blink out, and they are left in darkness.

Like cattle, the girls begin to settle in for the journey, lying down and falling asleep. Sniffles and gentle sobs fill the room. Hana and the young girl lie close together; the girl links her arm through Hana's.

'That way you'll wake if they come for me, and I'll wake if they return for you.'

Her words touch Hana in their simplicity. She is taking control of her situation the only way she knows how, by making sure she at least knows when to be afraid. She doesn't want to be asleep when the terrible things happen. She wants to see them coming, even though she knows she will be powerless against them when they do. They are all powerless here.

'My name is Noriko, but my mother calls me SangSoo,' the girl whispers into Hana's hair. Her breath warms the nape of Hana's neck.

She doesn't reply. She tries, but she can't speak, as though her lips are sealed shut to keep in the pain of what happened to her. Sang-Soo's mother calls her by her true Korean name at home. Like so many Koreans forced to assimilate, SangSoo's family speaks Korean in the privacy of their home, only speaking the required Japanese in public. Hana always thought she was lucky to have been named by a clever mother. In Korean, *hana* means 'one', or in her case 'firstborn', but in Japanese, *hana* also means 'flower'. So Hana never has to change her name, in public or in private. Her younger sister is not so lucky, and neither is SangSoo.

'Goodnight, Big Sister.'

In the darkness, SangSoo's voice could be her own little sister's. Hana suddenly feels crushed beneath the weight of her captivity. Her sister is so far away. Each moment spent locked up on the ferry takes her even further. A small hand slides into hers, and Hana squeezes it tight.

》《

Hana wakes with a start. It is still dark in the cabin, but a faint glow from beneath the door illuminates the sleeping shadows on the floor. She has no idea how long she has been asleep. Gently, she unhooks her arm from SangSoo's and sits up. She needs to use the toilet but has no idea what to do. The urgency presses against her bladder and threatens to flow.

'I need the toilet,' she whispers to the room at large. At first no one answers. A few bodies turn and shift positions. When still no one answers, she repeats her statement a little louder.

'Hush, stupid girl,' comes a response in the darkness.

'I'm sorry, I have to—'

'I know, I heard you both times,' the woman cuts her off. 'Can't you smell? We all have to use the toilet.'

Hana is taken aback by the woman's harsh response. She inhales slowly. Nothing. She doesn't smell anything. Is there something wrong with her nose?

'I don't smell anything.'

'That's because she smells like cologne. She can't smell above the reek of a man,' says a different voice in the darkness.

'Yeah, I smell her, too. He must have poured the bottle over his head.'

Their words sting her, and her skin feels inflamed. Hana lifts the collar of her dress up to her nose and breathes in. She smells like *him*. He is in her clothes. She wants to rip them off her body and tear them to shreds, but his words echo in her head. *Is that what you want, travelling for days and days on a train full of soldiers without a single piece of clothing to cover your beautiful body?*

Instead of stripping his scent from her, Hana lets her bladder go, not caring if she smells like a toilet. SangSoo must have woken up when they were talking because she links her arm back through Hana's without a word about the mess she has made of herself. Her silence comforts Hana, and she tightens her arm around SangSoo's. They lie together, side by side in Hana's sour wetness, and soon fall back asleep.

A loud thud against the metal door wakes everyone in the cabin with a start. A few girls yelp in surprise. The overhead lights flicker on, flooding them in a greenish glow. Four soldiers enter and three yank a girl each to her feet. Cries of resistance wash over the room but do nothing to sway the soldiers' resolve. The last soldier looks at Hana and beelines towards her. He reaches down for her but then suddenly cringes backwards, covering his nose.

'She pissed herself!' he cries out to the other soldiers, and kicks her in disgust. 'You Koreans are animals.' His eyes fall on SangSoo. 'You'll have to do,' he says, and grabs her wrist, yanking her over Hana.

'She's just a child,' Hana pleads with the soldier.

SangSoo looks down at Hana with sorrowful eyes.

'Don't worry, Big Sister, I will be OK, just like you.' Her voice is shaking yet brave. It breaks Hana's heart.

'I will take her place. I volunteer,' Hana says, rising to her feet and meeting the soldier's eyes.

The whole room watches the scene; not even a breath can be heard in the seconds that follow. It is as though they are all waiting for the sun to fall out of the sky and burn Hana to ash. She has stood up to a Japanese soldier. They all know better than to do that. Seconds stretch by as the tension from the stand-off thickens. Hana's knees turn to rubber, and she fears they will betray her. Then, before she knows it, other girls, older girls, the women, are volunteering to take SangSoo's place.

Their voices echo in the small space like a cacophony of seabirds, each one offering her body in the place of the child's. A few of the stronger girls try to wrench SangSoo's arm free and convince the soldier to take them, but he won't budge. Without warning, he punches one of the women in the gut. She doubles over, panting for breath.

'The next girl to open her mouth will get worse,' he warns, wrenching SangSoo's arm behind her as he marches her out of the cabin.

The metal door slams shut with such finality that the darkness that follows as they switch off the lights feels like a reckoning. Cries fill the darkness, soft and heartfelt, grieving for the little girl – chosen because Hana soiled herself.

》·《

The ferry docks on the mainland, and Hana can't contain her worry. The soldier never returned SangSoo to the cabin. The other three girls came back one by one, but the youngest girl, the girl everyone volunteered for, was still missing. When the soldiers arrive and order everyone out of the cabin, Hana is desperate to know what has happened to her. But she keeps her mouth shut.

With heavy feet, Hana follows the others as they disembark the ferry and are led towards a motorcade of military trucks. Hana's eyes scan the faces of the girls she passes, hoping to find SangSoo's familiar terrified brown eyes. The trucks take them a short distance to a railway station, where Hana is placed into a train compartment with another girl. Newspaper has been taped over the glass and then painted black so they can't see out. Hana asks her in whispers if she has seen SangSoo and describes the young girl. The other girl shakes her head. She wasn't in Hana's cabin on the ferry. She was in one with forty other girls who were supposed to be going to Tokyo to work in a uniform factory. For some reason she has been separated from that group and stuck on this train with Hana. She doesn't know why.

She is Hana's age, perhaps only a year or so older, and attractive, what her mother would have called moon-faced, with white skin and pink lips. Her teeth are mostly straight, not protruding, and her eyes are larger than the average Korean's. All the boys in Hana's village would have fallen in love with her.

'Did they take you from the cabin?' Hana asks in a quiet voice.

'No. They didn't take anyone. Why, did they take you from yours?' The girl looks alarmed.

'Yes, and my friend, the little girl, SangSoo. But they never brought her back.'

'Why did they take you?' she asks warily. Her eyes dart about the train compartment as though someone might be listening.

Hana can't say the word aloud. It is one small word, and certainly this girl, older than her, would know what it means. Still, she can't muster the courage to say it. Hana turns away from her and sinks back into the seat. She sits there worrying about SangSoo, wishing she hadn't soiled herself, yet simultaneously relieved that she did – and hating herself for the thought.

The train edges out of the station with a slow start, and the compartment door slides open. Two soldiers enter, one dragging SangSoo in with him. Hana immediately moves over so she can sit next to her.

SangSoo's face is pale, and her bottom lip is swollen. A thin line of dried blood has crusted along one edge. Her neck is bruised, and she can't stop shivering. Her dress is torn and fastened together with pins where the buttons should be. Hana leans her shoulder gently against SangSoo's, and the young girl emits a pitiful sob. She clasps SangSoo's hand in hers without a word. *She survived*, Hana thinks, but her happiness is muted by the state of the poor girl.

One of the soldiers sits across from them, next to the other girl. The other soldier steps over Hana's legs and squeezes next to her beside the window. She is too afraid to look at the man's face, but as the train gains speed and begins to glide over the tracks, she knows exactly who he is. She recognises his cologne. She stiffens at the sudden realisation and glances at his hand. Morimoto fingers the hem of her dress, playing with it like a cat toying with a trapped mouse, flicking its tail and blocking its escape without ever directly looking at its prey.

Throughout the journey, he smokes cigarettes non-stop, tobacco smoke filling their compartment. His fingertips constantly graze the hem of her skirt, taunting her, but he doesn't look at her. Her heart thuds in her chest, erratic beats that make her strain for breath. She does her best not to move, except when his fingers come too close and threaten to touch her skin, and then she very slowly edges her leg away from him.

The train travels through the night, and soon everyone in the small compartment dozes off, except Hana. Anger and fear swarm through her body, radiating in hot waves towards the soldier beside her. He stole her from her seaside home, from everything she knows and loves, and then raped her. All she can think about is murdering him in his sleep. The more time passes by, the more she cannot get the thought out of her head. Slowly, she turns to face him. Did he rape SangSoo, too? Hana looks at the other soldier sitting across from her. Did they both hurt her?

Hana turns back to Morimoto. His chest rises with each deep intake of breath, and Hana imagines his heart beating beneath the buttons of his uniform. At his waist, she spies a pistol safely tucked in its holster. Can she retrieve it without waking him? Hana stares at the black pistol barely visible in the leather holster. She imagines what it might feel like in her hands, aiming it at his heart. Will it be heavy? Does she merely have to pull the trigger or is there something more technical she has to do first? Could she really shoot him? No, she thinks, finally, but she could stab him. The thought feels right, comforting somehow.

A knife she knows how to wield. She dived with one every day, cutting abalone from the reef beds, harvesting seaweed, and even prising open the odd oyster left behind by the Japanese oyster boats. She would carve out his heart as if it were a pearl tucked deep inside an oyster's flesh. The thought sends trickles up her spine, fingers of revenge dancing on her vertebrae. Is this what courage feels like? She imagines stabbing him in the chest, the surprise on his face. Her anger courses through her veins. And then, she thinks, she and SangSoo can flee the compartment, hide on the train or jump from an open window, and escape. Hana wishes she had a knife to make it all come true.

Morimoto shifts in his sleep, startling her. Hana jerks, accidentally nudging SangSoo, asleep beside her. Struck by the chill of her skin, Hana notices SangSoo has stopped shivering. Hana places the flat of her palm on the girl's forehead. It is cool to the touch. Her lips are flesh-coloured. Stifling the rising panic in her gut, Hana bends her head forward, placing her ear in front of SangSoo's mouth to listen for breath. Nothing.

Hana suddenly can't swallow. She begins to choke in panic. The noise wakes the others in the compartment.

'What's going on?' Morimoto demands. 'What's wrong with you?'

He stands and pulls Hana to face him. She continues choking, grasping her throat. He shouts again, incoherent words, and Hana merely points to SangSoo's still body. He follows her finger and glances at the young girl. He releases Hana, his eyes on the small girl sitting still through all the commotion. He remains silent for a long while. Then the girl across from them cries out.

'She's dead! She, she's dead!' she shouts again and again. Terror animates her face and she is no longer pretty.

A clatter outside the compartment announces the approach of more soldiers. The door slides open and two questioning faces appear. Morimoto finally speaks.

'This one's dead. Take her to the back until we arrive at the next station. Then bury her.'

'Bury her?' one of the soldiers repeats.

'Yes, bury her. Put her with the others.'

'Of course, sir.'

The two men lift SangSoo's body as though it is nothing but a sack of rice and carry her out of the compartment. The door slides shut and Morimoto resumes sleeping as though nothing has happened. Staring at him, incredulous, Hana recalls his words. He said *others*. How many more dead girls are on the train?

The thought of SangSoo's tiny body being dumped is too much, and Hana begins to cry. She has been holding back her fear and sorrow – holding back her guilt. Now she can't stop the sobs; it's as though the sounds are being wrenched from her stomach by an invisible fist. No one says a word to hush her. Instead, Morimoto begins to snore.

The girl sitting across from her pats Hana's knee from time to time, sniffling in between Hana's mournful sobs, but nothing else in the small compartment acknowledges the loss of SangSoo's life. Not the blackened newspaper on the windows or the swaying light shade above their heads. Not the walls heaving with the movement of the train or the soldiers fast asleep.

Somewhere beyond that train snaking through unknown lands, far across a sea, back on their small island, SangSoo's parents, too, remain ignorant of her death. Perhaps they are asleep in their homes, dreaming of her imminent return, hoping beyond hope that they will see her one day, that time will return her to them. Hana imagines them, waiting for a daughter who will never return home, dead after only a few days away. They will wonder about her for ages and may never know how long ago she left them.

It takes two days for the train to arrive at the next station. The soldiers bury SangSoo beside the tracks in an unmarked grave with four other bodies. They make the girls watch, to see what happens to girls who do not obey orders. The dead are wrapped in sheets, but Hana knows which is SangSoo's because it is the smallest, the most insignificant. That is how the soldiers see her, how they see all of the girls.

Morimoto says she died of an infection from a cut on her leg, but Hana knows the truth. Once Hana's grief quietened down, she noticed the blood on the seat. It had soaked into the leather, and rivulets had streamed like veins down the sides onto the floor. SangSoo bled to death. She was too small, too young, to endure such torture. How many men raped this little girl?

Hana can't help but compare SangSoo to her little sister, Emiko. If Hana had not gone with Morimoto, he would have taken her sister. The thought that she could have suffered the same fate as SangSoo, dying a terrible death so far from home, makes Hana's stomach feel as though it has dropped down to the ground. But it isn't so; she is safe.

On her island, a burial ceremony would have taken place, and the gods would have been called upon to guide SangSoo's spirit onward to her ancestors. Hana doesn't know who the girl's ancestors are. She knows nothing about her except that she is from Jeju Island, and her Japanese name is Noriko. SangSoo, Noriko, Little Sister. Hana knows she will never forget her.

She closes her eyes and wishes SangSoo's spirit a safe journey home, wishes it not to be restless from such a painful death, and especially wishes it not to haunt her dreams searching for revenge on the girl who should have been taken in her place.

Two new girls join them in their compartment, and the train soon commences its journey. Hana does her best to keep her mind off SangSoo. Instead, she thinks of her little sister, and how she is still safe at home where Hana longs to be. At least she saved one girl from the soldiers. She aimed too high in thinking she could save two.

Hana keeps Emi's face in her mind so that she won't see SangSoo's pale skin. She thinks of diving in the sea so she won't feel the chill against her fingertips. She thinks of black seaweed swaying with the currents and miles of deepest blue water, so she won't see red, the colour of death. When Hana finally submits to the call of sleep, she dreams of her family, swimming at the bottom of a dark ocean, but at times she isn't certain if they are swimming or merely swaying with the current, eyes lifeless and skin cold as the water swirling around them.

Emi

Seoul, December 2011

Emi's daughter, YoonHui, lives near Ewha Womans University in Seoul. Emi helped her with the down payment to purchase the small one-bedroom apartment fifteen years ago. It seemed like a good investment, so Emi sold their family home near the tangerine grove and moved into the shack beside the road. YoonHui is a professor of Korean literature at the university, and she is doing well. She offers to pay the deposit back every time they see one another, but Emi won't accept the money. Her needs are met by what she finds in the sea, and that is enough to sustain her. Today, YoonHui's friend is over. She's feeding the dog at the coffee table with chopsticks.

'You remember Lane, don't you? She's an anthropology professor at the university.'

YoonHui has given the same introduction each time Emi has visited. Emi finds it peculiar that Lane is always there, always fawning over the dog, and always looking very much at home. She suspects they have been friends much longer than Emi has known of her.

'Hello, Mother, you look well.'

'Hello, Lane,' Emi replies. Lane has lived in South Korea for over a decade and has adopted most of the country's customs. No one is called by their name in Korean culture; instead they are all mothers, fathers, big and little sisters and brothers, aunts and uncles, or grandmothers and grandfathers. Even strangers are given such names. If YoonHui had married and had children like most women her age, Lane would be calling Emi Grandmother instead of Mother, but there are no children in YoonHui's home, so she is merely Mother. Even her son forgets and calls her Mother instead of Grandmother when their grandson is around. Perhaps if she visited more, made an effort to be a larger part of his life, she would have earned the title.

Lane also speaks impeccable Korean. Her city accent makes her sound sophisticated for an American. Most Americans have a heavy accent and sound dim-witted to Emi's ear, like the tourists who visit the *haenyeo* on Jeju Island. They arrive in groups, taxied in from the airport, and take photos of the *haenyeo* with their phones and expensive digital cameras. A few of them are confident enough to try out their basic Korean on the divers, who always giggle and smile at their attempts to converse. JinHee is happiest when a tourist makes an effort, but Emi is nonplussed.

'You should be more grateful to them,' JinHee said once when Emi complained. 'At least they try to speak to us.'

'They stare at us like we are zoo animals,' Emi replied, without looking at her friend.

'Hush, they do not! And anyway, they help keep our way of life alive.'

Emi laughed, incredulous. 'How do *they* keep our way of life alive when *we* are the ones who must do all the work?'

JinHee gently patted Emi's shoulder. 'Their excitement for our work travels with them back to their home countries. They share our way of life with their friends and tell stories about their time with us. If we are still spoken about, then we can never disappear.'

Emi stared at JinHee, marvelling at her ability to always see the bigger picture.

Emi's daughter interrupts her thoughts. 'Are you hungry? I can prepare some lunch for you.'

'Nonsense, I ate lunch on the plane. I packed some dried squid and *kimbap* in my bag,' Emi answers, still thinking about her friend. How odd that she suddenly misses her, now that she has arrived at her daughter's home.

'Where's Hyoung?' her daughter asks.

'He had to return to work. He said he'd see us at dinner. He took YoungSook to basketball practice.' Emi misses her grandson already. 'He's grown so tall.'

'YoungSook wants to be a professional basketball player in America, doesn't he, Lane?' her daughter says. She's sitting beside Emi on the sofa, and they are both watching Lane expertly insert servings of rice into the dog's awaiting mouth.

'If that boy keeps growing at the rate he is now, he just might make it,' Lane says. 'He'll be like a Korean Yao Ming.'

The dog barks, the two friends laugh, and Emi thinks she sees Lane wink at her daughter.

'Oh, Mother, your hair,' her daughter says, returning her attention to Emi. 'You need another perm. Let me take you before dinner. We're going to Jungsik, so we can get your hair done nearby.'

Her daughter touches Emi's hair, making her laugh.

'No, no, I don't need a hair appointment. I'm too old for vanity.' She laughs again.

'Mother, you're never too old to look good,' Lane says as she stands to put away her lunch dishes.

The dog barks, running and leaping into Emi's lap. It's a toy poodle, white, with a cotton-wool ball for a tail. Emi pats the dog's soft head. Then she reaches into her shopping bag and pulls out the plush cat she bought on the plane.

'Can he have this?' she asks before giving it to the dog.

'Of course,' Lane says. 'Oh, how cute, look, YoonHui.'

Emi's daughter takes the toy and tears off the tags. 'Fetch, Snowball. Go get it.'

The dog races down the hallway and retrieves the cat, bringing it back to Emi. She tosses the cat across the room again and again, until he tires and plops down beside her feet, gnawing contentedly on the cat's stuffed head.

》-《

The chemicals from the perm emanate in waves each time Emi moves, so she tries to sit as still as possible as they dine at the restaurant. It's too fancy for her, and she understands why her daughter wanted to fix her up. She even suggested Emi change from her pink trousers because they were stained with the green tea. Emi only brought one other pair of trousers for her short stay in Seoul, so she put on the black pair she had planned to wear the next day. She was already wearing a black sweater, and her daughter's expression showed her disapproval.

'You're not going to a funeral, Mother. Don't you have another sweater?' Emi looked down at her clothes. She hadn't planned on wearing the two garments together, but suddenly she felt like she *was* going to a funeral. The heaviness in her heart became too much to bear, and though she didn't want to, she started to cry.

'Mother, I'm sorry. I didn't mean it.'

'No, no, it's not your fault. It's just . . .'

But Emi didn't have the words to explain. She accepted the tissue YoonHui held out to her and wiped her tears away. Her daughter sat silently in front of her, looking ashamed.

'It's nothing you said,' Emi told her daughter when she felt like herself again. 'Come, let's go and make me presentable.' She took YoonHui's hand and led her to her suitcase. 'What should I wear to dinner?'

YoonHui laughed and sifted through her mother's meagre belongings. In the end, they agreed on a cream sweater her daughter had hanging in her wardrobe. The sleeves were a little too long, so YoonHui folded the cuffs over, and Emi was reminded of her own mother. She had always thought YoonHui looked more like her husband, but sitting there in her daughter's capable hands, Emi saw her mother's face looking back at her. It eased her burden a little, lifting her spirits enough for her to smile when she gazed at herself in the beauty salon's mirror with her newly permed hair.

The waiter brings the tea and sets the tray in front of Emi. He pours the hot liquid into each ceramic cup, while YoonHui passes them around the table. Emi is surrounded by the faces of her family, her daughter-in-law and Lane. The faces are older than the ones she sees in her mind when she is at home. Her son should be a grandfather already, her daughter a grandmother. Her grandson should be a great-grandson. They are all talking and laughing and ordering food. Lane is telling a story about her last publication on the rise of female genital mutilation in Western countries and how more women are speaking out because of the Internet. Her daughter-in-law is fussing with her grandson's shirt collar. Her son is ordering whiskey after whiskey, neat. Emi is listening and not listening, until everyone is suddenly quiet and looking at her.

'Did you hear me?' her son asks.

She shakes her head.

'I said what are your plans tomorrow?'

'Tomorrow?' Emi asks, and she has suddenly forgotten why she has come. The restaurant seems unusually hushed. Her grandson blushes as though he is embarrassed for her.

'Yes, tomorrow,' YoonHui says, and caresses Emi's hand. 'Lane and I want to go with you.'

Emi feels confused. The fumes from her hair are making her light-headed. Too many eyes are studying her. She needs air. She makes a move to stand, and her daughter rises with her. Leaning on YoonHui, Emi shuffles away from the table and into the cold night air. Cars whizz by under bright city lights, flashing and buzzing on all the buildings. She is homesick for the quiet of her lonely hut, the roar of the ocean waves, and the simple laughter of her diving friends.

'I didn't want to fly,' she tells YoonHui. 'But I had to.' She touches the bruise above her eye.

YoonHui doesn't reply, but her arm tightens around Emi's shoulders. Side by side, they watch the city rush by in shiny imported cars on the street and designer heels clicking against the pavement. Emi recalls the ground far beneath her as she flew in the plane. The black of the runway was surrounded by the crumpled brown stalks of winter grass, and Emi could not stop her mind from imagining what lay beneath the tarmac, buried for too many years. *Who, not what.* There were many faces looking up from the earth as she flew overhead. Emi doesn't want to remember them. She pushes their vacant stares away, allowing the sounds of the city to distract her. Her mind eagerly wanders back to the twinkling lights and the comfort of her daughter's arm.

〉〉-〈〈

Emi awakens in the middle of the night. There was a noise or a voice; she thinks someone shouted her name. She sits up, clutching her nightshirt around her neck. The room is black, except for the glowing red numbers of the alarm clock. It's 3 a.m. Her daughter is gently snoring beside her. Emi slips out from beneath the blankets, careful not to wake her. Hands out in front of her, she feels her way through empty space towards the bedroom door.

In the compact kitchen, she boils water in the kettle. Snowball comes to see what she is up to and trails after her feet as she shuffles around. Emi sits at the breakfast table and the little dog hops onto her lap. She pats his fluffy head. She stares at the blankness of the kitchen wall, painted sky blue. Stroking the dog's soft fur, she recalls the dream that woke her in the night.

A girl is swimming in the ocean, diving for seashells. She waves at Emi and shows her the starfish she has found. Emi is standing on the shore, but she isn't wearing her wetsuit. Instead she is in a white cotton dress that falls just below her knees. The dress does little to camouflage her old woman's fleshy folds. On her feet are shiny black shoes that she has never seen before. In the water, the girl laughs and dives again. She resembles a dolphin, rising up and diving down, again and again, with effortless elegance. *Is that me in an earlier time?* Emi wonders.

In the distance, a black cloud rushes towards them. It swells around them like an angry sea, building in height and strength. Emi shouts for the young girl to come ashore. She yells to her that a storm is coming, but the girl cannot hear her above the wind. She dives again, and then the rain and thunder and lightning crash all around. The beach is pummelled with hail, and Emi tries to find shelter beneath a rock overhang, while keeping a lookout for the girl to resurface. But she doesn't emerge from the water.

Minutes pass, and Emi begins to fear the girl has drowned. The storm is gathering energy. Powerful waves crash into the shore. Emi knows the girl doesn't have a chance. She removes her shoes. Then she pulls the dress over her head. Naked, she runs towards the swirling sea and dives in. As her head plunges beneath the cold water, someone screams her name.

The kettle whistles, making Snowball bark. Emi quietens the dog and quickly removes the kettle from the stove. She pours the hot water into a mug and steeps a bag of green tea. As she sits back down, the dog leaps back onto her lap. Emi warms her hands around the mug as she waits for the water to turn a dark shade of yellow green. In all her years, she has never worn a pair of shiny black shoes like the ones in her dream. She might have worn a white dress, but not the shoes.

Emi sips from her mug and wonders what new shoes mean in dreams. JinHee would know. She interprets everyone's dreams whether they welcome it or not. And who was the young girl in the sea? Was it her younger self? Is the dream about the death of her childhood or perhaps her impending death?

You know who she is, the voice in her mind says accusatorily. Emi tries to block it out, but she thinks of the girl's face, conjuring it back into her mind.

'Hana,' she whispers to the empty room. It's a name she hasn't said for over sixty years.

Snowball cocks his head sideways. Emi shuffles into the living room with her tea. She sits down on the sofa so she won't disturb her daughter's sleep. Snowball hops up beside her and snuggles against her leg. Emi doesn't want to close her eyes. She's afraid that she'll see the dead girl floating in the ocean, black lifeless eyes staring up at her. She pats the dog's head and sips her tea until the sun's early rays glint upon the windowsill.

Hana

Korea, Summer 1943

The train travels only during the night, when the bombers flying overhead can't see it driving supplies north. There are many stops along the way, but the girls are forced to remain on the train. They are given very little food and water. Hana is starving. Her stomach feels like it is eating itself from the inside out. Waiting for daylight to pass is excruciating. The girls are ordered to sit in silence, while the soldiers smoke, eat and joke.

The two girls who joined them when the train paused in the station are friendly, but Hana isn't very talkative after what happened to SangSoo. The moon-faced girl who witnessed SangSoo's death seems relieved to have new friends to talk to. Her expression is pretty once more; the shock has worn away. Sometimes, the four of them are left alone, and it is then they share their stories.

The three girls seem desperate to tell their life histories to one another. Hana sits quietly and listens, one eye trained on a sliver of sunlight streaming through the blacked-out window. Shadows pass across the thin line, and she wonders if they are from passing soldiers or civilians, civilians who might be inclined to help.

'My mother sent me to keep house for my aunt in Seoul, but I never made it there,' one girl says. She is the oldest of the group, probably nineteen, and she has a dimple in one cheek. Her hair is curly and frizzed into an unruly mass, which she ties at the nape of her neck.

'I was waiting for the bus at a station along my route. I had three stops before I would arrive at Seoul, and this army officer drove up. He asked me where I was going, and I told him. He said the bus was delayed and it would be hours before it would arrive. He offered me a ride.' She looks guiltily at the others, waiting for them to judge her, but no one says a word, so she continues.

'I know I shouldn't have believed him. My mother said not to believe a Japanese. That they're not really our friends because they see Koreans as inferior citizens, but . . . he seemed so friendly. I thought he really meant to help me.' Her voice fades to a whisper. 'I've never been away from home before,' she adds.

Hana looks back at the sliver of light and the shadows dancing across it. She has never been away from home either. Her mother is also suspicious of the Japanese. She didn't let the girls out of her sight, except when she had to, and then Hana was placed in charge with very strict orders to stay away from strangers. Her father was often gone all day, fishing for the scraps the Japanese boats left behind. He often returned home late at night, long after Hana and her mother and sister returned from the market, and he revealed his haul to them with great fanfare.

'Look what I have brought for our feast tonight!' he would call as he entered their small traditional house.

Hana and her sister would squeal with delight and run to him before he could even step over the threshold, each attaching to one of his legs. He would stomp into the house like a sea monster rising from the dark ocean depths. Even at sixteen, Hana continued the tradition, for her sister's amusement. Her sister would giggle with delight as their father struggled to move his overburdened leg. Hana would have to help him along, just enough so that her sister wouldn't notice. The small performance was their way of incorporating happiness into their home, even though their father was bone tired and prematurely ageing from exhaustion and stress.

'Where's my queen?' he would say before settling down to open his sack.

'In the kitchen, where else?' her sister would shout, and her mother would peek her head through the doorway.

'Ah, there is my fair bride, and what a lovely scent permeates through our palace tonight. Here, my soldiers of fortune, our feastly spoils are yours to bestow upon my beautiful cooking wife.'

That was the cue for Hana and her sister to rummage through the sack and emit sounds of pleasure and surprise at each fish, morsel of seaweed, or bag of rice pulled from it. Sometimes, her father would surprise them with pears he had managed to trade fish for, but those were a special treat not revealed more than once or twice a year. The night before her abduction, her father had brought home two large pears. She can almost taste their juicy flesh, the flavour sitting on the edge of her memory.

'He took me to an army depot, and they made me sign a form, but I can't read Japanese. I never went to school,' the girl continues shamefully. 'I had no idea what was going on. He left me there with a Korean man who told me my aunt no longer needed my services. He said the emperor needed me now. That I was to work for the glory of Japan.'

Hana looks at the girl's face and sees innocence in her eyes. The soldiers haven't raped her. Hana wonders if the soldiers only raided the cabin she was held in on the ferry. She can't possibly tell these girls what happened to her. They are silent, waiting for her to speak because it is her turn to share her story. Hana glances at each of their expectant faces, apologises, and turns away, focusing on the fading sunlight.

By the end of the week-long train journey, Hana finds herself alone in the compartment. The other three girls were removed at earlier stations. Morimoto hasn't spoken to her the entire way; he has hardly even looked at her. It is as though he has forgotten she is there, until they arrive at their destination in Manchuria. Suddenly, he is all business: ordering her off the train, handing her paperwork to the officer in charge, and marching away as though he has not dragged her halfway across the world. The new soldier leaves to procure a transport vehicle, and she is for the briefest of moments left alone.

She scans her surroundings and very nearly darts across the road, when she sees Morimoto already on his way back. He is holding a packet of cigarettes. Standing next to her, he lights one. He takes a few drags and then holds the cigarette out to her.

'Do you know how to smoke?'

Hana stares at the cigarette and then at him, wondering if it is some sort of trick. He laughs at her, a light sound, as though he is a casual friend offering a silly girl nothing more sinister than a cigarette.

'It's easy, watch me,' he says, and takes a long puff. He squints as the smoke curls upwards into the night sky.

He then takes the cigarette from between his lips and slowly pushes it into her mouth. She remains still, afraid he might burn her or worse.

'Breathe in,' he says.

Hana shakes her head, and he drops the cigarette. He smacks her. The sting brings tears to her stunned eyes. He retrieves the cigarette from the dirt and lights it again. He pushes it between her lips.

'You will learn to do as you are told. Breathe in.'

To refuse him would be madness, so she does as he wishes and inhales, immediately coughing as the burning smoke singes her tender throat.

He laughs, slapping her on the back like a big brother would. The cigarette falls from her lips back into the dirt. He smashes it with the toe of his boot. When the other soldier returns, Morimoto chats with him as though Hana isn't there. Morimoto pats him on the shoulder, they laugh, the soldier salutes, and Morimoto returns the gesture. The other soldier leads Hana towards a jeep parked beside the train station. Morimoto lights another cigarette, exhaling a cloud of smoke as they pass him on the dirt road. Hana tastes the tobacco on her tongue as they drive away.

>-<

It is dark, so she can't see very much of the Manchurian countryside besides shadows of scattered bushes and tall grassy pastures as they drive past. The night sky is darker than she has seen in a long time, with no moon to light their way. The truck's headlamps barely help the driver navigate the bumpy dirt road. Hana falls asleep and is surprised when a rough hand shakes her awake.

'We're here, get out,' the soldier orders.

Lit up by the truck's headlights, a large wooden inn looms over them. It is two storeys tall with barred windows along the upper floor. The door opens and another soldier steps out, beckoning them inside.

'Is this the replacement girl?' he asks as they gather in the entrance hall.

'Yes, from Corporal Morimoto.'

'Of course,' he says with a grin.

They salute one another, and without glancing at Hana, the

soldier jumps back into the truck. Hana watches as he revs the engine and drives away. The soldier in the inn shuts the door behind her and bolts it. He calls for someone, and an old woman appears, wearing Chinese-style clothes. She places one arm around Hana and steers her further into the inn. Hana follows her, relieved to be with a woman. Perhaps she is at a workhouse. The thought gives her a small amount of courage.

'Can you tell me where I am?' Hana asks, speaking in the mandated Japanese.

The woman doesn't reply. Hana tries again, but the woman just leads Hana into a large entrance hallway and ushers her towards an old wooden staircase. It leads to the upper floor, which is bathed in darkness.

'What's up there?' Hana asks.

The woman lights a candle and begins ascending the staircase. At the foot of the staircase, Hana pauses. Framed portraits of girls hang in two rows on the wall above the first step. Each girl has identically bobbed hair and a solemn, unsmiling expression. There is a number beneath each frame. Their dark eyes seem to watch her as she follows the woman up the stairs, and she does her best not to feel afraid.

The candle flickers on the walls of the gloomy hallway, but it doesn't shine enough light for Hana to see all of her surroundings. They pass a few doors, and then the woman pauses in front of one and opens it with a key. Hana steps inside and the woman turns to leave.

'Wait,' Hana calls to her. 'Please tell me where I am,' she begs, but the woman's slippers are already slapping against the wooden stairs as she heads back down.

Hana is left alone to inspect the small room in near darkness. It is barely large enough to contain the tatami mat laid out in one corner against the wall and the basin beside it. Hana rushes to the basin and finds it filled with cool water. She lifts it to her lips and the water rushes down her throat. She drinks and drinks, not questioning the cleanliness of the water or what it's there for. She swallows every last drop. Then she lies on the tatami mat and waits for the old woman to return.

Hana wakes from a fitful slumber when the old woman enters the room. She carries a bowl of soupy rice on a tray with a side dish of Japanese pickles. Hana sits up and a rush of questions fly from her lips.

'Where am I? Why am I here? When can I go home to my mother?' She is desperate for answers. She even repeats the questions in Korean.

The woman shakes her head. She speaks in another language that Hana assumes is Mandarin. She motions for Hana to eat the rice and turns to leave. When she opens the door, a deep, unearthly moan drifts into the room.

'What's that?' Hana can't help asking, but the woman again shakes her head. She leaves the room without saying anything more.

Hana goes to the door and peers out. The woman shuffles away, her small shoulders sagging inward. Hana feels certain it can't be such a bad place if the old woman didn't bother to lock the door to the room. It is as though Hana might be free to roam the inn, as though she is no longer a prisoner, or if she is still a prisoner, the woman might not care whether Hana tries to escape. Or perhaps there is nowhere to escape to, her mind interjects, stopping her hope from growing too large.

The sound comes again, a wail, inhumanly low, like death. Hana wants to shut the door and huddle in the furthest corner of the room, but she has to know what creature could make such a terrible sound. Perhaps if she finds the source of the sound, she will know where she is and why she was brought here.

The door to her room is one of many that opens onto a balcony that overlooks a small lounge with more doors leading off it. More candles have been lit downstairs, and Hana can see the space more clearly. It is bare, as though the inn's furniture has yet to arrive.

The moan comes again, and Hana thinks it came from the door nearest the bottom of the stairs. It sits ajar, and she can see shadows moving within. Without thinking of her safety or anything more than finding the source of that sound, she creeps down the wooden staircase, cringing after every creak of the wooden steps. She glances at the girls on the wall as she reaches the bottom step. They seem to hover above her, watchful and accusing. Hana turns away from them, tiptoeing to the door. She holds her breath and looks into the room.

A woman with her legs splayed and her thighs covered in blood lies on a mat against the far wall. A man with a cloth mask over his nose and mouth crouches between her legs. The hairs on Hana's neck stiffen when she realises the death moan is coming from the bloody woman.

'She must push,' the Japanese man says to someone next to him. Hana can't see the other person but hears her voice.

'The doctor says you must push,' she says in Korean.

Hana involuntarily sucks in a quick breath. The woman is Korean. She cries out, a deep, hollow sound that is more animal than human. Hana turns to run back up the stairs, partly afraid of the woman giving birth and partly relieved that she has ended up somewhere with other Koreans.

'She's not going to make it,' the doctor says in Japanese, and Hana freezes.

'What about the baby?' the woman beside him asks.

'It's already dead.'

'Can you save her by operating?'

'The risk of infection is too high.'

'What's to be done about her, then?'

'Either she pushes it out, or she dies with it. Tell her if she wants to live, she must push harder.'

Hana doesn't wait to hear more. She rushes up the stairs quietly, ducks into her room, and sits, shaking, with her knees pulled into her chest. Even as she listens to the labouring woman's cries of pain, Hana's eyes keep drifting to the bowl of soupy rice and the pickles on the tray. Her stomach grumbles. It sickens her to recognise her hunger in the midst of another woman's death throes. Yet, that is not enough to stop her from satisfying it. The train journey was too long.

She reaches for the bowl and slurps up the rice. When the bowl is empty, she eats the pickles, all at once, and then she wipes her face with the hem of her dress. Another moan slides beneath the shut door, and Hana feels sick. Nausea overwhelms her, and she crawls to the basin against the wall and vomits.

Rice, water and pickles splash into the curve of the metal basin. Wiping her mouth with the back of her hand, she rises to her feet to carry the basin downstairs to dump it. Halfway to the staircase, she hears the woman again and can't bear to go down. She rushes back to the room.

As she nears the door, she notices a wooden plaque next to it. It is carved with the name of a flower in Japanese script and a number: Sakura (cherry blossom) – 2. The other doors on the landing have a plaque with the name of a flower next to them, too. She passes them one by one: Tsubaki (camellia) – 3, Hinata (sunflower) – 4, Kiku (chrysanthemum) – 5, Ayame (iris) – 6 and Riko (jasmine) – 7. When she reaches the last one, she hears a noise at the other end of the hallway, near her room.

Hana is hesitant to investigate but heads back towards her room and sees another door beyond hers. The plaque beside it displays not a flower but a name: Keiko (blessing) – 1. Hana hears a shuffling noise inside. Desperate to find someone who will tell her where she is and why she was brought to this place, she quickly places the basin on the floor and reaches for the door handle. Fear sends her heart into an unsteady beat, too fast, too hard, restricting the air to her lungs, but the handle turns easily.

The room is identical to the one she was placed in. A candle burns on the floor beside a woman kneeling on the mat with her hands covering her face. She is crying without making a sound. Her shoulders shudder with each muted sob. Hana starts to shut the door, but the woman notices her presence and lowers her hands. They stare at one another.

'You must be the new Sakura,' the woman says in Japanese.

Hana is relieved that they can communicate.

'Are you Keiko?' Hana asks, recalling the plaque outside the door. The woman nods. The plaques are names. Hana's is now Sakura.

'You're so young,' Keiko says, shaking her head. 'How many years are you?'

'Sixteen,' Hana answers, embarrassed at the quaver in her voice. By the light of the candle, Hana estimates Keiko's age as somewhere in her thirties.

'I was your age once. It seems like a lifetime ago.'

The woman downstairs moans, and Keiko covers her mouth with her hands, stifling a sob.

'Do you know her?' Hana asks.

'She is my friend,' Keiko says after a long pause, her voice trembling.

'The baby is dead,' Hana says, before she can stop herself. Her stomach churns.

'Good.' A dark expression sweeps over her porcelain features.

Hana is taken aback by Keiko's anger.

'She might die, too,' she says, wondering if Keiko will be glad at that news, as well.

Keiko's face softens, and she looks down at her hands lying limp on her lap.

'That would be good, too.'

The woman sounds as though it would be the worst thing to happen, the very opposite of the words she spoke.

'I don't understand,' Hana says softly.

'You will soon enough,' Keiko answers without looking up. 'Go back to your room. If they find you here, we will both answer for it.'

Hana wants to ask what she means, but a man's voice comes from below.

'Go!' Keiko whispers harshly.

Hana quickly leaves Keiko's room, picks up the basin, and slips back into her designated room. It soon begins to smell of bile, and she wonders if she should pour the vomit out of the window, but she recalls Keiko's fear and thinks better of it. Hana lies down on the tatami mat and wonders about the ominous words Keiko said to her. No one else enters her room that night, and Hana falls asleep clutching her empty stomach.

The next day Hana learns that Keiko's friend died in labour, but not before she understands why she was brought to this place.

Emi

Seoul, December 2011

Emi's daughter awakens her with a gentle squeeze on her arm. Her eyes feel dry and scratchy.

'Breakfast is ready,' YoonHui says.

Emi smells freshly brewed coffee, along with boiled rice and pan-fried whitefish. Her stomach grumbles. Rising from the sofa, her knees pop. Snowball wags his tail and follows her into the bathroom. He doesn't seem to mind watching her go about her morning business. It's like they're old companions with years of intimacy behind them. She splashes water onto her face and then cups her hands over her eyes, soaking them in cold water. Refreshed, she picks up the little dog and shuffles into the kitchen.

Her daughter has outdone herself. An array of dishes on small porcelain plates sits on the breakfast table next to two steaming bowls of rice.

'You made my favourite *banchan*,' Emi exclaims, motioning towards the seasoned bean sprouts.

'I spent yesterday morning cooking,' YoonHui admits, and sits across from her mother.

Emi picks up her chopsticks and retrieves a portion of bean sprouts. They taste excellent, and she tells her daughter so. They eat in silence for a while, although Snowball intermittently makes his presence known. YoonHui feeds the dog a few morsels of fish.

After breakfast, they take their coffee to the living room, and her daughter puts on a CD. Classical piano music drifts about the room, and she turns the volume down.

'This is pretty music,' Emi says.

'It's Chopin. You liked it last time, too.'

'Yes, it's very good.'

YoonHui smiles and looks out the window. Emi thinks Lane must be arriving soon.

'Mother, are you sure it's OK if Lane comes with us today? You don't mind?'

'I told you, I don't mind. Don't worry about me. Is your brother coming?'

'No, he has to work.'

'And my grandson?'

'He has school. We'll meet them again for dinner tonight.'

Her daughter audibly releases a heavy breath. Emi thinks she's upset. She doesn't know why, so she sits and waits, even though she has finished her coffee and wants to get dressed.

'Mother? Can I ask you something?'

She looks afraid to speak. Even after all these years, her daughter, a fifty-eight-year-old woman, is afraid to speak to her own mother. Emi wonders what she must have done to make her daughter so fearful.

'Of course, ask me anything.'

YoonHui swallows and stares at her coffee mug. She licks her lips and doesn't look up when she speaks.

'Were you a "comfort woman"?' Silence falls between them like an invisible sheet.

Emi does not immediately answer; instead she looks at her hands.

'Is that why you've started going to the Wednesday Demonstrations whenever you visit us?' her daughter continues. Concern wrinkles her forehead.

Emi touches the table. It feels solid and smooth. Her heart clenches. The Wednesday Demonstrations have been held every week since the first so-called comfort woman came forward twenty years ago, though Emi has only attended once a year for the last three years. The demonstration calls for justice, for the Japanese government to admit their war crimes committed against thousands of women during the Second World War.

So many years have passed since the war ended, since the protests began, yet still the crimes go unpunished. What does it require to deserve an apology? To give one? Emi touches her chest. Her heart unclenches. Today's demonstration is special, the one thousandth protest.

'Why can't you talk to me?' Her daughter's voice aches with hurt.

Emi places her palms onto her thighs. She has never known how to talk to her own daughter. YoonHui is an academic, ruled by logic. Her every decision is painfully researched and carried out with calculated precision. That's why she couldn't follow Emi into the sea to make her living as a *haenyeo*. Instead she left for university in search of a world that made sense to her. Emi could never understand the world her daughter inhabits. Just as her daughter could never understand the secrets Emi has kept from her for her entire life. She doesn't know enough words to explain to her daughter a lifetime of silence. But she cannot tell more lies.

'I was never a "comfort woman". You shouldn't doubt me.' Emi looks at her daughter as she speaks, hoping it will be enough.

'I – I don't doubt you, I just . . . I want you to share your life with me. Some part of you.' YoonHui looks down at her coffee. She looks ashamed and a little angry.

'YoonHui.' Emi says her name softly.

YoonHui looks up. She doesn't hide her anger. Instead she seems to dare her mother to lie to her. The fierce tiger still resides in her, and Emi feels a surge of pride.

'I'm searching for someone, that's all. I hope to find word of her there.'

'Who is it? A friend?'

The girl from her dream flashes into her mind. She sees the young face. Who is she looking for? A girl lost so many years ago? A woman grown old in another land? Yet, if she answers her daughter truthfully, Emi knows she will open a vault that has been sealed for over six decades, and there will be no way to close it once opened. Behind that sealed door lie deceit, pain, fear, worry, shame, everything from her past life that she hid from her children, and as she grew older, even from herself. It suddenly overcomes her, as though a heavy military boot worn by a faceless soldier has just kicked her breath away. Her shoulders sag, and she can't look at her daughter. She stares beyond her at the linoleum floor, covered in marbled lines that converge like delicate flowers.

It was a flower that sent Emi to the Wednesday Demonstrations in the first place. Three years ago JinHee convinced her to attend the inaugural ceremony for the opening of the Jeju Peace Park. The park was created to commemorate the 1948 Jeju Uprising, which led to the massacre of over twenty thousand islanders. So many of those killed were unjustly accused. She still remembers the fear that plagued her village, everyone afraid to become labelled as a red, a communist. Anyone seen as sympathetic to Soviet-supported North Korea was thrown into prisons, beaten, tortured, and then killed when the South Korean interim government, supported by the United States military, ordered the mass execution of suspected leftists as a pre-emptive measure at the outbreak of the Korean War.

Emi was just fourteen when her family home was burned to the ground. Her village was one of many suspected of harbouring leftist rebels fighting for the communist North. She never spoke about it, but JinHee lived through it, too. She knew the painful memories in Emi's heart because she had to bear her own. The opening ceremony at the Peace Park was the first step in healing the wounds of the island's blood-filled past, and JinHee did not rest until Emi agreed to attend.

'Those nightmares you're having won't go away on their own,' JinHee said after a long morning of diving. They were sitting at the market selling their catch. Emi had filled an extra bucketful of abalone, a lucky day's find. 'You need to confront your past. This may help.'

'Past is past,' Emi replied, watching the shoppers stroll by. A little girl holding her mother's index finger caught her attention. They were tourists from the mainland. The girl's bright eyes fixed on her. She smiled, and Emi looked away. She had been having nightmares for a long while. She couldn't remember when they had begun, but she knew they had started sometime after her husband had died.

'Nothing can be done about it,' Emi answered.

'So stubborn. You cling to your *han* like it owns you.' JinHee shook her head in dismay, then waved to the little girl, who covered her mouth and giggled.

'I do not,' Emi replied, stopping short and sitting a little taller, kneading her lame leg with one hand.

'We're all going. We're renting a van to take us there.'

Emi didn't reply. She looked back at the little girl, who appeared carefree and light as air as she skipped beside her mother through the crowded market. The pang of jealousy Emi repressed each time she saw a happy child throbbed. Everyone had suffered during the Japanese occupation of Korea. Many had survived the Second World War only to die in the Korean War. But if, like Emi, they had managed to live through both, they forever after carried a burden of helplessness and overwhelming regret. Family members murdered, starved, stolen, neighbours turning on one another – all this was their *han*, a word every Korean knew and a burden they each held within them. Everyone, even JinHee and the other divers, carried this *han*, but it was no one's business how Emi dealt with hers.

JinHee touched Emi's good leg. 'Don't let your stubbornness keep you from finding peace.'

Emi was about to argue her case, but JinHee held her hands in the air, surrendering.

'I'll shut up, I promise—'

'Good,' Emi said, prematurely.

'But only if you come with us,' JinHee shouted, and clapped her hands in the air. 'You'll never have peace otherwise, with yourself or with me!' Then she let out her famous laugh, which echoed among the stalls. Eyes had fallen upon them, and Emi had no choice but to smile.

The drive to the memorial was filled with storytelling and tears as they recalled the uprising and the subsequent slaughter. Many of the divers had been young girls at the time and had lost parents, aunts, uncles, siblings and grandparents. Emi sat in the front seat of the van, staring out of the window but listening. She didn't join in because her memories of that time wouldn't come. When she tried to conjure an image of the period after Korea's liberation from the Japanese, a haze covered her mind. It was as though the fifty years of strict governmental suppression that had followed had done their work. Not even the freedoms of the current government had changed her inability to speak about it. Emi's mind had blocked out the memories of her painful past so that she could raise her children and survive. But that didn't stop the dreams.

'You OK?' JinHee asked when they arrived at the park.

Emi shrugged, and when JinHee kept hovering near her as though looking after a child, Emi batted her away.

More than five thousand people attended the ceremony. Emi peered through the crowd, wondering how many had once lived on Jeju Island and left because of the atrocities committed by their own countrymen. A woman passed by her carrying a bouquet of white flowers. Suddenly, it seemed as if everyone was carrying the same white flowers. Emi didn't know why the innocent blooms disconcerted her, but as people passed her carrying them in their arms, she began to feel out of breath. Clutching her chest, she noticed they were all headed in the same direction and began to follow them.

Her heart quickened again as she neared a mass of people crowded around a table. It was covered in white chrysanthemums, a symbol of mourning. Burial flowers were amassed before her as hundreds of visitors offered them to the long-lost dead. The flurry of white and darkest green loosened a memory in Emi's mind. Another ceremony, long ago. She saw her mother handing her one of these white, ghostly blooms.

The dreams increased in intensity every night thereafter, and Jin-Hee was sorry she had forced Emi to go to the remembrance ceremony. The memories Emi had repressed for too long began to haunt her beyond her dreams. They came to her during the day, while she cooked her breakfast or even as she dived in the sea. They were small flashes at first, an image of a girl swimming towards a rocky beach, a soldier standing on the shore, voices trailing away, until one day she couldn't hold them back any longer. They affected her productivity, threatened to knock her off her feet. Her entire history crashed back into her consciousness so painfully that she had her first heart attack. The doctor warned her she needed to take it easy and to minimise stress at all costs. But the memories began to plague her, and she couldn't ignore them any longer. So the next time she boarded a bus to Seoul to visit her daughter, she snuck away and went to her first Wednesday Demonstration in search of a girl lost long ago.

The dog barks, pulling Emi's attention back to the present. Her daughter is waiting for an explanation. Emi reaches down and picks up the dog and hugs him close to her stomach. The silky fur and small, warm body ease her mind, just a little.

'Mother?'

'It was a long time ago, during the war; the Japanese took a girl from our village, and she never came back.'

'Who was she?'

'Someone I loved.'

Her daughter remains quiet, but the anger has dissipated, leaving her eyes full of questions. Emi says no more. She places the little poodle onto the floor and eases herself to her feet. As she shuffles to the bedroom to change her clothes, her daughter calls out to her.

'You know that I love Lane, right?'

Emi stops a moment and looks back at her daughter. She can still see the little girl she once taught to swim in the cold waters of the South Sea, her perfectly round face smiling up at Emi as they splashed each other and swam circles around the *haenyeo* coming in from a long day of diving. Emi dreamed her daughter would one day dive beside her like the other girls did with their mothers, like she had with her own mother. But then YoonHui grew up so quickly and was so full of ideas, Emi couldn't keep up with the new and ever-changing thoughts from her maturing mind. The day she told Emi that she didn't want to learn to dive was the worst day Emi ever experienced as a mother. She should have expected it. YoonHui was nothing like the other girls. She looked up into the sky instead of down into the waters.

'Why can't I continue to go to school?' YoonHui asked one afternoon.

She was ten years old, only a year into her training as a *haenyeo*. It was also her final year at school. Emi had just finished diving for the day and was sorting her catch on the shore. The other women were nearby emptying their nets, too, and Emi knew they were all listening.

'Because I can teach you everything you need to know about diving here in the sea. A school cannot do this.'

YoonHui was thoughtful for a moment before replying. She seemed to weigh her words carefully. Emi continued sorting her catch. She remarked on how many more abalone she had found the day before. JinHee and a few others agreed with her.

'Mother,' YoonHui interrupted, demanding Emi's attention again.

'What, daughter?'

'I've decided . . . well, after very careful consideration, I've decided I want to go to school like Big Brother.'

Emi stopped gutting the squid in her hand. She looked at her daughter for a long time, saying nothing.

'Don't be angry. I have thought this through. I want to go to university one day. I want to be a teacher.'

'Is that so?' Emi went back to gutting and sorting, her hands methodically working through her catch.

'Yes, Mother. It is so. It is very so.'

YoonHui placed her hands on her narrow hips and straightened her thin shoulders. She held her head high and looked directly into Emi's eyes. It took all of Emi's self-control not to beam with pride at her silly, stubborn daughter, even as she simultaneously fought to conceal the hurt YoonHui's decision caused her.

'All the women of our family become *haenyeo*. We are women of the sea. It is in our blood. We don't become teachers. This is our gift and our destiny.' Emi eyed her daughter, impressing the importance of her words through her expression. YoonHui barely blinked.

'That was before the war. Now there's more opportunity. I am a smart girl, and my teacher says I'm even smarter than Big Brother was at my age. He says I'm too smart to waste my talents working like a field hand in the ocean, risking my life in the perils of the sea. No, Mother, I belong in school.'

'Field hand?' a few of the other *haenyeo* repeated in surprise.

'Who's calling us field hands?'

'What's that man's name?'

'Your teacher is a man,' Emi said in a controlled yet strong voice. The others hushed to listen. 'He is not from our island. He is from the mainland, and a mainlander cannot possibly understand what it means to be a *haenyeo*.'

'Yes, that's right!' replied a chorus of women.

'We dive in the sea like our mothers and grandmothers and great-grandmothers have for hundreds of years. This gift is our pride, for we answer to no one, not our fathers, our husbands, our older brothers, even the Japanese soldiers during the war. We catch our own food, make our own money, and survive with the harvest given to us from the sea. We live in harmony with this world; how many men teachers can say the same? It is our money that pays his salary. Without us "field hands" he would starve.'

Heads nodded in unison as Emi spoke. There were shouts of agreement and laughter. YoonHui's face turned bright red, her hands clenched into tiny fists, and tears wet her eyes but did not fall.

'It doesn't matter what he said. It matters what I want,' YoonHui said. 'I've already spoken to Father, and he agreed. I just wanted to tell you, before I go. Today is my last day diving with you. Father has paid my tuition for school. One day, I *am* going to university.'

Her father. It was Emi's turn to blush. He had gone behind her back and supported her daughter's break from her family heritage. It was a strategic move on his part, and YoonHui could have had no idea of his intention to assert his authority over Emi. The blade in her hand began to tremble. The other women hushed and turned away.

'I will miss you swimming beside me.' They were true words. Jin-Hee reached across and steadied Emi's blade.

Her daughter's tears fell, but in happiness. She rushed to her mother's side and hugged her. 'Oh, thank you, Mother. You won't be sorry. I will make you proud.'

That night, Emi couldn't bear to sleep beside her husband. He knew the conversation had taken place, for later that day he had taken his daughter into town to buy her school supplies and a school uniform. Emi watched as her daughter smiled up at him before bedtime, thankful for the chance to leave the sea behind, ignorant of what she had helped him do.

Sitting on the stoop, listening to the sounds of her sleeping family, Emi wept. She grieved with a mixture of sorrow and pride. Sorrow for her daughter's choice, but pride in her strength to make such a difficult one. Her daughter was an excellent swimmer. Of all her friends, she could hold her breath the longest, swim the furthest, and fill her net the fastest. She would have surpassed Emi's diving skills had she given the *haenyeo* life a chance. Now she would never know. Emi looked up into the sky, straining to see what her daughter saw when she looked out into the world. A black void greeted her, but there was consolation hidden in its vastness. YoonHui had pleaded for her mother's approval; even though she didn't need it, she had wanted it. Her determination did not outweigh her need for her mother's acceptance.

When Emi looks at YoonHui now, she sees that little girl again, eyes full of determination but also still beseeching her mother's approval. She has found love – few are blessed with such a gift – and she is happy. Emi has known so little happiness in her own life. Now that democracy and a sort of peace have settled across her nation, it seems only fair that her children should find some happiness. It would be a break in the cycle of suffering her country endured for so long. Emi nods her head at her daughter and ambles to the bedroom, her bad leg dragging slightly behind her, to get dressed for the day ahead.

Her daughter has laundered her pink trousers, and she puts them on. Emi pulls on the black sweater and gazes at her reflection in the mirror. An old woman stares back at her. Emi looks at her chest and wonders when the heart inside it decided to give up. She touches the mirror, her palm over the old woman's heart.

Lane is waiting for them outside the apartment building. The cold wind whips her scarf around her neck. She holds out a paper bag filled with coffee-cake squares towards YoonHui.

'We already ate,' YoonHui says, apologetic, but Emi interrupts.

'I'll have some cake with you, Lane.'

'I knew you would, Mother. It's the best coffee cake around. We order it at the university for special events. Be careful, though. You'll get addicted.'

Emi huddles next to Lane and takes one of the squares from the bag. She is full from the enormous breakfast her daughter prepared, and she rarely eats cakes. She hasn't had much of a sweet tooth since she had four molars pulled by a dentist last year. She takes a bite and smiles. It tastes more like a cinnamon bun. She licks her fingers when it is gone.

'Want another one?' Lane asks, her nose red and dripping from the cold.

'No, one is enough. It was very good.'

'Come on, let's go before we freeze to death,' her daughter says, linking one arm into Emi's and her other into Lane's.

Lane looks quickly at Emi, and Emi smiles at her. Warmth spreads through her chest as they walk with arms linked, three across, towards the subway. Her daughter is like a little girl again, bouncing along next to Emi. It's as though a weight has been lifted from her, and someone lighter and happier has emerged. Emi keeps the image in her mind, never wanting it to fade, and she heads to the demonstration, full of hope.

Hana

Manchuria, Summer 1943

Hana is finishing her breakfast of soupy rice and flecks of dried squash in the kitchen when she notices some of the other girls eyeing her without speaking. They are the faces that greeted her on the wall at the bottom of the staircase last night. Before she can say anything, Keiko comes up behind her.

'It's time to cut your hair,' she says. 'So that you fit in with the rest of us.'

Keiko brandishes a pair of gardening shears, and Hana already regrets the loss of her beautiful long hair. Keiko raises the shears, and Hana is preparing herself for the first snip when the guard, a soldier, disrupts them.

'There's no time for this. Just tie it back,' he says to Keiko.

She does as he says before he orders them all up to their rooms to prepare. No one looks at Hana as they rinse their plates and file past her towards the staircase. She lags behind them, wondering what she is supposed to prepare for.

'Wait a moment,' the soldier says to Hana before pulling a camera out of a bag on the counter. 'Sit still,' he says as he fiddles with the lens. 'Don't smile,' he orders before snapping two quick shots.

Hana barely has time to register that the photo was taken when he orders her to go back to her room and roughly shoves her towards the staircase. She ascends the stairs, but not before eyeing the faces peering back at her from the picture frames. One of the frames is missing. Hana notices it at the last moment, and her mind recalls the number beneath the empty space – 2.

Keiko halts in her doorway and appears to want to tell Hana something, but then bows her head and quietly disappears into her room. Hana touches the number beside her door. Her photograph will hang with the others. She is the face behind the door in room 2. A shudder runs down her arms.

As Hana sits on her tatami mat, she listens to the sounds beyond her thin wooden door. A murmur of men's voices, low at first, reaches her ears. It's coming from the lounge below, but then the intensity grows as they climb the staircase and soon it sounds like there are masses of people congregating on the landing. She fights the urge to go to the door and find out what is happening; it feels safer to remain still, as though if they can't hear her, then they won't know she is there. But it is all in vain.

The door swings open and she sees them, soldiers lining up for the new Sakura. Hana later learns that a new girl's arrival spreads like wildfire through the camp, and all the soldiers show up early, racing to be the first to try her out.

The first soldier enters her room. He is large, his hands already pulling down his trousers. Hana doesn't retreat into her mind as she did on the ferry when Morimoto raped her. She opens her mouth and screams. He freezes, just for an instant, and then he smiles.

'It's OK, it's OK, it will be quick, I promise. I'm always quick.'

His trousers slide down to his ankles, and he kneels on the tatami mat. Hana's back is pressed against the furthest corner of the tiny room, but it is not far enough. He just looks at her, and slowly, his penis begins to harden into an erection.

'You're a beautiful one,' he says, and grabs at her ankle.

Hana kicks his hand, but it doesn't deter him. He gets hold of her foot and slides her across the floor to the mat. Before she can scream again, he is on top of her. The weight of his body crushes her, but she wriggles beneath him, pounds on his back with her fists, claws his skin, and then bites his shoulder.

He lifts himself up, a brief moment of respite, and then punches her in the gut. The air rushes out of her. He doesn't wait. As she gasps for breath, he shoves his hands between her legs and forces himself inside.

She still cannot pull air into her lungs. Yet he continues, thrusting again and again. Hana struggles to regain control of her body, her lungs, her limbs, but nothing responds. It is like dying.

He stops suddenly, his muscles tensed, and then slowly gets off her. Hana rolls onto her side, gasping for air.

'I told you I'd be fast,' he says, and pulls up his trousers.

As he leaves, another soldier enters the room. He takes one look at Hana and shouts out the door.

'Hey, you didn't use a condom!'

'She didn't ask,' comes the reply.

The new soldier shakes his head and grabs Hana's legs. His trousers are already around his ankles.

'Please, stop,' she says, finding her breath at last. 'Help me, help me escape from this place. They stole me, I'm only sixteen, help me find my parents . . .'

Her words fall on deaf ears. He is already thrusting into her, rapidly, as though her pleas for help are calls for him to go faster, harder and longer. The second soldier uses his allotted thirty minutes. When the third soldier enters, Hana has started to bleed. She touches the red trail dripping down her inner thigh.

'Look what they did,' she says to the third soldier, holding up her bloody fingers.

He pulls down his trousers and doesn't look at her face. He pushes away her hand, turns her onto her stomach, and takes her. She screams, but he doesn't stop. None of them do. Hana falls silent. She lies still as they plunder her body one after the other.

By the time the procession of soldiers finally ends, night has descended. Hana lies semi-conscious on her bloodstained mat, lost in unspeakable darkness. Morimoto's words taunt her dreams. *I'm doing you a favour . . . breaking you in . . . At least this way, you will know what to expect.*

》-《

The sun slowly rises above the wooden fence encircling the compound. Keiko stands behind Hana, cutting her long hair with the shears. Small yellow birds perch above their heads on sagging laundry lines criss-crossing the yard. A dry wind ruffles their tiny yellow feathers as they chirp their pretty songs. The wind blows Hana's hair across her face as she kneels in the dirt, listening to the birds. She wonders how such cheerful sounds can exist in a place filled with so much horror and pain.

'It's over now, little Sakura,' Keiko says, dusting strands of hair from Hana's bare shoulders with a dry cloth. 'Now you are like the rest of us.'

She holds up a hand mirror that fits in her palm, and Hana can't help but look at her reflection. The ends of her hair grace the soft line of her jaw, but that isn't what catches her attention. A purple bruise has sprouted around her right eye, and a red mark in the shape of a heart stains her left cheek. Her bottom lip is cut and swollen, and her neck is rubbed raw from hands and forearms that choked her into submission. So this is what her pain looks like to others. She turns away from her reflection. It is no longer hers; it is now the broken image of a girl called Sakura.

Hana runs her fingers through the black dirt beneath her knees. Her fingernails are bloody and torn. If she keeps still as she kneels in the yard, her injuries hurt less, but she can't stop clawing the earth. All her muscles ache; her most private parts throb from the violations committed over and over too many times. She could barely walk down the stairs when Keiko woke her. Now she's sitting in the dirt, wondering if it will happen all over again.

'Don't fight them,' Keiko says. 'It won't be as bad if you don't fight them. They won't leave until they're satisfied. Fighting them will only make your suffering greater. Sakura, can you hear me?' Keiko places her hand on Hana's shoulder.

Hana shrugs Keiko's hand away. She stops clawing the earth. She recalls learning to dive, how she once waited too long before swimming back to the surface and involuntarily gasped for breath, swallowing water into her lungs. If her mother hadn't been nearby, she would have drowned. The excruciating pain in her lungs and the fear of drowning ensured she learned her lesson. It never happened to her again. Even when she ran out of breath deep beneath the water's surface, she made certain to drift slowly upwards, to keep herself calm as her lungs screamed for air. She learned to endure because the pain from nearly drowning was worse. Pain is a teacher. The question is whether she can accept what she has learned from it, to stop fighting. It seems unfathomable.

'How long have you allowed yourself to suffer here?' Hana asks.

'Too long,' Keiko replies.

The bitterness in her tone catches Hana's attention, and she looks up at the Japanese woman, who might be beautiful if she weren't so thin.

Keiko's hair is jet black, except for a stripe of silver at each temple, which frames her face. She is taller than the other girls, and in contrast to their plain beige cotton dresses, she wears a colourful silk kimono. Hana touches the hem of Keiko's kimono. It's smooth and soothing.

'I was once a geisha,' Keiko says. 'In Japan, I made a handsome living entertaining rich businessmen. This kimono was a gift from my favourite patron.'

She runs her hands down the sides of the kimono, and Hana is reminded of a white crane, standing by the water's edge, its regal head lifted slightly, ignoring all around it, the trees, the birds in the sky, the air.

'And where did they find you, little Sakura?' Keiko asks, her eyes watchful.

Hana is tormented by this new Japanese name. All the other girls are named after the flowers nailed beside their doors, too, all except Keiko.

'Is Keiko your real name?'

'Of course, but you've changed the subject.'

'Why do you keep yours and we lose ours?'

'You don't want to tell me where you're from, little Sakura?' Keiko raises one pencilled eyebrow, but Hana says nothing. The older woman reaches for a broom and sweeps the freshly cut locks of hair littering the ground into a pile. After a long pause, she finally answers.

'You require a Japanese name, so you are given one. I didn't require one.'

Watching her sweep the last strands of hair from the dirt, Hana suspects Keiko is lying. The wooden plaques next to their doors were all carved long ago and secured to the walls with nails long rusted over. Girls are given rooms, thereby given names. If Keiko has been there as long as the plaques, she should be rusted over, too. Keiko cannot be her real name. Perhaps they always keep a Japanese girl in that room, finding a new one when the old one moves out or dies.

'How did you end up here?' Hana asks. 'Did they steal you?'

Keiko stiffens.

'I grew old,' she says simply. 'An old geisha is worse than an old woman. A tragedy of the profession. I came here believing it would be a better opportunity. I would do my patriotic duty to Japan and service the soldiers, while paying back the debts I had accumulated when my patrons ceased to visit me.'

She looks across the yard, her eyes settling upon a sad persimmon tree with its branches nearly bare, struggling to exist in the poor soil. A shudder blows through her and her gaze suddenly pierces Hana's.

'Never trust a man you owe money to.'

Hana thinks she may never trust any man again. She looks to the ground and she watches her fingers scratch grooves into the dirt. She finds she no longer cares about Keiko or the plaques beside the doors and the names. She can only think about what the day ahead will bring. Perhaps it would be better to die now than to endure being raped over and over, day after day, until she dies like the woman giving birth.

'Come, Sakura. Let's eat breakfast,' Keiko says, pulling Hana from her dark thoughts. She motions for Hana to come inside.

Through the back door, Hana can see the other girls gathered around a small table in the kitchen eating quietly. A few of them peer out at her, past the armed guard leaning against the door frame. Their faces are full of pity as they take in Hana's bruises. She turns away, unable to meet their gazes.

That sort of pity has never been directed at Hana or anyone in her family before. Her island village is full of strong, proud people; even the children hold their heads up high. The Japanese occupation threatened to starve them by unfairly taxing their day's catch from the sea, but they managed to bring in more and more with each new tax decree, feeding themselves nevertheless. It meant remaining out on the water for longer hours and risking their lives even during bad weather, but with the increased peril came pride in their hard work and earned success. They were colonised in name only.

Her island is filled with strong fishermen and diving women, the *haenyeo*, and she is one of them – at least, she thought she was. It never occurred to her that it could be taken away, that she would be forced to become . . . this.

Inside, the other girls talk about her as though she can't hear them. They are Korean girls but speak in the mandated Japanese. They are all older than her; some appear to be in their twenties, though two seem closer in age to Hana. Keiko is the eldest, and now that Hana sees her in the sunlight, she thinks she is in her forties. Hana remains seated in the dirt yard, so Keiko carries a meal out to her in a small metal bowl: rice gruel with flecks of dried meat. Hana is starving, but she doesn't touch the food.

'She is too strong. That's her problem,' one of the girls says to the others at the table loudly enough for Hana to hear her. Her name plaque calls her Riko. 'I heard her fighting them like a little lion.'

'That's no good,' the rest of them chime in, agreeing.

'Better to be a weak girl and give in easily,' the girl called Hinata says.

'It's easier than fighting. They enjoy beating us too much,' Riko says.

'Yes, they're monstrous beasts, not men,' Hinata says, and they all agree in between mouthfuls of rice.

'She must be a farmhand . . . with those broad shoulders,' Tsubaki says. There are general noises of agreement.

'And her legs, they're so muscular. Do you know where she's from?' Hinata asks Keiko.

Hana's eyes meet Keiko's. She is a striking woman and looks back at Hana with a sorrowful expression. Her eyes are soft, but her voice is strong.

'Leave her be. She'll get used to it before long, just as we were forced to. Or she will never survive this place.'

They nod and a few agree in apologetic tones. Hana detects no animosity from the girls, no ill will. Their curiosity seems genuine, but she can't help feeling they betrayed her. They knew what was going to happen to her after breakfast the previous morning, yet no one warned her. And not one of them attempted to stop it.

As she kneels in the yard, Hana tries to remember the other girls who travelled with her on the train. Are they suffering the same fate? Hana was the last one to arrive at her destination, making her the last to know. She could laugh at her ignorance during those final few hours travelling north, but the sounds won't come. Laughter has become a foreign language. Then she remembers SangSoo. They buried her tiny body in the middle of nowhere, so far from home. It is too much. Hana begins to scream.

The sounds escaping her mouth are inhumanly wretched, but she can't stop. Her screams disturb the little yellow birds, and they take flight like a gust of wind, disappearing into the sun. The soldier leaning against the door frame orders the girls to shut her up. Keiko and Hinata rush outside and put their arms around Hana.

'Quiet,' Keiko hushes her, cupping Hana's face in her hands. 'Stop shouting, girl.'

They huddle around her, hugging her, stroking her hair, but she struggles against them. Her throat is soon raw, but Hana continues to scream. Keiko finally slaps her cheek.

The smack is followed by a heavy silence, and then muffled sobs as a few of the girls in the kitchen begin to cry. The soldier orders them all back up to their rooms. Keiko guides Hana into the brothel and up the stairs, depositing her into the room where the girl she once was died.

Emi

Seoul, December 2011

Everywhere Emi looks, banners with *One Thousand Wednesdays* emblazoned across them greet her eyes as she stands with the crowd in front of the Japanese embassy. The weekly demonstrations began in 1992, and today, the one thousandth Wednesday, there is still no resolution for the surviving women.

There are already many demonstrators and supporters gathered even though it is still early, but the buzz of energy feels muted, like the funeral of a great leader where a kind of celebratory sadness permeates the crowd. Emi looks up at the hulking embassy building. All the windows are shut and the blinds are drawn. Emi catches other women eyeing the embassy windows, and she knows they are all wondering the same thing: Are they in there, watching? Do they feel remorse or did they call a holiday for their embassy workers? Perhaps they are all on her island enjoying a day off. Bitterness settles in her stomach, slowly burning like coals at the end of a blazing fire.

'Are you too cold? Shall we sit over there, sheltered from the wind inside one of the tents?' Lane asks.

'No, this is fine.' Emi didn't realise she was shivering, but now that Lane has pointed it out, the cold is all she can think about. She shoves her hands into her coat pockets.

'I'll buy us some hot chocolate,' Lane offers, and disappears into the crowd.

A man taps on a microphone. 'Test, testing, hello, hello . . .'

Emi zones out in the midst of the hubbub. The man's voice booming through the speakers, the murmur of the crowd, the Japanese eyes hiding behind shut windows, they all blur into the background. The only sensation Emi cannot block out is the cold. It penetrates the layers of fabric wrapped around her body and pierces through her thin and wrinkled skin. It was cold like this the night she lost her father. The memory catches her off guard, and she is forced to let it in.

It's a strange and terrifying thing, witnessing a person's death. One moment he is there, breathing, thinking, full of motion, but then the next moment there's nothing. No breath, no thought, no heart beating. The face slack, emotionless. Emi saw her father's face like that, wiped of the terror it had held only a moment before. He was gone in the blink of an eye. She had closed her eyelids, a mere flutter, opened them, and he was dead.

She has never told anyone the story. It was easier never to think of it, to block it out so that she didn't have to relive it. But now she's too old to keep the memories back. Her body is worn out, just like her mind. They are starting to resurface at all hours of the day, invading her solitude with pain and regret. Sometimes, old wounds need to be reopened to let them properly heal – that's what JinHee says – and Emi still has not healed from watching her father die.

In the midst of the crowd, Emi lets her father's face fill her mind. His kind, peaceful eyes look back at her, and she sees him like he was, full of life and grace rarely seen in times of turmoil. It was 1948, and Emi was fourteen years old. The Korean War had not yet begun, but the tension on her island between the police the South Korean government had sent to keep order and the leftist rebels had grown into a fierce guerrilla war. The Jeju Uprising had begun, leaving many dead on both sides.

The police came into her village under cover of darkness. The howling December winds concealed their approach. A bang and then the front door to the house flew open. Policemen rushed in and pulled Emi and her parents from their blankets. They dragged them out into the frozen night air. She was crying and confused, but the policemen smacked her and beat her parents, shouting at them to shut up. The men were young and angry, but Emi didn't know why they were targeting her family. She had no brother or uncle to join the leftist rebels, no one to bring the wrath of the police down upon her family. They were merely citizens existing in a country torn in two by powers greater than themselves.

One of the policemen grabbed her father and pulled him out in front of Emi, facing her mother. He pushed her father down onto his knees and held a curved knife to his throat.

'This is for hiding the rebels,' he said, and then time stopped.

Emi watched in disbelief as the blade sliced across her father's neck from left to right. Blood streamed, staining his nightshirt black in the dim night. His terrified eyes didn't leave her mother's, and Emi thought he looked more afraid for her than for himself. Then they glazed over into lifelessness. Her mother wailed into the sleeting sky, but another young policeman kicked her in the side of the head. She fell into silence. Emi screamed and crawled to her father.

'Don't be dead,' she cried over and over again. 'Father, don't be dead.'

A policeman wrestled her off of her father's limp body. Emi tried to slip out of his grip, but he only held on to her tighter, bruising her arms.

'Stop fighting me, or I'll cut your throat, too,' he warned.

'Leave her. She's covered in blood,' another policeman said in a commanding voice.

Emi looked up at him. He appeared older than the others, and he seemed in charge.

'Killing makes me need it,' the policeman said, wrenching her arms until she knelt in front of him.

'We aren't finished yet. There are more houses to visit. Then you can do as you wish.' He glanced at Emi and then walked away.

The policeman holding her seemed to think about it a moment. He spat on the ground and then nodded. He kicked Emi in the centre of her back. She fell over onto all fours, and he kicked her again. She slammed into the cold, wet ground and covered her face with her arms.

'Get yourself cleaned up and maybe I'll return for you,' he laughed. He adjusted his trousers and straightened his coat.

They left as quietly as they had arrived, like tigers in the night. Emi and her mother held her father's body between them as they sat silently watching their home burn down. It had all happened so fast that Emi didn't have a chance to see who had lit the fire. When she looked around, she was shocked to see bright lights dotting the hills as other homes burned. If she listened very carefully, she could hear distant cries beneath the howling wind, or perhaps it was her mother's silenced voice screaming inside Emi's head.

The policemen had burned down nearly her entire village. She buried her father in a shallow grave, covered with sand she had carried by the bucketful from the beach because the earth was too hard to penetrate beyond a few inches. Her mother knelt beside the grave and wept. Others came to help, a few old women and even older men. The policemen had carried away most of the young men and women, along with the boys and the girls. No one wanted to think about where they had been taken. They just wanted to bury their dead and find shelter. Emi didn't know why the policeman had helped her the way he had. He had saved her from a terrible fate.

'How can they do this to their own countrymen?' an old woman asked no one in particular as Emi scattered the sand over her father's body.

A few old men tried to explain the fear that existed between the Soviet Union and the United States, but no one could explain away the death dealt by blood brothers.

'We are all Koreans,' the old woman said again. 'The Japanese have gone.' Her face was lined with time and hardship. She had survived colonisation only to suffer a new kind of occupation.

Emi returned to burying her father. Like the rest of the people in her small village, her family had done its best not to get involved with the guerrilla rebels or the police. All she could think about was the fact that her father had survived the Japanese occupation and the war but had died by his own countrymen's hands.

Emi and her mother followed the small group of survivors out of the village and down near the coast. The old man who had spoken earlier said that he had lived on the island for nearly eighty years and knew of a cave, hidden off an inlet along the shore. Her mother barely managed the day-long journey. It was as though a tether attached her to her dead husband and pulled her backwards two steps for each one she managed to take away from him. Emi had been diving for five years, and her body was lean and muscular. She used her diving strength to half carry, half drag her mother to the safety of the cave.

》《

The cave sheltered nineteen people. Emi recognised a few faces, but most were from the other side of the cove. She wondered whether her best friend, JinHee, had survived the massacre, but no one dared leave the safety of the cave to search for others, except for one woman. A mother left to search for her daughter, stolen as their home burned down. She returned to the cave broken, her face ashen-grey. No amount of coaxing could persuade her to tell them what she had found, but Emi imagined the worst.

At night, the mother would wake up screaming her daughter's name. Emi would cry herself to sleep, covering her ears to block out the woman's agony.

Afraid to light a fire in case the policemen located their hiding place, they froze through the night, teeth chattering, deep within the cave. Emi and her mother huddled together with two elderly women to share their body heat. The men lay together, too, but the December winter was too harsh. The oldest among them soon began to die, quietly slipping away as they slept.

Emi and her mother helped the old men move the frozen bodies to the back of the cave, where they remained preserved by the cold. Emi made herself think of JinHee's wild stories just before falling asleep, as though remembering them would ensure her friend survived. Imagining her friend alive in another cave on the island kept Emi going, even in the face of her grief for her father and her changed mother.

They ate what they could find inside the cave, moss growing on the walls, insects creeping in the dirt, and a few creatures Emi suspected were probably rats or worse. After four weeks of near starvation, Emi's mother decided it was time to go back. They leaned on one another, blinking in the January sunlight, as they exited their hiding place.

They were both weakened and suffered in the wretched cold, walking all the way home through newly fallen snow, passing buildings burned to the ground without encountering a single soul. When she saw the black cinders that were once her family home poking through white tufts of snow, Emi felt too numb to cry. Everything was gone. Everything. The place that had once housed her family, had held memories of each of them within its walls – her sister's serious expression as she taught Emi how to read, her father's voice as he sang while playing his zither, her mother's delicious dishes cooked with tenderness – all was burned to ash.

Where were they now, Emi wondered, her father's spirit and her sister's absent body? Her mother knelt in the ruins and covered her face with her hands. After a long silence, Emi led her mother to the site where they had buried her father.

The mound was covered over with a layer of virgin snow. Tiny twiglike footprints trailed zigzag tracks across the small hump. Emi looked up into the white sky, where seagulls soared, gliding on the cold January wind. Were they visiting her father, perhaps paying homage to his departing spirit?

Her mother knelt beside the mound and bowed her forehead to the ground, touching the snow. Gentle sobs escaped her, and Emi knelt next to her, hugging her shaking body. She felt so thin, like an old woman. Her mother was not yet forty, but the war had stolen too much from her, her eldest daughter, then her husband, and now what was left of her youth drained away into the frozen earth with her home. Emi sobbed, too, mourning for them all, the living and the dead.

Voices drifted towards Emi, and she sat up, listening. The wind seemed to die down into silence, and the seagulls overhead cried their high-pitched warnings. Then she heard it again, men's voices.

'Mother, someone's coming,' Emi whispered just as the voices sounded behind them. The tips of rifles held aloft marched towards them.

'We must go,' Emi whispered, and attempted to lift her mother to her feet, but she wouldn't budge.

Emi's heart raced. It had been a mistake to leave the cave. If they survived this, they would return to its safety. A small grove of tangerine trees blackened from the fires remained standing below a rise in the terrain. If she could just get her mother to her feet, they could hide behind the trees and wait for the policemen to pass, Emi thought, forgetting the fresh layer of snowfall.

'Please, Mother,' she begged, pulling her with all her strength. 'We must hurry.'

They rushed over the small rise and down into the tangerine grove. They hid behind a tree that loomed above the rest, even though half its branches had burned to dust in piles on the ground. The cold weather had kept the roots from burning, but it would never recover.

The policemen's voices ceased as they came upon the ruins of the house. Emi listened as they sifted through the ashes. She crouched protectively over her mother as they knelt, shivering from the cold.

'Look here,' a policeman called to the others.

'What is it?' another one answered.

'Fresh footprints.'

Then silence. Emi imagined them inspecting her footprints, following them over the hill, being led to her hiding place. She had been foolish to let her mother go back. She knew her mother wasn't in her right mind; they were frozen, starving and grieving. Surrounded by death, Emi had been glad to leave the cave that had become like a tomb. She had so desperately wanted to see what was left of her home.

The teenage boy who rounded the tree first wore a thick, padded coat with a yellow scarf around his neck. He spoke to her in a soft tone.

'Are you injured?' he asked. He glanced beneath her at her mother, pressed against the tree. 'Is she OK? Is that your mother you're protecting?'

Emi couldn't respond. She simply kept her arms around her mother. The other policemen came near, and their silent curiosity hung heavy. Emi waited for the harsh words, the cruel fists, and the pain that would follow. She bowed her head.

'Is she deaf?' one of the policemen asked.

'I think she's in shock,' the younger one answered. 'It's OK. We're not here to harm you. We're searching for survivors. Come with us. We'll take you somewhere safe.'

He reached out his hand, and Emi shrank away. Her mother lifted her face and spat on his coat. He took a step backwards. The other two policemen shouted at her mother and started towards her with their rifles high in the air, preparing to smash them against her.

'No, stay back. It's all right. They're just afraid. They're covered in ash,' he told the men. 'Remember the house we passed, and the burial mound . . .' His voice faded as he inspected Emi's face.

'They murdered him,' Emi said.

The three policemen froze and stared at her.

'Who did?' the boy with the soft voice asked. He lowered himself so that they were eye level. 'Did you see who did this?'

'Don't tell him anything,' her mother whispered.

Emi looked into her mother's dark eyes. They flashed a warning at Emi. She looked back at the young man.

'They came in the middle of the night. We could see nothing. It was too dark.'

'Are you sure?' he asked, his voice still kind, as though he wanted to help her. As though he truly cared.

She nodded. He stood up and seemed to think about her words for a moment. He looked out over the fire-ravaged tangerine trees. Emi followed his gaze and couldn't help remembering running through the shady grove during hot summers with her sister, laughing at nothing. The sudden memory took her by surprise, and she couldn't shake the feeling she would never see it like that again. Everything was gone. The policeman took in a breath, and it rushed out heavily through his nostrils.

'Bring them,' he said.

Emi was taken aback by his altered tone. His soft demeanour was instantly replaced by military efficiency. The other two policemen lifted Emi and her mother to their feet and led them away from their home. As they passed her father's grave, her eyes lingered on the smallness of the mound. In her mind he was a large, robust man who towered over her with strong, protective arms, but death had taken that image away, leaving behind a small rise that in time would become barely noticeable. She stared at the ground as they led her past familiar stones and seashells along the path, her treasures brought up from the sea. She struggled when she saw the truck, but it was too late.

The policemen took them to the local station, which was a swirl of bodies, some uniformed, others in bloodied rags, their voices a cacophony of anger, pain and fear.

An old woman sat against the wall, cradling her son's blood-soaked head in her lap. She was still and silent, while all around her chaos raged. Emi clasped her mother's hand in hers as tightly as she could, as the policeman dragged them to a makeshift waiting area. People huddled together in small groups, some crying, others shocked into silence. He left them and spoke to the officer at the reception desk. He looked over his shoulder a few times as he filled out a form.

Emi looked at each face around her and recognised no one. Where were the people of her village? Emi suddenly feared they were all dead, then pushed the thought from her mind. She glanced at her mother but couldn't bear seeing the vacant expression on her prematurely aged face.

The policeman returned and Emi squared her shoulders, trying to express her disdain for him, but he seemed not to notice.

'We'll wait here until they call us.'

'Why, what have we done wrong?' Emi asked.

'Nothing,' he answered, clearing his throat. He seemed uncertain.

'Then why have you brought us here?' Emi felt bolder the more sheepish he became. He was once again the soft-spoken young man who had first approached her in the tangerine grove, not the policeman who had ordered her into the truck.

'That is not your concern. It's government business.'

'We have nothing to do with the government—'

'Stop talking,' he interrupted, grabbing her arm. His eyes darted around the room, surveying the people listening to their conversation. 'You are here on my orders. That is all you need to know.'

She glared at him until he finally released her arm.

The desk officer called to them, and the three of them were ushered into a small office at the rear of the station. When the policeman shut the door, the misery of the world beyond that room was suddenly muted, leaving a patch of foggy quiet in Emi's head. A large desk dominated the room, and behind it sat a man in a decorated uniform. Numerous medals and ribbons adorned his chest, and Emi wondered which countrymen he had killed to have earned such heavy badges of honour. She studied his face and waited for him to speak.

'I have been told you are a *haenyeo*. Is that correct?' he said, not looking up from the pile of paperwork in front of him. He seemed to keep reading even as he awaited her reply.

'Yes,' Emi answered, wondering how they had checked her family's records so quickly.

'And is this your mother?' He looked up for a moment and glanced at Emi's mother.

'Yes.'

'She is a *haenyeo*, too?'

'Yes.'

'Ah, you are very agreeable, I must say. HyunMo, you are a lucky one! She will make a suitable wife, I think. As long as you ask her the right questions, that is. Ha!'

He slapped his knee as he chuckled to himself.

'Tell me, what is your family name?'

Emi paused. He had said wife. She didn't understand.

'Her father was Jang,' HyunMo answered before she could speak. He did not look at her but kept his eyes on the desk.

'Jang? Good, strong family name,' the officer said, and wrote it down on the form. He signed the bottom of the form and slid it across the desk towards Emi. 'Good, now sign here.' He offered her the pen.

The policeman knew her father's name. Emi stared at him; her ears prickled with heat, and her mouth felt dry.

'Take the pen, girl, and sign your name on the line, just there above mine. See? Right there,' the officer instructed, placing the pen in Emi's hand.

'What is this?' Emi finally asked. She looked at her mother, but she was no help, staring at the floor, silently weeping.

'It's your marriage licence. Sign there.'

'But, who am I marrying?' Emi asked.

'Why, him of course,' he said, pointing to the policeman, the boy who had taken her away from her burned-down home, who knew her father's name and her occupation. 'Come, come, I don't have all day. Sign it. HyunMo, you'll sign next to her name.'

Emi turned to stare at HyunMo. He was much older than her but still a teenage boy. They expected her to marry him? She simply stood there, holding the pen, when the officer suddenly slapped her so hard that she fell to the floor. He had moved so quickly, rising to his feet like a striking snake, whipping his hand across her face with such power.

'Get her to her feet.'

HyunMo carefully lifted her and kept a supporting arm around her as he nudged her back towards the desk. He seemed as astonished as Emi at the sudden violence. Her cheek throbbed, and her vision blurred.

'You will sign this, now. HyunMo will be your husband. And then all three of you will exit my office, so that I may deal with the next citizens on my list. Do it now, or I will have him arrest you, and by the state of you two,' he said, motioning towards their emaciated figures, 'you won't last very long in jail.'

Emi's mother seemed to focus on the officer. She leaned over the desk, her hands gripping the edge of it. Her face became animated, her expression filled with vitriol. Emi was afraid of what she might say, but the officer cut her off before she could speak.

'Do not attempt it, Mother. I wield the power of life and death over your daughter. One displeasing word from either of you, and I will not hesitate to send you in front of a firing squad. Tell her to sign the form,' he ordered HyunMo.

'Just do as he says,' HyunMo urged, the look in his eyes apologetic.

Emi gripped the pen, but it shook in her trembling hand. HyunMo guided it to the correct line, and she signed her name. He took the pen from her and signed his name next to hers, *Lee, HyunMo*.

'Good. Now get out. I have a busy day.'

HyunMo led Emi and her mother out of the office, back through the scene of despair in the crowded station, and into the cold January air. The blustering wind cooled the heat in her assaulted cheek. She rubbed it with her hand, still trembling from signing her life away.

'Why?' she asked after the silence between them dragged on longer than she could bear. They were walking back to the truck parked behind the station. 'Why did you force a marriage between us?'

'Our sons will inherit this island,' he said without pausing. He opened the door to the truck and ushered her mother in.

'Our sons?' She was shocked that he expected them to engage in a real marriage, like the one her parents had. The notion was surreal.

'Yes, and your land, the village's, will be inherited back by us through our children.'

'Us?'

'The other policemen. Like many of them, I had to leave my home in the North and flee south of the line before the communists murdered me like they did my family. They took everything from me. From all of us. So we are marrying you to regain what we lost, but more importantly, to keep the communists out of the South, we must breed them out. It's for your own good . . . and the good of Korea.'

'I'm not a communist,' she said, hoping that someone who had suffered so much might understand what she was suffering in that moment.

He looked at her directly, and his expression was void of emotion.

'This island is full of communists. You are one whether you know it or not. By marrying me, you are no longer a threat. Get in.'

He held the door open and waited for her to climb into the truck, but she couldn't move. The policemen had killed her father. Emi thought back to the darkness of that night. Was HyunMo there? Was that how he knew to come looking for her at the ashes of her home? Her stomach turned over and her knees gave way. HyunMo caught her in his arms and helped her into the truck.

Emi sat beside her mother, trying to remember. It was so dark that night, the sleet had pelted her eyes, and fear had blurred all the men's faces. She tried to recall HyunMo's image from that terrible scene, but it wasn't familiar. Surely she would recognise her father's killer if she saw him again. When HyunMo climbed into the driver's seat, she gazed at him, trying to see him through the fog of memory.

Ignoring her, he started the engine and drove away from the station without another word. Emi couldn't make his features match any of the men from that night. Slowly, she tore her eyes away from him and blankly stared out of the windscreen. Emi didn't know where HyunMo was taking them, and the longer they drove, the more lost she felt.

》《

Shivering in the square, recollecting events from long ago, Emi feels her age weigh heavily upon her. Her leg aches with a terrible pain, running up the back of her thigh and spiralling in fiery stabs upwards into her hip. The cold doesn't help the pains of age or the memories flooding in from her past.

Lane returns bearing three cups of hot chocolate. Emi accepts hers readily, enjoying the heat that penetrates her mittens. She glances at the faces surrounding her. She is searching for something and nothing at once, hoping yet not believing she will notice something familiar, a smile, a gesture, anything that reminds her of her childhood. She has come to the demonstration three times, and as she searches through the crowd, she feels like she is looking for something as obscure as happiness.

Emi sips from her cup; her tongue stings from the sweet, hot liquid, and her eyes keep moving over the bodies amassing around her, never resting on one face or hand for too long, afraid she might miss something – someone. Lane and her daughter sip from their cups, too, ever watchful of Emi's eyes, but neither woman interrupts Emi's quiet search.

Emi gazes at the people in the crowd, hoping that one of them will look back and that she will find her sister.

Hana

Hana's photograph now hangs with the others at the bottom of the staircase. Her face looks upon visiting soldiers who will know to queue in front of door 2 if they choose her for their allotted time. Enlisted soldiers get up to thirty minutes alone with her, officers an hour. She is like an item on a menu, perused, purchased and consumed.

The routine at the brothel is simple. Rise, wash, eat, then wait in the room for the soldiers to arrive. When the hour grows late, usually after nine o'clock at night, the remaining men will be sent home. Then she washes herself and the used condoms, disinfects and dresses her wounds if she accumulated any that day. They eat a meagre meal, then go to bed to start the day again. Ten hours a day, six days a week, she 'services' soldiers. She is raped by twenty men a day. The seventh day is chore day. She cleans her room and launders her ragged dress, and together with the other girls she cleans the brothel and tends to the tired vegetable patch in the yard, while awaiting the doctor's visit every other chore day.

It took Hana two weeks to accept that there was no escaping the routine. The first week was the hardest. For three straight days, Hana ate nothing, and for three straight nights she cried uncontrollably. She later learned she was lucky not to have been put in solitary confinement in the basement, where they sometimes put girls who refused to conform or who required punishment beyond a lashing. On the third night of her tears, a knock at the door interrupted her dark thoughts.

'Stop crying, little Sakura. It is enough.' Keiko walked in. The woman's voice startled Hana and she turned to look at her. Keiko risked punishment by coming to Hana's room. They could throw her into the horrid solitary confinement cell beneath the brothel, and the thought that Keiko would take that chance stopped Hana's weeping.

'You must pull yourself together,' Keiko scolded her, though her harsh tone didn't match the pitying expression on her face. She leaned towards Hana and swept a lock of hair from her face. 'I know what you're thinking right now. That you want to die. We all wanted to die after our first few nights.' When Hana didn't respond, Keiko continued. 'Don't you want to see your mother again?'

Her mother. The word was a stab in the heart.

'I'll never see her again. I know that,' Hana whispered, turning away from Keiko. The women's voices at the market echoed in Hana's mind then. Even if Hana lived through this and returned home one day, would that not drive her own parents to early deaths?

'You won't see her again if you die, that's for certain. And you must think of your mother. She'll never know what happened to you. She'll be left wondering for the rest of her life.'

The image of her mother's distraught face when her uncle's sword arrived at their home filled Hana's mind. She would have saved her sister from this horrible fate only to leave her with a broken mother.

Hana would rather endure the worst torture imaginable than to destroy her family.

But the alternative surfaced in her mind. She would suffer day after day at the hands of soldiers, until – she wasn't sure how long it would last. Until the war ended? Until she got pregnant? Or until she died? Her mother might never learn what happened to her.

'I promise, you'll see her again. You won't be here forever. None of us will. We just have to put in our time, and then we can go home.'

Keiko continued talking, but Hana could no longer hear her. *Home*. It sounded so far away, like a place in a dream she once had. Was it really possible that she would ever find her way back? Was Keiko telling the truth? Would they send her home?

'Let's get you cleaned up.'

Keiko instructed her on how to wash herself, and when Hana didn't respond, Keiko did it for her.

Hana didn't have the energy to stop her. The antiseptic solution burned worse than salt water in a cut, but Hana didn't cry out. Keiko talked throughout, as though filling the silence between them would make everything OK.

'This war won't last forever, nor will your time here. Take care of yourself in here, survive, and one day, you will be set free, and you will see your mother again.'

Hana looked into the woman's eyes. This was the second time she had mentioned being set free. She still couldn't judge whether Keiko was telling the truth, but the geisha didn't look away. She seemed to dare Hana to dispute her. Hana remained silent. After a long moment, Keiko spoke again as though nothing had passed between them.

'If you are to make the journey home one day, you will have to take care of yourself the best you can while you are here. And that requires cleaning yourself after each soldier's visit, eating as much food as you are given, and washing your clothing and your room so that bugs cannot infect you with sickness. That is how we all will survive.'

When Keiko left her, Hana lay back down on the thin mat and stared into the darkness of her room. She listened to the new sounds that encompassed her: the other women in their rooms, the creaking of the roof above her head, the wind rushing through the eaves.

'Please, Mother. Come and find me. Take me away from this place,' Hana whispered to the empty room. She repeated the words over and over until they became a monotonous chant buried deep in her mind.

Now, two weeks later, Hana has learned to follow Keiko's guidance and manages not to think too long on the notion of dying. Instead, she holds on to Keiko's promise that they will all be set free one day and she will see her family again. The soldiers continue to line up outside her door. They don't beat her if she lies still on the mat. It is as though they don't care if she is dead or alive, just that she is physically present so that they can do what they have come to do.

One of the other girls, Hinata, offers Hana a special tea to numb the pain between her legs and along the length of her body. She takes a few sips but doesn't like how it makes her feel afterwards. Dizzy, light-headed, and not quite present. She finds it difficult to stay awake. She learns later that it is opium tea and makes certain not to accept it a second time. In Hana's school, the children were warned against opium. They were told that it was a sign of inferiority to consume opium, and that is why their enemy, the inferior Chinese, were all addicted to it.

Hana refuses the tea partly because she is afraid she may become addicted, but mostly because she needs to keep control of her mind. Hinata drinks the opium tea continuously throughout the day and night. It's how she copes with the demands of the soldiers. It's how she survives. But Hana knows it won't work for her. She will lose control of her mind and slip back into thoughts of death. Her memory of home is strong, but so is the pain of remaining in the brothel.

Turning down the tea is her first step towards staying alive. With a clear head, she has the power to make herself retreat into her imagination. As the men visit her each day she withdraws from reality and sees herself diving deep beneath the ocean, escaping her surroundings. She learns to hold her breath as a soldier invades her body, and she feels as if she is really struggling to breathe before rising to the surface for air to fill her lungs. She never looks the men in their faces. It is better not to even think of them as people. Instead, they are machines sent to her throughout the day. She focuses on the promise that it will all come to an end, because it always does, and then she sleeps. She can control her mind and choose what she lets in.

When Hana rises each morning, her first thought is of the sea. The sound of the waves splashing against the rocky shore fills her mind. And then she wonders whether her mother is also rising with the morning sun. Is she preparing breakfast for her sister and father? Most mornings her mother makes rice porridge with flakes of seaweed and fish from the previous night's dinner. Sometimes she fries an egg and slices it into thin strips to mix into the porridge. Hana can taste the salty broth on her tongue, and she finds herself salivating at the memory. In the brothel, they rarely have more than a couple of rice balls or a bowl of soupy rice prepared by the old Chinese woman. If they are lucky, a few Japanese pickles can be found lurking beneath. Their paltry vegetable patch is often raided by the soldiers, who are also desperate for food.

Water is drawn from a well located at the far end of the dirt yard. The girls take turns retrieving a fresh bucket throughout the day. When it is her turn, Hana takes as long as she can to carry out the chore. Even five minutes of respite is worth it.

If she isn't stealing time by fetching water, she finds a reason to wash herself extra carefully before the next soldier enters the room.

When they try to hurry her, she follows Riko's advice and mentions venereal disease prevention, and if they press her, she lies and says she noticed red bumps or pus-filled sores on the previous soldier. Most of the time, she gets away with the lies, but once in a while the soldier won't care. Those are the worst men to deal with. She quickly learns to say nothing and do as they wish. The quicker they are satisfied, the sooner they leave.

Late at night, after the soldiers are gone, Hana misses home the most. Lying on her musty tatami mat with her threadbare blanket pulled up to her chin, she yearns for the warmth of her little sister's body lying next to her, the slow draws of breath of her snoring father nearby, and the constant rustle of her mother's restless body searching for abalone in her dreams. Hana also thinks of her friends, the other *haenyeo* divers she worked with every day. She misses them all.

These memories distress her and yet sustain her. They invade the silence within her tiny prison, each comforting memory cutting her as though a blade is slashing across her flesh. The pain reminds her of her sacrifice. If she weren't trapped in the brothel, her sister would be. She will endure the brothel because one day she will find her way back home. She will see her family again.

Chore day comes, and Hana rises early to wash her clothes in the yard. The guard stops her at the kitchen door.

'Go back upstairs. The doctor comes today.' He blocks her way with his body.

Hana knows not to question the guard. She goes back upstairs and waits in her room. It is her first visit with the doctor. The Chinese woman comes in first, bringing Hana a pitcher of water and pours it into Hana's basin. She motions for her to clean herself.

As the woman leaves, Hana wonders why she and her husband manage the brothel. Are they forced to run it? Are they prisoners, too? A light knock at the door interrupts her thoughts.

A soldier enters her room, and Hana leaps to her feet. The soldier must see the alarm on her face because he raises his hand in a surrender motion.

'I'm the physician,' he says quickly. 'I'm here to check your health.'

He holds up his other hand to show a black satchel. He motions for her to sit back down. Tentatively, she does as he wishes, but she is still prepared to flee. He sets down his satchel and sits in front of her.

'Open your mouth,' he says, and then proceeds to inspect her throat, her teeth and gums and tongue. 'Good, all good. Now, lie down.'

Hana stiffens. She has never been to a doctor and is still not certain this man is who he claims to be. His military uniform unnerves her, but slowly, she obeys and lies down on the mat. He lifts her dress, and Hana sits back up.

'What are you doing?' she demands.

'I need to examine you.' If he is insulted or angry, he does not show it. 'Lie back down, bend your knees and lift your dress. I need to examine your vagina, and don't waste any more of my time.'

'No, I don't want you to,' Hana says, and scoots away from him.

'You don't have a choice. I am required to examine all of you every two weeks. I have to check you for venereal diseases, infections, pregnancies, wounds. It's for your own good. For your health, and the soldiers' health.'

Hana stares at him. The health of the soldiers. That's what he's really here for.

'Now, lie back down, bend your knees and lift your dress.'

She lies down in humiliation. The examination goes quickly after that. He inserts a cold metal instrument into her vagina, feels inside her with his fingers, and then douches her with an orange liquid. Then he inoculates her left arm with a serum he says will ward off future venereal diseases.

After a fourth week passes, officers arrive in a jeep late one evening. They have been drinking, and two are falling-down drunk. The others help carry them, half walking, half stumbling, into the brothel, where they stagger straight upstairs, shoving the queuing soldiers aside as they force their way to the front.

'Everyone, go back to your barracks,' the captain shouts above the dissenting grumbles. 'We are taking command of this outpost for the remainder of the evening.'

The soldiers at the front of the line aggressively protest, claiming they have been waiting for hours. The soldier in Hana's room opens the door and peers out. When the captain's first lieutenant unsheathes his sabre, the soldiers grow quiet, but no one turns to leave. The soldier retreats back into Hana's room and quietly begins to dress. Hana moves so that she can see out the door.

'Go on, get out of here,' the captain shouts, pointing his sword at a private standing at the front of the line.

The private is undecorated. His uniform is neat but shabby. He takes a step backwards but does not immediately leave.

'You have a problem, Private?' the captain asks as he moves beside the first lieutenant. The two of them standing together is an impressive sight. They are taller than most of the non-commissioned soldiers, and their decorated chests shine as though gilded with silver- and gold-encrusted gems. The private seems to shrink in stature beneath their gaze.

'We are going to the battle lines in the morning, sir,' the private says, his voice low and unchallenging.

'Is that so?' the captain responds.

'Yes, sir,' a few of the men mumble in unison.

'Well, that's good to know. First Lieutenant, don't you agree that's good to know?'

'Yes, yes, very good intelligence, Private. Solid work,' he says mockingly.

The captain takes a step towards the private, towering above him. The men behind the private shrink away.

'And who do you think will be leading you onto this battlefield, soldier? Any thoughts as to who your superior officers might be? You know, the ones who will lead the charge and die first should the battle not turn out successfully?'

The soldiers within hearing distance begin to slink away before the captain finishes his tirade, but the poor private and the few soldiers caught in the firing line are forced to remain at attention.

'Yes, sir, my apologies, sir,' the soldier says, saluting the captain.

'Your apologies? Do you hear that, First Lieutenant? He apologises.' He laughs in the private's face, leaning dangerously close to the trembling man. 'I could have your head on a bayonet if I wanted it. Perhaps to warn future privates of your ignorance and remind them not to question an officer, ever. Now bow,' the captain orders, his voice a low growl in the private's face.

The soldier bows deeply, exposing the vulnerable nape of his neck. The first lieutenant places his sword against the skin with increasing pressure. A hairline of blood sprouts beneath the blade.

'What is your command?' the first lieutenant asks the captain.

The soldier trembles beneath the first lieutenant's blade, which pushes the razor-sharp edge deeper. Blood drips down one side of his neck, staining his collar.

'I'm in a good mood. I don't want to spoil the evening. Send them away.'

'You heard the captain. Get out,' the first lieutenant shouts, shoving the private against the wall. 'All of you, get out, before I charge you with insubordination.'

A clatter of retreating boots hurries down the stairs. The soldier in Hana's room swiftly exits as the first lieutenant marches in. The captain heads towards Keiko's room next door.

Hana does not look up at the officer. She keeps silent, waiting for him to come to her. She tries not to notice the sabre gripped tightly in his right hand or the sway in his step as he moves towards her. They all have scars on their bodies from drunk and angry soldiers. Hana has heard a few of the assaults through the thin walls as she serviced a soldier in her room. The first lieutenant kneels in front of her and orders her to get to her feet. She does as she is told and stands shivering in front of him. He stares at the triangle of hair between her legs. He leans in as though to inspect her, and using the tip of his sword, he searches through her pubic hair.

'This will have to go,' he says. 'Remain still, or I will cut you.'

Using the sword, he proceeds to shave her, nicking the tender skin, drawing blood. Hana trembles as the cold blade scrapes across her skin. She bites her tongue when it cuts her.

'Your kind are all diseased,' he mutters as he works. 'You practise improper hygiene. You're full of parasites. I will not be infested.'

Hana closes her eyes. She's infested? The soldiers are the ones who bring their diseases to the brothel. Every girl here arrived innocent and clean. The soldiers are the infested monsters, the reason the girls are subjected to humiliating medical check-ups and injected with chemicals so harsh their arms sometimes swell and grow numb. This soldier is the infested one. Hana squeezes her eyes even more tightly to keep her rage from spilling out.

When he finishes shaving her, he tosses the sword to the floor and orders her to wash herself. She goes to the basin of water in the corner of the room, which she has learned is for soaking used condoms, and crouches over it. She uses a hand towel. He watches as she washes, instructing her at times to scrub harder, to clean herself more thoroughly, and to ensure she is sanitised. When he is satisfied, he orders her to help him undress. Once naked, he lies down on the mattress and instructs her to straddle him.

'Ride me until Yasukuni is in my sight. If I die tomorrow, I want to see the shrine where my soul is going!' He is too drunk to climax. After an hour of useless intercourse, he shoves her off him and falls into a deep slumber.

Soldiers often call out to the sacred Japanese shrine in Tokyo – that is not new for Hana – but the humiliation the officer inflicted upon her is. The officers stay overnight. As Hana lies on her tatami mat, listening to the first lieutenant's rumbling snores, she is too angry to sleep. Instead, she remains awake all night, listening to him breathe. Each intake of breath disgusts her, each alcohol-infused exhalation turns her stomach. Each of her own breaths makes her wounds cry out for attention.

The cock crows at dawn, rousing the soldier, and he orders her to help him dress. When Hana finishes tying his bootlaces, he kicks her aside. She remains on her hands and knees, hoping he is too hungover to do any more harm. He stands, runs his fingers through his scruffy hair, and then calls loudly for his friend to join him as he exits her room. After a moment, they descend the stairs together, laughing about their respective nights. When she hears the front door shut and the jeep's engine speed away from the brothel, Hana leaves her room and quietly heads downstairs.

Keiko follows Hana to the kitchen.

'I heard what he did to you,' she whispers into Hana's ear.

Hana's shoulders sag inwards.

'Let me see,' Keiko says.

'I'll be fine.' Hana pulls away.

'Don't do that. If he cut you badly, it'll get infected. Come,' she says, taking Hana's hand. She leads her into the storage cupboard and shuts the door. 'Lift your dress.'

Hana does as she is told. Keiko sucks air through her teeth, shaking her head.

'The bastard butchered you,' she whispers vehemently.

Keiko swiftly retrieves disinfectant and soaks a small towel in the solution. Gingerly, she washes Hana's wounds. The other girls arrive in the kitchen to prepare their morning meal just as Keiko finishes.

'Don't tell the others,' Hana says, her eyes downcast.

'Why not? They should be warned about him.'

'Please, I don't want them to pity me more than they already do.'

Keiko cups Hana's face in her hands and looks into her eyes. Her hands are soft and strong and her gaze fierce. Chatter from the kitchen drifts towards them. Hana worries one of the girls will open the cupboard door at any moment, but she doesn't want to upset Keiko by pulling away.

'Pity is a kindness,' Keiko says, her voice absolute. 'Each of us deserves pity, but no one in this forsaken land has the compassion to give us this kindness. So we are stuck here in this humiliation, tortured day after day. There is nothing left for us but to bestow what little kindness we have onto one another.'

Hana reflects on Keiko's words. None of the other girls have shown her ill will, but neither are they as kind to her as Keiko has been since her arrival. Like Hana, the other girls are all Korean, and that should have created an instant bond between them, but it hasn't. Hana has kept to herself, offered almost nothing and therefore received nothing. Lost in her own misery, she has failed to notice that the other girls are experiencing the same miseries, too. There is no difference between any of them. They are all trapped in this unspeakable prison together. Perhaps if she allows the others to see her humiliation and pain, it will bring recognition. Like looking in a mirror, the others would see themselves, bloody and ashamed, and welcome her into their circle.

When Keiko exits the cupboard, Hinata comes to the door to see what has happened, and Hana does not hide herself. Riko comes up behind Hinata and peers over her shoulder. Her hand goes quickly to her mouth. As Hana finishes dressing her wounds, she exits the storage cupboard and the girls all sit around the table, waiting for her to join them. When Hana sits, Tsubaki sets about making a pot of rice tea. As the water boils, she recounts the time an officer decided to carve his name into her back with his bayonet before he went to the front line.

'He didn't die, as he had feared he would,' Tsubaki says, her eyes narrowed. 'When he returned he came out of hours and I refused to service him, not that I would have ever let him touch me again. But then he threatened to kill me!' She shook her head, recalling her anger. 'So I grabbed the bayonet from his hands before he knew what was happening, and I stabbed him in the neck.'

Tsubaki grins with pleasure at the memory.

'We buried him in the garden in the middle of the night. We disguised the grave as a vegetable patch.'

The girls giggle at that, covering their mouths.

'When the night guard questioned us later, wondering where the officer had disappeared to in the middle of the night, we all feigned ignorance,' Keiko says.

'Which is easy to do when they already have such low opinions of us,' Hinata says, and they all laugh.

'That year, we had a bountiful vegetable crop, so now, whenever the garden refuses to flourish, we are tempted to do it again,' Tsubaki says, nudging Keiko's shoulder. 'So if that first lieutenant is not killed in battle and returns, you let me know, and I will help you put an end to him. Then we will eat well!'

Hearty laughter follows Tsubaki's words, and Hana finds she can't suppress a smile. It is her first since arriving at the brothel.

Emi

Seoul, December 2011

Demonstrators chant in front of the Japanese embassy. Bundled up in their warmest winter coats and hats, their gloved hands waving banners, they shout: *Japan must admit its crimes. Reparation for the grandmothers.* A man shouts through a megaphone, *Admit your war crimes, no peace with Japan without admission of guilt!* Someone near the gate cries out, *All wars are crimes against the world's women and girls!*

The red-brick building seems to hide behind the wrought-iron gate in shame. There are more policemen than usual stationed in front of it, standing shoulder to shoulder in an orderly line. Their emotionless faces disguise their humanity.

'We should have made some signs,' Lane says. 'Everyone seems to have one.'

Emi scans the crowd. Even the children have something in their hands to wave.

'Perhaps there's a station to make one,' YoonHui replies. 'Look there, in that tent.'

Emi's daughter points to a white tent set up beside a makeshift stage. Chairs are set up in front of the stage, shrouded in banners that call for *reparation, admission of crimes against humanity, admission of guilt, admission of crimes against the Geneva Conventions.* Large speakers emit white noise into the charged air, electric with discontent.

'Shall we go and see?' her daughter asks, stopping to touch Emi's arm. 'Mother?'

'What?' Emi asks.

'Perhaps we can make some signs, too?'

Emi follows her daughter's lead towards the tent. Two women standing behind a large table covered in poster boards and markers welcome them. Lane picks up a red marker and begins writing Japanese characters across the white poster board. Emi watches the fluid lines spilling from Lane's red marker, marvelling at her perfect handwriting.

'You know Japanese?' Emi says.

'She does, and Mandarin, too,' her daughter answers for Lane.

Emi nods appreciatively, though she wonders why an American would want to learn these languages. What drives her to go so far away from home and surround herself with foreignness? Lane looks up at Emi and offers her the marker.

'Do you want to make one?' she asks.

Emi shakes her head. Her daughter concentrates on her own sign written in English, as though not to be outdone by Lane. Emi cannot read it.

'For the cameras,' YoonHui explains as she motions towards the news trucks lining the street.

Anxious to get a good look at the group of old women gathering near the side of the stage, Emi slowly fades out of the tent, and no one notices her exit. As she shuffles in the direction of the stage, her bad leg gives her trouble. The pain slows her pace, but she doesn't stop. She recognises three of the grandmothers from past demonstrations. The survivors. Two others are not familiar to her, and she moves closer to get a clearer view of their faces.

They are Emi's age and even older. Time has obscured their once-youthful skin. Unsure she would recognise an aged version of her sister, Emi pays close attention to their mannerisms. The shorter one gestures with her hand, which is clad in a red mitten. The other one nods her pink-hatted head while toeing the ground with one pointed boot. Emi watches, waiting for déjà vu. Then one of them laughs. Has she heard that laugh before, perhaps in a higher pitch from a younger throat?

She cranes her neck to get a better view of the grandmother, waiting for that sound again. The old woman is telling a story and gesturing with her red mittens. She claps them together and laughs again. The sound is unusual, raspy and harsh. It's not familiar after all. Emi turns her attention to the other survivor. She is a little taller than the first one, but her back is to Emi. She has just taken a few steps to one side, hoping to get a better view of her face, when the woman turns round. They all stare at Emi.

'We know you?' one woman calls out.

'No, I don't think so,' Emi says apologetically, and begins to turn away.

'You sure? Come over here,' the woman wearing the red mittens kindly says.

Emi stalls, looking back towards the white tent. Lane is talking to the women behind the table, and her daughter is still working on her sign. The old women whisper among themselves but never take their eyes off her. She starts towards them. Her leg drags behind her a little more dramatically than usual, and no matter how hard she tries, she cannot make it obey her. She wishes she could go for a swim; that would loosen her joints up and give her some relief.

'You were here before, weren't you? I recognise your face,' says one of the more famous survivors.

'Last year, I met you here last year,' Emi admits.

'Yes, I remember,' she says, and glances at Emi's lame leg. 'You were looking for someone? Your friend?'

Emi blushes. Does she really remember, or is she merely being polite?

'Yes, my friend. Hana. Her name is Hana.'

'Hana, do any of you remember meeting a girl named Hana during the war?'

The women mutter among themselves, and Emi waits for them to travel back in time to that horrible place of memories shared between them.

'I knew a Hinata,' one of the newer ladies says, the one whose face Emi had yet to see. She turns to Emi and they search each other's eyes for recognition.

'Hinata?' Emi says absent-mindedly, studying her aged face, trying to see it with younger skin, fewer marks, brighter eyes . . .

'Yes. Sunflower,' she says, interpreting the Japanese name into Korean.

'We were all called flowers then, not our real names,' one woman says without disguising her bitterness.

'I hate flowers to this day,' another one replies.

'Yes, me too. I can't enjoy them.'

'Too many memories,' another says.

'None of us knew each other's real names,' the woman in the mittens tells Emi. 'No one would know your friend's given name unless she had a chance to tell them.'

'But perhaps she spoke of her home . . . or me? My name is Emi, Emiko.'

The ladies repeat her name and one by one begin shaking their heads.

'She was from Jeju Island. She was a *haenyeo*,' Emi states, as though that makes all the difference in the world.

'*Haenyeo*? They took her from so far away?' one woman exclaims.

'From all over,' another answers. 'Even China, the Philippines and Malaysia.'

'And the Dutch girls, too. Remember that one who spoke out?'

'Yes, the Dutch woman. She was brave to come forward.'

Emi remembers seeing the Dutch woman in the newspaper. Like so many of the other 'comfort women', she had hidden her story of rape and humiliation from her family for over fifty years. When the first Korean 'comfort woman', Kim Hak-sun, came forward in 1991, giving her grim testimony, she was followed by others. They were met with disbelief and branded as money-seeking prostitutes. It was then the Dutch woman, Jan Ruff O'Herne, joined them in a bold move, telling her story at the International Public Hearing on Japanese War Crimes in Tokyo in 1992, and the Western world took notice.

At that time, Emi was not yet ready to admit to herself that the hole in her heart was her sister's absence. Nor was she ready to accept that her sister could have been one of these women.

'Mother?' Emi's daughter arrives carrying her newly inscribed sign.

'Your daughter?' the red-mittened woman asks.

'Yes, this is YoonHui,' Emi replies, and smiles proudly at her daughter.

The women exchange polite greetings, but Emi soon loses interest in them. They cannot help her. She turns away and again searches the crowd, straining to see something familiar, a head held like Hana once held hers, a laugh, a certain way she had of walking, sitting, anything that might remind her of the girl who was lost.

The woman with the red mittens falls away from the group and stands next to Emi. 'Do you know where they took her?'

'I was told perhaps China or Manchuria, but I never knew for certain.'

'She must have been a very close friend to you if you're looking for her after all this time. I'm so sorry.'

Emi nods absently, remembering the day her mother told her what she knew of Hana's whereabouts. It was a cold January afternoon, and Hana had been missing for months. Emi's parents were too afraid to leave Emi alone on the shore or even at home. Soldiers had returned to the village not long after Hana's abduction and stolen two more girls from a family on the other side of the tangerine grove. That was the day Emi learned to dive in the deep waters. She was only nine, but her mother wouldn't let her out of her sight.

'At least out here they will have to risk drowning before they dare take you from me,' she said to Emi as they swam out beyond the shallow reefs.

That year was unusually dry, and the farms had suffered. The divers, however, managed not to go hungry by working longer hours even in winter. Instead of remaining in the water for the one-to-two-hour time slots they usually adhered to, they remained two and sometimes three hours in the freezing sea, warming themselves afterwards at campfires on the shore. Emi had learned to prop herself onto the buoy while guarding the net when her mother dived in the deep waters. Her mother allowed her to dive in tandem with her nearer the shore, where she could find oysters and sea urchins along the reef. Emi took to the water quicker than her mother had expected. She had a smaller build than her big sister, and she had not previously been a strong swimmer. It was as though Emi had no choice but to thrive in her new circumstances. Her mother seemed pleased, the only positive emotion she had expressed since her sister was taken.

After a long morning of diving, they had swum back to shore to bring in their catch and to rest near a blazing fire. Emi had found an oyster on the reef and was prising it open with a small knife. Inside, she found a pearl hidden in the flesh.

'A pearl,' she exclaimed, and held it out to her mother.

The other divers leaned in for a glimpse of Emi's find.

'Ha!' they exclaimed. 'It's so small, nothing to be so excited about.'

Her mother glanced at the tiny pearl, too. 'Too bad you couldn't have found it a few years from now. It would have been a magnificent pearl. Such a waste.' She shook her head and went back to counting and separating her catch.

After Hana's abduction, her mother had grown distant and quiet. Though even in her distance, she kept Emi close to her side, which made playing with her friends more difficult.

'It wouldn't be here in a few years,' one of the women said, her tone filled with resentment. 'Those Japanese oyster hunters, they leave nothing for us to find. Enjoy your little pearl, Emi. It may be the only one left in these waters.'

Emi held it up to the bright winter sun. She had never seen a pearl up close before, and only two divers had ever found one that she knew of. The Japanese had ravaged the oyster beds for pearls since they first arrived over thirty years ago, leaving none for the *haenyeo* to find. Now they searched for seaweed and abalone and creatures living deeper than the Japanese cared to fish.

What if she hadn't pulled the oyster from the reef that morning and instead found it years from now as her mother had said? She rolled the tiny sphere between her thumb and forefinger in the sunlight.

'I wish Hana was here,' she said. 'She would have been happy for me.' She kissed the pearl and let it fall into the sand.

At the mention of Hana's name, Emi's mother dropped the sea urchin she was cleaning and sucked in a breath through her front teeth. She glared at Emi. The other divers averted their eyes, giving them privacy without actually moving away. Unfazed by her mother's evident animosity, she continued.

'You never talk about what happened to her. Why don't you?'

Her mother reached down to retrieve the sea urchin. She quickly gutted its edible flesh with her knife and tossed its remains into a bucket. Without a word, she continued separating, gutting and counting.

Emi shivered from the cold. She usually helped her mother with the tasks so they could quickly get the catch to market, then head home for a hot bath and warm clothes. But she was too angry to drop the topic.

'You know what happened to her, don't you? That's why you won't speak her name. Tell me where they took her.'

Her mother didn't look up. She kept sorting and gutting and discarding. When she dropped another sea urchin onto the sand, she audibly expelled her breath in exasperation. Emi prepared herself for a reprimand, but her mother didn't speak right away. Instead she looked out over the sea. Emi followed her gaze, shielding her eyes from the sunlight glinting on the ocean waves. They seemed to freeze beneath her mother's sharp glare, the white crests unmoving in the distance. It was as though time had ceased. Even the wind died into silence. Emi and the other divers held their breath, anticipating her mother's wrath. Finally, her mother looked at her.

'They took her to the front lines in China, or possibly even Manchuria, we'll never know. But I do know that she will not come back.'

The last thing Emi had expected was an answer to her question, and it caught her off guard.

'You know where she is? You've known all this time?' she cried out too loudly. The other divers shrank away from her raised voice. 'Then why didn't Father bring her back?'

'Hush, child. You don't understand. He couldn't bring her back. Not from . . . there.'

'Then I will go! I'm not afraid. Just tell me where to find her.' Emi stood, ready to begin the search for Hana.

Her mother grabbed her by the elbow. 'It is too late. They took her to the front lines of the war. That means she is already dead.'

She spoke so matter-of-factly that Emi was struck dumb. Her knees went weak. She sank back down onto the rock. The waves began to swell and the winds began to roar once again. The seabirds cried their childlike calls above their heads, and the women began chatting among themselves to talk away the strangeness.

Emi stared at her mother's muted face, trying to determine whether what she had said was a known fact or a supposition. She was concentrating so fervently that she didn't realise she was squeezing the blade of her knife in the palm of her hand.

'What are you doing?' her mother shouted, rushing to Emi's side and seizing the knife. Blood oozed from the cut in her palm. As her mother bound the wound in scraps of rags torn from her own swimming shirt, Emi searched her mother's face until she finally found her voice.

'Why did they take her to the front lines? She's not a soldier. She's a girl. They only take boys to fight.'

Her mother tied the makeshift bandage before speaking. She held her daughter's injured hand in her lap. She seemed to think about her words, while gently caressing the top of Emi's hand. The wind had begun to blow again, and a chill settled in Emi's thin bones.

'There are things in this world you should never have to know, and I will shield you from these things for as long as I am able. That is my duty as a mother. Do not ask me this again. Hana is dead. Miss her, mourn her, but never speak of her to me.' Her mother suddenly stood up, lifted her bucket and walked away. When her mother looked back over her shoulder, Emi knew she needed to follow. Even though no more words would be spoken, she would never leave Emi on her own.

When her father arrived at the market, Emi was sent home with him. She couldn't explain to him why her mother was angry. Instead they ate a light meal of fish soup with seaweed and oyster mushrooms. Her father had grown quiet when Hana was taken. He no longer sang, recited poetry, or even played his much-loved zither. Once in a while, he would catch Emi's gaze, and the two of them would exchange a sad smile, neither knowing how to cheer up the other.

Night fell before her mother returned home from the market. Emi had stayed awake sitting with her father.

'Come, daughter,' she said as soon as she walked through the door, as though she knew Emi would still be awake.

'Where are we going?' Emi asked, afraid her mother was still angry with her for asking about her sister.

'Husband, come, too.'

The three of them walked down towards the sea, guided only by the stars. The rush of waves crashing along the shore far below the cliffs warned them to turn away in case they fell down into the rocky waves. As they neared the edge of the cliff, Emi realised where they stood. It was a high perch overlooking the beach and the black rocks below where she once guarded their catch several long months ago.

Her mother lit an oil lamp and set it on the ground. Then she opened her bag and retrieved a flower. It was a chrysanthemum, a symbol of mourning for Koreans. The imperial seal of Japan was the yellow chrysanthemum, a crest symbolising the imperial family's power. Emi had wondered which came first, the symbol of power or mourning. Her father lifted the lamp and held it aloft to illuminate the white bloom against the hazy, starlit sky.

'We offer this flower to the Dragon Sea God in the name of Hana, our child and a daughter of the sea. Aid her spirit, great one, so she may find her way in the afterlife; guide her to our ancestors.' She tossed the flower over the edge of the cliff, where it disappeared as though into oblivion, gone forever. Just like Hana.

Her mother turned to Emi and bade her to perform *sebae* to the Dragon Sea God. The three of them faced the sea, executing three deep, ceremonial bows. When they stood for the final time, tears streamed down their faces as they prayed to an omnipotent god to bring their loved one's spirit home to rest.

The walk back to the warmth of their house was slow and dreamlike, reminding Emi of the *gut* ritual for her sister's induction as a *haenyeo* so many years ago. Emi had been just four years old, but she remembered the shaman's circling ribbons and the ache in her heart to follow her sister and become a *haenyeo*, too. *You will be standing here one day soon, Little Sister, and I will be right beside you to welcome you* . . . Her sister's words from that night echoed through her mind.

'You lied,' Emi whispered to no one, and for the first time, Emi felt that Hana was dead. In that moment, she decided never to think of her again, because the pain felt like her heart might implode and kill her. Breathless, she doubled over and fell to her knees, saying farewell to her sister for the final time.

》-《

Emi recalls that pain as she stands before the red-mittened grandmother. She feels a hint of it even now. The moment the flower disappeared over the cliff, the shock of it, and then the certainty that followed when she truly believed her sister was dead. Like the grandmothers, she, too, has not been able to enjoy flowers since that day, especially chrysanthemums, white or yellow. Looking up at the grandmother, she shakes these memories from her mind. The old woman's quiet patience warms Emi's heart.

Hana

As the weeks pass, Hana finds herself trapped in the numbing routine despite the increased camaraderie with the other girls. The only
variation in her day comes with the brothel's bad-tempered rooster.
The old Chinese couple also keeps hens locked up in cages; the captive hens lay eggs that the girls are never offered. Hana has come to
hate the scruffy creature, which stalks the grounds like a sentry.

The cock hounds her whenever she goes outside. When she washes
her dress in the yard, the mean-spirited bird sneaks up behind her
and pecks the backs of her legs, drawing blood, before she can turn to
kick it away. Sometimes, when she is fetching water from the well, it
jumps onto her back as she leans over to haul out the bucket, scaring
her, and she drops the bucket and has to draw the water all over again.
The bird seems to possess an angry spirit determined to make her life
at the brothel more miserable than it already is.

Each morning when the rooster crows, she awakens with the thought that SangSoo's spirit has indeed followed her to this place and is haunting her. She tries to make peace with the cock. She even starts saving a few grains of rice in her pocket to offer to the cruel bird. It merely pecks the grains until they disappear into its gullet and then proceeds to peck at the flesh of her palm.

Nearly two months have passed when the crowing of the demonic creature rouses Hana from a fitful sleep one night. Lying in the dark, she waits for the intolerable bird to crow again, for its habit is to crow three times in slow procession, concluded by a final, longer herald, but nothing follows. Hana begins to doubt whether it is the cock that woke her in the first place. Perhaps it is something else that disturbed her.

Two stars whose names she does not know flicker their dying light beyond the iron bars of the narrow window, high on the wall. The night sky tells her it is well past midnight but not yet near dawn. Hana listens through the silence, concentrating on the familiar noises of the brothel. The ceiling creaks overhead with each gust of wind, crickets chirp in unison under the floorboards, and the constant pitter-patter of the mice's tiny feet inside the walls and floors suggest all is as it should be. Then, somewhere beneath her room, a door clicks shut, and footsteps trail through the main room on the ground floor.

It is too early for a change of the night guard, which happens at dawn. The footsteps are muffled. None of the guards care enough to step quietly through the house. In contrast, they seem to want to announce their presence, marching throughout the wood-planked rooms below without a thought for the sleeping girls above their heads.

The careful footsteps reach the staircase, and Hana quickly lies back down. The footsteps draw closer and closer, until all at once they stop outside her door. She pulls her blanket up to her neck. It can't be an officer's visit. Their presence is usually announced with dinner, drinks and ceremony as they choose a girl and take her upstairs. The thin gap beneath the wooden door glows with the dim light of a torch. She begins to wish she hadn't shunned all of the soldiers who vied for her attentions, that she had chosen a protector. With a protector, unscheduled visits are not allowed, for fear of retaliation by the man who has claimed the girl. Perhaps this is one of the soldiers she rebuffed, returning to take his revenge. How can she explain to him before he murders her that it isn't personal, that she equally loathes them all?

The doorknob squeaks as it turns, and Hana feigns sleep. The door swings open and a stream of light shines on her shut eyelids. She relaxes the muscles in her face and mimics the deep breaths of slumber, forcing her chest to rise and fall in a slow, steady rhythm. The torch flicks off. The room falls back into darkness. Footsteps pad inside. The door clicks shut. Hana stops breathing.

A ghostly wind howls through the rafters above their heads. The brothel seems to gasp, and the wind rushes through the window. Hana opens her eyes and stares into the darkness. A black shape stands by the door. For a long time, it doesn't move. The crickets have stopped chirping, and the mice seem to have frozen mid-step. The intruder's shallow breaths fill the void left by their silence.

He takes a step towards her, and she clutches the blanket tighter. He takes another step and before she can stop herself, she sits up and backs away from him, cowering in the far corner.

'Do not be afraid,' he whispers. 'It's me.'

Hana instantly recognises the voice. She shakes her head violently. He pauses in front of the window. Faint starlight streams across his face. Morimoto has returned.

'It's me,' he repeats, kneeling in front of her. 'I finally made it back for you.'

He touches her trembling knee, and the warmth from his fingertips sends a shock of electricity through her skin. She shrinks away from him, still shaking her head in horror at his return. He is the monster that invades her dreams as she relives her abduction and imprisonment. She has promised herself every morning that if she ever lays eyes on Morimoto again, she will stab him in the heart – or die trying.

Now the moment is upon her, yet her courage falters. She cannot keep herself from trembling. She wishes she'd simply vanish. When he reaches his other hand towards her, she has to bite her tongue to stifle a scream.

'I've come back for you,' he says, wrapping one hand around her wrist and pulling her towards him.

His tone confuses her. He sounds as though he thinks she should be happy to see him. She kicks and struggles against his grip, but soon he is on top of her, crushing her on the bare floor.

'Why are you fighting me?' he asks, not bothering to keep his voice at a whisper. If Keiko is awake, she will have heard him. 'Don't you understand? I came back for you.'

His face hovers above her, cloaked in shadow, and she fills in the black void with the man in her memory. The one who raped her first and called it a kindness, before condemning her to this unimaginable life. Not life, but purgatory in the underworld. Morimoto is Gangnim, the death god, reaper of souls, and he has come to claim hers.

He unbuckles his belt. Hana squirms beneath him, and he fumbles with the buttons of his trousers. She presses against his chest with the heels of her palms, heaving him upwards, and he nearly falls off her. He quickly regains his balance and punches her in the stomach, knocking the wind out of her. She doubles over, choking for breath.

'Don't make me do that,' he says, shoving his trousers down to his knees.

'I'll scream,' Hana manages through painful breaths. 'And if the night guard finds you up here, you will be punished.'

Morimoto forces her to the floor, climbing on top of her once more. His face hovers above hers, their noses nearly touching.

'I am the night guard,' he says.

》-《

Afterwards, Morimoto lies next to her. Hana turns her back to him so he cannot see her cry. Countless men have used her since she arrived at the brothel – more than fifteen that first day alone. She hates them all. Their lust disgusts her. Their fear of death and of the emperor's jubilant war sickens her. She wishes for each one to die a slow, painful death and be forced to suffer in his afterlife. But the hate she feels towards Morimoto outstrips any she has felt thus far. It consumes her entire being, paralysing her, and she can do nothing to release the force of her growing wrath but cry silent, pitiful tears.

His breathing slows, and she thinks he has fallen asleep. She wipes her face with a corner of the ragged blanket. The crickets have begun to sing again, and the mice scurry through the crawl spaces of the flimsy clapboard brothel. Her shoulders sag. She has no control over Morimoto's whims or desires. If he wishes to visit her in the middle of the night, he can do so. If he wishes to beat her senseless every time he comes, he can do that, too. She has no dominion over her own body.

Her thoughts drift to the well behind the vegetable garden. If Hana falls head first, she might knock herself unconscious before drowning in the well's dark depths. She sees herself hurrying down the brothel's staircase, breaking through the glass in the kitchen window, running across the yard before Corporal Morimoto can rush downstairs to stop her, and then she sees the black water greeting her broken, unconscious face. This is within her power to do. This is how she can regain control of her own body.

Hana rises to her feet. She shivers with the sudden loss of Morimoto's heat. He turns over, and she waits until his breaths resume the slow rhythm of sleep. The well looms in her mind. If she is lucky, it will be a quick, painless death, and she will never have to endure his touch again. When she is certain he is asleep, she steps over his naked body and heads towards the door. The floorboards creak beneath her feet, the noise of each step too loud for the quiet of the night. She is nearly at the door when she hears someone speak.

Wake up, daughter. Prickles ripple down her limbs. It's her mother's voice. She sounds so near. Hana closes her eyes, listening for her mother to speak once more.

It's time, her mother says, and suddenly Hana can see her. She is home, and her mother is beside her, urging her to awaken from a deep slumber. Hana feels her mother's hand gently shaking her arm, until finally she opens her eyes. The memory feels so real as Hana stands in the small room deciding between life in the brothel and the freedom waiting for her at the bottom of a well.

Come, her mother says, and Hana loses herself in the memory, a young girl, eleven years old.

The wind whirls through the cracks in the brothel's rafters, and Hana remembers the shaman twirling on the shore, white ribbons dancing on the sea wind, and her sister's hand held tightly in her own. Hana promised they would dive together one day. She felt it as a certainty. There was no question in her heart that she would one day stand on the shore watching her sister's own ceremony as a fully-fledged *haenyeo*. The image of her sister standing tall in the early dawn light sends a jolt of warmth through Hana's veins. She is suddenly desperate to see the ceremony, to watch it happen with her own eyes. There is nothing she wants more in that moment than to see her little sister, Emiko, join the *haenyeo*. Hana returns to Morimoto's side. As she lies down, she decides that if she must die, then she will die trying to get home, not flinging herself down a well. She lies awake all night, imagining her escape.

》-《

Over the next few weeks, Morimoto visits Hana's room each night he is on duty. She tries to resist him at first, but he easily overpowers her each time, leaving a parting reminder on her body before he leaves. The last time she resists, he nearly chokes her to death. After that Hana stops fighting. Morimoto will come and go as he pleases. There is nothing she can do about it.

With each visit, he grows more and more bold, speaking to her as though she is his lover and not his captive. It is as though her acceptance of her powerless situation has soothed him, making him less volatile towards her. And soon, he begins to speak of his discontent with the war.

'The emperor has sentenced his soldiers to death. The Americans are defeating us in the South Pacific. No one knows if he is even aware of the losses we have suffered.'

Morimoto often speaks harshly as he stands at attention, waiting for Hana to finish undressing him. His voice is low, but never a whisper, and Hana often wonders if the other girls listen to him through the walls or whether they block him out so they can sleep. They never mention his late-night visits. It is as though nothing that happens in their rooms, unless blood is spilled, can be spoken about.

'I have to get out of Manchuria. I refuse to die for a doomed cause. Not for the emperor or anyone else.'

It is an odd way for a Japanese soldier to speak. Most of the soldiers she encounters worship the emperor as though he is a true god. They gladly lay their lives at his feet to shed their blood as the deity wishes. Only a few ever speak against the emperor, and those men are usually touched with mental instability. They have seen slaughter first-hand and committed atrocities at the front lines, breaking something in their minds. Hana begins to believe Morimoto is among those psychologically broken soldiers.

'I'll take you with me,' Morimoto says one night. When he speaks of leaving Manchuria, Hana reminds herself that his talk of leaving may be a lure to get her to fall for him in some way, to trust him, or something else his deranged mind has devised. Her disgust for him is always present, but her desire to return home exceeds her hatred, so still she listens.

'We can leave this place together. Escape to Mongolia. I know people there. I have connections.' He touches her thigh, the palm of his hand unwelcome on her skin. 'What do you think? Do you want to come with me?'

Hana remains silent. This is the first time he has asked what she wants. He might be tricking her. If she says she does want to leave the brothel, he could send her to solitary confinement for planning to escape, but if she says she doesn't, he may beat her for rejecting his proposal. There is no right answer.

'Did you hear me?' he asks, his voice too loud in the darkness.

His hand grips her arm, and she can feel him daring her to upset him.

'If it pleases you,' she whispers.

His hand relaxes, slides down her arm, caressing her skin.

'Being with you pleases me,' he says, and kisses her, deep and probing.

Hana holds her breath when he kisses her or touches her. She often holds her breath so long that she nearly faints. Sometimes, she counts to see how high she can reach before she is forced to take in air. Her highest count so far is one hundred and fifty-two. Tonight she has counted to eighty-four when he finally climaxes and rolls off her.

As he dresses, she looks past him, imagining the myriad escape plots she has planned if he really does free her from this brothel.

)>-((

'Don't go,' Keiko says as they kneel in the yard washing their used condoms.

They have finished servicing the soldiers and are now tending to the only barrier they have between the men and the threats of pregnancy and disease. Hana hates touching them. Even though the soldiers are gone for the night, it is like they are still around, like they have left a part of themselves behind so that she won't forget that they will be back in the morning. They always come back – like she can possibly forget.

Hana concentrates on the sudsy water, rinsing the used condoms as quickly as she can.

'I don't know what you mean,' Hana replies.

'Don't lie to me,' Keiko says, reaching out and holding on to Hana's forearm. 'And don't leave me alone. You can't trust him. He's like all the rest. They'll say anything to get what they want from you. They thrive on love affairs, they make you believe they want to help you to escape so you will hand them your heart. For what? A false promise. You'll lose your leg . . . or more.'

Hana gently pulls her forearm out of Keiko's now-tightened grip. She returns to rinsing the condoms. 'I never listen to what any of them have to say.'

Keiko's sharp eyes narrow. 'Not even Corporal Morimoto?'

Hana is taken aback to hear his name on Keiko's lips. They have never spoken about his nightly visits. She looks at Keiko and tries to see what she is feeling. Is it fear or anger or something more sinister . . . can she be jealous that a soldier like Morimoto chooses to visit

Hana instead of her? Hana keeps silent, uncertain what to say or even to feel.

'Learn from my mistake: never trust a man. Especially one in this place.' Keiko gathers the condoms from her basin and dumps the murky water into the dirt. Without a word, she marches back inside.

Is Hana foolish for believing, even for a moment, that Morimoto is not a liar? That he isn't leading her into a trap just to take pleasure in her punishment? Or that he isn't merely a madman, leading them both to their deaths?

》-《

Hana fixes her gaze on the clear midnight sky. Tonight is the night. She is standing on her tiptoes, pulling herself up by the bars of her prison cell, so that she can peer over the window's high ledge. The bars are rusty and scrape the skin on her palms as she grips them tight, lifting herself higher. The Manchurian summer is quickly dissipating, and with it, a cool breeze brushes against her face. On her island it is still the rainy season, and the night air would be wet with humidity. The early September heat would be rising from the volcanic rocks that form her stone home, and she would be sweating from the exertion. The crisp scent from the grasslands of the Manchurian plains rushes through her nostrils, pushing the thought away.

She holds on a moment longer to catch a glimpse of the dirt path beyond the perimeter wall. It's too dark to see it, but she knows it's there. In daylight, she can make out the skinny path stamped into the earth by hundreds of soldiers' boots. Hana releases the bars and sinks to the floor. She hugs her knees to her chest and stares at a neat line of tiny crescents, barely noticeable in the floorboard closest to the wall. Her fingertips count each mark, painstakingly pressed into the worn wood . . . twenty-four . . . forty-eight . . . eighty-three. She presses her thumbnail into the floorboard to mark one more day turned into night. Eighty-four days. Her fingers trace over the evidence of her incarceration as her mind drifts towards the door and who lies beyond it. Hana listens for the noises of the brothel, but they, too, have been silenced. Or perhaps it's the looming decision that seems to mute the familiar din from her ears as though she is submerged beneath a great ocean with only the pressure of the water sounding against her eardrums.

Footsteps interrupt her thoughts. Morimoto is downstairs, preparing to leave. Hana's heartbeat quickens. He said he'd end his shift five minutes early and walk down the dirt path without turning his key in the dead bolt, five whole minutes before the next night guard would arrive to take his place, so that Hana could slip out and be free.

He is like a conquering king and has finally offered Hana terms: follow him through the unlocked door and into his arms. His terms are a second kind of death.

Sitting beneath the window, staring at the bedroom door, Hana hears him again as he moves through the common rooms below. She tiptoes to the door and slowly opens it. Silence greets her in the hallway. The other girls usually sleep like the dead, but she must still take care not to awaken them. Edging her feet around the boards that creak, Hana makes her way to the landing and listens to his boots go out the side door. The hinges squeal shut and the doorknob is released. Hana leans over the railing, straining her ears to hear the familiar slide of the key into the lock, the turning of the dead bolt as it shrieks into place, and the silence that follows. But there is nothing, except whistling. Hana listens to his song as it slowly fades away.

She has less than five minutes before the next soldier arrives to take Morimoto's place as the night guard. Hana is tormented with indecision. If they find her out of her room, they will punish her with ten lashes of the whip and then throw her into solitary confinement. But if they realise she is trying to escape, they will saw off one of her legs. There is no judge or jury, just a group of men to hold her down. Her fear of getting caught does not outweigh the memories that plague her, memories of home. Do her parents miss her? Are they searching for her?

Her feet are cold from standing barefoot on the landing. How much time has passed? A minute? Two? Hana creeps back inside her room. Hidden in a hollowed-out cavity underneath the sweat-stained mat is everything valuable she has acquired in her captivity, wrapped carefully in a square of cloth: coins tossed to her by grateful young men, a gold necklace left by a commander, a ring left by a homesick private, a silver hair comb left by another faceless, nameless soldier. These are the only things of worth she has, and yet they are not enough to get her very far on her own.

'Don't you want me to take you away from this place?' he asked before he left her for the night. Confidence radiated from him like the sun's heat. She only had to nod to satisfy his ego. One slight motion to send him contentedly on his way.

As hard as she tried, she couldn't make herself do it. Her mind screamed at her to simply nod so that he would leave, but she stood frozen, staring back at him, her distaste threatening to appear on her face. He began to look confused. His confidence faltered, and his eyebrows drew together.

'What's the matter, my little Sakura? Don't you trust me?' His grip on her arms began to tighten.

When his grip was threatening to bruise, she blinked, breaking the tension between them. Then she bowed her head in a submissive nod.

'Who am I not to trust you?' she said, her voice so low she wondered if she had actually spoken.

He released her arms, satisfied with himself once more, and left her alone in her room.

Holding her meagre belongings, recalling his confident step as he marched from her room, Hana knows he is already out there, hiding beneath the bridge in the shadows of the night and waiting for her to come to him. He has no doubt she will do as he bids. She glances one last time at the darkness beyond the window, willing the universe to help her. Her mother's voice, clear as if she were beside her, rings out: *Look to the shore. If you see her, you are safe.* She sees her sister standing on the shore . . . Emiko.

Hana clenches her jaw at the memory. Why would she think of that now? Her mother's image fills her mind, followed by her sister's and then her father's. They are all with her now; their ghostly forms stand side by side in her tiny cell, as though waiting for her to make this decision: remain in this brothel and service the never-ending lines of soldiers or risk life and limb to escape with the man who brought her here. Their hollow eyes sparkle in the darkness. *Make the decision,* they seem to say. Hana takes a step away from them.

'You're not really here,' she whispers. They only gaze back at her, unblinking phantoms. She squeezes her eyes shut. In her mind she sees them as they were before Morimoto captured her – before she became Sakura. She sees them on her island, living beside the sea when she was still Hana, a name she has not told anyone.

Before she can think of reasons not to go, Hana stuffs the cloth bundle into her underwear. Then she flies down the staircase two steps at a time. The eyes of the girls trapped in frames on the wall stare at her as she nears the bottom step, and she pauses to look at her own face. The thought that her photograph will remain there for even one more night makes her chest tighten.

She stands on her tiptoes on the edge of the bottom step and reaches for the frame. It tips upwards and then slides down the wall. Hana catches it and quickly slips the photograph out of the wooden frame. She shoves it into her knickers with the bundle and then runs through the lounge towards the kitchen.

Hana is nearly to the back door when she feels a deep certainty that there will be a voice behind her, a rifle aimed at her back, and her muscles seize. Her steps falter, and she falls to the floor. On her knees, Hana is prepared for the inevitable.

Her heart flutters like hummingbird wings, but only gentle snores drift to her ears. Suddenly, she wants to turn back. The reasons to stay crowd her mind. Losing a leg if she is caught, potential death. And if she leaves, the other girls will suffer. They will be punished, thrown into solitary confinement, and maybe even die because of her selfish act. Keiko's pleading voice cuts through the images. *Don't leave me alone.*

The front door opens on the other side of the brothel. Heavy boots stamp on the wooden porch before entering. She has to cross the lounge to get back to the stairs if she chooses to stay, and the night guard will see her. Her legs burn at the thought of the saw's jagged edge against her skin.

It is too late. She cannot stay, not even to spare her sleeping friends. She rises to her feet and hurries to the door. She lets out a shaky breath as she tries the metal doorknob. It squeaks, and she cringes, holding her breath until it stops turning. She breathes out, and then she pulls it. The door doesn't budge. Heat prickles her cheeks. She pulls it again as hard as she can. It doesn't move. The door is still bolted shut. She is a fool. Morimoto is laughing at her.

This is her punishment for believing a Japanese soldier – for being so naive. She sees Keiko's disappointment in her as clearly as if she is standing in front of her now. Hana has betrayed her. She chose to trust a man.

Resigned to her fate, Hana leans her forehead against the door. She deserves to be punished. She deserves to die. She feels the cold edge of the knife against her thigh, making her feel faint. Before Hana realises what is happening, the door slowly pushes open. *Push, not pull.*

The door is open. Morimoto didn't lie. Footsteps march towards the kitchen. Hana doesn't look back. She slides through the open door, shuts it behind her, and disappears into the night. There is no burden now, just the elation of escape.

Hana knows the way to the bridge where Morimoto is waiting for her. It is at the end of the dirt path she can see from her room. The path leads a mile to the north, and he will meet her where it forks, just before the ramshackle military barracks. She can picture him as he waits for her in the darkness, his smile as she approaches. She can see him coming forward to grab her and kiss her cheek, her neck, her forehead, his embrace like a stranglehold, before hurrying her along the river to the life that he has planned for them in Mongolia. She can see him, and his question echoes in her mind.

Don't you want me to take you away from this place? She sees his face as he stared back at her, and now, standing outside beneath the night sky, she is free to answer his question.

'No,' she says firmly, 'I don't want you to take me away,' and then she begins to run.

The stars light her path. Hana runs as fast as her legs can carry her, not north up the narrow trail where Morimoto waits, but south, back to Korea and to her island in the sea. Her legs seem to know it will not take him long to realise she is not coming, and they are swift. They will not stop until she can see the shore where her sister once stood, anchoring Hana's life to hers.

She keeps Emiko's image in her mind as she races through the darkness, but sometimes the face transforms, and she becomes Hana's other sisters, the ones she's left behind. She sees their horror when it dawns on them that she is gone, she sees Keiko's horror. But Hana keeps running until her lungs burn and her chest aches. She pushes through the pain, as though it's the deepest dive of her life, and she is swimming out of the ocean's dark depths towards the light.

Emi

Seoul, December 2011

An old woman sobs a few steps away from where Emi stands. A woman on the stage speaks into the microphone. It squeals with feedback, and the crowd moans while children cover their ears.

'For the one thousandth Wednesday demonstration, we have a special unveiling. Two artists have created the *Statue of Peace* to remember the plight of the so-called comfort women. This monument is for all the women and girls who were forced into military sexual slavery, losing their childhood, their families, their health and dignity, and, for many whose stories we will never know, their lives.'

She motions towards a group of women and they quickly move out of the way, revealing a blanket-covered statue. Two women in beautiful white-and-pink traditional *hanbok* gowns lift the blanket with a flourish. Emi strains her eyes to see the statue.

Gasps and appreciative laughter ripple through the audience as they applaud the statue. Emi lifts up onto her tiptoes, struggling to see above the people standing in front of her, blocking her view, but she is too short. Slowly, she shuffles towards the statue, clumsily bumping into people as she stumbles past them.

'Where are you going?' YoonHui calls after her.

Emi doesn't answer her daughter. She just keeps going. She has to see it. She doesn't know why it's so important to her to see the statue, but she is suddenly filled with a determination to set her eyes upon it. She pushes past people, weaving a path through the crowd, her eyes fixed in the direction of the bronze figure. The crowd seems to melt away at her touch, as though they, too, feel the determination within her. She flows past them without difficulty until she is standing in front of the statue.

Emi is breathless after pushing through so many people. The thin winter air is icy in her heaving lungs. She is face-to-face with the life-size sculpture of a young girl, no older than sixteen, seated alone beside an empty chair, her gently fisted hands placed neatly in her lap, her eyes gazing straight ahead, into Emi's. She gasps, clutches her heart, and sinks to her knees. *Hana* . . .

Snow flurries fall from the grey afternoon sky, swirling in lazy circles, descending in soundless wonder upon the scurrying crowd below. Her daughter shouts to her, a piercing cry trembling with fear. Hands seize Emi as she slumps forward, her face nearly crashing into the pavement.

'Mother!' YoonHui cries, running up beside her.

They turn her onto her back, and YoonHui cradles her head in her lap. Lane arrives and their two heads hover above Emi like guardian angels. A halo of winter sunlight casts their faces in shadow. Emi sees her parents looking down on her, beckoning her to them from the great beyond. The urge to follow them pulls at her like an undercurrent. If she fights it, she will drown, but if she lets it sweep her out to sea she will disappear in a gentle lull. The statue's sombre face sits above them all, and Emi turns to steal a last glimpse of it through a break in the mass of people huddled around her. Her eyes alight upon the young girl's face, at once breathtaking and familiar. Recognition settles in her mind. *Not yet, Mother. Father, not yet. Hana has finally found me. How can I leave her when she has come such a long way?*

Hana

The sun's early rays creep across the horizon. Hana moves further away from the road. Her feet are bloody from the stones and sticks on the rugged path. The night was quiet, with only a single truck rumbling down the road. She hid behind a shrub in the ditch as it passed, but she knows that as morning nears, a shrub won't hide her from their eyes. She suffered from a bitterly cold wind that suddenly swept through overnight, and the bright sun is a welcoming sight.

The dry grass pokes through the sores on her feet. If Morimoto is looking for her, he will only have to follow the trail of blood she is leaving behind. Hana stops and listens to the empty countryside every ten minutes as she catches her breath, on the alert for footsteps, heavy in boots, behind her. He's out there somewhere, enraged that she would dare betray him. The thought of his anger sends prickles across her skin. She runs faster as the sun rises on her first day of freedom.

Careful to keep the road to her left, she continues heading south. The land is beautiful. Gentle hills rise and fall in the distance. The grass on the plains reaches up to her waist. She can sit in the field and hide from intruding eyes. After a few miles, her feet cannot go any further, so she sinks to her knees and relishes her new hiding space, careful not to look at her bloody feet. Insects buzz and chirrup all around her. Tiny yellow flowers bloom on tall stalks. Arms from the earth beckon her towards the ground. Lying here like this, safe from the world, she could have already left this life. Only the pain from her throbbing feet reminds her that she is indeed still alive.

Hana knows she must keep moving as Morimoto is surely hunting her down, but her feet beg her to stay put, just a while longer. She gazes into the sky and watches the clouds transform themselves into an assortment of shapes. A serpent erupts from the mouth of a whale, which splits into a sea of burial mounds before fading into faint wisps. They remind her of Morimoto's cigarette smoke, drifting out of the cracks of her room window. The thought of him gives her chills, his hands on her body, his hunger sucking the breath from her lungs. Hatred fills her and her heartbeat quickens. She sits up and listens to the sounds around her. Would she hear him coming?

She looks down at her swollen feet. Caked in black earth mixed with blood, they cannot be ignored any longer. She grabs a handful of grass and rubs them mostly clean. She endures the pain without making a sound. A bird sings its song nearby. The wind kisses her face. She finds a thorn lodged in a wound in the ball of her foot. It's in quite deep, and she has to dig her fingers nearly past the first layer of flesh before she reaches it.

At first she can't grasp it because her fingers slip with blood. She wipes them on the grass. With dry fingers, she inserts them into the wound again. This time, the thorn pulls free. Recovering for a moment, Hana touches the grasses. They bend with the gentle wind, and she strums them like they're a delicate instrument.

Her father was musical. Before he became a fisherman, he studied poetry and often performed his poems to music. His words were lyrical and full of history, which made them political. When the Japanese began their world war by invading China, they grew tougher on the colonised Koreans, reinforcing the ban on all Korean history books and literature, prohibiting the study of Korean culture. Her father became an outlaw, and he fled from the mainland to Jeju Island, where he reinvented himself as a struggling fisherman. That is where he met her mother.

After a fruitless day out at sea, he would sit on the beach with an empty net at his feet and sing an old forbidden folk song. Most of the other people on the beach distanced themselves from him, wary that a Japanese policeman might stroll by and see them listening to the Korean words of a Korean song, but not Hana's mother. She stood up and shaded her eyes to get a clearer look at the fool singing such a ridiculous song, and when she saw the young fisherman with the empty net at his feet, she tilted her head back and laughed. He looked up but didn't stop singing, and when she came near and sat beside him on the warm rock, he decided in that moment that he never wanted her to leave his side again. They were married and Hana was born within a year. It took longer for her sister to come along, but when she did their family was complete.

At night, when the dinner dishes were washed and the four of them sat together warming themselves by the hearth, he would play the zither. Sometimes, when he was in a good mood, he would sing that old folk song that had made her mother laugh.

> *Leaving? Are you leaving?*
> *Are you leaving me behind?*
> *How can I live without you?*
> *Are you leaving me behind?*

I want to hold on to you.
But if I do so, you won't come back.
I have to let you go, my love!
Please go and return swiftly!

The song is a whisper on her lips. The forbidden words roll off her tongue. She feels defiant, singing in her native language, and she recalls how her mother made sure to close the shutters tight when her father picked up his zither. Hana keeps her voice low so only she can hear her song. She lifts her head above the grasses a few times, scanning the field for prying eyes. Seeing none, she continues to sing until her throat is parched.

She has to find water, but her feet are too sore to go anywhere. Willing herself to move, she plays with the long grass, weaving it through her fingers. The stalks are sturdy, like bamboo strips, and she has an idea. Pulling a handful from the ground, she binds one end together with a few strands of grass and then weaves them into a thin braid. When it's long enough, she wraps it once around the ball of her foot and ties it across the top.

Rising to her feet, she takes a few steps to test her makeshift shoe. Her excitement grows with each step, and just as she squats to the ground in order to make a second one, the ties rip apart and the weave unravels. Not yet disheartened, she sits and weaves together a second shoe, and when it, too, falls apart, she weaves a third and a fourth, until her efforts fade with the sun's dying light. She lays her head on the pile of withered and broken grass shoes, resting her tired eyes.

Her sleep is plagued with dreams. Nightmares and happy memories swim together, mixing storylines and jumbling feelings so that she awakens with a scream in her mouth. A shock of orange birds launches into the early-evening sky. The insects keep silent. She doesn't know if she has screamed or whether it was something else that spooked the birds into flight. She lies still, listening, waiting for something or someone to make a sound.

It is distant at first. Just a slight sweep of grass pushed aside as though by the wind. But the longer she listens, the louder and closer the sweeps become, until she hears the crunch of stiff stalks beneath boots. Her heart lurches in her chest, and she wants to leap into the sky and follow the orange birds to safety. She forces herself to remain where she lies, still as a corpse. Any motion will move the tall grass surrounding her, signalling her location. Men's voices whisper to each other, commands and responses. She strains her ears to hear *his* voice. Is Morimoto with them? Are they searching for her or someone else?

Hana fears one of them will step on her arm or face or stumble over her and stab her through her heart with his bayonet. She closes her eyes and waits for the inevitable. They will find her, and then they will torture her. How long will they keep her alive before setting her spirit free from her abused flesh?

A soldier is standing in the grass beside her. She can see his tan uniform through the blades of grass. His back is to her. He hasn't seen her yet. Another soldier is whispering something to him and clutching his rifle.

He steps backwards, the heel of his boot standing on the hem of her dress. She cannot close her eyes. She has to see his face. Is it him? She must see what expression crosses his face when their eyes meet. Will it be surprise? Or will it be triumph, lust or hate? She waits for him to turn round and stumble upon her.

Then suddenly, another man shouts from across the field, and the soldier near her takes off, freeing her dress. She hears them running away from her. Their shouts increase in frequency, and then a gunshot cracks through the chaos. She remains still as a newborn deer hidden in the tall grass, holding her breath, listening and waiting for the sounds to fade away, for darkness to fall and for night to hide her once again.

It wasn't him. She is certain. If it was Morimoto, he would have turned round and found her. There is no way he could stand so close to her without sensing her presence. He is like an animal. He would have smelled her.

She watches the hours creep by in the changing hues of the sky. Pale dusky blue darkens into deep sapphire and then the purple blue of night. Too afraid to move for fear the soldiers are still lurking nearby, she urinates on herself. The stink attracts flies. They crawl on her dress, buzzing, as they taste the soiled cotton. The odour is dark yellow like the stench in the outhouse at the brothel. No matter how much they scrub it down, the stink never leaves the rotting wooden floorboards.

An owl hoots, and she imagines it swooping above the field in search of moles and mice. She listens for the rustle of feathers gliding on the wind. It hoots again and she finds her courage. She sits up, and very slowly, she stands. There is nothing to see beneath the night-time sky but darkness. Hands in front of her like a blind girl, she takes her first step, and then a second. Soon she is running; her shredded feet scream for her to stop, but her mind refuses their pleas.

Hana is no longer certain she is continuing along the same direction as the road. She's not even sure she's still headed south. She was never able to commit the map in the sky to memory. Her father attempted to give her a sense of place in the vast heavens, but she always resisted. Her attentions were drawn down into the sea, into the calming darkness and the creatures within. She wanted to listen to the other fishermen's stories about blue whales and swordfish and sharks. Her father's stars never made an impression. Hana looks up into the sky, and the stars shine back at her in silence.

》《

After running uncertainly through the field, Hana hears a cry in the dark, low at first, transforming into a high-pitched screech. She hears the rhythmic chug of wheels turning on a track. The train. She has found her way. She darts after the sound, a sharp turn, following her ears. The clatter of metal against metal grows louder as she nears the railway tracks, until the train passes in a rush of air and sound.

She wants to go in the direction it has come from. All the night trains head north. They're full of supplies for the field, and travelling at night is their only cover from aerial bombers. At the brothel, she would listen late at night for the train's whistle as it crossed the railway bridge into the military base. It announced its arrival once every week, or sometimes every two weeks if it was delayed by bombings of the tracks, and Hana's stomach never failed to turn over. She arrived on one of those trains, labelled as 'necessary supplies' on their inventory checklist. When she dreamed of escape, she knew the railway tracks would aid her passage back home.

She slows to a careful pace, her hands out in front of her again. She will run into the rail ties and surely trip onto the tracks if she isn't careful. Threadbare grass beneath her feet reveals rocks that stab her tender sores, but she ignores them, focusing on the dark path ahead of her. She stubs her toe on something hard. Quickly, she kneels and touches solid, smooth metal. She puts her ear to the tracks and listens for the train. Which way is it going, and which direction is the way she came?

A low hum reaches her ears. She places her hands on the metal rail and senses a weak vibration. The low hum fades to nothing. The tracks become still, dead in her hands. She is surrounded by silence. A slow panic builds in her chest. Which way? The wind is the only sound, the stars the only light in the darkness. Then a faint whistle shrieks like a faraway phantom. Did it come from the right? She turns her head in that direction and listens for the spirit's ghostly cry, but it doesn't come again. Hana rises to her feet and turns, trusting her ears, her heart and the vast silence that presses on her skin as she heads left, following the railway tracks, hoping they will lead her south.

She walks through the night. Afraid to lose her way, she endures the pain of walking on the wooden ties and the rocks between them. She hasn't had anything to drink for two nights, and she is light-headed, her tongue swollen in her mouth. Water is all she can think about. In the morning, she tells herself; she must wait until daylight to find water. Right now, she must keep moving, while she has the cover of darkness. Wait until morning.

When the sun is high, she will find water, and perhaps a place to rest. There must be a lake or a river to keep the land fertile and the birds flying in the sky. She will find it in the morning. *Don't stop, not yet.* The distance to the sea is further than she can imagine. Her only hope of reaching it is to keep moving. One step after the other, she makes her feet move, even as they cry out to her for rest.

When dawn approaches, the night transforms into a hazy grey, and at first Hana can barely see the outlines of her pale hands splayed in front of her. As the sun rises further, she can see the railway tracks beneath her feet and soon the landscape around her. The tall grass has fallen away to rolling fields of yellow flowers.

To her dismay, she sees a gravel road following the path of the railway track. A convoy of soldiers could have driven by at any time, and she would have had nowhere to hide. Quickly, she darts off the tracks away from the road and heads into the flower fields. They only reach up to her knees, so she continues running further away from the tracks until they are a distant feature on the horizon. She warns herself to stay parallel to the tracks so she won't lose her way, or she could end up walking in circles.

In the distance, she notices brown shapes huddled in the grass. The deep bellow of an ox pierces the silence. She crouches on her knees and searches the fields for farmers or herding nomads. The sun lights up the countryside, but the beauty is lost on her. Her eyes scan the field for signs of people, but the oxen are alone. A low moan escapes one of them, and Hana thinks it might be giving birth. *Milk*, she suddenly thinks, and runs towards the labouring creature, never resting her eyes as she searches for any sign of people who might help or hurt her.

When she reaches the ox, her hopes fade as she realises it isn't in labour. It has fallen prey to an old hunter's trap, and the rusted metal jaws have snapped closed on the ox's leg. The lower hind-leg bone juts through a flap of skin. It has become separated and hangs lifelessly next to the other leg. The ox cries again, and Hana covers her ears. The sound is a death moan.

She backs away from the pitiful creature, her hands shutting the terrible, deep groan out of her mind, but she can't keep it out. When she hears it again, it's as though it rises from her memories – the night she first arrived at the brothel and witnessed the Korean woman give birth to a dead baby. She hears the woman's inhuman moans as though she is peering into the candlelit room once more. There was so much blood between the woman's splayed legs. Hana remembers running upstairs and meeting Keiko for the first time, the geisha kneeling on her tatami mat and crying into her hands.

The ox moans again and startles Hana. She is not at the brothel anymore. She is free of that place, and she must do what she has to in order to remain free. Gathering her courage, Hana walks around the animal towards its head. The ox's eyes roll wildly in its sockets, and it thrashes its legs as she approaches it. Fresh blood seeps from the wound where the skin has torn further from the ox's frantic attempt to get away.

'Hush, poor creature,' she whispers in a soothing tone.

She kneels next to its head and pats its brow. The ox grows quiet.

Its breath is shallow. Flies congregate on the wound, and wriggling maggots infest the flesh. She strokes its neck in long, slow motions. It must have been lying here for days. Hana can imagine its pain. She can feel it, as she feels the caress of wind on her face. She knows what it is like to lie helpless while her body is broken. Hana leans in close to the ox and whispers into its ear.

'Go to sleep, dear ox. Please, go to sleep. Rest your heavy head on this earth. Give up your tired spirit and flee this wretched place. Go soon, dear ox, go soon. And forgive me, please . . . forgive me.'

Hana presses her lips to the ox's ear before crawling towards its broken leg. She makes sure to keep one hand on its hide as she moves behind it, still making soothing sounds as she nears its leg. The ox snorts but doesn't kick. It may not have enough energy to fight, but she can't be sure. She reaches slowly towards the broken leg.

Before she can change her mind, she seizes it and, in one quick motion, twists it while yanking as hard as she can. The skin doesn't tear away as she hoped. Hana is leaning backwards, halfway to the ground, her heels digging into the earth to keep from sliding across the grass into the thrashing ox. The metal trap is rattling about, but the chain keeps it secure to the ground. The ox is screaming, and the sound is worse than the low moan. Hana pulls and yanks and twists, while the ox scrambles desperately to get away from her. She is suspended in a kind of tug of war.

The ox bellows its death moan. The trap clatters against her foot. Her arms threaten to give in – she is so tired. Fearing she can't hold on much longer, she contemplates letting go, but then, in one mighty rip, the hide splits in two.

She falls to the ground clasping the severed leg. The ox continues to kick at the earth, desperate to crawl away from her. She cannot bring herself to look at the terrified creature. Instead, she stares at the patch of crushed yellow flowers left in its wake as it inches away from her. As though resigned to its fate at her hands, it lies still with only its chest heaving and nostrils flaring.

Disgusted with herself, she releases the severed leg from the trap. The leg is heavy in her hand. She tries not to think about what she has done. Hana quickly rises to her feet and runs away from the poor animal, still clutching the hoofed leg in her hand. This is no time to think about the violation she has committed. She looks down at the leg, and to her horror, her empty stomach grumbles. A wail escapes her mouth. Just one. And then there is nothing but the sound of her feet pounding the earth as she flees the scene of her transgression.

When she can go no further, Hanna sinks to her knees and stares at the bloody leg. She doesn't know what to do with it or how to eat it. Her only good fortune is that most of the maggots have fallen off. Her stomach growls, and she feels disgusted. She squeezes her eyes shut. It's not a leg, she tells herself. It's not a leg. It's – a fish, a thin, long ocean creature that found its way into her net. Her father taught her to skin and debone countless fish, and that is what this is. A dead fish. Her father's dark, suntanned hands appear in her mind. They hold a mackerel and a sharp blade, and she watches as he expertly fillets the creature in sure, steady motions.

As though his hands are her own, she begins to skin the leg. Her fingers peel the hide from the broken end, tentatively at first, but then with more force, and using all her might, she pulls it down towards the hoof. The hide doesn't peel easily, and she must work it free from the flesh with harsh jerking motions. When the hide is halfway down the bone, Hana cannot wait any longer. She raises the leg to her mouth and takes a bite.

The flesh does not tear away easily either, and she has to rip it from the bone. Blood seeps down her throat. She tries not to taste it on her tongue. She tries not to remember where the flesh came from. In her mind, it is just a fish.

It was a skinny ox, and it doesn't take her long to pick the bone clean of meat. She sucks the bloody marrow from the end of the bone as well and is surprised to find that she doesn't mind the dark, heavy flavour. She hasn't tasted fresh, bloody meat since her captivity began, eating only flecks of dried fish if they were lucky.

Sometimes, a soldier at the brothel would bring in a small bag of fresh fruit or vegetables to treat his favourite girl. Keiko often received these gifts, and she would share with Hana each time. What is Keiko doing now? Hana imagines the elegant geisha crouching in the solitary-confinement cell in the basement of the brothel. The prison cells were half a man high, so they had to remain seated the entire time. How many days and nights will Keiko suffer for Hana's escape? And the other girls, will they suffer, too?

She closes her eyes and physically wipes the image away with her bloodstained hand. She cannot think of Keiko or her other sisters. In order to keep going, she can only think of home.

Hana buries the bone in the dirt as though hiding her offence, but she keeps the strips of hide skinned from the flesh. She rubs the fur against the ground to scratch off the ox's blood. At first the dirt mixes with the blood and soils the fur, but with repeated scrubbing, the bloody dirt dries and finally rubs off. Using her teeth, she tears the hide into shorter strips and then ties them in successive layers around the balls of her feet. Taking a few steps to make sure they are on tight, she traces her path back to where she first heard the ox and continues on her journey, running parallel to the railway tracks.

Hana keeps an eye out for people, trucks and trains, but also for waterfowl. She is so very thirsty now, the blood having done little to assuage her.

≫ ≪

The afternoon feels hotter than it should. The clouds have bulked up into massive grey mountains in the sky. Hana is now walking so slowly, her feet shuffle in the grass. The hills are gone; everywhere is flat. She lost sight of the railway tracks miles back. They disappeared behind one of the hills and never reappeared. She wandered aimlessly in search of them, and now she is lost. No roads, no railway tracks, no sign of human development – Hana is alone in the wilds of Manchuria surrounded on all sides by fields of grass.

A high-pitched ringing in her ears sounds like the constant whistle of a lone train she cannot find. There are no signs of animal life either. Not even cattle tracks to lead her somewhere with hope. Once, she saw a pack of wild camels, but they disappeared so fast she couldn't be certain they weren't a mirage, her mind playing tricks on her. She has eaten handfuls of grass when they appeared different from the other grasses she has passed. Flowers, too, but after retching from a particularly peppery flower, she stopped trying to eat the vegetation surrounding her. Now she is walking. Nothing more.

Her thirst torments her. In the brothel, she awoke each morning and went downstairs to fetch water. At the time, it seemed so far away as she dragged her used body out of her room and to the kitchen. Keiko would always beat her there, and they would stand in silence and drink. Then the other girls would arrive and they would prepare their meagre breakfasts.

There was never enough food. The other girls said their starving condition was due to the difficulty of transporting supplies so far north. They said even the Japanese soldiers were nearly starving, but they never seemed to lack energy. Hana thought they filled out their uniforms better than the Japanese soldiers from home. It occurs to her that they were fed so little in the brothel so that they would have energy for nothing more than fulfilling their duties. There would be none left over for escape.

The girls were allowed to listen to a small radio during chore days. The stations consisted mainly of news reports that spewed nothing but Japanese propaganda. The girls didn't mind because in between reports they would play a song or two. They listened as they did their chores or ate their meals.

The news reports warned that the foreign armies were everywhere, arming against the Japanese, and the emperor needed as many volunteers as possible to hold them at bay. The Chinese, the Mongolians, the whole of Europe and America, they were all enemies of the emperor. Even the Soviets were suspicious, their tentative treaty with Japan weakening with each passing day. Fear was struck into the girls' minds, fear of the wilderness beyond the brothel and fear of the enemy lurking within it.

There is nowhere for Hana to run, except south to Korea. But home is a long way off. Perhaps if she can find some water. Thoughts of home cloud her vision. Water tumbling in bucketfuls from their well. Cold and delicious, crisp like melted snow. Closing her eyes, she can almost taste the memory.

'You spilled on me,' her little sister squealed, dropping her cup and darting away.

Hana laughs aloud at the memory. It was a hot summer day, they were thirsty, and Hana had doused her sister with the cold water from the well. She focuses on the memory as though she can see it, as though it is happening now, though her parched mouth aches for a hint of saliva.

'Come back, I promise I won't do it again,' she called out.

A small face peeked at her from behind the house. 'Really?'

Hana's heart leaps in her chest as she remembers those innocent brown eyes, so open to the world. Whenever she looked down into them, a surge of responsibility coursed through her. She made it her duty to keep those eyes from seeing the truth of the war. The death of their uncle would have cast a shadow over them for certain, so she had made their parents keep it from Emiko. Hana had helped her sister write letters to their uncle and then pretended to mail them. Once, she had even written a reply in her uncle's handwriting. When her mother had found out, she was less than pleased but did nothing more than make Hana promise not to write any more letters.

'Please, come back,' Hana called out again.

With tentative steps, her little sister returned to the well, holding her tin cup in front of her. Hana drew the bucket up and carefully set it on the ground.

'There, dip your cup in, that's the safest way,' Hana instructed.

Her sister crouched and plunged her whole hand into the bucket, then shivered.

'It's cold!'

Hana knelt beside her and dipped both hands beneath the water. It cooled the heated blood vessels in her hands and wrists. She bent her head down until her lips touched the curve of her cupped hands. The water smelled like ice. Before she could taste it, a small hand shoved Hana's head down into the bucket. Water surged up her nose. She stood, water dripping from her mouth, as she coughed and sneezed the cold liquid from her nostrils. Laughter trailed away as her sister flew into hiding.

Hana remembers the sound, like tinkling bells swaying in the breeze. A southerly wind picks up. It cools her skin. She stops walking, slightly swaying against the strong current of air that whips around her. It feels like a sea wind. Hana can taste the salty air on her lips, which are cracked and dry against her sandpaper tongue. Perhaps it is the salt of her blood she tastes, but closing her eyes, she pretends she has made it home.

She is standing on the black rocks piled high on the sandy shore, staring out over the vast dark sea. The waves are whirling dancers, celebrating her homecoming and crashing into the rocks beneath her like a massive applause. Voices travel on the wind, and she hears her mother call her name. She turns. Her mother is running towards her with arms outstretched. Her father is there, too. He's shouting her name above the roaring wind and the splashing waves.

'I'm here,' Hana calls to them. 'I'm here,' she cries, taking a step towards them. But her feet feel like they are buried in sand. She has travelled so far, and now, exhausted, they are too heavy for her to lift.

'Sakura,' her father calls. 'Sakura!'

A third voice rides the wind and reaches her ears. It is small, like a child's, and sounds as if it has travelled from a faraway island behind her. Hana turns back to the sea and shades her eyes against the blazing sun. A young girl in a white fishing boat in the tumultuous ocean calls her name. Hana squeezes her eyes to focus on the girl's face, and her heart leaps in her chest.

'Emiko!' she shouts. 'Little sister, I am home!' She waves and tries to jump for joy, but her feet will not lift out of the sand tethering her to the earth.

The girl climbs onto the bow of the boat, and Hana is instantly worried.

'Little Sister, be careful!' she shouts, afraid her sister cannot swim in such powerful waters.

The girl looks up once and calls her name before diving into the dark sea. For a moment, Hana is stunned by the girl's graceful dive, but in the next moment, she is taken aback. The girl called out for Hana. The name her mother chose and the one her family knew her by – not Sakura. That is the name carved on a wooden board, nailed beside a door: cherry blossom.

Hana turns to look back at her father, but the seaside vision fades away. On the horizon she sees not her parents running towards her, but a black horse galloping at full speed. The outline of a man sitting atop the beast is unmistakable, lashing its haunches with a whip. Morimoto has found her. It is too late to run, but still she turns away from the oncoming charge and tries to flee. Her muscles don't want to obey her frantic mind, but she doesn't give in.

One foot after the other lifts until she is sprinting. She has nothing left to fuel her besides adrenaline, and the burn in her muscles threatens to shut her body down. The horse's hooves pound against the earth in dark, echoing thuds as it swiftly approaches. She is no match for such a magnificent animal, yet even when Morimoto's hand grabs hold of the collar of her dress, her legs continue cycling, running through air. He drags her up onto the horse, like a sack of grain. She struggles in vain, legs and arms wild and useless against such a captor. Morimoto slows the horse to a halt and then yanks her round to look at him, one fist tangled in her hair.

'Sakura,' he says, breathless. 'You can never leave me.' His voice is rough like his hands. He drags her off the horse and wrestles her to the ground. She fights beneath him and he strikes her face over and over, until she is still.

'Don't you understand yet? . . . You're mine.'

A clap of thunder shocks the skies. Electricity crackles through the air. Thunderheads gather above them. He lies on top of her, the length of his body squeezing the breath from her heaving lungs. He whispers the name forced upon her, kissing her neck, gently now; his hands lift her dress.

If she is still struggling, she cannot feel it. Her limbs, numb from exertion, are disconnected from her mind. She turns her face away from his abrasive chin, gazing beyond in search of the sea.

The first drops of rain splash onto her lips, and they are cold like water from her father's well. She licks the raindrops, greedy for more, but the relief is short-lived. Sharp, burning pain sears through her with each eager thrust, plunging her back into painful memories of soldiers and flesh and mouths – all the images she has failed to escape. The clouds release a flood upon her worn-out body as she lies motionless in the grass.

》《

Hana is lying on the bottom of the ocean, looking upwards at the sunlight shimmering above the surface. The great ocean's heartbeat pulses against her eardrums. The current caresses her skin. A heaviness on her chest is an old ship's anchor she has found. She hugs it close to weigh her down. Her body is so small that normally it would naturally float back to the top, but not today; today she wants to remain in the deep until the sun fades into the ocean's depths. This is her favourite game, one she always wins. She can hold her breath until the other girls give up and swim back to the surface. Her last friend has held on for as long as she can but floats upwards, bubbles streaming after her. Hana watches her go. She has won the game. No one can beat her.

Except him. Morimoto is the anchor keeping her down. She lies beneath him, waiting for him to punish her further or kill her for her betrayal. His heaving body sinks deeper into hers, pressing her ribcage into the muddy earth as he catches his breath.

She can run, she thinks, she can scratch his face and prise him off in one last attempt to survive, but the raw sores on her feet plead for her journey to end in this peaceful place beneath a mountain of heaving flesh. *No more pain*, she agrees, and stares at the falling sky, waiting.

He lifts himself to look at her. Their eyes meet and she cannot look away.

'How could you leave me waiting for you by the bridge like a fool?' His voice seethes with rage. 'I risked my life to help you escape the brothel, and this is how you repay me? Running away?' He pauses as though waiting for an apology or an explanation.

When she doesn't answer, he laughs. The sound is bitter and dark.

'As if I couldn't track you down? I know this territory inside and out. You could never hide from me.'

He shakes her, demanding a response, but there is nothing she can say that could speak louder than her attempt to escape him. She lies beneath him wordless, lifeless, a hunter's fallen quarry. He leans over her, his breath in her face. Now he will kill her. She closes her eyes.

He wraps one hand around her neck; his thumb presses down on her throat. Her gag reflex takes over, and she struggles against her will. His other hand clamps down on her throat, too, and he begins to squeeze. Hana opens her eyes, searching the skies for the sun, but it's hidden behind the thunderclouds.

'I will kill you,' he whispers beside her ear. 'I will. If you ever make a fool of me again.' He doesn't release her. Instead he squeezes even harder, until there is no breath left in her lungs.

〉〉-〈〈

Hana is awakened by pain. Her cheek stings as though a thousand hot needles are burning into her skin. Her bottom lip is on fire. She tastes blood.

'Wake up,' he says, and hits her other cheek with his open hand. He yanks her to her feet, but she cannot stand on them and sinks to the sodden earth.

'You're useless,' he mutters under his breath, and lifts her off the ground as though she is nothing.

A horse snorts in the distance. Its hooves stamp into the ground. Hana has never seen a horse this close. It is black with white spots scattered like dust around its ankles.

Morimoto whistles, and the horse comes nearer. He leans Hana against the animal as he reaches into a satchel behind the saddle and retrieves a canteen. He opens the lid and pours water into the small cap. He holds it to her lips. Hana gulps the water, but it's not enough to quench her thirst. She wants to ask for more but resists. Morimoto smiles as though he knows, and then he very slowly screws the cap back on. His eyes never leave hers. Hana says nothing, but she cannot stop licking her lips.

He grabs her by the waist and lifts her up so she can climb onto the horse. Hana's mind is still clouded with exhaustion and thirst, and she struggles with the task. She can't understand why her arms are not obeying her.

'Get up,' he orders, and shoves her.

She manages to grab the saddle and then realises what is wrong. He has bound her hands together with rope. He shoves her again, thrusting her into the saddle. He pushes her leg over the horse's neck so that she is sitting astride it. He loops another rope around her waist and takes it with the reins in his hands.

'Don't think about making this horse run off.' He shows her the rope leading to her waist. 'I will yank you down so fast . . . and then we will both be walking,' he warns, touching the wounds on the sole of her foot for emphasis.

She winces at his touch. He stares at her, his gaze so intense she cannot look away. Then he reaches into his pocket and pulls out a square of cloth. It is the bundle she stashed in her knickers. She reaches for it but nearly slips off the horse. She grabs the saddle and steadies herself.

'I found this beneath you,' he says as he unwraps it, revealing the contents. 'Such lovely trinkets.'

Hana wants to reach for them again, but she will not give him the satisfaction of seeing her suffer. She looks straight ahead and focuses on the horizon.

'I should be jealous you kept these,' he says, and she begins to worry. He sifts through them one at a time, inspecting them as though searching for a sign. 'Were these all from one soldier in particular? Does he have a name?'

Hana shakes her head. His tone is dangerous. He stares at her, his eyes boring holes into her skull as though trying to read the truth inside. He looks back at the items and seems to think about it awhile before grinning up at her.

'You have no need of such things, now that you are with me.'

He tilts his hand and they fall, one by one, to the ground. Then he grinds them into the dirt with the heel of his boot. She turns to see the gold ring, necklace, coins and hair comb disappear into the earth. She has nothing left.

Morimoto looks pleased with himself, like a child who has won an award. She is the war prize he has claimed for himself. She wants to kick the horse in the side so hard that it will rear up and stomp him into the ground along with her lost belongings, but she is too weak even to frighten a horse.

'But this,' Morimoto says as though it's just an afterthought. 'This, I will treasure.'

He holds up the photograph of her, and the rush of anger surprises her. She wants to yank it out of his hands. She cannot stand his touching the photograph. It was taken before the line of soldiers visited her; Keiko hadn't yet cut her hair in the yard, she had not yet learned to lie still until they were done – she was still Hana in that photograph. It belongs to her.

Hana stops herself from giving him the reaction he so desperately desires, even though every fibre within her is itching to leap off the horse and knock him to the ground. It takes every ounce of restraint she can muster to leave the last piece of her old self in his possession. Hana slowly turns away and stares straight ahead. She can feel his satisfaction as he slips the photograph into his breast pocket.

The moment is over, and Morimoto clicks his tongue, urging the horse forward. He leads the horse, walking in front of it, and Hana turns her eyes away from him, refusing to stare at the man who will never let her go.

The thunderstorm intensifies, and they travel in silence. Hana opens her mouth to the rain as lightning cracks above their heads. She doesn't care that she might be struck: it would be a welcome end. He is sticking to his plan. They are going north to Mongolia, trudging through the pouring rain as though that was always what they were meant to do.

》《

Sheets of grey cover the land, hiding them even from themselves. Hana gulps the rainwater tumbling from the skies. Her stomach begins to bloat, but she cannot stop. With her face lifted upwards, she drinks her fill. When her stomach is nearly bursting, she hangs her head, too exhausted to hold it up any longer. Morimoto holds the reins tighter and yanks the beast onwards.

As they march across the steppe, Hana's face and feet are chilled from the cold rain and no longer throb. She thinks she might be able to run again with a day's rest, but she has no idea how long the journey to Mongolia will be. She doesn't know if he will be meeting someone, an accomplice perhaps, Mongolian or Soviet, one or many. He could even have made arrangements with the Chinese.

Fear sets in as she imagines their joining a group of faceless, nationless men. What has he promised them? Is she part of the bargain? Hana stares at the back of his head. Would he force her to service them all? Images of barbarians ripping at her ragged dress overwhelm her. She bows her head, but even with her eyes closed she sees him arriving late at night after the other men have all had their fill.

She doubles over and vomits the contents of her waterlogged stomach. Her frail shoulders shudder as she heaves the rainwater from her churning stomach. Before she realises it, her body slides from the horse. Her hands are bound, and she cannot soften her landing. She hits the ground on her right shoulder. Sudden, shocking pain knocks the air from her lungs. The horse rears up, but Morimoto quickly gets it under control. He sees her huddled form on the ground and rushes to her side.

'What are you doing?' he demands.

Gingerly, he turns her onto her back. Rain pours onto her face. She cannot breathe from the pain, the invading wetness, and the vision of her future with him. He grabs her by the shoulders to lift her to her feet, but her right arm collapses and she cries out in pain. He releases her, and it subsides. She winces as he presses around her shoulder. His fingers investigate the flesh and quickly find the source of her injury.

'It's dislocated. I have to push it back in.'

His voice is tender, concerned. She doesn't care. She stares straight ahead into grey nothingness. He loosens the rope around her wrists; it unravels and slips to the ground. He lifts her up until she is seated. The horse turns its head to the side as if watching the scene with one great black eye. Morimoto massages her bicep, gently kneading the muscles, and then he massages the top of her shoulder. His hand is assured, practised. She feels little pain.

'Shrug your shoulders, slowly,' he tells her.

She does as he instructs and feels her arm sink back into place within the socket. Using the rope that once bound her wrists, he ties a sling around her arm to support her shoulder.

'You must be more careful. You could have landed on your neck and broken it. Then where would we be?' He shakes his head, as if resigned to the fact that she is bound to disappoint him.

'We?' she says, her voice thick with non-use.

'It's you and me now,' he says.

She stares at him, dumbfounded.

He ties the final knot and smiles, staring at her through the rain. He seems to be waiting for an expression of thanks from her. Hana recalls the first time he declared his intention to help her. He said he would leave the side door unlocked so she could escape. She did her best not to let her body give away her nervousness. She stopped her heart from beating too fast by slowing its rhythm as she would after a fast swim back to shore. She kept her hands from trembling by chanting to herself over and over, *He lies, he lies, he lies*, until her body believed her. His words were empty, and in the morning, she knew she would wake up, still a captive in that prison, and a line of depraved soldiers would be waiting.

'You don't seem pleased at the chance I've offered you to escape this place. Is there someone else who keeps you here, another soldier, perhaps?' His question startled her. He lifted her chin and gazed into her eyes. The room was silent except for their breaths, his calm and steady, hers threatening to take flight. 'Have you finally picked a favourite?'

Morimoto's jealousy sickened her. He had brought her to the brothel to be repeatedly raped by soldiers, and yet suddenly he was angry that some of them would show her gratitude before marching to their deaths? But he had mentioned escape. The possibility that he could aid her in what she sought more than anything else helped her hold her tongue.

'There is no man in the whole of the emperor's army who could take your place in my heart,' she replied. In truth, she hated no man more than she hated him. He would always occupy a space within her heart as the most vile of the men who visited her room.

Hana escaped from the brothel, but she didn't escape from him. He's still waiting for her gratitude for bandaging her arm. She turns away, pulling from his grasp, and lies back down on the saturated earth, her face half submerged in a puddle. The muddy water tastes heavy and dark, like the marrow of the dying ox, like a grave. Morimoto lifts her from the mud and turns her face back to his.

'When we reach Mongolia, we will start a new life. Together. I will make you my wife.'

He searches her eyes as though waiting for her to smile, but his plan for the future turns her stomach. He is so certain that she would want that life. She is desperate to throw his words back in his face, to hurt him. The only way to reach him is through his pride.

'It doesn't matter what you do. You will never be more than a Japanese soldier to me,' she whispers into his ear in Korean, as he so often has whispered into hers.

He pulls away in shock, and she spits rainwater into his face. His hand tightens its grip on her injured shoulder. Hana refuses to cry out. She bites her lip and tastes fresh blood. He squeezes even tighter, and she holds her breath, nearly fainting from the pain. When he finally releases her, bright spots dance in front of her eyes.

'One day, you'll understand,' he says, lifting her from the ground and forcing her onto the horse.

I will never understand you. The words trace outlines across her tongue as she bites down to keep from saying them aloud. The horse moves, trudging towards a future she cannot possibly endure as Morimoto leads on foot. Hana droops forward against the horse's neck, watching the terrain pass beneath her. Its heady animal scent fills her nostrils, and she drifts in and out of consciousness, as if her life is a dream she wishes to awaken from.

》《

Hana opens her eyes when they cross a railway track. Hoof on wood, a distinct break in the monotony of sodden earth, rouses her from her fevered slumber. The rain has settled into a light drizzle, and sunlight threatens to break through in patches across the grey clouds. She lifts her face up to the sky. The horse stalls at her movement, alerting Morimoto she is awake. He brings the horse to a standstill, pats its nose, and feeds it a handful of something from his coat pocket. His footsteps stop beside her.

He pulls her down from the horse, and at first her legs won't take her weight. He holds her close, and the familiarity of his scent frightens her. She doesn't want to recognise him in any way, and yet she smells tobacco and sweat and grass and salt and rain. She turns away and breathes from her mouth.

'We're making good progress,' he says.

Hana says nothing. She wants to know more, where they are headed to – is it a town or encampment or another military base? – and what will happen when they reach it. Her legs feel like themselves again, and she stands on her own, taking a step away from him. She breathes in the late-afternoon air, cleansing her nose of his odour. She rests her forehead on the horse's thick neck. It stamps the ground with its front hoof but doesn't nudge her away. She wishes she could lean on the strength of this creature forever.

'Here,' he says, turning her to face him. He hands her an apple. She stares at it as though it is a figment of her imagination. The bloody redness contrasts with the muted grey covering the land. 'Take it,' he commands.

Slowly, she reaches for the apple with her good arm. When her fingertips touch it, she understands it indeed is real and snatches it from him, devouring it, core and all. He watches her with greedy eyes. She doesn't care. He can't do anything more to her than he has already done. She licks her fingertips and her lips. She stares at his hand as he reaches deep into his coat pocket. Like a magic trick, it appears in front of her with another bright red apple. Her eyes follow the apple as he takes a bite.

She cannot stop the drool dripping from her lips. She doesn't care enough to try. Instead, she watches him take another bite.

She steps towards him. A hint of a smile touches one corner of his mouth. She leans into him, her lips nearing the apple, but he moves it slowly towards his lips, leading her back to him. She follows his lead, letting her lips touch his. He kisses her. His tongue is alive in her mouth. She lets him have his fill, but her eyes never leave the apple.

She reaches for it. He holds on to the apple at first. She freezes, letting him kiss her, but her unblinking eyes remain on the fruit held tightly in his hand. When he finally pulls away, he smiles at her and releases the fruit. She turns away from him, hunching her shoulders towards the horse, as she devours the half-eaten apple. He lifts her dress as she swallows the last of the crisp fruit, and she leans her forehead against the horse's black mane as his hands touch her.

He kisses her neck and presses up behind her, pushing her against the horse. She listens to his breath, alternating with hers. She listens to the rain falling in a delicate patter all around them. She hears the wind push the clouds away. He wraps his arms around her in a fierce embrace so tight, Hana thinks he means to crush her body into his until there is nothing left of her, merely a memory living within him, the last person in this world to see her alive.

Her heart thumps inside her chest. His embrace threatens to suffocate her, but her heart continues to beat strongly against his arms. She sucks in a deep breath through her open mouth. Her chest expands against his stranglehold.

A beam of sunlight breaks through the departing clouds, revealing a slice of green in the distance. He finally releases her, and she breathes deeply. The air tastes different, sunlit, warm and fresh. The throbbing pain in her shoulder reminds her she is still alive, that her body is healing. She swears to herself Morimoto's will not be the last human face she sees.

Morimoto lifts her onto the horse. He surprises her by climbing up behind her and holding her close to his chest so they ride together as one. She ignores his constant touch and his nearness, but when he begins to whistle, the familiar tune that often drifted through her barred window as he ended his shift at the brothel, she can't suppress her repugnance. She leans away from him, hugging the horse's neck, gripping its hair in her fisted hands. Her shoulder protests against the motion, but she doesn't give in. She welcomes the pain because it does its work, screaming into her head, blocking out his nauseating song.

Emi

Seoul, December 2011

Emi awakens as the echo of a girl's voice fades into silence. She shivers and glances around a sterile room. A heart monitor beeps beside her. She reaches out to touch it but notices a small device clamped onto the tip of her finger. It is connected to a wire that disappears over the edge of the bed. She touches her forehead with her other hand, and she slowly begins to recall the demonstration. The crowd of unfamiliar people swarms in her mind, the sudden shock of recognition.

The statue looms in her memory. Its bronze face, Hana's face, shines like gold reflecting iridescent sunlight. She sits up, the heart monitor beeps erratically, and then she spies her son asleep in an armchair in the far corner of the room. The mechanical beeps slow, find a regular rhythm once again, and she calls to him.

'You're awake.' He coughs and she smiles at him as he sits next to her on the hospital bed.

'I need to go back,' she says.

'Go back?' he repeats. 'Go back where? Home? Because you can't fly home. The doctor says' he begins before she cuts him off.

'No, to the demonstration.'

'The demonstration is over, Mother. You have been in hospital for two days.'

The news is a shock. Her heart skips a beat on the monitor, and her son looks at it, concerned. He taps the plastic screen, but the beats are regular again. He turns to her, and there is uncertainty in his eyes. He looks like a child questioning what he should say next.

'Mother, you're not well. The doctor says your heart has suffered a shock. You need to rest here for a few more days ... especially ... because of your heart condition.' He pats her arm, as though unsure what else to do with his hands. 'I'll get YoonHui. She can explain better than me. She went to get a coffee.' He rises, looks at her carefully as though assessing whether he should stay, pats her arm again. 'I'll be right back,' he says reassuringly, and runs his hand through his thinning silver hair before heading for the door.

The door whispers shut, and Emi is alone. *Hana.* She has to see her again. Hyoung said it has been two whole days. Will the statue still be there? She can't remember if it is a permanent fixture or a travelling art exhibit. Surely it will still be there one day more either way, but she knows she has to hurry. Time was not her friend when she left her island, and waking up in a hospital only emphasises that fact.

When the village doctor informed her she had heart disease and only months to live, she laughed. Of course she would die from a broken heart. Then the bitterness within her turned into desperation. She needed to search for her sister, just one more time, even if she never truly believed she would find her. But now she has; Hana is out there, waiting for Emi to come to her.

Emi throws the covers off her legs. They are bare. She is wearing a hospital gown with nothing underneath. She removes the clip from her finger, but then the heart monitor goes flat, issuing an alert. Reaching over, she pushes a few buttons, desperate to silence the high-pitched alarm. Finally, she turns a knob and the sound disappears into nothing.

Carefully, she slips out of the bed and searches the room for her clothes. She finds them in the en suite bathroom, neatly folded next to the sink. Her daughter's work. She dresses as quickly as her ailing body will allow, but she cannot find her handbag. She searches through the wardrobe, the drawers, even underneath the hospital bed, but it is nowhere to be found. She cannot leave without her handbag.

In the hallway, the medical staff rushes past Emi as she shuffles towards the nurses' station. Lane is standing in the waiting room, staring out of the window at the grey sky. It is snowing again. Emi makes her way to her.

'Mother, you're awake. What are you doing out here?' Lane sounds alarmed.

'Where's my handbag?' Emi asks, careful to sound calm and in control of her senses, as if nothing has happened.

'Your handbag?' Lane repeats as though she does not understand the meaning of the word.

'I need my handbag so that I can go back,' Emi explains.

'Slow down, you're not well, Mother. Have a seat, here.' Lane helps Emi into a chair. 'I have your handbag. It's right here,' Lane says, and digs beneath a pile of coats on the chair next to her. She lifts Emi's handbag from the bottom and gives it to her.

Relief and calm flood over Emi as she clasps it to her chest. She looks at Lane and wonders how to explain herself so that she will be understood. A nurse passes them, and Emi sits a little taller, as though sitting straight is a sign of health. When the nurse is out of earshot, she leans towards Lane.

'I need to go back to the statue. My children won't understand, but perhaps you will.'

Lane looks sceptical, but she leans in towards Emi.

'I don't have much time left,' Emi confesses. 'I've known for a while that my heart is diseased.'

She looks at Lane meaningfully, and it takes a few seconds for her to understand. When she does, her hand flies to her mouth. Emi nods.

'How long have you known?' Lane asks. She touches Emi's forearm.

'That doesn't matter. What matters is this is my last trip to Seoul,' Emi confesses. 'My last chance to find her.'

'It does matter!' Lane nearly shouts. She looks past Emi, searching for YoonHui. 'You have to tell your children. How much time do you have?' Lane keeps spouting clipped sentences and questions at Emi until she suddenly stops and focuses on Emi's face. 'You can't die. Not yet. Your daughter needs you.'

'My daughter is a grown woman. She is successful and secure,' Emi says, and then touches Lane's shoulder. 'And she has you.'

Lane seems not to know how to respond. Emi continues.

'I need to finish what I came here to do.'

'And what is that, exactly?' Lane asks, cradling Emi's hand in both of hers.

'I need to see my sister again.'

Lane remains silent. She turns her head and stares out the window. The grey light casts a filtered shadow across her pale skin.

'YoonHui will never understand,' Lane says finally.

'I know, that's why I have to leave before she can stop me.'

'No,' Lane says, releasing Emi's hand. 'She will never understand why you didn't tell her about your sister.' Lane looks at her accusingly.

'Each of the last three years you've gone to a Wednesday Demonstration, and you've lied to YoonHui and to me . . . You should have told us you were looking for your sister.'

Emi looks down at the linoleum floor. She doesn't have time to argue with Lane or her daughter and son. She fears getting stuck in the hospital. If she falls seriously ill in this place, she will never escape it.

'I have kept my sister a secret for so long. I didn't know how to tell YoonHui the truth. I didn't know how to tell anyone the truth.'

'You could have told us anything about your family and your past, anything at all, and I know that YoonHui would have understood. Especially something like this. We could have helped you look for her.'

Emi pauses. She stares down at her hands, still clutching her handbag.

'I don't know if you're right,' Emi says honestly.

'I am right. I know her.'

Lane's salt-and-pepper hair is tied up into a careless ponytail. Loose strands stand on end and frame her face like a sparse lion's mane. Emi stares at this outspoken woman who seems to know more about her daughter than Emi ever will. Perhaps she couldn't tell her children what happened to their aunt because Emi half wanted to believe it wasn't true. She didn't want to believe that her silence that day on the beach resulted in her sister being forced into sexual slavery. In the beginning, her guilt kept her silent. But after so many years of secrecy, it became impossible to reveal the truth. Emi's shoulders sag, and a dull pain throbs in her chest.

'I don't have time to explain things, not right now,' Emi says. 'But I promise, I will. Tell her that I will explain everything when I return.'

'You tell her,' Lane says, motioning towards the nurses' station.

YoonHui is frantically shouting at the nurse behind the counter that her mother is missing. Emi watches the scene as though it is on a television screen. The pitch of her daughter's voice edges higher and higher with each hysterical statement. Then her son's gruff voice cuts in, and Emi knows she cannot leave now. She will have to convince her children to let her go, as though she is the child requiring permission.

Hana

Mongolia, Summer 1943

The rare thunderstorm disappears, and blue sky fills the horizon like a great calm lake hanging above their heads. Hana holds her breath and pretends she is sinking to the bottom of the sea. The earthy thud of the horse's hooves is like a heartbeat in her ears. Eyes closed, breath held, she could be somewhere else. They have travelled through two nights or more, the horse slowing but never stopping. Morimoto has alternated between riding and walking in order to rest the horse. They stopped at a river to drink, but that was more than a day ago. The pain in her shoulder is strong, blocking out the passage of time.

The late-afternoon sun is already leaning towards slumber. Hana is saddle-sore, her swollen face and bloody feet adding to her misery, though the discomfort recedes when she retreats into her mind. There she can be free of pain. Her body slides through the ocean. Her legs kick with strength against the current, strength she once relied upon to help feed her family. She is miles away beneath a blue sea when the horse snorts, and her eyes open. On the horizon, she sees a dwelling and movement.

Hana keeps her eyes on the structure as they near it, and step by step, it grows in size. Beginning as a small oblong in the distance, it gradually takes a new shape, rounded with a taut, domed roof. Morimoto tells her they are in Mongolia. A huddle of men salutes them as they approach. There are four of them, dressed in colourful coats. A wolfish dog barks and runs in tight circles. It takes a moment for Hana to realise the animal is tethered to a stake in the ground. The great beast growls as the horse passes by. One of the men kicks grass at it, shouting something in Mongolian, and the dog lies down with its tongue lolling from one side of its open mouth. The men greet her captor like they are old friends. None look up at her. A boy, perhaps near her own age, takes the horse's reins and waits for Morimoto to help her down. The boy leads the horse to a pen encircling a few ponies and an ox.

Standing on the ground, she feels their eyes on her now, assessing the broken girl dressed in rags, her beaten face, her arm in a sling. Morimoto's hand rests on her waist as he speaks to the nomads in their language. They nod in understanding, and she imagines he is selling her or, worse, granting them temporary use while they remain at the camp. Looking down at the bloodstained hide strapped to her feet, she feels humiliated and weak.

When he finishes speaking, he ushers her towards the domed tent, which she later learns is called a *ger*. The curtained door opens as they approach it. A woman greets them when Hana steps inside. Morimoto doesn't follow her in but nods his head at the woman and lets the heavy curtain fall closed without saying a word to Hana. She suddenly feels abandoned, and the feeling is a slap in the face.

Inside, the Mongolian woman is all she sees at first. The woman's ruddy face is lined, with sun more than time. She's no older than Hana's mother. She touches Hana's injured arm, and the softness of the woman's skin surprises her. There are no calluses on her fingers, no roughness along the edges of her palms, and she imagines this woman is also soft inside. She allows herself to be led deeper into the *ger*, sat down upon a silk floor pillow, and undressed and washed with a hand towel. First her face, then working down her body, finishing at her feet, Hana is washed and then dressed in a deep-purple coat with silk embroidery, sleeves that hang beyond her hands, and a hem that falls well below her knees.

Hana thinks of nothing but what is physically happening to her, the woman's hands on her skin, the bone comb sliding through her hair. The only sounds are the woman's breathing, the wind rushing past the *ger*, and the fire crackling in the pot-bellied stove in the centre of the round, tented space. The semi-darkness and quiet are like being in a womb, warm and comforting, and Hana closes her eyes, feeling safe for the first time since her capture. She wonders if this was Morimoto's intention, this feeling of safety, but thoughts of him threaten to break her serenity. She pushes them away, focusing on nothing but what is happening in the moment. Slowly, she welcomes in the stillness.

The woman says something, startling Hana from her restful state. She doesn't understand a word of the woman's foreign tongue. She is wearing a coat similar in style and colour to the one Hana now wears. She must have shared her own clothing. Touching the finely crafted coat, Hana bows her head to her in thanks. The woman smiles. Her teeth are white and straight, except for her left canine, which has grown in crooked. Hana thinks the imperfection makes her beautiful.

The woman leaves her and tends the fire. The burning wood sends smoke upwards through the metal pipe and escapes through a large hole at the top of the *ger*. The woman motions with one hand towards her mouth and says something in her language. Hana nods. The woman opens a large leather trunk beside a small altar in the back. Inside are parcels of food, wrapped and tied in animal skins, woven cotton or straw baskets. She gives Hana one of the baskets and opens the lid.

Inside is dried meat of some sort, and Hana again bows her head in thanks. She falls upon the meat strips, starving, and the salt tingles on her tongue. Her mouth fills with saliva. She watches as the woman tears a few pieces of bread from a large, unleavened loaf and places them into Hana's basket. The woman then nods and rises to her feet. She dons a pair of suede boots and disappears through the thick curtain made of heavy woven wool and animal skin.

Seizing a piece of bread, Hana follows the woman's trail to the door and pauses beside the curtain. She eats the bread and then places her hand on the door flap separating her from the men. She hears the dog's bark, a man's laugh and the wind. The horse snorts from further away, and she has a sense of where they all are in that outside space. The urge to open the flap and slip outside, too, sends electric pulses into her fingertips.

A few moments pass, and no one enters the *ger*. Hana remains standing beside the door, fighting with her curiosity, until finally she turns round, retraces her footsteps, and sits back down on the silk pillow to continue eating the dried meat. When the small food basket is empty, the woman returns, lifting the door flap high enough for Hana to catch a glimpse outside. The black horse that brought them here is framed in the triangular opening. Morimoto sits in the saddle. She notices a bundle tied behind him. He is leaving her behind. His eyes meet hers for a fleeting moment, before the flap falls shut and she is again alone with the woman inside the warm circle of light and shadow.

Fine prickles dance on her skin, sending rays of heat into her ears.

He must have sold her. Hana doesn't know if she should be afraid or relieved. At least the woman is kind. Her soft and caring hands give Hana hope that perhaps these Mongolians will set her free once they understand she has been kidnapped from her home.

The woman brings Hana a bowl of water. The cold liquid runs down her throat, filling her stomach, expanding its salted contents, until she feels full for the first time in many months. The sound of the horse's hooves galloping away soothes her. She imagines Morimoto disappearing across the plain, never to return.

Her eyes feel heavy, and although her injured shoulder still throbs, Hana wants to lie down and sleep and never reawaken. As though reading her thoughts, the woman brings her a fur pelt and motions for her to lie on it. The silken fur feels luxurious after too many nights held captive within her barren cell in the brothel and three or more astride a horse. She runs her hands through it, sinking into the softness. The woman covers her with a homespun blanket, and Hana can barely keep her eyes open. Humming somewhere nearby, the woman busies herself with yarn. The constant rustle of her coat as she moves lulls Hana to sleep.

She dreams she is floating in a warm pool next to the shore enclosed by an outcrop of black rocks. The water is shallow, and the absorbed warmth from the afternoon sun flows through her limbs. She can feel the heat on her cheeks and hear the seabirds cry overhead. A sea lion barks somewhere nearby, and Hana thinks she should open her eyes and find her mother. The impulse to do so is strong, but try as she might they are glued shut, and she is floating in darkness beneath a radiating sun.

》-《

Hana awakens in the night. The heavy breathing of the sleeping Mongolians fills the hot air. Her eyes adjust to the dim light of the embers still glowing in the fire. Even in the mild autumn evening, they keep the fire alive, but with only a hint of life. Slowly, she lifts her head and makes out three people sleeping nearby.

The woman is lying nearest to her. A dark mound to the left of her is too deep in shadow for Hana to see the face, but its size is definitely male. Beyond that mound is a smaller one, not much larger than the woman. It must be the boy who took the horse from them when they arrived. With no sign of the other two Mongolian men, Hana feels content to lie back down and settles deeper into the blanket.

Unable to go back to sleep, she listens to the sounds around her. The man's deep rumble at the end of each sonorous intake of breath; the woman's quiet exhalation, which cuts off in a soft sigh; and the boy's constant tossing, as though he's suffering through a nightmare. The winds outside have calmed, and even the dog seems to have gone to sleep, but the ponies occasionally stamp their feet, and the thud of earth reminds her of her journey to this place. Where has Morimoto gone, she wonders, and what will happen to her when the sun rises?

Hana, come home . . . Her sister's voice sounds close, as though she is standing just outside. Hana sits up and listens for it again, but nothing rises above the snores, the breathing and the intermittent crackle of the fire. Uncertain whether the voice was real or where it came from, she takes her time deciding whether she should go outside to investigate. Hana almost lies back down, but then an owl screeches high above the *ger* and she crawls to the door and slips outside.

The stars beyond the *ger* light up the night sky, and outside is brighter than within. Thousands of white pinpricks illuminate the black ether, and she sinks to her knees. After the peaceful moments the Mongolian woman bestowed upon her and the restful sleep she awoke from, the beauty of the night overwhelms Hana, and she can only gaze, wide-eyed, at the speckled sky.

The dog interrupts her reverie, growling somewhere nearby. She turns her head in the direction of the low grumble. A small mound not far away changes shape as the mongrel rises. Its full size is cast in shadow against the glowing backdrop of starlight on the flat plain. It growls again, barely audible, a warning. Hana takes a last glance at the starlit heavens and ducks back inside the *ger*. She crawls to the fur pelt and covers herself with the soft blanket. The woman stirs beside her, the man is no longer snoring, and the boy is still. They are awake but say nothing. After a long pause, the tension eases out of the *ger*, the fire's embers intermittently crackle, and they are all clothed in a red glow. Hana cannot forget the stars shining brightly in the night sky. Staring up above her through the smoke hole in the centre of the *ger*'s roof, she glimpses one, perhaps two, white eyes peering back at her.

>-((

The Mongolian woman wakes Hana with a gentle squeeze on her hand. She sits up immediately, her heart already racing. The woman smiles and softly touches Hana's cheek, calming her. She hands Hana a pair of suede boots and motions for her to put them on. Then she bids her to follow through the door flap.

Outside the sun has barely breached the flat horizon. The deep-purple sky is empty of stars. The dog growls when she emerges, but the woman hushes it with a hand signal. It lies down, its tail rapidly beating the dirt. Still tethered to the stake in the ground, the dog stays as near to the *ger* as the rope allows. The woman hugs Hana, a grand motion, and then she takes Hana's hand in hers and leads her towards the waiting dog. Alarmed at the woman's intentions, Hana instinctively pulls back, but the woman looks her in the eyes and shakes her head, her face an open smile. Hana relents.

As they near the mongrel, the woman speaks softly to it. The dog responds in kind, and it is as though they are talking to one another, the woman with words and the dog in wistful whines and half-barks. When they are within touching distance, it lets out a low growl, the same warning it gave Hana last night. She hesitates, but the woman insists and slowly places Hana's hand near the dog's nose. Hana watches the dog closely, fully expecting it to snap at her hand and rip it from her arm.

The dog's silken grey fur stands upright like the fur of an angry cat. It sniffs her hand and sneezes three times, as though allergic to her foreign scent. The woman says something to it. It lets out a long and mournful whine. Hana wonders if the mongrel is really related to a wolf. Its yellow eyes glare at her, but it lowers its snout and bows its head.

The woman releases Hana's hand and motions for her to follow her lead and pet the dog. As the woman runs her fingers through its thick fur, she speaks softly and curiously to the mongrel. Hana leans in very slowly, preparing her hand to touch the top of the dog's head. Perhaps if she grazes just the tips of the fur on its forehead, and it decides to bite her, she can yank her hand away quickly enough before its teeth can sink into her fingers.

It feels like ages pass before the tips of her fingers come into contact with the mongrel's fur. She pauses, giving the creature a moment to decide whether it likes her or not, but when it does nothing, she pets it in one long motion from head to neck. After a second daring stroke, its tongue lolls sideways in its teeth-filled jaws, and it flops onto its back, revealing a soft underbelly. The woman motions for Hana to continue petting it, and she does, enjoying the downy fur and the genuine pleasure spreading through her own limbs. Before she knows it, she, too, is speaking gently to the dog.

'You're a magnificent animal,' she says, gently scratching its stomach. 'Please remember this moment, when you and I became friends.'

They linger with the dog a few minutes longer, but when it licks

Hana's hand, the woman motions for them to rise. The meeting successful, it is time to move on. Hana follows the woman behind the *ger*. She stops suddenly, amazed by the sight before her. Far beyond the rolling plains, blue mountains rise up into the morning sky. The majestic scenery leaves her breathless. The woman urges her towards a small pen. Hana is still marvelling at how she didn't see the mountains yesterday.

Inside the pen, a shaggy ox with engorged udders lifts its head as they pass through the gate. Four ponies of short, stocky stature and various colours greet them with quiet, alert eyes. Behind the pen is a second, smaller *ger* with three double-humped camels tethered to a stake near the door frame. Hana guesses the other two men must be asleep inside. Perhaps they are not blood relatives, she thinks, while taking the bucket the woman holds out to her. With their metal pails, they enter the pen and corner the ox.

It bellows at them but seems to consent to the milking. Hana tries not to think of the leg she stole from the injured ox after her escape. She focuses on the woman as she kneels and milks it. Hana watches, taking mental notes. When the pail is nearly full, she rises and motions for Hana to give it a try.

She dutifully kneels just as the woman did, places the pail beneath the udder, and takes hold of two teats. Her shoulder smarts, but she pushes past the pain. Nothing happens with the first few squeezes, and the woman helps her with the technique, squeezing softly higher up the teat and gently tugging downward until a stream of milk squirts out. After a few successful tries, the woman picks up her pail and heads out of the pen towards the *ger*, leaving Hana alone with this chore.

At first she struggles with the teats and begins to wonder if the milk is dried up, but after she tries two different teats, the milk flows again and the pail slowly but surely fills up. Before attempting to lift the heavy pail, Hana wipes the sweat from her brow. Her sore shoulder throbs with heat, protesting against the motion. She massages it while gazing at the brightening landscape. Undulating waves of green capture her attention. Heavy shadows drift lazily across the flat grassland as billowing clouds pass overhead. It could be the ocean, and Hana imagines the South Sea.

A gust of wind blows a lock of her hair into her eyes. As she tucks it behind her ear, she senses movement to her right. The ox steps away and she turns, her heart speeding up as she expects to find the mongrel preparing to leap onto her and tear out her throat. Instead a boy leans against the pen, his chin resting on his crossed arms, smiling down at her.

Hana recognises him as the boy who took the horse the day before and the same boy asleep in the *ger* across from the woman. She turns quickly away and stands, lifting the pail in one swift motion. It takes two hands, but she manages not to stumble as she leaves the pen and heads back to the *ger*. Her shoulder is angry at the task, but she doesn't let it show.

Before she knows it, the boy is next to her, trying to take the pail from her hands. She stops walking and jerks the handle away from him. Milk spills over the metal rim and splashes onto the ground. He reaches for the pail once more, but she takes a step away, holding it out of his reach. He smiles at her, bemused, and then places his hands behind his back. She carefully sidesteps around him and continues towards the *ger*.

Like a curious dog, the boy follows her. He remains far enough behind her not to cause alarm. She peers over her shoulder only once to ensure he isn't sneaking up on her, and when she reaches the *ger*, she ducks through the curtain without looking back at him. He doesn't enter the *ger* immediately, but after she manages to pour the milk into a container near the door as instructed by the woman through hand motions, he slips inside and sits next to his rolled-up bed mat. When the woman notices him watching them, she chastises him, and he quickly exits the *ger*, though not before making eye contact with Hana. His peculiar actions keep Hana on alert. She hasn't seen the other men yet, but this one, even though quite young, seems to be attempting to make a claim on her.

For the remainder of the day, she makes sure she stays close to the woman, following her around like a dutiful child. The day's chores are simple enough: gather fresh water from the stream beyond the first rise to the east of the camp; feed the ponies, ox and camels; churn the fresh milk into butter, cheese and fermented drink; rework and repair footwear and clothes and parts of the *ger*. The day passes quickly into night. The approaching dark unnerves her.

The men are gathered in the interior of the main *ger*. They have just finished their meal; the dishes are wiped clean and the men begin to sing around the stove, enjoying the fermented milk. Their laughter dances through the quiet air, and their festive mood fills Hana's gut with dread.

She loiters outside the *ger*, hidden in the dark night, and pets the pony tethered to the stake near the door, as though it is there in preparation for an imminent journey. Though fully grown, it is the size of a young horse and reminds her of the breed she has seen from afar on her home island. The Jeju horse is prized among the islanders, and she feels an affinity for this creature that reminds her of home. She saved a few pieces of pear from her meal and holds them in her palm. The pony's soft nose nudges her hand before its lips pick up the first piece. The sound of its teeth grinding the pear's flesh into pulp reminds her of the wooden wind chimes clacking beside the door to her home. A wave of homesickness rushes through her.

As she runs her hands over the smooth coat, they come to rest upon the peculiar wooden saddle. Unlike the soldier's black horse, this Mongolian breed is short enough for her to mount without much trouble. One leap and she would be astride it. Her hand finds the horn of the saddle. She holds on to it tightly, feeling the aged wood beneath her palm. She could ride off into the night. It would be difficult for them to follow her in the dark. She could do it.

The dog whines behind her, and she turns. Someone leans down and pats its head. The shadow reveals a slender outline. The boy. Turning back to the pony, she drops her hands to her sides. Has he seen what she wanted to do? His footsteps approach her, crunching the sparse grass beneath his leather boots. She feels his presence behind her and turns.

She looks towards the *ger*'s door, listening for the men inside. The curtain is held partially open with a rope to let in the cool night air. Their guttural songs drift towards her. The dim light from the triangular opening illuminates the boy's face. He is not smiling. Instead, he appears apprehensive, perhaps nervous. Then he motions for her to enter the *ger*. Examining the entrance, she wishes she had slipped away with the pony. Her feet are heavy as she heads towards the *ger*. She feels as though she is wading through wet sand. After what seems an eternity, she ducks beneath the curtain flap and enters the circle of light and warmth beneath the wide canopy.

Inside the *ger*, silk pillows are arranged in a semicircle around the stove. The woman is seated at the far end of the circular room. She motions for Hana to sit on the pillow beside her. Hana tiptoes around the seated men, who continue singing through the interruption. The woman glances at the boy as he follows Hana in. He plops onto a pillow nearest the door, and the stove partially conceals him from where Hana sits. The royal blue of his coat shines in the firelight as he joins the men in song, clapping and swaying side to side, intermittently revealing his happy face.

Without joining in, Hana watches and listens to the foreign songs of her new captors. The men grow more inebriated with each refilled mug of fermented brew. They slap one another's knees, direct smiles and laughter towards the woman, who refills their cups when empty. As the stove's dying light threatens to snuff out, Hana prepares herself for the inevitable attack, which she has learned follows drunken men enjoying themselves. Her hands held stiffly in front of her, palms facing down onto her lap, she does not sway along with them during their songs. A smile does not grace her lips. Her eyes remain sharp, preparing for the moment when her new clothes will be torn from her body and the stink of these foreign men will permanently imprint on her mind. This was her purpose after all, the real reason Morimoto brought her here.

The pony remains tethered outside. The men are drunk. She could get up and quietly step past them, exiting as though to relieve herself. Once outside, she could silently lead the pony away, mount it, and ride off into the darkness before they know what's happened. She could, she thinks, but then the boy catches her eye, and she realises he is not drunk. And he is watching her closely. He would hear the pony's hooves. He would stop her.

The last of the fire's orange light fades, replaced by a red glow. Their faces now in darkness, silence descends upon the sombre group like a heavy fog. The singing suddenly stops, and a hand touches her arm. It's useless to shrink away. *It's happening now*, she thinks, but the hand lifts her to her feet and leads her away from the men, who have begun to stir. It is the woman's hand, and she leads Hana to the same sleeping space as the night before. The woman places the thick fur pelt onto the floor, and Hana lies upon it, waiting. To her surprise, the men exit the *ger*. Their voices float back inside, and she listens intently, wondering which man will come for her first and how they will decide.

The pony snorts. Its hooves clomp against the dirt as it is led away.

Its steps quicken into a gallop, which begins to fade. One man re-enters the *ger*. His footsteps softly pad past where Hana lies and he finds the woman. His silk coat, stiff with padding, crinkles as he kneels. He undresses and lies down beside the woman. A faint murmur escapes the woman's lips, and then Hana listens no more.

The familiar sounds of man and wife remind her of her parents. She recalls the quiet of their lovemaking in her home as she lay falling asleep beside her sister. Before her capture, it was a mystery what went on between them under night's cover. Now she blocks out what she assumes is consensual desire, and possibly love, between the man and woman. Her parents loved like this. Like her, the boy is silent, but she knows he has yet to fall asleep. The man and woman soon grow quiet, and then snores fill the dark spaces within the *ger*. Hana closes her eyes. Sleep does not come. She cannot stop wondering whether Morimoto has truly left her here for good, or if he intends to return.

Emi

Emi is sitting on the edge of the bed in her small hospital room. Surrounded by her family, she tells her children the story of their aunt's abduction when she was a young girl. She tells them how their aunt sprang from the sea, hiding their mother beneath the rocky cliff. The story rolls off her tongue as though in one long breath, with no pauses for thought, and when she finishes, the silence that follows is broken only by her daughter's discreet sniffs each time she wipes her tearful eyes.

Her son speaks first. 'All these years we thought you were an only child.'

'I know, I'm sorry.'

He doesn't pause. 'Now you tell us you have a sister who you think might still be alive? And you've been coming to these demonstrations hoping to find her? I mean, what are we supposed to think?'

'Calm down,' Lane says, her voice soft. 'Remember, your mother's not well.'

'Why didn't you tell us any of this before?'

His words are heavy with scorn. His anger fills the room with heat. Emi forgot about her son's temper. Anger is the emotion he expresses first, before thought and understanding can follow. She waits for him to calm down before she answers him. A stiff silence fills the small hospital room. Her daughter sniffles a few times and blows her nose into a tissue. Lane's arm never leaves YoonHui's shoulders. Emi finally answers her son.

'I couldn't bear to burden you with my shame.'

'Your shame?' Her daughter suddenly finds her voice. 'Mother, you did nothing to be ashamed of.' She takes her mother's hand and steadies it.

Her son says nothing, though he is unable to disguise his anger. The tips of his ears flare a deep red.

'You can't understand, I know,' Emi says softly.

'Mother,' YoonHui whispers. 'We want to. Help us understand.'

Emi cannot look at them. She stares at the tiny yellow flowers dotting the white bedsheet. She touches them with her fingertips, each little flower a replica of the next. They remind her of yellow chrysanthemums, and her hand flinches away from them. The flowers blur into a mass of specks against a white background, and she wipes her tears away. It takes all her willpower to speak.

'It *is* my shame,' Emi says, each word more painful than the last. Her heart aches.

'No, it's their shame ... the Japanese,' her daughter says in a strange high-pitched voice Emi does not recognise. 'They are the ones who should feel ashamed for what they did, not you.'

Emi wipes her eyes with the back of one trembling hand. She looks up at the ceiling and squeezes her eyes shut before confessing her heart's deepest, darkest secret. A secret she has never confessed to herself, not even quietly in her mind.

'I crouched below the rock that day and let them take her in my place. She offered herself as a sacrifice to save me . . . and I let her. That is why I could never tell you . . . or anyone. Because I was ashamed of my cowardice.'

Emi's head falls down into her hands and her shoulders hunch together as though she might fold into herself and disappear. The fear that coursed through her that day rears its head and spreads through her limbs again, as though she is there now, cowering below the rocks. Hana stood up to the soldier, and her words drifted down to Emi's ears. Her sister lied to the Japanese soldier, and then two more approached and dragged her away. Emi could hear their voices fade the further they retreated from the shore, back towards the road. She knew they wouldn't be able to see her if she rose and peered above the rocks to watch them go, but she was too afraid. She remained lying beneath the rock until her mother rushed to her side.

'Are you hurt? Emi, what's happened to you?' The alarm in her voice did nothing to snap Emi out of her fearful trance. 'Emi?' Her mother's voice grew in concern.

Emi suddenly began to cry. Huge sobs wrenched from her chest. Her mother's concern increased to alarm.

'Emi, where's Hana?'

'They took her,' Emi finally answered in between hiccups and sobs.

'Who took her?'

'The soldiers.'

Emi remembers the horror on her mother's face in minute detail. Her eyes widened into black inkwells that seemed to pour into Emi's own eyes. The edges of her mouth sagged into a child's frown, her lips trembling, and then she exploded into a grief-stricken wail that not even the wind could blow away. It was then the shame filled young Emi, shame for hiding in the sand, covered in seaweed, as her mother's first daughter, the source of her pride and her partner in the sea, disappeared with the Japanese soldiers, while she did nothing.

'Your sister saved you,' YoonHui says gently, nudging Emi's head up from her hands. She caresses her mother's cheek. 'And I'm grateful to her for that. Mother, I'm grateful to your sister . . . to my aunt. She chose to save you by going with them. She was the big sister, and you were just a child. She did her duty to you, and she deserves to be remembered for it, yes. But you owe her no guilt. She wouldn't want that from her little sister.'

Emi can't accept her daughter's readily given absolution. She remembers waking up the day after Hana was taken. She sat up slowly, rubbed the sleep from her eyes, and turned to wake her sister. At first the empty blankets confused her, but in a split second, she remembered.

'Hana! Where's Hana!' she shouted over and over again, until her mother rushed into the room and encircled her in her arms, rocking her back and forth, soothing her into silence.

They remained in that embrace, swaying to and fro in collective grief. When she peered up at her mother's face, she saw silent tears trailing down her soft cheeks.

'Don't cry, Mother. Father will find her. I know he will.' She stood and walked through the still house, without really seeing anything. She headed outside and sat on the wooden stoop, waiting for her father to bring her sister home.

Night took ages to arrive, yet still her father did not return. Her mother sat with her on the stoop, and they gazed in silence at the dimming horizon. Emi must have fallen asleep, and when she awoke the following morning, she found herself alone in her blankets and again cried out for Hana. Her mother rushed to her side and held her until she quietened. Then they sat on the stoop watching the sun arc across the sky like a silent witness, as they waited another day for her father to return.

After a couple of weeks, Emi awoke already aware Hana would not be next to her. She covered her head with the blanket and tried to go back to sleep. Her mother found her later in the morning and gently rubbed her back, urging her to rise.

'Not until Father brings Hana home,' she protested from beneath the blanket.

'We will go hungry if I do not dive today,' her mother said matter-of-factly, removing her hand from Emi's back.

Emi instantly missed her mother's soothing hand, but she fought the urge to turn.

'I won't eat again until Father returns home with Hana.'

Her mother didn't immediately respond. The silence unnerved Emi, but she stood her ground and refused to turn round.

'I have to return to the sea. I must do my part to keep us fed. We cannot rely on the charity of our friends forever.'

'I'm not hungry,' Emi lied, even as her stomach groaned with morning hunger pangs.

'Well, I'm hungry. Come, daughter, off to work we must go,' she said, nudging Emi softly at the small of her back.

'You go, I'm waiting for Father.'

The silence was thick with something Emi could not discern. Had she angered her mother or saddened her? She could not tell. This time, she did turn over and gaze at her mother's face. Her expression was unreadable. Emi feared she might be in trouble.

'I cannot leave you here. It's not safe,' her mother said in a voice so low that Emi wasn't certain she had heard her correctly.

'Not safe?' Emi repeated.

'The soldiers may come back.'

Images of faceless men in Japanese military uniforms sifted through her mind and she quickly sat up.

'Why will they come back, Mother?'

'For the rest of our girls. For you and anyone they left behind.' Her mother touched Emi's cheek with such tenderness that she finally understood. Her mother was afraid of losing her, too.

'They'll never get me, Mother. I know I'm not a strong swimmer, but I promise I can become one. Like Hana was. And I will stay beside you in the sea. I can do it.' She stood and towered above her kneeling mother. She held her head up high and straightened her back so that she seemed to grow a whole inch.

'I know, daughter. I know.' Her mother's smile wasn't the same one Emi was used to; it was a weak imitation that never touched her eyes.

They walked down to the sea together that day and every day thereafter.

When her father finally returned home a month later, he was alone. She knew from the thinness of his face that he had travelled far searching for Hana. She didn't ask why he had given up. She couldn't bring herself to hurt him when he was already heartbroken.

》《

Emi holds her hand to heart, remembering the first day she became a *haenyeo*. It was her mother's fear that gave her strength. If only she had had that strength before Hana allowed herself to be taken.

'You have no shame to bear for her choice and your survival,' YoonHui says again, tearing Emi away from her memories. 'And there's no shame if your sister was forced to serve as a "comfort woman". You went through so much. You deserve to be happy. Let it go, so at last you can be happy in what's left of this life.'

Shame is a heavy word in Emi's mind. It hurts her ears to hear it spoken. The shame she feels is wholly ingrained and has nothing to do with her sister's forced prostitution. It is deeper than that and has become a part of her that she knows will never disappear. Her shame is her *han*. Shame for surviving two wars while those around her suffered and perished, shame for never speaking out for justice, and shame for continuing to live when she never understood the point of her life.

Sometimes, she has felt as though she was born into the world merely to suffer. People these days seem content to search for happiness in life. That is something her generation never fathomed, that happiness is a basic human right, but now it seems like a possibility. She sees it in her daughter and her life with Lane. Even her son is happy, in his way, though he is often like his father, a policeman used to carrying out tasks as though they are orders from a commander. But it suits him, and Emi is satisfied. That is more than she ever hoped for, until now. The image of the bronze girl haunts her. She must see it, one more time.

Hana

Mongolia, Autumn 1943

For a week, each morning begins the same as the last, and Hana follows the woman throughout the day and falls asleep in the *ger* at night wondering how long this routine will continue. Then one morning, Hana awakens at the woman's touch, and they exit the *ger* while the others remain asleep. This time Hana is given both metal pails. The woman nods towards the pen before heading in the other direction. Hana is now on her own.

A pail hangs from each hand, but her injured shoulder hardly notices the extra weight. The sun has barely crested above the horizon of the flat land. The woman shimmers in the distance. Hana searches beyond the *ger*, shielding her eyes against the sun. Endless grassy fields roll into the faraway mountains. The woman's deep-purple coat, which Hana has learned is called a *del*, appears black so far away.

Slowly, she turns and heads towards the pen. She has learned a few Mongolian words. Dog is *nokhoi*. Horse is *mori*. And hungry is *olon*. She lets the unfamiliar words repeat in her head so she can remember them when needed.

The dog yaps at her as she passes. *Nokhoi*, she thinks, and sets down one of the pails to offer her hand in greeting. He licks it happily, and she kneels to rub his exposed stomach. He is off his leash, free to wander, but doesn't. Scratching the dog's stomach fills her with a peculiar warmth she hasn't felt in so long. When she realises she is smiling, Hana abruptly stops, takes the pail's handle, and trudges off. The dog rolls onto his feet and trots in the direction the woman has gone.

The ox sniffs the air upon her arrival. The ponies greet her, their soft noses nudging her arms.

'I have nothing for you yet,' she says, patting the littlest one's neck.

She pushes through them and kneels beside the ox. Footsteps approach, and she doesn't have to turn to know it is the boy. He has kept his distance from her while his mother was near, but she has left Hana on her own, making him bold. The boy is light of foot, unlike the Mongolian men, who stamp about like soldiers. He greets her. She ignores him, concentrating on her task as though milking the ox is the most important duty in the world, but her ears follow his movements. He hovers beside her awhile, his chin on his arms as he leans on the outside of the pen looking in.

'Altan,' he says.

She looks at him then, and he touches his chest.

'Altan,' he says again, patting his chest with his open hand. Then he motions towards her, and his expression changes into one of questioning. He waits, but she doesn't want to speak. He tries again, going through the same motions, but she remains silent.

When he begins a third time, a giggle escapes her, and she covers her mouth. Laughter spills out of her as though a dam has burst from intense pressure, and soon she is holding her stomach, unable to keep it back. She hasn't laughed for so long. It's as though she can't control herself. Tears stream from her eyes. The boy's face is blurred, and she cannot tell if he is upset. He climbs the pen and leaps over it, heading towards her. Her laughter fades to nothing as he approaches. She stands up to meet him, wiping her eyes dry with the back of her hand.

Face-to-face, they are nearly the same height. He is only slightly taller in the shoulders and his head tilts downwards when he stares into her eyes. She knows her face must still be bruised from Morimoto's beating and her neck as well from his hands, but she doesn't let her appearance make her weak. Preparing herself for anything he might decide to do to her, she clenches her jaw and balls her fists. She isn't certain if she should fight back. This boy is not as strong as a grown man, but he would be a formidable opponent. She gives him her most defiant stare, hoping if she stands up to him, he will learn to leave her alone.

He lifts his hand, and she flinches. He touches his chest.

'Altan.'

He smiles at her with a genuine, wide grin that reaches his eyes. He touches her chest in the same manner and raises his eyebrows. It is a question no one has asked her since her capture. She isn't sure what her name is any longer. Should she use the name they gave her at the brothel or tell him her real name? As she contemplates which name she should say, she is aware that his fingertips still rest on her chest. She touches his hand gently, pushing it away. His arm falls to his side.

'Hana,' she finally says.

He repeats her name a few times, and she laughs at his pronunciation.

'Ha-nah,' she says deliberately, correcting him.

He repeats her name again, then he points at himself without a sound. She smiles.

'Altan,' she says.

He seems pleased when she pronounces it correctly. The ponies stamp their feet, and Hana realises they have an audience. The young man from the other *ger* is watching from his doorway. He has a smirk on his face. Hana blushes, but the boy waves at the man, who shakes his head and retreats behind the *ger* to relieve himself. The sound of his urine stream against the dry earth embarrasses her. She returns to the milking, and her silence signals to Altan that their conversation is over. Dutifully, he leaves her alone in the pen. She watches him jog after the woman. *Ekh*, Hana corrects herself. Mother.

Words are power, her father once told her after reciting one of his political poems. *The more words you know, the more powerful you become. That is why the Japanese outlaw our native language. They are limiting our power by limiting our words.* Hana repeats the new Mongolian words in her head as she works, concentrating on each one, increasing her power.

Once both the pails are full, she tries to lift them, one in each hand, to return to the *ger*, but they are too heavy. She lifts one pail with both hands and carries it back. She is careful not to awaken the man still asleep next to the stove. His grumbling snores soothe her nerves. As long as he is asleep, she feels safe in his company. She hurries to the pen to retrieve the second pail, but the young man from the other *ger* is inside with the ponies.

She hesitates before entering the pen, watching him smooth his hands over the first pony's coat, checking it for burrs or thorns. He plucks a couple from its thick fur, then he lifts each hoof, one by one, to check its foot health, before walking twice around it, eyeing it up and down, and then moving on to the next pony. Hana remains by the pen's opening, waiting for him to finish. He moves on to the third pony before he acknowledges her presence.

He grunts at her, but she doesn't react. He points to the pail next to the ox. The stoic creature still stands obediently next to the pail as though urging her to return. The sun is well up by now, and she notices he is not much older than some of the youngest soldiers from the brothel. Perhaps he is Altan's big brother. He is much taller than her, at least a head higher. His shoulders are broad, his legs stocky and thick like tree trunks. She wouldn't stand a chance against him.

When she doesn't enter the pen, he laughs and mutters something to the pony. He tugs its tail, and it starts towards the gate at a trot. The other two ponies follow, and soon they are galloping past the *ger* and heading out into the fields. Hana watches with surprise at the ponies' freedom. The fourth pony loiters behind the others, watching Hana as though curious.

The man says something to her. Hana jumps, frightened by his sudden communication. He laughs at her as he walks towards her. She stands tall, feigning indifference. He pauses in front of her. They stand toe-to-toe in silence. He looks her in the eyes, and she stares back, again defiant. He smiles, and his teeth are tinged yellow with tobacco. His tanned skin shines with exertion. He speaks again, patting his chest.

'Ganbaatar.'

He smiles, and she realises he is teasing her after witnessing her exchange with Altan. She narrows her eyes but says nothing. The wind picks up, blowing dried grasses from the fields into the air. She turns away from him and hurries to the pail to shield it from the debris. He chuckles again and leads the last pony out of the pen. He, too, heads towards the mountains, in the same direction as Altan and the woman.

When Hana returns to the *ger* with the second pail, she is startled by the silence. The Mongolian man sits beside the stove, half undressed, eating his morning meal of cheese and salted meat. As quickly as she can, she empties the milk into the cistern and whirls round to leave.

'Wait,' he says.

Hana pauses. He spoke in Japanese. She turns back to him. He stands and pulls on his cotton undershirt. He's still chewing on the dried meat. Her stomach grumbles. When he is dressed and his *del* is properly pinned at his shoulder, he sits back down.

'Join me,' he says, indicating a pillow beside him.

Hana weighs her choices. She can run from him now and hope to find where the woman and the rest of the camp have gone, but he would still be there when she returns. Or she can face up to him now and get it over with. Her fingers clench into tight fists, her fingernails digging into her palms.

She lowers her eyes and follows the invisible trail leading to the pillow beside the man.

'You haven't said a word since you arrived,' he says as she sits. He doesn't look at her; instead he continues to chew on the meat and inspects it after each bite as though it is interesting and new. He offers her a strip, which she declines.

'I didn't know you spoke Japanese,' she responds, keeping her eyes on the floor in front of her knees.

'Ah, you speak so well, so softly. It is good for a girl to have a soft voice.'

Hana stiffens. Compliments lead to unpleasant things, but she tries not to show her dismay.

'I'm not certain why you are here,' he says, and finally looks at her.

His eyes are surrounded by delicate wrinkles that give him a kindly appearance. His thick, tanned skin reveals his age, and she wonders if perhaps he is Altan's grandfather, instead of his father. When she says nothing, he continues.

'I know why Corporal Morimoto tells me he brought you here, but that doesn't mean that is why you are really here.'

Hana looks up at him. He is staring at her as though she is a peculiar animal he has never seen before and is trying to make out what she eats or where her kind originates. She thinks he isn't as scary as she first believed and lets her shoulders relax.

'What reason did he give you?' she ventures, careful to avoid eye contact.

'He says you are an orphan. Rescued from the Kwantung Army in Manchuria. He's returning you to your uncle out west. Why is your uncle in Western Mongolia? That's a question I'd like answered.'

Morimoto told him she is an orphan, not a prostitute. Relief washes through her entire body. These are good men. They would never rape an orphan. Perhaps that's why Morimoto told him this. He never intended her to be harmed. He meant to leave her in this safe place until his return. Hana covers her face with her hands so he can't read her emotions.

'Ah, it is still a sore subject,' he says, mistaking her gesture for sadness. 'We can talk again another time.' He rises to his feet. 'Come,' he says, motioning towards the door.

She follows him, and he leads her in the direction of the others. The soles of her feet are still sore, and she fears a few of the wounds have broken open again. She doesn't want to expose her weaknesses, however, and speeds up so that she doesn't lag too far behind him. All the while, she turns over in her mind the fact that Morimoto intends to return for her. *Of course he will return*, she thinks, and can't breathe as easily as she did only a few hours before.

They seem to have travelled at least a mile when the long grass dwindles into short scrub. The mountains hang over them, blocking out the sky. A small incline strains her calves, but she pushes herself onwards, careful not to get too close to the man. He may not be taking her to the same place that the family disappeared to, instead leading her into a secluded wilderness. Although older than the others in the encampment, he somehow appears more powerful.

He slows as he reaches the top of the small hill and stands with his hands on his hips. Stopping beside him, just out of arm's reach, Hana takes in the view of the valley below them. As far as her eyes can see, green stalks adorned with large round pods flood the valley, all the way to the base of the nearest mountain. Blood-red flowers are dotted among them, though most of the bulbs have lost their petals. Altan and the woman, along with Ganbaatar and the other young man, are there, too, walking slowly up and down the rows, stopping at each pod.

'What are you harvesting?' she asks.

'Do you not recognise a poppy field?'

Hana shakes her head. He scrutinises her face, and she blushes.

'You've never seen a poppy? Do you know what we harvest them for?' He turns to face her. She takes a step away, towards the field and nearer to Altan. 'Opium,' he says, and smiles. 'Come, my young son will teach you all you need to know.'

He heads down the small hill before she can reply. She remains rooted to the ground, watching him go. Altan's mother looks up and waves, and Hana knows she is smiling, even though her face is too far away to make out for certain. Altan then looks in her direction and waves, too. He calls her name, *Hana*, and suddenly she feels like herself again. Not like the girl who was trapped at the brothel. Here she is simply Hana because these people are not like the soldiers. She follows Altan's father down into the poppy field and greets Altan with a smile.

They may be harvesting opium, the plague of China, but that means nothing to Hana. She thinks of Hinata and her tea and is thankful she had it to help her endure the brothel. In the field, Altan shows her how they score the poppy bulbs with a knife to let the sap seep out. Many of the bulbs in the field have already been cut, and Ganbaatar collects the sap in small scraps of cloth. Altan and Hana's job is to cut the bulbs that haven't been harvested yet. They work in parallel rows so he can keep an eye on her technique, although there isn't really much to it. Once in a while, he comes over to her and corrects the angle of her blade. By twilight, they have covered nearly three-quarters of the field. Altan shared his afternoon meal with her, yet at the end of the day she is still famished.

Altan replies to a call from his father. Then Altan's parents head towards the camp. The ponies emerge from nowhere and follow behind the couple like obedient dogs. They nip at each other's necks and tails as they trot dutifully back to their pen. Hana gazes up at the dimly lit sky. The black shadow of a bird with an immense wingspan glides along the field. It could be one of the hawks that Morimoto spoke of. Ganbaatar comes near them and gives Altan a flask. He unscrews the lid and presses it to his lips before catching himself. Altan laughs shyly and offers it to Hana.

'Water?' she asks.

He shrugs. She takes the flask from him and sniffs the opening. A pungent waft of fermented milk hits her nostrils and she recoils, handing it back to him. He laughs again and takes a long swig. With a smile, he offers it to her again. He says something she doesn't understand, nudging her with the flask. Ganbaatar laughs and shakes his head. Curiosity wins her over, and she takes the flask again. She lifts it to her lips and takes a sip.

The fermented drink has a bite, and she coughs as it warms her throat. Altan grins and urges her to drink more. She takes a big gulp and then hands the flask back to him. Sharing seems to have made his day, and he takes another long drink before tucking the flask into an inner pocket of his *del*.

The bird circles again, and Hana looks up into the sky. Ganbaatar lets out a high-pitched whistle and holds out his arm. Hana watches with surprise as the immense bird circles twice and then lands on his forearm. It is a golden eagle. Altan smiles at her and strokes the feathers on the eagle's neck. It is a magnificent creature, perched regally on Ganbaatar's forearm. He says something to Hana, and she looks at him. He motions towards the eagle, and she hesitates. He wants her to pet it, just as the woman wanted her to befriend the dog.

Hana steps closer, wary the eagle may not take a liking to her and may scratch out her eyes with its enormous talons. Its reddish-brown feathers shimmer in the twilight. She wants to touch the bird, to feel the softness of its feathers. Lifting her hand, she slowly reaches towards it.

When the bird snaps at her finger, she snatches her hand away as Ganbaatar and Altan howl with laughter. She takes a step backwards, staring at the boys, incredulous at their idea of a joke.

'It could have pecked off my finger,' she shouts at them, angry they are still laughing.

Altan stops laughing immediately when he sees her anger, and he nudges Ganbaatar's arm, to no avail. The older boy continues laughing as he strokes the bird's neck.

Hana starts to leave, but Altan stops her. He has taken hold of her wrist and won't let go. She begins to yank it free, but he smiles at her, before smacking Ganbaatar's arm. He says something to the older boy that makes his laughter cease. Ganbaatar appears ashamed and can't look Hana in the eye. Instead, he busies himself with placing a hood on the eagle. Once its eyes are covered, Altan again motions for Hana to pet the bird.

She doesn't immediately want to. Instead, Hana thinks it might be better to walk away now, to refuse to fall for another trick, but something in Altan's expression changes her mind. Hana reaches out once more to pet the eagle. She watches the bird's beak, preparing for it to stretch open to peck at her again, but this time, her fingers land on its soft throat feathers without reaction.

A surprised laugh escapes her, and she doesn't care that she has expressed pleasure in their presence. Powerful muscles ripple beneath the eagle's soft feathers, and Hana is awestruck at its magnificence. Ganbaatar eventually smiles and he, too, strokes the bird. She smiles at him and, for the first time, doesn't care what he is thinking because there is nothing but this moment, appreciating a creature grander than themselves.

》-《

The three of them head up the small hill towards the camp. They walk in silence most of the way. Birds chirp overhead as they fly back to their nests. A cool breeze rushes through the tall grass, tickling her fingertips. Hana cannot stop thinking about Altan's proximity. He keeps just the right distance between them to make her feel comfortable instead of dominated or threatened. He is like the boy from her village who visited her mother's table at the market. Polite, inquisitive, yet intelligent enough to know where the boundaries lie.

Even though they cannot communicate, Hana instinctively feels they have taken the first tentative steps on the road towards friendship. She stares at everything around her to avoid looking at him, but she feels his every move beside her, as though a small part of him has penetrated her armour.

As they near the camp, the dog barks and runs in circles around their legs. He jumps with joy because he senses dinner is near. He licks Hana's hand and then rushes to Altan, jumping up, nipping at his ear. Altan pushes the mongrel away, laughing. Ganbaatar waves to Hana and heads to his *ger*.

Altan follows him and places the basket inside with him, then comes back out and rushes after the dog. Hana finds herself smiling at them. She stops beside the pen and pats the smallest of the ponies, watching the boy play with his dog, as night continues to fall.

The evening is much like the others, except this time Altan sits beside her in his mother's former seat. Hana pretends she does not notice, but he makes it difficult, often smiling at her as he sings, nudging her shoulder gently, and encouraging her to join in. The others act as though they don't notice his exuberance, and the strangeness of these people and this foreign place dissipates, leaving Hana with a sense of family and togetherness once again. But she refuses to sing or smile or laugh in their presence. That would be too much for her to give in to just yet, but she does allow herself to sway to the music, just a little, enough so that Altan grins wider and the men sing louder and his mother's eyes twinkle brighter in the firelight.

Ganbaatar gets up to leave when the last of the embers glow a deep red. Altan's father walks him out, followed by the other young man who stayed behind in the camp. Hana has yet to learn his name. Their singing continues beyond the *ger*. Altan goes to a chest near the far wall and retrieves something. He returns to Hana's side and offers it to her. It's a small leather satchel. Hesitant to accept it, she looks at his mother for approval, but she has turned her back, busying herself with cleaning up. Altan nudges Hana's hand with the satchel again and, afraid to offend him, she accepts it. Carefully, she unties the leather strap and opens the flap. She peers inside and touches something soft as silk. Eager for her to see his gift, Altan pulls it out and reveals a finely crafted sash.

Even in the semi-darkness, the colourful patterns are brilliant. Bright blues, reds and oranges are radiant. The sash gleams between them. He motions towards her waist. Uncertain, she remains still. He tries again but then smiles, shaking his head. Gently, he wraps the sash around her waist, securing it with a double knot. Her heart flutters from his nearness. Altan leans back, examining her appearance, and then nods as though pleased.

He abruptly leaves and follows the men outside. Hana blushes when his mother acknowledges the sash. She nods and smiles at Hana. Together, the two of them set out the fur pelts for everyone's sleeping areas. When she thinks his mother isn't looking, Hana touches the smooth silk, inspecting the colourful swirls that delight her eyes. The dark colours highlighted with red and yellow flowers and green leaves and black vines are beautiful. It's hand-stitched, and she wonders if his mother toiled away on this piece of beauty for Altan, and what she must be thinking now that it adorns Hana's waist.

Later in the night, Hana's dreams are warm and musical. She can hear her father playing his zither, her mother's laughter echoing through their small hut, and she is dancing with her little sister, their bare feet turning circles on tiptoes. Everything is real, the heat of the fire, her father's song, his fingers plucking the zither's taut strings, and she can even smell the salty sea wafting in through the open shutters. She is back home, as though she has never left and nothing unpleasant has happened to her. Dancing with her sister's small hands held in each of hers, she throws her head back and sings the words she knows by heart. Her mother claps along, and Hana wants to dance forever.

A dog barks nearby. The familiar baritone strikes a chord in her memory. It barks again, three deep bursts of sound. She stops dancing. Her arms hang limply by her sides, but no one notices. The merriment continues without her. Her sister swirls around her like a leaf caught in a tempest. Laughter erupts from her mother's mouth, sweet and gentle and full of glee. She is dreaming. She doesn't want to leave them, but she is waking up. *Please don't stop*, she tells her father when he stops playing. His eyes find hers and they are full of sorrow. She can hear the early-morning birds outside the *ger* now, calling the inhabitants of the steppes from slumber. She tosses on her fur pelt, and then suddenly, she is awake.

Emi

Seoul, December 2011

The faces around the small hospital room all concentrate on Emi. The attention is too much, and Emi wishes they would just take her to the statue.

'I'm thirsty,' Emi says, and Lane offers to fetch her some water.

'Mother, why don't you lie down and rest?' YoonHui asks. She tries to encourage Emi to lie back.

'No, I don't have time to rest. I need to see the statue.'

'It doesn't have to be today. Rest, give yourself a chance to recover, and then we'll take you to the statue in a few weeks' time.'

'A few weeks?' Emi cries out, louder than she intended. 'I don't have a few weeks. Don't you understand?' She pulls the covers off her legs and threatens to get out of the bed.

'Hold on,' her son says, rushing to her side and preventing her escape. 'You're not going anywhere. I'll chain you to this bed if I have to.'

Emi freezes. He sounds just like his father in that moment. She looks at his face, stricken with the sudden similarity.

'You're just like your father,' she whispers before she can stop herself.

He looks taken aback. His eyebrows furrow and anger sweeps across his face.

'Why did you hate him so much?' he chokes out.

Too many wounds scar Emi's soul. And now she realises they have scarred her children's, no matter how hard she tried to prevent it. Her final journey to Seoul to find her lost sister has smashed the door to her past into pieces.

'There are many reasons why your father and I didn't get along. Too many to tell. But they are between him and me.'

'He's dead,' her son says quietly. 'He's been gone for nearly five years. Can you not forgive a dead man?'

The small room heaves with a collective unease. Lane slipped in during this statement and couldn't decide whether to give Emi the glass of water or to stay by the door. Emi motions for her to come forward. Lane hands Emi the glass, and everyone watches as she gulps it down. Emi doesn't stop until she has swallowed the last drop. When she sets the glass on the bedside tray, her son takes her hand.

'Just tell me. What did he do that was so unforgivable? I need to know the truth. I deserve to know it, we both deserve to know.'

He reaches for YoonHui. She stands beside him, and they look like children again. The years are erased from their faces, and Emi can only see the two loves of her life. They were the reason she survived a loveless marriage. They kept her from looking backwards. She knows she owes them the truth, but she's terrified of revealing it.

'I never told you how your grandmother died,' she says.

'Mother—' her son begins, but YoonHui hushes him.

'Go on, Mother, tell us how she died,' her daughter says, taking hold of Emi's hand.

'It was just before the Korean War began. Your father and I had recently married, but he didn't trust your grandmother. He often accused her of being red.'

'Red? You mean communist?' Lane interjects.

'Yes, a North Korean sympathiser. A rebel.'

'But Father was a simple fisherman, wasn't he?' her son interrupts. He looks as though his childhood is either falling apart or just beginning to make sense.

'A policeman first,' Emi says. 'Not a very good fisherman, second.'

Emi's daughter knows much about the history of the Korean War. It is her speciality as a professor of Korean literature. She remains silent, but Emi knows she must be running the facts of the war through her mind.

'How did our grandmother die?' her son asks, impatient as always.

'The communist rebels used to come into the villages at night, hidden by the smoke still rising from the embers of the homes burned down by policemen. They were recruiting members, the survivors whose homes were just destroyed. They also went door-to-door to gather supplies. As a policeman, your father was tasked with finding the rebels and also punishing anyone who aided them. He never trusted your grandmother; no matter what I said to convince him otherwise, he always believed your grandmother was helping them. He called her rebel and red – sometimes to her face.'

'Was she?' her son interrupts.

Emi pauses, shifting position in the uncomfortable hospital bed. Now that she has allowed herself to think about that time and those days, the memories feel so close. The pain is near, too. Visions of the airport swim beneath her hospital bed as though she is in the aeroplane and the shiny hospital floor is a thousand miles beneath her.

The runway appears as a field, newly turned with black earthen mounds dotting its landscape.

'I don't know. I was diving long hours in the sea. Your father wouldn't let your grandmother dive with me. He didn't trust her. So I worked alone, and at night I slept like a rock, exhausted. And I was young. Many things didn't make sense to me. Still more escaped my attention.

'I returned home one day, and she was gone. Your father wouldn't tell me where she was. I searched the village for any news of her. No one would tell me anything. They were too scared of your father.' Emi touches her forehead, recalling their faces as she passed them on the road.

'I remember that,' her daughter suddenly says. 'Everyone used to look at him in such a way. I didn't understand it as a child . . . but now that you say it, I do. They were all afraid of him.'

The look on her daughter's face pains Emi. So many secrets, so many lies, all hidden away in one small heart. She wishes her heart could have been larger, like her friend JinHee's; her laughter over the waves is like joy come alive.

'He turned her in, didn't he?' YoonHui says.

Her voice is so certain, as though she has known all along, but it's impossible. She wasn't even born yet.

'He never admitted it to me. Never. Not even on his deathbed,' Emi says, staring into her hands. She looks up and meets her daughter's eyes. 'But I knew, deep down, that it was his doing. I always knew.

'My marriage to your father wasn't a love match. I'm sure you noticed that. We were forced to marry because of the war. He was a policeman. He worked for the government after that.' Emi hopes her children won't ask about the day she was forced to marry their father; she fears it will hurt them too much. Her hands tremble slightly, and she cannot make them still. Her son takes them in his. The warmth gives her courage.

'I was fourteen and newly married to your father, and another war was on the verge of breaking out. Your grandmother went missing only a few months into this new life. I was distraught. Left alone in the house with this stranger who petrified me. I needed her. I was desperate to find her. Months passed, and then years with no sign of her. It was like she just vanished.'

Emi pauses, remembering the effort it took for her not to lose her mind. The Japanese took her sister away. Then the Koreans took her father. Now someone had taken her mother. Emi was suddenly alone.

'I was pregnant with you when I finally learned that she had been executed,' she says, looking at Hyoung. 'Over two years had passed without a word of her whereabouts, and then one day a friend came to the house to tell me they had killed all of the political prisoners. I rushed to the police station, desperate to find out if she was one of the dead. They wouldn't tell me, so I demanded to see the list of prisoners. The government loved their paperwork. They documented everything. Your father followed me to the station. He wouldn't let them show me the list. I threatened him, said I would kill myself and his unborn child if he didn't make them give me the list. It was the first time I revealed that I was pregnant.'

As she speaks the words, she can no longer look at her son. Her guilt is magnified. It is as though she is on trial for failing in her motherly duties. If she were in front of a jury, she would most certainly not succeed in securing their sympathy vote.

Her husband looked at Emi as though she had daggered him in the gut.

'You're pregnant?' he asked, incredulous.

The office had grown quiet and a few of the police officers left the room. Emi couldn't look him in the eyes. She stared at the desk, and it occurred to her that it was the very desk where she had signed the marriage contract to HyunMo.

'I am.'

'How long have you known?'

He looked at her tenderly, as though he was in love with her, but Emi didn't believe he could love her when he had only married her to claim her family's land. He reached for her arm, but she moved away from his touch. At night, he took advantage of his marital privileges, but during the day, he couldn't touch her against her will. That was the deal they had struck so that she would cease to fight against him and they could bear living together in their forced life.

'Just a few months. I need my mother. I can't do this without her.'

Emi beseeched him with her eyes, unable to express with words how much she needed her mother. She was sixteen years old, afraid of giving birth, afraid of mothering, but most of all, afraid of raising a child while feeling isolated in a life that was no longer her own.

'And now you're threatening our child?'

He looked betrayed, but Emi didn't care. He had betrayed her first. He had stolen her land, her innocence, and now he stood in the way of the truth. Emi lifted her chin and glared at him.

'Yes.'

HyunMo's shoulders sagged, but he said nothing more. He opened the door to the office and called in a policeman.

'Let her see the list.'

'But, sir,' the policeman stammered. His eyes nervously darted between Emi and HyunMo.

'Do it.'

Emi watched HyunMo leave the room a broken man. It was the only time she ever saw him like that. Afterwards, he closed himself off from her, making it impossible for her to hurt him. He became a father who made decisions without her consent, like sending their daughter to school. Once in a while he would reach out, to try to touch her physically or emotionally, but she always shrank from him.

She never forgave him for his part in her mother's disappearance and death. Emi searches her children's faces as she finishes the story.

'He left the police station after giving me permission to view the list, all the while knowing her name was on it because he had put her there. I didn't even have to look at it to know. But I did anyway, my eyes scanning hundreds of names until I found hers. She had been held prisoner all that time. And then one day, they executed her.'

After reading her mother's name on the list, she walked to the seashore, determined to fling herself from the highest cliff. She was alone in the world and pregnant by a new enemy. Yet, as she stood there, swaying in the strong October breeze, she couldn't do it. She realised that she loved the baby growing inside her.

'You saved my life,' she says, looking up at her son. 'If I hadn't been pregnant, I don't know how I could have survived. I had you to look forward to. You, who would be a part of me and my mother and father and even my sister. Their blood runs through your veins. I believed it then, and I see it now. I buried them in my heart that day. I had to. For you and for me. And then I went back home to your father, and I never spoke of this to anyone . . . until now.'

'Mother,' her son says quietly. His eyes are rimmed in red. In all his adult years, Emi has never seen her son look at her so tenderly. 'I never knew.'

'Of course you didn't. He was your father, and it was right for you to love him. I could never have taken that away from you.'

'But he killed your mother . . . our grandmother.' His words fall flat in the quiet that follows.

Emi knows what he must be thinking. Both of her children are running their childhoods through their heads, making sense of all the moments she did not respond to their father's affectionate advances or the times she did not laugh at his best jokes, or even sleep by his side. They often found her sitting on the front porch late at night, unable to sleep, but also never able to tell them why. It was her way of protecting them, insulating them against the terrors of the world. She never wanted her children to know suffering as she had. Keeping them in the dark was the most selfless thing she ever did. And she did it out of love.

'Yes, his actions killed your grandmother, but he was a government puppet. He did what he was told. It was wartime. People committed atrocious acts against one another. And many, many died. But that is war. People are killed. All those who survive have been wronged, one way or another.'

The Korean War was a bloodbath. Emi remembers how neighbours turned against one another – years before it even officially began in 1950 – accusing one another of spying before the other had a chance to make the same accusation. Many of her mother's old diving companions were lost. Everyone with sons lost them, everyone with daughters lost them or gained new sons they could never trust. The whole island wept with collective grief.

Emi's grief was buried beneath Jeju International Airport. At the time it was a military airfield, abandoned by the Japanese imperial air force when they left the island after the Second World War ended. More than seven hundred political dissidents were held there, including her mother, Emi learned. The prisoners were executed by firing squad, and their bodies were buried in a massive pit, one on top of the other.

No one ever mentioned what was beneath the brand-new runways when the airfield was expanded into the current international airport, but those who had lived through the massacres never forgot. That's why Emi could never fly. The idea that her aeroplane could be rolling over her mother's unmarked grave made her stomach shrivel and her mouth run dry.

At sixteen years old, Emi found herself orphaned with no family left to love, but there was hope growing within her. Her son was born the year the Korean War officially began, 1950, and then her daughter followed when it finally ended three years later. HyunMo and Emi lived together through the war and for years afterwards without ever baring their souls to one another. Only on his deathbed did he reveal his true feelings.

He was dying of cancer. His lungs and liver were riddled with tumours. He used to smoke his pipe all day long, even while waiting for the fish to swim into his nets. In the end he weighed barely ninety pounds and could hardly lift his head to gaze at his children and his only grandchild.

'Thank you for our children,' he managed to say through shallow breaths.

Emi had been wiping his forehead with a cool cloth. She paused mid-wipe and looked into his eyes, something she had not done since her daughter had refused to become a *haenyeo*. A milky cataract threatened to cover the whole of his right pupil, and the whites of his eyes were tinged yellow and streaked with angry red blood vessels. He looked much older than his years. Emi wondered how much harder his life had been compared to hers.

'I always loved you,' HyunMo whispered. He reached out for her hand, which she instinctively snatched away. He blinked, slowly, with a determination she was used to.

'In my way, I did,' he said, and lowered his hand onto his concave chest.

Emi looked down at him and wondered when he had become an old man.

'Don't hate me so much after I die,' he said, catching her off guard. He laughed at her expression of surprise, but his laughter quickly turned into a bout of wet coughs.

Emi pressed her hands gently against his chest to keep him from shuddering too violently. When the coughs subsided, he placed his palms on top of her hands and lightly gripped her wrists.

'Burn incense for my ancestors if you ever find that you can forgive me.' His red eyes searched hers as though asking for her to breathe life back into his frail body.

Looking into his eyes was like sifting through a stranger's memories. When she finally found her voice, it was harsh and filled with bitterness.

'Forgive you for what? For my mother?'

He released her wrists, his hands sliding down to his sides. He blinked his slow blink, and the seconds between his eyelids' closing and opening seemed to edge into days. A deep cough rattled his congested lungs. He spat up black blood that looked more like motor oil. Emi dutifully wiped it from his mouth.

'Forgive me ... for so much more than I can say ... for everything.'

Those were the last words he ever said to her. He hung on to the thinnest thread of life for two more weeks, his sickly body torturing him in ways she would never have wished upon her worst enemy. When he finally died, it was a relief, but Emi was surprised to find that she also felt a pang of sadness as they buried him. It could have been the tears falling from her grown children's eyes that made her feel sad, but she wasn't certain.

Even now, thinking about his wretched death, she isn't sure how she felt when he was finally gone. Looking back so intently, she feels detachment once more, her familiar dispassion for her own husband. She did what she had to at the time because her anger threatened to overwhelm her. Instead, she swallowed her emotions, until she was able to continue to exist.

Her sister once called her a dancing butterfly, full of life and laughter and free like the birds of the sky. Emi thinks back to the moment that little girl disappeared, leaving behind this husk of a woman. She sees the painful moments of her childhood and knows that the final straw was standing in the police station and seeing her mother's name on the list. They both died that day.

'Will you burn incense for your grandmother?' Emi suddenly says to her daughter.

'What?' YoonHui replies, her expression filled with worry and pain.

'I – I never did burn incense for our ancestors . . .' Emi's voice fades. She sees her mother's dead face and wonders if she ever found peace in the afterlife.

'Don't worry about such things, Mother,' Hyoung says, an undercurrent of anger in his voice. 'You just focus on getting well.' He tries to smile, but she can see the war battling in his mind.

It's too much, the task of revealing the truth of her past. The pull of the eternal sleep tugs at Emi's eyelids, bidding them to shut once and for all. She touches her forehead, pressing her fingertips into the skin until the pain brings her senses back to the living. Her time is short, but her willpower remains strong. She will not wait until her children are at peace with their father's crime or her own secrecy. She has something she needs to do.

'I want to go to the statue. I have to see it again,' she says suddenly.

'You can't leave the hospital, you're ill, it's too much of a strain on your heart,' YoonHui says, sounding more like a mother than a dutiful child. 'We can go in a few days, after you've recovered.'

'No, I must go today. Now. I need to see it now.'

'Mother, you can't. You're not well!' YoonHui is shouting, Lane is trying to calm her down, Hyoung is silent, staring at his feet.

'I will take you.' Her son's voice is a whisper, yet it cuts through his sister's high-pitched cries.

'You can't,' YoonHui shouts. 'She needs to stay in hospital so they can treat her condition. She can't go, not yet.'

She is on the verge of breaking down. Lane places her arm around YoonHui's shoulders. She comforts Emi's daughter like a mother comforting a wounded child, except the graze is not on her knee but on her heart.

No more words are spoken. Her son leaves the room to organise the use of a wheelchair, and YoonHui is silent when she realises she has no more to say. She goes to Emi's side and kisses her cheek. She reaches for Emi's hand, and they are mother and daughter again, sitting in their village home near the sea. A rush of waves crashes against the rocky coast as they wait together in peace.

'I should have followed you into the sea. It was my duty. I failed you.'

YoonHui's voice is riddled with guilt. Tears drip from her chin. Lane wipes them with her hand. The tenderness between them touches Emi deep within her heart. In her long life, she has never experienced such intimacy. Her daughter's relationship gives her a sort of reconciliation with the struggles within her own life. She thinks perhaps it was worth it, if her daughter has found someone in the world to share her life with, someone she chose for herself, and someone who loves her back.

'You followed your heart. That is all I ever wished for both of my children. I'm proud of you . . . of your choices for your own lives. I'm happy that they were yours to make. Nothing could give me more satisfaction as your mother. You have what I never dreamed of.'

Hyoung arrives with the wheelchair, and it is time to go. He commandeers the chair and wheels her out of the room towards the elevator. YoonHui and Lane follow without further complaint, but she does not see them. She can only see ahead of her, the face beckoning her to return.

Emi concentrates on that golden face, so much like her sister's. She lets herself get lost in the possibility that her sister is still alive, that the likeness it bears to her cannot be without a reason. Emi feels it in her bones that her sister is somehow linked to the statue, but she must look upon its face again to be certain.

Hana

The dog's low growl rouses the rest of the *ger*. The Mongolian man –
aav ni, 'father', another word Hana has learned – lights an oil lamp.
His wife stirs. Hana feigns sleep, watching him through her eyelashes.
The dog barks a warning. Dressing in a hurry, he nudges Altan
awake with his foot. Together they slip on their boots and duck outside with the lamp. A man shouts a greeting to them before the door
flap falls shut, again cloaking her in darkness. A gust of predawn air
slips into the *ger*, chilling Hana's skin. She pulls her blanket close
around her neck.

A bird's shrill song pierces the quiet of the *ger*. A trotting horse
approaches. Careful not to awaken Altan's mother, Hana crawls to
the door and listens. Altan's father calls out to the approaching rider,
who responds in greeting. Hana recognises the voice.

Her heart seems to stop mid-pump, draining the blood from her head. She can't breathe. Panicking, she gasps like a fish out of the sea. Morimoto has returned.

It takes too much time before her heart unclenches. She is on her knees, forehead to the carpeted floor, desperate for air. She has lost all sense of hearing or touch. It is as though she is lost in a vacuum. Then, as suddenly as the panic began, it dissipates. Very slowly, her lungs fill with oxygen, and she can breathe once again. When she has stopped trembling, she leans her ear closer to the door flap.

The men converse in Mongolian. The dog runs his tireless circles. Hana pushes the edge of the door flap over just enough to peer through a crack. Light from the oil lamp shines into the *ger*. She looks over at Altan's mother, but she is still sound asleep.

Outside, the horse is gone, and Hana assumes Altan is leading it to the pen for the night. His father stands in front of the *ger* and hands Morimoto a flask. He takes a few gulps, his exposed throat white in the lamplight. He wipes his mouth with the back of his hand and offers the flask to Altan's father, who drinks from it before returning it to his breast pocket. Morimoto unfolds a piece of paper and holds it out so Altan's father can see it. Hana can't make out what is written on it. A map, military plans? It could be anything.

Holding the oil lamp high, Altan's father hunches over the paper, studying it. Morimoto points to a few places and talks in a hushed voice, as though keeping their conversation secret. When Altan returns, Morimoto quickly folds the paper and tucks it into his trouser pocket. Altan's father straightens up and motions to the *ger*. Altan nods and heads towards the door.

Hana darts back to her sleeping space and covers herself with the blanket just before he enters. He grumbles under his breath and flops onto his sleeping pelt. He yawns, adjusts his blanket a few times, and then drifts off, already breathing heavily before his father re-enters the *ger*. Hana waits for Morimoto to follow, but he doesn't appear.

Altan's father snuffs out the oil lamp and settles down next to his wife. Soon he, too, is snoring.

Lying in the darkness, Hana prepares herself for Morimoto's sudden appearance beside her. There is nowhere to hide, so she tucks the edges of the blanket tightly beneath her, like wrapping a corpse, to keep herself safe from invading hands. He is out there, and she is certain he will not leave her be even for one night. Minutes pass into hours, and he doesn't come. Her eyelids are heavy, and no matter how much she tries to keep them open, they keep slipping closed.

Early-morning birds chirp above them and fly high up in a bright sky in her dreams. Altan's father's snores seem louder than usual, as though he is lying close beside her. She is drifting further and further away from the *ger*, swaddled in the soft hands of sleep, but the hands aren't so soft anymore. They tug at her, pulling her from the longing arms of slumber. She tosses in her sleep, trying to push them away, when aggressive fingers force her legs apart. Her eyes open, and Morimoto is next to her.

'Did they violate you?' he whispers, his stubble scratching her cheek.

The shock of him renders her mute. She twists away from him, but he holds her down.

'Did they put their hands on you?' he asks, his voice hoarse.

She manages to shake her head.

'You're sure?' he asks, still touching her.

In the midst of this sudden attack, anger rises into her throat. He, who has violated her beyond imagination, accuses the only kind men she has met since her abduction. Her body tenses, and she finds her voice.

'They did not rape me. These are noble men, not like soldiers . . . not like you.'

His fingers halt their aggressive exploration. He removes his hand.

Even in the darkness she knows he is pulsating with anger. She hurriedly closes her *del* and ties the silk sash into a double knot. Without a word, Morimoto rises and exits the *ger*. She cannot fall asleep. Instead she listens to the sounds of the family sleeping next to her and imagines what it could have been like had he never returned.

》-《

In the morning, Altan's father is the first to rise. He nudges Altan awake and they leave together. Hana watches them go and sees Altan turn to look back at her. She quickly shuts her eyes, and then he is gone. Altan's mother is still asleep. Hana doesn't know what Morimoto has planned, whether he intends to take her away today or to stay for a few days more. With her eyes closed, his face looms in her mind like an evil spirit, menacing and deadly. She abruptly sits up, pushing the image away. She decides to carry out her chores as though nothing has changed.

After lighting the fire in the stove, she stows her bedding, along with Altan's and his father's into the trunks. Altan's mother slowly awakens and sits up. She smiles at Hana. The warm greeting, so simply given, is too much for Hana to lose. The impulse to fall into a sobbing heap in front of her is strong, but she swallows it down. Instead, Hana bows deeply, performing *sebae*, a Korean ritual bow, honouring her for her kindness. A sound of surprise escapes the woman. Three times, Hana bows, and when she stands, Altan's mother nods her head in thanks. Then Hana turns to exit the *ger* and commences her morning chores, as though Morimoto has not returned to take her away.

She fills the metal buckets with ox milk. She carries both buckets at once and pours the fresh milk into the cistern. She returns to the pen to feed apple slices to the ponies. She does all this under the watchful eye of Morimoto, Altan's father, Altan, Ganbaatar, the man with no name and Altan's mother. Even the dog seems to follow her every move. It is as though everyone knows that her time here is nearly over.

Altan doesn't visit her in the pen as he has done the last few days. Instead he keeps his distance. He binds brushwood with twine as Ganbaatar plays with his eagle. She catches Altan staring at her at times, but he quickly looks away when she does. Morimoto sits on a stool taking apart and cleaning his pistol. He methodically wipes down each piece and lays them in straight rows on a small rag.

Ganbaatar releases the eagle and it flies into the sky with a great cry. Everyone watches it soar high above them. Morimoto breaks the awed silence.

'Magnificent creature, isn't it?'

He is speaking in Japanese. Hana knows he is speaking to her, watching her, waiting for her to acknowledge him, but she doesn't take her eyes off the eagle.

'He raised it from a mere eaglet,' he continues, as though her silence doesn't bother him. 'And now it is his eyes and his arrow, hunting for him in the dead of winter so they don't starve.'

Circling above them in growing, concentric rings, it could fly away never to return, but it doesn't. It seems as though an invisible rope chains it to Ganbaatar in an ever-increasing radius.

'He sleeps with it in his tent, feeds it hand to mouth, cradles it for comfort; it is a member of the family, prized above even a wife or child.'

Hana looks at Morimoto then. The idea that an animal could be more valuable than a wife or child surprises her. She wonders if he is telling the truth or trying to make the Mongolians out as backward barbarians. But then she recalls their relationship with the ponies, the way the animals follow them like ducklings follow their mother duck, the care and gentle handling Ganbaatar shows them each morning. Perhaps what he says is true.

Ganbaatar calls to the eagle, and it lets out a piercing cry before landing obediently on his arm. He strokes its breast and carries it into his *ger*.

The others nod to Morimoto and head down to the poppy field; Hana quickly sets out to follow them so she won't be left alone with him. She rounds the *ger*, but Morimoto steps in front of her, blocking her path.

'Where are you going?' He smells of grease and metal.

'I have chores to do in the field.' She takes a few steps away from him and looks past his shoulder at the back of Altan's head, wishing he would stop and wait for her.

'Your chores have come to an end,' he says, and ushers her towards the *ger*'s door.

She knows his intentions, that he has thought only of her the whole time he was travelling back here. If she does as he wishes, he will be quick. He will satisfy himself, and then she can go down to the field as though nothing has happened.

She catches herself on the door frame. Her hand clenches it, her nails digging into the wood. He lifts the flap and tries to guide her inside. Her hand clings to the door frame, and she braces against him. He looks down at her.

'Have you not missed me?'

He smiles, and it seems genuine. It is as though he is a different man, one who has forgotten he has not been a friend to her. She cannot comprehend his expression.

'Well?' he asks, clearly waiting for her to respond.

She licks her lips, thinking how best to answer. Nothing comes to her mind. She stares back at him in dumb silence. A cloud seems to cross his face. His expression darkens. He grabs her arm and yanks her into the *ger* after him.

Morimoto pushes her down onto the bare floor and unties the silk sash Altan gave her. She lies on the ground beneath him in the lifeless state that has become her refuge. Does giving in to him without a fight make her a prostitute? He kisses her neck. If she does not fight, is she then giving him her permission?

Hana's instincts tell her to lie still so he will not hurt her – or kill her. His hands could wring her neck with hardly any effort, and then she would never see her mother again. Altan's face appears in her mind. She would never see Altan again. The sadness she feels surprises her.

Morimoto kisses her mouth, but she doesn't kiss him back.

'I thought you would be more eager to see me,' he says.

Hana closes her eyes, blocking him out of her sight. She's tired of his delusions.

'I brought you something,' he whispers into her ear. 'I'll give it to you after.'

He reinstates his possession of her body, paying attention to every inch of her with the same detail he gave to the cleaning of his pistol. Hana keeps her eyes shut the entire time. This time, she reaches a new record, holding her breath for one hundred and sixty-three seconds, and nearly faints.

>>-<<

He smokes a pipe as she dresses herself, then focuses in on the sash as she ties it around her waist. She doesn't double-knot it as she wants to so as not to draw too much attention to it, but he notices anyway.

'Where did you get that?'

'This? The Mongolian woman gave it to me because I had no clothes. She burned the rags you brought me in.' She turns away quickly and slips her boots on one by one.

He chews on the end of the pipe, not rising to the bait.

'No, not the coat. The pretty belt. What is it, silk?' he asks, and motions for her to come to him.

Hana hesitates before obeying. He lifts an eyebrow, questioning her pause. She looks down at the ground and pads towards him. She kneels in front of him. Morimoto rubs the silken material between his thumb and forefinger as though assessing its worth. He balances the pipe on his knee and begins to untie the sash. She keeps the *del* closed with both hands, afraid he means to undress her a second time. Instead, he holds the sash out in front of him, taking in the full length of the delicate design.

'This is an ornament of honour,' he says, still gazing at the intricate needlework. 'Who gave you this?'

'Is it really so important?'

'Yes. It's a gift. A valuable one.'

'Perhaps they are more generous than you knew.'

He lowers the sash and inspects her expression. His hawkish gaze unnerves her. She turns away. 'Women don't wear sashes. For ease of access,' he finally says with a smirk. 'So whoever gave you this did so with a purpose.'

'The Mongolian woman wears one.'

'Ah, but hers is a belt to hang her work tools from. This, well, this is more, shall we say, decorative?'

His eyes accuse her of lying, yet he says nothing. The silence between them unsettles her. He laughs and tosses the sash at her face. It slips to the floor. She leaves it there. He lifts his pipe to his lips, takes a puff, and blows a stream of smoke into her face. Her eyes water. She coughs.

'So, someone has claimed you, have they? Which one, the young man, Ganbaatar's friend? The little boy? Who wants you as his own?'

Afraid for Altan, she thinks quickly. Perhaps if she can anger him, Morimoto will direct his hate towards her instead of him.

'None here are like you. You are the only one who claims me as your own even though you know I would do anything to escape from your grasp.'

He sits up straight and looks as though he might strike her. She stiffens, prepared for the blow. He seems to change his tactic and smiles, like a snake preparing to strike.

'We can stay here all day if you want. Or you can go ahead and tell me which one gave this to you.'

She doesn't look at him, instead staring at the brilliant blues and yellows adorning the sash. Her heart already aches with a magnified sense of homesickness.

'We leave in the morning,' he says, trying to get a reaction from her.

When she still says nothing, he adds, 'I guess he'll have one last night to dream about a future with you that will never come to pass.'

The truth behind his words crushes her. Hana can't help sagging inwardly. Outwardly, she holds her shoulders stiff, refusing to let him see how much he has hurt her.

'Why must I go with you?'

If he is taken aback by her sudden question, he doesn't let it show. He puffs on the pipe and waves one hand dismissively.

'I need you. Only you can take away my misery.'

His misery? In the brothel, he forced her to listen to his complaints on many sleepless nights when all she wanted was to rest from the torture of her day. Morimoto would appear in her room like a phantom, awaken her from her slumber, and demand she service him, too. Afterwards, she would have to remain awake to listen to his words. She wants to spit in his face, but Morimoto touches her cheek. He will tell her his story, and once again, she will have to listen.

'The Americans killed my family,' he says, and his expression looks like he is far away. 'My wife, my young son. I sent them to live with my brother in California before the war broke out, so they would be safe.'

His demeanour changes. He seems subdued.

'How did they die?' Hana asks before she can stop herself. He has never mentioned his family.

He takes in a deep breath and exhales it so slowly that she wonders if she's angered him, but then he continues.

'Japan bombed America. Did you know that? Sunk their battleships in their naval base in Hawaii. It was a defensive strike, to keep them out of the war, but it didn't work. It made them angry, you see, so they joined the war instead. And they declared all Japanese subjects in America traitors and spies. They put them into detention camps, forcing them to leave their homes and belongings behind to live in squalor in these camps. My son starved to death, and then my wife, stricken with grief – abandoned by me so I could fight in the emperor's war – hanged herself.'

Hana takes in his words, trying to imagine the sorrow he must have felt upon hearing of their deaths. Morimoto sent his family to America for safety, but instead they suffered and died. She looks upon his face in the dim light of the *ger*, but as hard as she tries, she still cannot see a man worthy of pity. There is no humanity left in him. His humanity died with them.

'I knew when I saw you in the sea that the gods had gifted you to me. I am certain that they meant you for me and that one day you will bear me another son.'

He will never let her go. The future he has planned sickens her. She could let him take her away, and then when he least suspects it, she could try to escape. Images of that future play through her mind, but in the end, she sees herself trying to run away while carrying a baby in her arms. His baby. She would rather die than give birth to his child. But then another thought enters her mind. She would rather kill him, or die trying.

He lowers his pipe and removes a pouch from his coat pocket. As she watches him open it, she half hopes inside will be her photograph. It is a senseless thought, but it makes her appear keen to see what he has brought her.

'These are for you,' he says, pulling out two gold bracelets like a proud suitor.

Disappointed, Hana stares at the trinkets. Morimoto reaches for her arm and slides the bracelets onto her slim wrist. They clink together, and the sound reminds Hana of chains.

'Do you like them?' he asks.

Hana knows how to please him, and that by simply nodding her head, he will be satisfied. It takes all her effort to do it.

》-《

In the poppy field, Hana keeps her distance from Altan and the others. Part of her fears they may smell sex on her or that they may sense it if they get too close. Would they turn into animals, too, if they knew what she really was to Morimoto? The knife, which felt light yesterday, feels heavy and unwieldy in her hand as she slits the bulbs. Morimoto is busy talking to Altan's father but intermittently looks in her direction.

Altan passes her in the field. His shadow falls across her face, but she doesn't acknowledge him. Instead, she moves away, heading in the opposite direction. Now that she has started walking, it is as though she cannot stop. Her feet have a mind of their own, and soon she is out of the poppy field, heading away from them and towards the mountains. The vast rocky mass seems to beckon her, and she is unable to ignore its call. Morimoto follows her, but she doesn't stop.

He's riding on one of the ponies and cuts her off. She tries to walk around him, but he cuts her off again. It is a game of cat and mouse, but she refuses to be the mouse. She doesn't run. She walks patiently around the pony time and again. He tires of the game and slides off the animal. It heads back towards its people in the poppy field. He grabs her by the elbow and drags her backwards. She fights against him. He hugs her to him. She is like a fish, wriggling in vain against a fisherman's assured grasp. For if the fisherman is hungrier than the fish, it does not stand a chance, and Morimoto is so hungry, she cannot escape.

'Don't make me bind your hands and legs in front of them. I will if I have to, but I don't want to.' His breath is ragged in her ear.

'I don't care. Let them see what I am to you. Nothing but an animal.'

'Not an animal. My wife. Don't you understand yet?' He tries to kiss her, but she shoves him away.

'You had a wife. She died. She was fortunate.'

He slaps her, and she falls to the ground. Blood trickles into her mouth from her nose. She licks her lip. The taste reminds her that she has become strong again.

'I will never be your wife,' she says, and removes the bracelets from her arm. She throws them at his face.

'Look around you,' he says, spreading his arms wide. 'You have no choice.'

He laughs at her, turning his face up to the sky. Then he shakes his head as though she is the pitiful one. He picks the bracelets up from the ground before offering a hand to help her to her feet. She spits on it. He pauses, then straightens himself to his full height. Without taking his eyes from hers, he licks her spit off his hand. Then he walks back towards the poppy field.

Hana doesn't immediately follow him. She watches for a long time, thinking about what will happen next. He will take her away in the morning, and then their life together as man and wife will begin. It will be like living in a cage. Altan stands still among the poppy stalks, and she cannot see his expression as Morimoto passes him, continuing onwards to the camp. Altan does not move until she finally heads back to the field. His questioning expression greets her, but she does not answer him. He is too young, too innocent, to understand what is going on. He has not lived as much as she has in these last months. She keeps her head down as she slashes the poppy bulbs, one by one.

〉〈

Tonight, there is no singing. Altan's father and Morimoto go over plans, while Altan sulks in the corner. Hana's mind wanders through the memories of the last few days. They drop like leaves into a swirling puddle, floating round and round in an endless spiral. She is the vortex, pulling them inwards, refusing to let them go. If she never saw her home again, she could be happy in this place, and this realisation frightens her. She would forsake her mother, her father, even her sister to never see Morimoto, or any other soldier like him, again.

When they all lie down to sleep, she is surprised when Morimoto is invited to join them in the family *ger*. He sleeps near Altan on the other side of the stove. His presence stifles her. He has invaded the serenity she felt among these people. She tries to recall the first moment she felt at peace, but her mind goes blank, as though the memories have left her. Panicking, she opens her eyes and is searching through the darkened *ger* when a single thought blooms in her mind: *I know where Altan's mother keeps the harvesting knives.*

Hana can picture the one she wants. The short one with the bone handle has the sharpest blade – the one Altan uses. He lent it to her their first morning in the poppy field. It slides through the bulbs' flesh without resistance, a clean cut, quick and precise. It is small in her hand, easy to manoeuvre. She could get close to Morimoto, hide the knife in her long sleeves, and kneel beside him without his suspecting her motive until it is too late. It would be as simple as cutting a mollusc from the reef. One clean slice, deep and controlled, and she would be free.

Hana imagines holding the blade against his throat. She watches the blade slide from left to right, imagining the pressure needed in order to cut through flesh. She repeats the image again and again until her hand is moving through the air in quick, assured strokes, practising.

Hana presses against the soft fur beneath her and rises to her knees. She pauses, waiting for the sleeping bodies to sense her movement. The two men are snoring, and in between their pauses, Hana can just make out Altan's mother's steady breaths. Altan is huddled against the wall, unmoving. Rising to her feet, she surveys the curved room. The sounds of sleeping bodies reassure her. Her own breaths are quiet and deep, steadying the pitter-pattering of her heart, as she tiptoes around Altan's mother and carefully navigates through the sleeping bodies.

The knives are tucked away in a wooden box beside the trunk of food. She knows the hinges squeak when it is opened so she spits on them, hoping her saliva will lubricate the metal. The lid lifts with barely a sound. Inside, the small blade with the bone-white handle glows as though it knows it has been chosen for this deadly task. She lifts it out of the box, and a current seems to flow from the smooth bone into her hand, travelling up her arm and into her chest, fortifying her resolve with a new-found sense of power.

Closing the box, she grips the knife and mimics what she intends to do. It feels good in her hand, the slicing motion a natural movement. She must step around Altan's father's head to reach Morimoto. Carefully, she edges her toes around his fur pelt, keeping her movements slow so that the breeze of her passing will not blow the pelt's hair against his cheek. Step by step, she inches past him, her eyes watchful for any movement within the *ger*. Breaths disguise her footsteps. Nearing Morimoto, she forces herself to remain calm. One step, two steps. Three more, and she is there, towering over him. She listens to his sleep rhythms; his familiarity infuriates her. She grips the knife even tighter. She sees her hand slide past his neck, both graceful and powerful at once, and her resolve is set.

She takes in a deep breath before kneeling next to him. She has lain beside him on too many occasions. She knows when he is dreaming, when she can leave his side and clean herself up or relieve herself. She watches him, his face lit only by the red embers dying in the stove. His eyelids flutter. Hate fills her with each flickering movement. It is time.

The knife assumes a life of its own and hovers above his exposed throat. Her hand tingles as though it has fallen asleep. *One cut. That's all it will take. Do it now.* Her father's voice surprises her. It's an echo from her childhood. The first time she gutted a fish. It was wet and slimy and flopping side to side in her hand, trying to swim away. This will be like that. And like the dying ox. Terrible but necessary. So she can live, free of him.

Hana lightly presses the blade against Morimoto's neck. Holding her breath, she calculates the amount of pressure needed to cut through his windpipe so he can't scream. She exhales fully, tenses her stomach and arm, before her hand begins to slide from left to right – just as she saw in her mind. But without warning, her arms are lifted high into the air. Her body is jerked backwards. The sudden force disorientates her, and she falls to the ground. It takes a moment for her to realise she has landed on someone. They struggle for the knife. His hands are powerful and assured. She twists round to see his face. It is Altan.

He squeezes a pressure point in her wrist. She drops the blade. He snatches it up before she can recover, tucking it into his belt. They are both breathless. She wants to shout at him but cannot risk waking the others. Altan says nothing, but his expression is enough. He is incredulous, or perhaps he is disgusted.

She glares back at him, even though in her mind she wants to explain. But he would never understand. There are no common words that can travel between them.

Altan rises and quickly exits the *ger*. She does not follow him. There are other knives in the box. Hana could get a new one and finish the job, but the look on Altan's face stops her. He would never forgive her. She turns back to Morimoto, the man who has reduced her to a would-be killer. If she goes through with her plan, she will be no better than him and the other men who tortured her. The thought is difficult to swallow. Is it worth it, to be better than them?

Staring at Morimoto, she grinds her teeth in frustration, anger and hate. She clenches her hands into balled fists, relishing the sting of her fingernails biting into her flesh. Pain; she has gained an intimate relationship with this sense. It tears her away from her haze of hatred. Altan's face rises in her mind like an ill-fated moon. His expression stains her memory. The innocence in his eyes lost. What has she become?

Morimoto continues sleeping. She watches herself in her mind slitting his throat one last time, before she crawls back to her pelt and lies down. Her body slumps against the soft padding as though she has trekked a thousand miles. She could sleep an entire day and still not recover from the effort it takes to make herself lie back down knowing that in the morning Morimoto will take her away.

She will never see Altan again, and the last image she will have of him is the horror on his face when she looked into his eyes. She imagines what he must have seen, watching her prowl through the darkness, preparing to murder a man in his sleep. He must think her the lowest of creatures. He must despise her. She closes her eyes and hopes she won't see him in the morning, that he will be so disgusted by her that he will wait until she has gone before returning to the *ger*. She closes her eyes even tighter and tries to convince herself she doesn't care.

》《

Later in the night, Hana is awakened. She fears it is Morimoto. She thrashes against the hand on her arm, but a young voice hushes her. Altan holds his finger over his lips and urges her to follow him. He is dressed and a leather satchel hangs on one shoulder. She sits up. Without looking at her, he hands her the suede boots his mother has given her to wear. She puts them on, and then he leads her out of the *ger*.

Outside, Ganbaatar stands next to the door, and Hana is taken aback. He puts one finger to his lips, just as Altan did, and she pauses, trying to understand what they are up to. Altan is still holding her hand, pulling her away from the *ger*. Ganbaatar follows them, and as they head towards the smaller *ger* set behind the pen, Hana slowly realises she may not be safe with them.

She pulls away from Altan, but Ganbaatar is behind her, holding her by both shoulders and pushing her forward. She struggles against him, but he doesn't hurt her. Instead, he whispers something softly into her ear. She doesn't understand him but knows she cannot wait to find out what he intends. She strikes her head against his. The blow jars her vision. He releases her and she turns to run, but Altan grabs the silk sash tied around her waist. She tries to yank it from him, but he holds on, slowly shaking his head. His expression isn't angry but worried. He keeps glancing back at the *ger*.

'Hana,' he says, trying to calm her, before he releases the sash.

She stops struggling, waiting for him to explain what he wants. He points to the smaller *ger*. Two ponies are tethered to the post, both animals fully saddled as though prepared for a journey. Lifting his satchel, he opens it so she can see inside. It is packed with food rations, water flasks and other travelling items. Slowly, his intentions dawn on her. He means to help her get away.

Rubbing the side of his face, Ganbaatar smiles at her and points to her head. She smiles back at him and rubs her head as well, acknowledging the pain. The three of them walk in silence to the ponies. Ganbaatar helps her onto the white one with black feet. Altan removes the blade from his belt and hands it to her. He says something to Ganbaatar, who nods and pats him on the shoulder, then unties the ponies from the post. Altan leaps behind Hana on the pony, surprising her. She looks at him over her shoulder, but he merely nudges the pony, and they depart together. The spare pony follows them dutifully, as though he also knows the way.

When they are beyond the poppy field, Altan urges the pony into a gallop. Soon it is flying at top speed, navigating through the dark as though it has travelled the route time and again. Altan kicks it in the sides when it slows from the change in terrain. His anxiety is contagious, and soon Hana is urging the pony onwards with sheer will. They travel up a rocky incline, and she suspects they must be climbing up the base of the mountain behind their encampment.

The stars glisten above them. She listens for approaching hooves, and the image of Morimoto in pursuit makes the suspense even harder to endure. A few times she thinks she does hear his black horse galloping behind them, but it is only in her imagination.

When the sun decides to awaken the land, her eyes can finally see the path the pony has found. A skinny goat trail winds through the rocky outcrops of the mountain pass. They are only a quarter of the way up the mountain, so she cannot see much beyond the immediate trees and boulders surrounding them. The need to know if they are being pursued strangles her stomach until it twists into a knot.

Altan's arms encircle her as he holds on to the reins, giving her a small amount of comfort. She doesn't know where he plans to take her or how long he will remain with her, but she is glad he has come. The expression of disgust on his face when he stopped her from killing Morimoto hangs in her mind. She wants to shrink into herself from shame and guilt. Her only consolation is the fact that Altan doesn't know what she has experienced because of Morimoto. He also has no idea what the future held for her. Perhaps if she could have communicated these things to him, then he would have let her hand slide the knife across Morimoto's throat, and they wouldn't have to run away. All these thoughts pass through her mind over and over as the sun rises and the pony tires, until they finally come to a stop.

Altan helps her dismount before removing the saddle and placing it onto the reserve pony. He gives the exhausted pony a handful of water from one of his pouches before mounting Hana onto the fresh pony and climbing on behind her. They continue their speedy escape ever upwards through the craggy mountain pass, ignoring the aches of riding at such speed over that distance. Part of the anxiety pitted in her stomach is the small chance that they might get away, that Morimoto might have slept through the night and is only now waking to find that she has gone, and that with Altan's help, she may truly be free. The thought is too wonderful to believe, so she tempers her emotions, pressing the hope down into herself, and focuses only on the rising sun, the pony's sure-footed steps, and Altan's arms encircling her as he guides the pony through the misty dawn.

The narrow path crests, and then the pony's nose leads them down the other side of the mountain pass. It is easier going down than it was to climb, and the pony is nearly at a full gallop. It dodges obstacles along the path with deft agility, and it is all Hana can do to hang on.

Altan seems to sense she is having difficulty and leans his chest against her back. They move as one down the mountain; rolling prairie spreads beneath them like a green ocean. She could live in this land, and the moment she thinks it, she hears a rock tumble behind them.

At first she thinks it must be the other pony trailing after them, but when she looks over her shoulder to be certain, she loses her breath. It's as though a vice has clamped down upon her lungs. Morimoto's black horse is speeding down the path behind them. The lashing of the riding crop snaps through the thick air. Altan hears it, too, and he kicks the pony into full speed. The sturdy little horse obeys and soon they are bounding across the prairie.

They are travelling too fast for her to look behind them, but the black horse's progress can be gauged by the slap of the crop against its flesh. It is closing in. The pony is overburdened with two passengers. At a full sprint across the flat plain, it is still too slow to outrun Morimoto's steed.

Altan steals a glance over his shoulder and shouts what must be a curse. He kicks the pony again and again, urging it to go faster, but it cannot give him what he wants. Without warning, Altan is knocked backwards, off the pony. Hana glances behind her and sees him in a heap on the ground. Morimoto has lassoed him like a prize pony. His horse halts beside Altan. The pony is still galloping at full speed, and Hana takes the reins. She urges it onwards, desperate to get away, but she can't stop herself from looking back once more. Morimoto is on the ground, beating Altan with his fists. He will surely kill the boy.

Hana cannot leave him behind. She cries out with rage and sorrow and regret. The sound echoes across the steppe, and the pony rears up in a sudden halt. She guides it in a U-turn, heading back the way she came, back to Altan, and to captivity, or perhaps her death.

Morimoto is on top of Altan, his arms animated in powerful strikes against the form lying still beneath him. The pony is galloping back towards them, but Hana fears it will not arrive in time to stop the beating before it's too late. The sounds of Morimoto's fist against Altan's face reach her, even beneath the pony's thundering hooves. As she nears them, she remembers the knife tucked into the sash tied around her waist. She runs her hand over it to check it is still there before the pony skids to a halt, and she slips down on quivering legs.

Upon her arrival, Morimoto climbs off Altan and forces him onto his knees. His fists stained with Altan's blood, Morimoto turns to face Hana, one hand resting on the hilt of the sword hanging from his belt. She touches the knife tucked into her sash. The slick bone handle reassures her as she prepares to sacrifice herself.

Altan's face swells before Hana's eyes, his right eye closing. He's shouting at Morimoto with words that sound like bullet strikes, but they miss their target. Morimoto's attention is solely on Hana as she approaches the pair. His eyes shine at her, black and glittering, reflecting the noon sun. She remembers the day he first stole her away, standing on the black rocks that hid her sister from his view. She went to him voluntarily on that day, too. It seems it is her fate to surrender to him.

For a moment, she imagines herself turning back to the pony, leaping onto it, and flying away in a cloud of dust. It thrills her senses to imagine the possibility. Even as she enjoys the image, she knows it will never come to pass. Her life would be worthless if she let Altan die. He is still shouting, words that sound like curses, boyish threats against the power of a trained soldier. Morimoto's hand sits lightly on the hilt of his sword. When she is a few steps away, Altan gets to his feet, prompting Morimoto to unsheathe his blade.

'Stop,' Hana says, her voice soft yet firm.

Altan holds one hand out to her, as though to warn her away. She shakes her head slowly.

'Don't hurt him,' she says.

'Why shouldn't I?'

Morimoto's expression is as dark as his eyes. In it, she sees he wants to murder Altan. One quick motion and Altan's head would roll off his neck, never to see another Mongolian blue sky or to smile in that innocent way that makes the sun seem brighter.

'Because I came back. I'm here.'

'Maybe I'm going to kill you both.'

A grin spreads across his face, reminding her of the villain's mask in a *talchum* folk dance. He is an evil god who has come back to punish her for sins from another life.

'Kill me if you must, but he is just a boy. He is blameless.'

Morimoto seems to weigh his choices but never takes his eyes off her. Hana begins to fear for both their lives. She nears Altan and touches his battered face.

'I'm so sorry,' she says, knowing he cannot understand her.

Altan pulls her away from Morimoto, pushing her back towards the pony. She resists him, her feet rooted to the earth. His tears mingle with the blood dripping from his mouth. He tries with all his might to get her back onto the pony, shouting at her all the while, but she is immovable. He slips and falls on the dry grass. He grabs hold of one of her legs and pulls her towards the pony. Their struggle is a pantomime on an empty stage, and their one audience member is grinning with wicked pleasure. It's a tragedy acted in real time, and Hana must endure it for Altan's sake. He is kneeling now, his forehead resting against her thigh. He's mumbling through sobs, words only Morimoto can decipher. She stares at her captor, bold and unmoving, and when he looks away, she finally allows herself to attend to Altan.

She bends towards him and gently lifts his face up to meet hers. She caresses his cheek and leans down, tenderly kissing his forehead. She takes his hands in hers and helps him to his feet. Altan pleads with her, but she shakes her head. It takes every ounce of her strength to force herself to smile at him.

'I'll be all right,' she says softly. 'Go home, Altan.'

He says something to her, clutching her hands in both of his. He peers over her shoulder and shouts at Morimoto. She turns his face back to her and looks into his eyes.

'Go home, Altan,' she repeats, more forcefully this time.

She urges him to mount the pony. He resists at first, but she insists, pushing him towards the animal until he has no choice but to take hold of the saddle and pull himself up. He looks down at her.

'Goodbye, Altan,' she says, and bows.

'Hana,' he says, his voice cracking.

She shakes her head. She points towards the way they came from, back over the mountain and back to the safety of his family. He stares at Morimoto, and for a moment, she fears he is going to charge at him. She steps slightly in front of the pony so that he would have to go around her in order to do so. He seems to think better of it and looks at her one last time. Then he turns the pony round and kicks it hard. The pony jerks into a gallop and speeds across the prairie, leaving her behind.

Hana watches him as though his life depends on it. Her eyes strain as he disappears into the shadow of the mountain. Even after he is gone, she searches for a speck of him in the distance against the vast rock. When she can no longer decipher the difference between him and the mountain she tightens her grip on the knife in her sash.

Morimoto's footsteps crunch on the brittle grass as he nears her, but she doesn't turn to face him. The after-image of Altan galloping away on the pony burns into her mind. Her shoulders sag, and her previous defiant stance melts. She stares at the ground, waiting for Morimoto to approach. He stops behind her. She grips the knife and turns to face him.

'You've disgraced me. Running away with that boy. And now you've ruined everything! I can never trust you again. Can't you see that?'

His face seethes with fury. He reaches for her wrist, but she is too quick. She unsheathes the knife and raises it in the air before driving it directly at his heart. Morimoto catches her by the arm. Hana struggles with all her might, pushing the blade towards his chest. As he presses against her, his face is incredulous, but he quickly regains his composure and twists her wrist. She drops the knife in the grass before he can snap her arm in two. He starts to say something, but Hana doesn't pause; she knees him in the groin before wriggling out of his grasp.

He doubles over and she backs away from him. Hana knows she cannot outrun his horse, that it is futile to try, but her legs don't seem to care about reality. She turns and starts running. She retraces Altan's steps, back towards the mountain, even though her rational mind knows she won't make it.

Morimoto doesn't chase her on the horse. He runs after her, and she is no match for his speed and physical strength. His fingers thread through her hair and yank her backwards off her feet. The ground meets her like a sack of rocks, knocking the air from her lungs. Dazed, she cries out when he drags her back to the horse by her hair. Her hands cling to his wrist, but it doesn't relieve the pain in her scalp. Her feet kick at the ground, scrabbling to keep up with his pace. He stops suddenly and releases her. She falls to the ground, cradling her face. He kicks her in the stomach.

'I should kill you.'

She's a tight ball on the ground, and he kicks her again, this time in her shins. He grabs her forearms and wrenches them away from her face. She kicks at him, but he overpowers her. He sits on her pelvis and presses her arms against the ground on either side of her face. She struggles like a rabid animal caught in a trap.

'Stop it,' he shouts, and quickly lifts her arms before slamming them back to the earth, banging her head against the ground. Stars explode in her open eyes. The sky above her swirls as though she is falling. The pressure of his weight on top of her feels like she is drowning in heavy air. It takes too much effort to breathe.

'Why do you keep running away from me? After everything I've told you, after everything I've planned for us?'

His head droops, resting beside hers. The stubble on his cheek scratches her temple. Lying together, they could be lovers picnicking in a grassland park. The horse and the spare pony nibbling grass together nearby are picturesque. It could be home. The comfort of the *ger* pulls at her senses. The wind rushes through her hair. The air smells of warm earth. There was kindness in this place that reminded her of home. She closes her eyes and recalls her sister's smiling face.

'I had a peaceful life. You took me from it. I will never forget that,' she says.

His body stiffens. She feels the tension along the length of him pressed against her. She looks up at him, preparing herself for another attack. She cannot read his face. His expression is empty.

'I no longer care,' he says.

Morimoto pushes off the ground and kneels next to her. Hana crouches, too, afraid of what he will do next. He gazes past her across the steppe, shielding his eyes as though focusing on something in the distance, and then suddenly he is on his feet. When Morimoto looks back at her, he appears panicked. He glances between Hana and the horizon as though deciding something, and then whistles to his horse. It trots towards him. As Morimoto mounts it, Hana wonders if he has decided to trample her to death.

It would be a fitting end, to die in this place after a brief encounter with kindness. She remains motionless; the wind rushes across her body. Her tangled hair flies into her face. The horse screeches above her, and then it gallops away. She stares in disbelief as Morimoto rides back towards the mountain. The sound of the horse's hooves grows faint and disappears into the wind.

He has left her behind. The ground seems to sway beneath her as she realises she is free. Her heartbeat pounds in the back of her head where he smacked it against the ground. She takes a few deep breaths and kneels on the soft grassy earth. He is gone. She can't believe that he truly is gone. That he has given up his delusion and has finally let her go. She is free. The thought makes her smile, even after everything she has just endured, and it feels good on her face.

The second pony is still nearby, eating its fill of grass. They know their way home, these Mongolian ponies. This one will take her back to the *ger*, back to the family and Altan. His face fills her mind. She cannot hear the trucks rumbling across the steppe towards her.

She stands and quickly mounts the pony, nudging it gently with her foot, but it does not move. Instead it turns its head to look behind them, and she follows its gaze. A convoy of troops is heading in their direction, and suddenly she understands. Morimoto did not leave her behind. He did not decide to free her. Less than a kilometre away are three heavy trucks, a tank and a squadron of mounted soldiers. Waving from the back of the tank is a flag, blood red, with a yellow star and sickle in one corner. A Soviet patrol convoy. Like a coward, Morimoto fled, leaving her to an unknown fate.

Hana shouts into the pony's ear, frantically kicks it in the sides, until it moves, slowly at first, and then finally galloping. She looks over her shoulder. Four horsemen leave the neat convoy and start after her. Their horses are large and swift. They will catch her. Ahead of her, far off towards the horizon, she sees a tiny speck, dark against the light-coloured sky. Morimoto is racing the heart out of his horse.

Her pony slows, but she doesn't let it stop. She kicks its sides, screams into its ear, and cries against its neck, pleading for it to keep running, to not give up. Horses' hooves beating the earth like deepest thunder rush towards her and overcome her small pony. But they fly past her without slowing. They continue at top speed, darting across the grassland as though she is invisible, but there are only three soldiers racing away from her.

The fourth horseman appears beside her, and a sheen of sweat covers his tawny horse. White foam lines its lips. The Soviet soldier takes the reins from her hands, easing her pony into a trot. The two creatures heave for breath, while Hana looks up into the strange soldier's face. He has large brown eyes, fair hair and a hooked nose. He doesn't speak to her. Instead, he points to his pistol, still sheathed in his belt. He wags his finger at her and smiles. Then he leads her pony in a tight U-turn, towards the convoy.

Hana glances over her shoulder at the horizon. The three dark spots close in on the fourth. He won't get away. Their horses are too swift. Morimoto will be taken prisoner, too. There is nothing new they can do to her, besides kill her, and that thought matters little in this moment. Instead, she thinks of Morimoto. Everything they do to him upon his capture will be new to him. The pain, the torture, the humiliation – Morimoto will endure it all for the first time. The thought tastes sweet in her mouth, like a ripe plucked apricot, warm with sunshine.

》-《

The Soviet soldier leads Hana to the last truck in the convoy. Piled practically on top of one another are prisoners. Most of them are Chinese, with their padded coats and high-necked collars, but Hana notices a pair of Korean girls sitting next to each other, clasping hands. They don't look at her as she approaches the tailgate, but she knows they have seen her. Two armed Soviets sit in the back with the prisoners. Careful not to step on anyone, she makes her way through the other prisoners to sit as far away from the two soldiers as she can.

One of the Korean girls moves over, leaving a space next to her, and Hana squeezes between them. Neither of the girls speaks. With heads bowed, their eyes never leave their knees. Hana gazes off into the distance. The three horsemen are returning. As they come nearer, she searches for Morimoto's face until she sees him mounted behind one of the Soviets. He didn't get away.

Her heart thrums inside her chest. His hands are tied behind his back. His lip is swollen. Blood soaks through the trousers of his left leg. He doesn't look at her as they pass. He sits straight, staring into the shoulder of the large Soviet, as though nothing has happened, as though he is not in danger and he is not afraid. His erect posture and bleeding leg betray him. She knows he is terrified of what will certainly come. They will interrogate him, torture him, and after he has told them all he knows or can think to make up, they may possibly kill him. Satisfaction swells within her.

The horsemen continue up the convoy line, and she loses sight of Morimoto. Looking back at the horizon, she suddenly wonders what happened to his magnificent horse. Surely they wouldn't leave behind such a strong, powerful animal. She wants to see its muscles rippling as it gallops freely across the grassland back to Altan and a content life far from these men. She clings to this image, but the warmth of the satisfaction she felt at Morimoto's capture slowly dissipates, until she is left shivering in a truck full of silent prisoners.

》-《

A wolf howls in the distance. Its lone cry echoes in the hills beyond the steppe. The convoy has been heading towards those hills all day. Blue-capped mountains rise up behind them, reminding Hana of her home and Mount Halla. Orange clouds reflect the setting sun as the sky fades into night. She watches the last of the light, as though burning the beauty of the bright swirls into memory. Horrors dwell in darkness. Her mother warned her never to dive after the sun set. That was when the creatures of the black depths awakened and hunted.

'With night come terrors of the deep searching for the light,' she said to Hana one evening as they swam back to the shore.

It was the longest day she had spent in the water so far, and the sun was beginning to set. But Hana wasn't ready to stop diving. She had only found two conches.

'JinSook found four yesterday. I can't return with just two in my net. She's a year younger than me.'

'Nonsense, you should be proud of the two you managed to find. The sun is dipping down. The day is done.'

Her mother continued swimming home. Hana dutifully followed but pestered her the whole way in.

'Just a little while longer, please? I'm certain I can find two more very quickly. There must be some hiding near the old ship's anchor where the seaweed has collected.'

Once on the shore, her mother lifted her mask and bent down a little so they were eye to eye. Hana abruptly stopped her begging.

'You don't want to be caught out there when the creatures rise from the deep.'

Hana was certain her mother was teasing her about the night creatures just to get her out of the water.

'You don't have to worry about me. They won't even notice me because I don't have any light to attract them,' Hana replied.

'Oh, but you do,' her mother said, raising her eyebrows.

'I do? Where?'

'Your skin.'

Hana was sceptical, but her mother continued.

'White like milk, fair as the purest down on a goose's breast. The brightest beacon in the darkest of seas,' she said, touching Hana's cheek.

Hana looked down at her arms and legs. They didn't look very white to her. In fact they were completely tanned from swimming so much.

'I'm brown, not white like Emiko anymore.'

Hana pointed to her sister, who waited for them, still guarding the buckets. Her pink cheeks glowed with exertion. Her hair stuck to her brow in sweaty clumps.

'I kept the seabirds away. They are really hungry today! Look at that one, it pecked my hand.' Emiko showed Hana a small cut on the back of her hand.

'Which one did it?' Hana asked, forgetting about the number of conches she still needed to catch. A rogue seagull had assaulted her sister, and it needed to be taught a lesson or the rest of them would follow suit.

'That one, with the grey circles around its eyes.'

The bird waddled towards something buried in the sand, unaware of the attention focused on its every move. Hana bent and picked up a small rock. She closed one eye and took aim. The rock pinged the bird in the back. It squawked and flew away in a flash.

'Let's get it!' Hana yelled, and she ran after it, following its path on the long stretch of beach beyond their little cove. 'Come on, Little Sister, run!'

'Wait for me,' her sister shouted behind her, running as fast as her shorter legs could go. 'I'm coming for you, bird,' she shouted at the sky, and they ran all the way down the coast until they couldn't run any further.

They collapsed onto the sand and gulped in great breaths of salty sea air. Hana stared up at the sky and watched the seagulls draw invisible circles below the clouds. Her sister's small hand slipped into Hana's, and they lay side by side watching the clouds glide by. When they had caught their breath, her sister jumped up. 'I'll race you back home,' she said and took off back towards the cove.

'Hey, no fair, you got a head start,' Hana called after her, but Emiko merely laughed and ran faster. She laughed all the way back home, and even louder when Hana sped past her.

Emiko's laughter fills Hana's mind, the sound of pure joy. A hand touches her arm, and she jerks away.

'What are you thinking about?' the girl sitting next to her whispers.

'What?' Hana replies, her eyes darting back and forth between the girl and the Soviets. One of the soldiers has fallen asleep, but the other is wiping down his weapon with an oiled rag.

The girl briefly touches Hana's mouth, her fingertips barely caressing her lips. 'You were smiling,' she whispers, and looks down at her hands, tucking them between her knees to stop their trembling.

'Was I?' Hana asks.

'Yes, you were. Smiling in a situation like this, you must have been remembering something wonderful,' the girl says.

Hana looks down at her feet. Emiko's laughter has disappeared. Even as she tries to conjure the sound back again, she cannot.

'It was wonderful,' Hana admits.

She feels the girl's eyes on her now. Her yearning is palpable. How long has the girl been travelling with these Soviets that the mere prospect of a happy memory fills her with such longing? She meets the girl's earnest gaze. The whites of her eyes are bloodshot. Yellowed bruises dot her arms. A purple welt blooms on her cheek.

'I was remembering my sister's laughter. She's only nine.'

'I have a little brother – he's five. I miss him.'

'I miss my sister, too.'

'What did her laugh sound like?'

Hana pauses, thinking about the sound that she can no longer hear. The grumble of the truck's engine drowns out any hope of bringing the laughter back to her. She looks in the girl's desolate eyes.

She deserves even a scrap of happiness, if Hana can manage it. Looking up into the night sky, she focuses on the first star to appear in the dark blue.

'It was like a bird floating gracefully on a summer breeze, rising and falling like the waves, teasing the tips of the trees as it glides by. It sounded . . . free.'

The girl is silent for a long time. She doesn't look at Hana. As the truck groans to a halt, the girl hastily wipes her cheeks before the soldier orders them all to stand. He yanks a few of them to their feet just as the tailgate swings down, and two Soviets order the prisoners out of the truck. Hana rises with the girl and strains to see her face.

'I'm so sorry if I made you sad,' Hana urgently whispers.

The girl looks back over her shoulder as she moves towards the tailgate. 'I could hear her,' she says, and smiles.

Her brief expression of happiness warms Hana, until she leaps down from the truck and follows the other prisoners. The feeling quickly sinks into fear as she stares at the two soldiers leading them through the darkness. They are barbarians, tall and thick with crude muscles. They could tear her in half in a tug of war. She envisions each man taking hold of one of her legs, ripping her in two, but her head cannot crack in half so it tears off with the left side, and that soldier cries out in victory. At least she would be dead. It would be easier then.

Campfires dot the horizon. In the darkness, she remembers her mother's words: *With night come terrors.* Her sister's laughter cannot exist in this place, yet she wishes she could hear it one last time. A girl behind her whimpers, but no one comforts her. Hana, too, walks in silence. They are like ghosts entering another realm.

The Soviets stop in front of a large beige tent and motion for the prisoners to enter it. They obey, ducking their heads dutifully beneath the low opening. When Hana reaches the doorway, one of the soldiers places a hand on her shoulder. Too afraid to look up into his face, she keeps her eyes focused on the people inside the tent. He says something to her, but she does not understand him. He repeats it, louder this time. She must tear her eyes away from the group.

He inspects her face before pulling her from the queue. He motions for the others to continue into the tent, though he never releases her arm.

The soldier barks something to the other guard, who then takes position in front of the door, rifle at the ready. Hana is led away, back the way they came. *It's going to happen now*, she thinks. They're going to 'break her in', just like Morimoto did on the ferry. She stumbles in the dark, stubbing her toe on rocks littering the trampled grass. His grip on her arm is a vice, keeping her from falling or getting away. Kidnapped again, but this time by a man twice her size and ten times her strength.

They pass many other soldiers on their way to the trucks. The men walk in groups of two and three. Some of them notice her as she passes, others are too busy to look. A thrum of electricity surrounds the men even as she is led further away from the camp. There's a charge in the air she didn't notice before, when she was cushioned by the other prisoners. Now that she is alone, she feels the taut energy from each soldier as they pass.

He stops her in front of a tank from the convoy. Its red flag droops in the still night air. Two Soviets stand on top of the metal beast, pointing their rifles at a man kneeling in the dirt. A campfire burns a few feet away, illuminating the Soviet soldiers in a semicircle near the kneeling man. The man's face is swollen to twice its normal size. A slit above one eye bleeds down the side of his cheek, covering half of his features like warpaint. He stares at the ground, and she wonders if he can see at all through his swollen, bleeding eyes.

Two men from the small crowd of Soviets step towards the beaten man. One of them says something to him. The other soldier, a large Soviet, then translates into Japanese.

'Save yourself from more agony and tell us what we want to know.'

The interpreter speaks in heavily accented and slightly broken Japanese. The first man, the leader of this interrogation, glances at her, and she begins to tremble. The bleeding man is Morimoto. She stares at his unrecognisable face, and her body begins to violently shake. There is no satisfaction in seeing him like this. Instead, she is filled with terror. Why have they brought her here? Will they beat her, too?

'She will tell us if you won't.'

The Soviet officer nods his head. The soldier guarding her wrenches her arm behind her back, forcing her to kneel on the ground. She is ten feet away from Morimoto. He does not lift his head or speak. He merely breathes through his broken nose. The sound is a painful rattle of air sliding through a river of blood.

The officer punches Morimoto, knocking him over. Two soldiers rush to his side and quickly sit him back onto his knees. Dirt and grass stick to the blood on his face. He looks like a creature now, all humanity beaten from his broken flesh. This is what men do to other men in times of war. Hana does not know if it is worse than what they do to women. She cannot tear her eyes from his monstrous face.

'Where are your accomplices?' the interpreter shouts. 'We know you are a spy, crossing the border to gather intelligence for your emperor. We know the Mongol traitors are helping you. Where are they? What are their names?'

Altan. He is in danger. If Morimoto confesses, they will be slaughtered. Altan, his mother and father, and Ganbaatar, ignorant of the Soviet troops only a few days' drive away. What loyalty remains in Morimoto to his Mongolian friends after Altan helped her to escape? Would he betray their location for revenge? He looks at her, and suddenly his eyes seem to focus. His expression is unreadable beneath the ravages of his battered face.

Afraid that any movement might trigger his confession, she remains completely still. They would hunt down the Mongolians like missiles in black waters, surprising them in the night and wiping them out without a moment's pause – and it would be Hana's fault. The officer shouts at Morimoto again while the interpreter translates, but then Morimoto lifts one hand. Hana's heart rises into her throat, beating like thunder in her ears.

'I told you,' he says, his voice hoarse. A dry click in the back of his throat seems to make his words stick, and they take more time to come out. 'I transport –'

'Yes, we know, you transport women,' the interpreter says, irritated. He sighs. 'Tell us,' he says to Hana. 'Is he speaking the truth? Are you a prostitute for the Japanese military?'

The question is like a knife in her stomach. Morimoto told them she was a camp whore for the emperor's soldiers. Memories of her captivity flash through her mind: the moment he seized her from the beach, the first time he raped her, the long line of men that followed, the beatings, the forced medical examinations, the starvation, the hunger, her escape – everything blurs into a golden light, which shines onto Altan's mother and her soft hands, and that first kindness glows like a good spirit. Time becomes thick, and it is as though she is reliving the memories ten times over before she can speak.

'I am what he says.'

The words taste like ashes in her mouth, but she holds on to Altan's image. Morimoto spits a mouthful of blood onto the dirt. She wishes she could look away from his mouth, full of broken teeth.

'So where was he taking you?'

She stares straight ahead, unable to look away from him. The story of one of the girls at the brothel leaps into her mind.

'He said I would repay my father's debts by working in Manchuria.'

The interpreter relays the information to the officer, and they converse for a few moments before returning their attention to Morimoto.

'How did you end up in Mongolia?'

Morimoto keeps his eyes fixed on Hana. He does not move as he answers. His words come out flat.

'She escaped . . . I tracked her here. I was about to take her back to Manchuria, but then you came upon us.'

'You want us to believe that this ragged, starved girl travelled here all the way from Manchuria on her own?'

'She's feisty,' he says, half laughing, half coughing. He doubles over and vomits blood. When he sits back up, he focuses his attention on the interpreter. 'I wouldn't let that one out of my sight if I were you.'

The interpreter relays the information in Russian. Hana feels all their eyes on her then, measuring her against his words. They are curious, but their curiosity is not as strong as the hate emanating from Morimoto's body towards her. If she ever had a chance, he has erased it by revealing her purpose for the Japanese army. He has ensured her continued suffering with these men.

The officer says something to the interpreter before heading back towards the camp. The interpreter and the other Soviets stay behind. An excited murmur erupts among them. The interpreter slowly unsheathes Morimoto's sword from the scabbard now hanging from his own belt. Hana wonders that she didn't notice it before. The metal blade glints in the firelight. Morimoto threatened to cut off Altan's head with that sword. The interpreter tosses the sword to the ground in front of Morimoto and takes a step back.

'Pick it up.'

Morimoto doesn't move. Hana wonders if he is too badly beaten to move, let alone lift it.

'We've often heard of your fascinating samurai rituals,' the interpreter says, as though not bothered Morimoto hasn't picked up the sword. 'Though none of us have been witness to one.' He glances at the small gathering crowd, who encourage him to continue.

'So you have a choice. You can perform this ancient ritual and have a chance at dying with dignity at your own hand, or you can let them kill you.' He motions towards the men crowded behind him. 'I promise you, it will be anything but dignified.'

Hana remains on her knees, watching Morimoto. Slowly, he reaches for his sword, nearly crashing to the ground with the effort. She holds in a gasp. He regains his balance and then straightens as he lays the sword across his knees. Visibly winded, he catches his breath. The sound is audible pain, air rushing through his destroyed face, gurgling through spilled blood.

Morimoto squares his shoulders and lifts the sword to inspect the blade. He slides his finger down the razor-sharp edge, drawing blood. Hana cringes, not wanting to continue looking at him but unable to turn away.

He looks in Hana's direction, but his swollen eyes give away nothing of his thoughts. She imagines he is smiling behind those puffy lids, enjoying his final act, as she will be left in the hands of an even greater enemy.

'Well, what have you decided?' the officer abruptly asks, but then Morimoto stabs himself in the stomach, and everyone freezes.

Even Hana seems rooted to the earth in that moment. The sword is buried deep within Morimoto's abdomen. Without uttering a sound, he cuts through his guts horizontally towards his right side. His face is contorted in pain. The white of his teeth appears jagged in the light of the campfire. His bloody, swollen face is grotesque in the flickering light. She wants to flee, but the Soviet grips her arm so tightly that she can only stare in horror as Morimoto completes the *seppuku*.

A Soviet soldier abruptly turns away and retches, but Morimoto is still not dead. With trembling hands, he slowly lifts the blade, and in one swift motion, he slices his own throat. Purged of life, his body falls limp to the earth, staining it black. Morimoto is no longer the death god. Instead, Gangnim has come to reap his soul.

Silence follows Morimoto's fall, uncomfortable and thick, like the lifeblood draining from his corpse. The relief Hana thought she would feel at his death does not come. There is merely emptiness now. Not even fear of what will happen to her next can penetrate the nothingness that fills her. It is as though the violence he enacted against his own flesh is infecting her with a sense of hopeless loss.

The remaining soldiers depart, one by one. Even the man holding her on her knees seems to disappear, as if they want to see what she does when she is left alone with the dead man. She rises to her feet and walks towards him. Hana kneels in front of Morimoto's lifeless body and pauses, taking in the grotesque carcass that was once a man who tortured her with his mere presence. Morimoto's once-crisp uniform is soaked with his blood. In death his beaten face has become more animal than human. His eyes glaze over like the eyes of a rotting fish. His stillness begins to unsettle her. Now he is nothing but a pile of blood and flesh on the Mongolian plain.

Without looking to see who might be watching, Hana reaches into his pocket. She pulls out the black-and-white photograph of the girl she used to be. It's covered in Morimoto's blood. Quickly, she wipes it on her *del* and slips it into her pocket, relief washing through her. He no longer has any part of her.

After a long moment, she finally looks away from Morimoto's remains. Just as she does, the interpreter appears beside her. He inspects her face as though surveying her thoughts. She saves him the effort.

'I hated him,' she says flatly, wondering if he saw her take the photograph.

Her words sound as empty as she feels. The interpreter doesn't respond. Instead he leads her back towards the camp. They reach the tent where the other prisoners were taken. The guard moves aside to let her enter. She takes one last look at the interpreter before ducking inside. If he has seen her take the photograph, he doesn't care.

Dozens of faces greet her as she steps inside. Some weep quietly into their hands, too afraid to make a sound, while others, seemingly numb to the events to come, absently stare at her with vacuous eyes. She searches the lamplit space for the Korean girls from the truck. They are tucked into the furthest corner, hidden behind two Chinese men whose hands are bound behind their backs. Hana squeezes past the men and sits beside the girls.

'There's blood on your coat,' the older girl says.

Hana looks down at the *del* and sees that the girl is staring at the upward spray of tiny dark droplets staining her chest. She wipes at it with her sleeve.

'What did they do?' Her eyes are full of innocence.

'They killed the man who kidnapped me. A Japanese soldier.'

Hana so often fantasised about Morimoto's death, and she nearly enacted it in the *ger*. It was Altan who preserved her humanity, or at least reminded her of its existence. His disgust at her actions brought her back from the brink of evil. He spared her from becoming the worst version of herself, at least for a little while longer. Out on the steppe, after watching Morimoto beat Altan to a pulp, she tried a second time to kill him, but she failed.

'No man should die like that,' she finally says.

The girl nods. She touches the sash around Hana's waist. 'This is lovely.'

Hana fingers the silk. The red and yellow flowers alighting each black and green swirl of vines against the dark blue silk seem to move, an endless pattern of beauty in this fearful place.

Morimoto told the interpreter that Hana was a prostitute. She knows he will send for her sooner or later. Her fate is sealed. Suddenly, she feels exhausted. This time, she will fight, she decides, and the thought ends with the realisation that it will probably mean her death.

'I have to tell you something,' Hana hurriedly whispers to both of them. 'In case they come for me and I don't return, I want someone to know my story.'

They both nod, urging Hana to continue.

'My name is Hana.'

Hana starts at the beginning. Her life as a *haenyeo*, swimming in the waters of her island and spying the Japanese soldier heading towards her sister on the beach – the words fall from her lips like water rushing over a cliff. The thought of perishing compels her to tell these girls everything. Hana tells them about the brothel, the other girls, and Keiko. She tells them about the Mongolian family and their animals and about her friend Altan. But to keep them safe, she says she hasn't seen them in over a month. When she finishes, she feels spent, as though she has emptied all the best parts of her, leaving her hollow.

The two Korean girls also share their stories with Hana. They tell her they are sisters from a village in northern Korea near the Man-churian border. They were tricked by the local police into climbing into their truck for a lift home one night after their duties in the apple orchard. The police drove them straight to the border and turned them over to a Japanese trafficker. He put them on a train with five other girls and sent them far north into Manchuria. Before they reached the station, the sisters managed to jump from the train at night and walked as far as they could. They crossed a mountain range and didn't realise they had crossed the border into Mongolia. They were caught at dawn, a few days before Hana was found.

The three girls clasp hands, forming a small circle in the cramped space. Their tears flow freely as they gaze at each other, memorising each nuance of the others' faces. The flap lifts open and the interpreter enters. The prisoners nearest the door scuttle backwards until they nearly sit upon the laps of those behind them. He ignores their fearful withdrawal, scanning the room until his eyes rest on Hana.

'You, come with me,' he orders.

The room follows his gaze. The two Chinese men in front of her turn to look at her. Their faces are apologetic. They know it is her turn to be tortured. Hana rises to her feet. She looks down at the sisters and whispers to them in earnest.

'Don't forget me,' she says, and reaches into her coat pocket. She retrieves the photograph of the girl she once was and truly wishes she could be again.

'Hurry up!' the soldier shouts.

Her hand trembling, Hana gives the photograph to the older sister before quickly turning away.

'We will never forget you,' their reply comes as Hana follows the soldier into the night.

She stumbles after the interpreter, deeper into the camp. He ushers her inside a small tent, which she thinks must be his personal sleeping quarters. He motions for her to sit upon a cot. The muffled activity outside the tent fills the air between them. Soldiers talking as they walk past, motors revving as trucks drive away, and yet Hana can still make out the quiet burning of a kerosene lamp inside the tent.

The interpreter stands at the far end, near the door, fishing for something from his pocket. He is a massive man and must duck his head to stand in the small tent. Hana has never seen men as large as the Soviets. Sitting so close to one feels like being in the gaze of a hungry bear. He leans against one of the metal poles, and Hana watches as he taps tobacco from a small canister onto a thin square of white paper. With practised fingers, he rolls the paper and then slowly licks the edge, sealing it.

He lights the cigarette and takes a drag. He smokes it as though she is not waiting and he has all the time in the world. When it is merely a nub between two fingers, he drops it to the ground and takes two steps towards her. Two more and he will be upon her. His expression is serious.

'Why are you dressed like a Mongolian?' he asks.

She looks down at the bloody and soiled *del*, then looks up at him, thinking how she could answer without putting Altan's family in danger.

'You are a Japanese, aren't you? Yet you wear that ridiculous costume,' he says, motioning towards her *del*.

He unbuttons the first two buttons of his uniform. She doesn't answer his question or tell him she is Korean. She watches his hand as it disappears inside his breast pocket and emerges with a brown metal flask.

'Vodka. The last of it, I'm afraid. I've had to conserve it over these last months in this godforsaken country. Now it is nearly gone.' He takes a sip, swishing it around his mouth before swallowing and letting out a sigh of satisfaction. 'Tell me the truth. I will know if you are lying.'

She takes in a small breath before responding and then lets the words rush out in one long sentence.

'The Mongolians found me crossing the mountain range. I was nearly naked because the brothel didn't provide us with clothes, so they gave me this to wear.'

'How long were you with them?'

'A few days.'

'And where is their camp?'

She hesitates.

'Don't think about it, just answer the question.'

'I don't know.'

'You're lying.'

'I'm not lying. Truly, I don't know where the camp is.'

'I told you not to lie to me.' He tucks the flask back into his pocket and steps towards her, his hand crossing his waist as though preparing to backhand her.

'I'm telling the truth. When – when I learned the soldier . . . ' she stutters, thinking of Morimoto's recent demise. His bloody face appears in her mind, and she has to physically shake her head to erase it. 'When I learned that he was in the Mongolians' camp, I escaped on the pony. All I could do was make it run as fast as it could so I could get away. It was dark. I couldn't see where I was going. I only knew that I had to escape or he would take me back to the brothel. I just ran . . .'

She waits for the impact, his hand against her face, but it doesn't come. Instead he straightens up and crosses his hands behind his back.

'He must have been a spy, I'm certain,' he says, staring at her as though she will answer. His expression shifts; one eyebrow arcs above his eye. 'Or perhaps he is an opium trafficker. That's how your emperor affords this war. Did you know that? That the great Hirohito smuggles opium like a lowly drug trafficker? The West buys it all up, turning it into other things, heroin, special tea . . . This man, he had opium packed in his belongings.' The interpreter reaches behind a small table and holds up Morimoto's pack. It is stained with blood. 'Not enough to pay for an army, but enough to sell for good cash. Did you know he had this?'

Exhaustion suddenly sweeps through her, and she rests her forehead on the cot. How long has she been in this nightmare? It feels like a thousand years have passed, and still she is trapped in this misery. Perhaps Morimoto was going to sell the opium and use the proceeds to start up their new life. Or perhaps he was a smuggler. She will never know.

'I don't know about any of that. I only know he took me from my home and sold me to a brothel. I can tell you nothing else.'

She realises her eyes have closed when she feels his hands untying the sash. *Forgive me*, Hana whispers to her family across the miles. She sees Emiko standing in the *haenyeo* ceremony all alone and it pains her heart, but she shakes the image from her mind. With all her might, Hana shoves against the Soviet's chest. Unprepared for her sudden attack, he loses his balance and falls to the ground. She scrambles over him and seizes the pistol from the holster on his belt. Standing above him, she points the gun at his chest.

'If you shoot me, you're dead. And they won't be as kind to you as I would have been.'

She laughs at him. The sound is bitter, like an old woman's scorn.

'You, show me kindness? You don't know the meaning of the word. You call us dogs. Your kind, soldiers, men, all of you are the worst creatures that plague this land. You bring your hatred and pain and suffering with you everywhere you go. I despise all of you.'

Before he can respond, she pulls the trigger. The gun doesn't fire. Tingling sweat seeps from her pores. She pulls the trigger again, harder, but still nothing happens. He makes a move towards her. She backs away, desperately searching the gun for a safety latch. He's on his feet and then lunges at her. Hana falls and struggles beneath him, but she is no match for his size and strength. He twists her wrist, prising the pistol from her hand. He smacks her in the head with the side of the barrel. Her mouth fills with blood.

'Get up. On your knees,' he orders.

Dazed, she does as he says. He unlocks the safety latch. Hana stares at his boots as blood trails down her chin. She is a hundred miles away on a black, pebbled beach. The sun shines above her, warming her long hair. Her sister's laughter rolls in with the waves of the sea.

'Any last words?' He is breathless. His chest heaves.

'I was never a prostitute.'

He laughs at her. 'Is that all you have to say? Who cares what you were? You are nothing.' He takes aim, his finger on the gun's trigger.

'I am a *haenyeo*,' she says, and glares at him. Her words rush over her lips like a confession. 'Like my mother, and her mother before her, like my sister will be and one day, her daughters, too – I was never anything but a woman of the sea. Neither you nor any man can make me less than that.'

He snorts, but she doesn't hear him. She is somewhere else, in another time. Hana closes her eyes. The sun's rays warm her blood, and she tastes them on her tongue. The wind rushes through her hair. The ocean swells beneath her, calling her name, *Hana*.

She feels the pain before she realises what has happened. Her eyes open, but her vision is clouded with blood. She focuses just in time to see the interpreter raise his hand and smash the gun against her temple once more. Hana falls to the ground. The last thing she sees is the tip of his boot as he steps towards her.

Emi

Seoul, December 2011

When they arrive in front of the Japanese embassy Emi doesn't want to sit in the wheelchair, but her son won't hear of her attempting to walk to the statue. The strain on her heart and her bad leg would be too great.

'Either I push you in the wheelchair, or I take you back to the hospital. Your choice.'

Emi doesn't remember talking to her son this way when he was a child, but she thinks she must have. She loved her children greatly, but she had difficulty showing her affection for them without also having to show that same affection to their father. He would have demanded it if he thought her capable of such actions. So it was easier to love them from within, so that she could survive.

Their father was never unkind to her after his son was born. Perhaps it was because they rarely spoke. Practically useless as a fisherman, he preferred to look after the children when she went diving. He would bring them to the market where she sold the day's catch. Her daughter would sit on his shoulders, clapping her hands to onlookers, elated at being so high up. Her son would follow his father's every step, like a shadow; they were inseparable. Perhaps that's why her son became so angry when his father died. He had lost his shade on this earth and was left to burn in the scorching sun.

Emi gives in to him, and he retrieves the wheelchair from the trunk of the car. Soon they are progressing across the road and up onto the pavement towards the memorial statue. As they pass the embassy, the red-brick building seems so small and unimposing. The windows no longer loom over her like vacant eyes. Tearing her gaze from the building, she sees the statue.

A young girl, ageless, sits in a straight-backed chair. Beside her is an empty chair waiting to be filled. The girl is wearing a traditional *hanbok* dress, and her bare feet dangle slightly above the ground. Someone has clothed the statue in winter gear, a knitted hat for her head and a scarf and blanket to keep her warm. A few yards away, Emi stops her son.

'I want to walk,' she tells him.

He begins to protest, but she holds up one hand. He falls silent. She grasps the armrests of the wheelchair and presses with all her might until her feet support her weight, and then she stands. Slowly, as though it is the early hours before sunrise and she is heading down to the water's edge, she shuffles towards the seated girl.

Her bad leg drags pitifully behind her, but she does not take her son's offered hand. Each step feels like wading through thick mud. Her eyes are locked on the young girl's face. She finds strength in the expression of deepest understanding, of pain and loss, of forgiveness and patience. The expression of endless, weary waiting.

When she finally reaches the statue, Emi flops into the empty chair beside it. She catches her breath, slowing her heaving chest into a resting state. Then she reaches for the bronze girl's hand. It is cold, and she rubs it gently, warming it with the heat from her wrinkled hand. They sit together in silence. Emi steals a few glances at the girl's profile. It is the girl she remembers from her childhood. It is Hana.

Her son smokes a cigarette a few feet away, coughing uncomfortably a few times before tossing the half-smoked cigarette onto the ground. He crushes it with the toe of his shoe. Emi smiles at him. She is transported back to a time when she knew nothing of war. Her innocence untouched, she was enveloped by her small family beside the sea, where she frolicked on the beach chasing seagulls. Her only job was to keep them away from the day's catch. Sitting hand in hand with her sister, Emi can feel the sun shining on her face, hot with summer's heat. She can smell the ocean breeze and taste the salt upon her tongue. It is no longer winter but summer, a summer's day before everything happened, when they were still a family.

'What is it about this statue that makes you smile so?'

Her daughter's voice sounds as though it is coming from somewhere far away across the ocean. She wants to focus her eyes upon YoonHui's face and see her again, but it takes too much effort to travel across time, away from that summer's day, and back to her.

'Tell me, Mother,' YoonHui says. Her voice is suddenly close and her breath warms Emi's ear.

'It's Hana, my sister. I have finally found her,' she whispers.

'You mean she reminds you of your sister?'

Her voice sounds closer now, as though it is coming from inside Emi's head and she is asking the question of herself. The sunshine begins to fade, and the ocean breeze ceases to blow against her cheek.

'It's Hana,' she says again. 'My sister, she's here.'

Emi's heart feels near to bursting. It's beating fast and hard inside her chest. She presses her hand against her breast, and the cold winter air rushes up the sleeve of her coat. Snowflakes cool her burning cheeks. When she opens her eyes, she knows she has returned. Her daughter kneels next to her, one hand on her shoulder. She is shivering from the cold.

'Mother?'

She is a little girl again, worried and uncertain. Emi leans towards her daughter and kisses her forehead. YoonHui looks up at her, and Emi sees her mother in the soft line of YoonHui's jaw. Emi is surprised when she does not feel sadness at the thought of her mother. Instead, she feels only peace.

She wishes it hadn't taken a lifetime to reach this moment, but the past is unchangeable. The present is all she has left.

'I was always proud you went to university,' she says, her voice a hoarse whisper.

YoonHui's face crumples, and she buries it in Emi's lap. Her rough wool coat catches her daughter's tears.

'I was proud of both of you,' she says, and turns to look at her son. He is kneeling in front of her, too, doing his best to refrain from crying.

Emi smiles and turns back to the statue. *I never forgot you*, she thinks, even though for so many years she pretended that she had. The statue sits beside her as though in forgiveness. Hana was always out there, waiting for Emi to find her. Emi wishes this moment would last a lifetime.

Hana

Mongolia, Autumn 1943

Hana drifts in and out of consciousness. When she manages to open her eyes she sees only dirt, black and solid. She tries to lift her head, her hand, her leg, something to signify she still inhabits this world, but nothing moves. Perhaps she is mistaken and is already dead, her body waiting for her spirit to rise and flee this wretched life.

Her mind skims through childhood memories; echoes of happiness fade in and out. She sees her mother's face looming above her, bright and shining, beaming like a brilliant sun countless worlds away. The heat reaches Hana's cheeks and warmth rises in her numbed skin. She turns her face towards the glow, a flower following the heat of sunlight. The light calls to her, *Hana, open your eyes.*

The late-morning sun dazzles her. A shout from far away pierces the air. A man's voice. Hana realises she is tied up and bound to a stake in the ground. The Soviets are breaking down the camp and preparing to set out. She is still alive. He did not shoot her after all.

She gazes at the morning sun, waiting to find out what they intend to do with her. When the final tent is packed away, the interpreter arrives, wielding a hunting knife.

'You're awake,' he says, the grin on his foreign face so similar to that of all the soldiers she has known in her short life.

Hana doesn't respond. Her head aches, and she has difficulty focusing for too long on one thing. He kneels behind her and cuts her hands free. Then he cuts the ropes from her ankles, before pulling her up into a seated position.

'Your freedom has been negotiated,' he says, and his voice holds an excited note.

Hana follows his gaze and starts when she sees Altan walking towards her. His father and Ganbaatar trail behind him. They came after her. A lump blocks her throat, and she suddenly finds it difficult to breathe. She is worried they are in danger but also grateful they are here. Did they truly convince the Soviets to release her?

'You have generous friends,' the interpreter says when they near.

Altan quickly bows his head at the soldier, who salutes him with a jovial laugh. The Mongolians don't even glance at Hana. It is as though they do not see her, although she knows that they must. She says nothing, following their lead, but she cannot stop staring at Altan's bruised face. Morimoto punished him dearly.

Altan's father steps ahead of his son and says something in Japanese to the interpreter. His voice is low, and she cannot hear him. She stares at his face as the two men communicate. The interpreter looks down at Hana and grins again.

'You're free to go,' he says, and walks away without looking back.

Only then do the Mongolians acknowledge Hana's presence. Altan and his father reach for her arms and help her onto her feet.

They carry her between them, helping her walk, and quickly exit the remnants of the Soviet camp. Their ponies stand in a huddle waiting for their masters, and Hana is overjoyed to see Morimoto's beautiful horse among them. Altan helps her onto one of the ponies and climbs on behind her. As the ponies begin to gallop away from the camp, an eagle's cry pierces through their hoof beats.

Hana looks over her shoulder and sees Ganbaatar's eagle perched on the interpreter's forearm. Her heart drops into her stomach. It squawks again, its sharp eyes easily making out its master galloping away. Ganbaatar traded his dearest possession for her freedom. Morimoto said Mongolians treasure their eagles above wives and children, yet Ganbaatar gave his away for a girl he hardly knows.

She tries to look at his face, but he races ahead of her, leading the small group back towards the mountains. Altan's arms encircle her as he urges the pony on. She doesn't know how much he gave up to convince Ganbaatar to trade his best possession for a girl. Hana only knows that she owes them both her life.

YoonHui

Jeju Island, February 2012

'I know, Auntie. I do,' YoonHui answers, and lowers her mother's old mask over her eyes. A crack in one corner obscures her view, but she doesn't care. She won't dive too deep, just far enough to remember what it is like to be a *haenyeo*, to be like her mother.

JinHee nods and lowers her mask, too. This signals to the other diving women that it is time. They wade out further into the sea and one by one somersault into the ocean and dive down to Earth's sea floor in search of treasures that will feed them, send their grandchildren to school, while keeping alive the memory of a favourite diver, a matriarch lost but never forgotten.

YoonHui dives and at first is shocked by the cold winter sea. She holds her breath, though she struggles against the current that threatens to lift her back to the surface. She releases a stream of bubbles from her nostrils in slow succession, allowing her to go further down, where the ocean pulses against her ears. The under-water world opens up in welcome as fish dart in and out of seaweed stalks swaying with the current. A crab scuttles on the seabed, scav-enging for food. A red octopus lurks nearby, watching, waiting for the crab to come near. Losing her breath, YoonHui rises slowly to the surface, watching the octopus creep ever so slowly across the ocean floor.

JinHee greets her as she heaves air into her lungs.

'Not bad for your first time.'

'I guess I still remember,' YoonHui says. She smiles, pleased to recall her mother's teachings. She was only a girl when she left; now she is a middle-aged woman. Why did it take her so long to find her way back home?

'She was proud of you,' JinHee says.

'I know,' YoonHui replies. She turns to look back at the shore. Some of the oldest women are sitting on rocks, waving at her. Their frail bodies won't allow them to stay in the cold February waters too long, but they came out of respect.

She left her brother in Seoul, and her nephew, too. But before she travelled to Jeju Island, YoonHui visited the statue for the first time after her mother's death. Lane went with her and so did her nephew. When they arrived at the site of her mother's final moments of peace, she was overwhelmed with sadness. The January wind dried her tears as soon as they fell, so she didn't have to try to hide them from her nephew. He looked so tall standing in front of the statue, staring at it as though he thought it might stand up and greet him.

YoonHui was surprised when he suddenly bowed to the statue, a deep, low bow full of filial respect. He lowered his face all the way to the ground, rose, and repeated this bow twice more. YoonHui grasped Lane's hand, watching with stunned pride. When he stood up, his shoulders slumped a little, from embarrassment or grief, YoonHui didn't know, but it made her love him even more. He wiped his nose before turning to her.

'Someone left flowers,' he said, pointing to the statue's lap.

White blooms poked out from beneath a knitted blanket someone had left to keep the statue warm. Nearing the statue, YoonHui lifted the blanket and revealed a bouquet of mourning flowers, white chrysanthemums. The petals were still supple, and she leaned down to touch them to her cheek.

In the days following her mother's funeral, Lane had tracked down the artists who created the statue. After a few email exchanges, they shared with her their inspiration. A black-and-white photograph, aged with time and stained with blood, that had found its way to the House of Sharing in Gyunggi-do, a home and museum for some of the 'comfort women' where their health is looked after and their stories are shared with visitors from all over the world.

The daughter of a woman who was captured by Russian soldiers during World War II had donated it to the Museum of Sexual Slavery by Japanese Military housed within the House of Sharing, and the artists had come across it during a research visit; it was labelled *Haenyeo girl, 1943*. The girl's expression had captured their attention, and so had the fact that her hair was tied behind her instead of cut short as it was in most of the other photographs of the girls they had seen. Of course they had changed her hairstyle for the statue to suit the true look of 'comfort women' at the time, but they had kept her face, her sombre expression, because something about the look in her eyes had touched them.

YoonHui gazed at the face that brought closure to her dying mother.

'Goodbye, Aunt Hana,' she whispered to the statue. 'I wish we could have met sooner.'

〉〈

Lane stands on the shore. She has already made friends with the *haenyeo* women. She looks up and waves. YoonHui waves back above the water, her hand arching across the sky so the elderly women can see her, too. She sees her mother in their faces, in their resting bodies, in their kindness. She feels her mother among these women, and she will remain here awhile and burn incense to her ancestors until she can be certain her mother's spirit has found its way back home to her island.

YoonHui turns back to her mother's oldest friend, and together they dive into the ocean's depths, the pressure pulsing against her eardrums like a heartbeat beneath the waves.

Hana

Mongolia, Winter 1943

Cold air brushes against Hana's skin. She can taste the grasses turned brown on the tip of her tongue. Her hair flies loose and tendrils lash against her face. Altan's hand wipes the wisps away, securing them behind her ear. His touch is gentle. He pulls the fur pelt snug around her shoulders.

'Cold?' he asks, one of the growing cache of Mongolian words she now recognises. She shakes her head.

The dog rests its head in her lap. He smells like morning dew. His wet fur brushes against the backs of her hands. Once she returned to the Mongolian camp, the dog refused to leave her side. It was as though it adopted her, a lost child returned, her spirit broken from the wilderness. Its favourite resting place is the tops of her hands quietly folded in her lap. Her bony knuckles poke the soft folds beneath its muzzle. Its eyes roll upwards as though to check on her well-being.

She bends her neck downwards and gazes back into the dark puddles, which blink each time she does. So much care and kindness have flooded into her since her return. She is born anew.

Altan leaves her side. They are packing up again. This is the fourth time they have moved location since they left the Soviet camp. She suspects they are playing it safe in case the Soviets change their minds, or they could be running from the Japanese. They don't share this information with her.

The dog licks her hand. It is time to go. A pony stands in front of her, waiting. Altan helps her to her feet. He has been treating her like an injured infant since the moment they arrived back at the Mongolian encampment. It took a few days after her return for her vision to grow clear once again, but the headaches sometimes come back, agonising migraines that knock her off her feet for hours on end. The swelling in his face went down quickly from poultices his mother applied each day. The bruises around his eyes have faded to a sickly yellow. He is nearly himself again.

Hana climbs aboard the speckled pony. It snorts and nods its head, shaking the fringe from its eyes. She reaches forward and gently combs its mane to one side. The stiff hairs slide through her fingers, and she is reminded of something from another time, the feeling of rough weeds beneath the sea gliding over her hands, dark waters surrounding her, floating. The pony shakes its head and starts its slow march. The image is gone, replaced by the vast blue of the sky above her and the brown of the grasses all around her like a moving tide.

The great beauty surrounding Hana envelops their small travelling group as though they are in a painting. She saw a caravan once in a schoolbook the teacher showed to her class. Peasants moving to a new home, a new land.

Hana remembers feeling grateful she would never have to see her home packed up into a cart like those children. She felt superior in her status as a *haenyeo*'s daughter, with the knowledge that she would one day, too, become the breadwinner in her family, matriarch of her home, and master of her own destiny. She would never be forced from the sea because it would always sustain her. She pushes the image out of her mind.

》《

Early snow blankets the Mongolian steppe. They make camp at the foot of a low and ragged range of bare-topped hills. A large lake shimmers blue and green on the horizon.

'The sea,' Hana says, forgetting they are in a landlocked region.

'No, that is Lake Uvs. It was once a great sea before the land appeared around it, separating it from the oceans. It's salty like the ocean.'

Altan's words are lost on Hana. She is already heading towards the familiar colours that beckon her. He calls her name, but she continues on, as though pulled by a magnetic force towards true north. Footsteps follow her, a guardian shadowing her, a light hand placed on the small of her back.

'Where are you going?' Altan asks. When she doesn't respond, he tries a different approach.

'We shouldn't go so far away from camp. There are predators out here. They're lured by the waterfowl in the wetlands.'

As though on cue, a flock of white gulls launches into the air crying as they spray across the sky. They startle a four-legged creature Hana has never seen before. She stops mid-step, staring at the intriguing animal, which resembles a sheep crossed with a deer.

'Hello, little friend,' Altan calls to the animal, sending it into a fast gallop away from them. 'That's called a *dzeren*,' he tells her. 'They're good to eat if you can catch one.' He laughs as though he has told her a joke, even though he knows she doesn't yet understand much of what he says.

She watches it scamper through the tall grass, blending into the brown stalks until it disappears. Turning her attention back towards the lake, Hana continues on her trek to the blue and green waters behind the wetland reeds. Gulls float on the placid lake, calling to their mates hovering above them on a cold winter wind. Tiny snowflakes melt on her lashes. Her boots sink into the sandy earth with each step. She is once again walking on a beach. The wind rushes through her hair; the fur pelt around her shoulders tickles her neck. She breathes in the salty air, and memories wash through her mind. Her first taste of the sea, her first dive, her mother's *sumbisori* whistle after each plunge, exhaling oxygen from her lungs, her laughter above the wind, and Emi dancing on the shore.

Hana unties her sash and begins to remove her *del*.

'What are you doing?' Altan asks, trying without success to stop her hands from stripping off her clothing. 'You mean to go in there? You'll freeze.'

The call of the sea overpowers her and blocks him from her mind. She feels no sense of embarrassment from her nakedness, only a pull towards the water. Freed from her clothes, she pushes him away and heads down towards the edge of the lake. He follows, grabbing her by the arm, but she yanks it out of his grasp. She rushes into the lake and gasps as the cold water knocks the air from her lungs. He charges in after her, but she is too quick. Instinct kicks in and soon she is diving deep beneath the surface and disappears into the murky depths.

It was always a dream; even if Hana had managed to make the journey, returning home would never have been safe. If she suddenly appeared at her mother's house, there would be questions. There is still a war on, the Soviets made that clear, and the Japanese are still in control of Korea. If they found her, they could ship her back to the brothel in Manchuria, or somewhere else even worse. She must remain in Mongolia with Altan and his family. She has resigned herself to this.

The realisation that she is content to stay with them relieves a burden from her bones. She is weary no longer. Instead, she feels weightless at the thought of this new life. Altan is the light summoning her towards the surface of the water. The light that will chase away the darkness she has endured for too long. A surge of energy courses through her limbs. Hana presses her feet against the soggy floor of the lake and thrusts herself upwards, trailing behind the rising bubbles.

Remembrance of My Beloved Sister (*Je Mang Me Ga*)*

You were afraid that the way of life or death had come,
So you went without even saying you were going.
Like falling leaves scattered by the early autumn wind,
Borne from one branch, no one knows where they are going.
Ah! I will wait for the day to meet you in Mitachal
While praying and seeking enlightenment!

---

* Song by Buddhist monk Master Wolmyeong in the eighth century, translated by Jeong Sook Lee, Korean translator and teacher at the Oriental and African Studies, University of London. Author's Note: This lyric poem is a *hyangaa* folk song composed after the death of Master Wolmyeong's sister. I read it often to remind myself of the universality of Emi's plight.

Author's Note

Some historians believe fifty thousand to two hundred thousand Korean women and girls were stolen, tricked or sold into military sexual slavery for and by the Japanese military during Japan's colonisation of Korea. Japan's armies were fighting for world domination, beginning in 1931, when Japan invaded Manchuria, leading to the Second Sino-Japanese War in 1937, and ending in 1945 with their defeat by the Allies at the end of World War II. In that time, countless lives were destroyed and lost by all the countries involved.

Of those tens of thousands of women and girls enslaved by the Japanese military, only forty-four South Korean survivors are still alive (at the writing of this book) to tell the world what happened during their captivity, how they survived, and how they returned home. We will never know what happened to the other women and girls who perished before getting the chance to let the world know what they suffered. Many died in foreign lands, and like Emi, their families never learned of their tragic stories.

Many of the '*halmoni*' ('grandmothers') who survived their enslavement were not free to tell their stories to their families or communities when they returned home. Korea was a patriarchal society based on Confucian ideology, and a woman's sexual purity was of the utmost importance. These survivors were forced to suffer from their past in silence. Many were left with medical issues, PTSD and an inability to re-enter society. Most lived in abject poverty with no family to care for them in their old age. Some historians believe the issue of the 'comfort women' was never a priority for the Korean government after World War II, because very soon after, the Korean War broke out, costing so many more lives during the fratricidal war between the North and the South. The Thirty-Eighth Parallel was drawn across the peninsula, and Korea was forever cut in two. The South Korean government was then left to rebuild a country whose infrastructure had been demolished by war. There were 'more important' issues at hand. It took a further forty years before the issue of the 'comfort women' was raised, when in 1991 Kim Hak-sun came forward to give an account of her story to the press. Many more 'comfort women' came forward following her bravery, more than two hundred in total.

In December of 2015, South Korea and Japan reached an 'agreement' over the 'comfort women' issue, and both countries hoped to resolve the conflict once and for all, so they could move forward in more amicable international relations. As Corporal Morimoto did with Hana, Japan offered South Korea terms, and one of them was the removal of the *Statue of Peace*, erected on private land across from the Japanese embassy in Seoul. Removing this statue is the first step towards the denial of women's history in South Korea. The *halmoni* rejected this 'agreement' and continue to seek a true resolution because they believe Japan wishes to simply erase the unsightly history of wartime military sexual slavery as though the atrocities never took place and up to two hundred thousand women did not suffer and possibly die in tragic, heartbreaking circumstances.

In March 2016, I travelled to Seoul to see *Pyeonghwabi* (the *Statue of Peace*) in person for the first, and possibly the last, time. It was a sort of pilgrimage for me to journey halfway across the world to set my eyes on the symbol representing, for me, wartime rape not only of Korean women and girls, but of all women and girls the world over: Uganda, Sierra Leone, Rwanda, Myanmar, Yugoslavia, Syria, Iraq, Afghanistan, Palestine and more. The list of women suffering wartime rape is long and will continue to grow unless we include women's wartime suffering in history books, commemorate the atrocities against them in museums, and remember the women and girls we lost by erecting monuments in their honour, like the *Statue of Peace*.

In the writing of this book, I fell in love with Hana, who for me came to represent all the women and girls who suffered her fate. I couldn't leave her dead in the Mongolian dirt by a soldier's hand; though the chances of the real-life Hanas reaching freedom are slim, my ending is what I wish could have happened to Hana and others like her. Writing Emi's story was my escape from the horrors of imagining Hana's world. Emi was my favourite character, and I think after all she suffered, it was only fair that, in the end, the statue was actually Hana. In real life, the statue was not sculpted in the image of a particular lost 'comfort woman', but it makes for a good story, one that I dedicate to all the women of the world who suffered in war and who suffer still.

〉〉·〈〈

The history of conflict in any nation is often mired in controversial truths and institutionalised falsehoods. The events I included in this book from South Korea's and Japan's histories are no different. I did my best to concentrate on direct consequences upon individuals rather than on an entire nation or people. I also hoped to impress that the wars in Korea were global in nature with many belligerents taking part, not just Korea and Japan. As this is a work of fiction, some historical inaccuracies may arise throughout, namely time and locations of certain events that took place. None were done on purpose or with intent. Growing up with a South Korean mother and influenced by her community of expat women friends, I am fascinated by their ability to overcome the hardships they faced as girls and young women in South Korea with laughter and community. As a tribute to those women, I included a song ('Ga Si Ri') and a lyric poem ('Je Mang Me Ga') in this book that were translated by my friend and teacher, Jeong Sook Lee. The song is of unknown authorship, originating between the tenth and fourteenth centuries, but it is well known among schoolchildren in South Korea. I wanted Hana to have a humorous memory during an uncertain moment by remembering her father being silly so that laughter filled their humble home. The lyric poem is about the loss of a dear sister and the hope to one day reunite with her in the afterlife. Losing a loved one touches each and every one of us at some point in our lives and, sometimes, the pain never diminishes. I know that for my mother and her friends, the pain will last a lifetime, but remembering their stories helps them to endure it.

War is terrible, brutal and unfair, and when it ends, apologies must be given, reparations made and survivors' experiences remembered. Germany set a positive example, admitting to and compensating for their government's crimes against the Jews perpetrated during World War II, while also committing to the remembrance of this dark part of their history. It is my hope that subsequent governments would follow in their footsteps. It is our duty to educate future generations of the real and terrible truths committed during war, not to hide them or pretend they never happened. We must remember them so that the mistakes of the past are not repeated. History books, songs, novels, plays, films and memorials are essential to help us to never forget, while also helping us to move forward in peace.

– Mary Lynn Bracht

Acknowledgements

A story often undergoes many transformations before it becomes a book, and I am grateful to have had the support of so many people during this amazing process. Double thanks to my editors, Tara Singh Carlson and Becky Hardie, for their support and suggestions throughout the editing process. I am so fortunate to have worked with you both, as well as with Charlotte Humphery and Helen Richard. My wonderful agent, Rowan Lawton, and the staff at Furniss Lawton, thank you for believing in my novel and in me. Liane-Louise Smith and Isha Karki, your dedication and positivity helped in so many ways, thank you. My friends in the Willesden Green Writers' Group – Lynn, Clare, Anne, Lily, Naa and Steve – thank you for listening to the many versions of this work in progress, your comments were so helpful. To my teachers at Birkbeck College – Mary Flanagan, Helen Harris, Courttia Newland and Sue Tyley – thank you for your guidance and instruction. To all my family and friends, thank you for your love and support over the years. A heartfelt thank-you to Tony for encouraging me to pursue my dream. And most of all, thank you to my wonderful son whose love and acceptance helped me to reach it.

Notable Dates

1905   Korea becomes protectorate of Japan, ending the Korean Empire.

1910   Japan annexes Korea; Korean traditions and culture are repressed.

1931   Japan invades and occupies Manchuria.

1932   The puppet state Manchukuo is created by Japan.

1937   Second Sino-Japanese War begins; China receives help from Germany, the Soviet Union and the United States, setting the stage for the conflict to merge into the Second World War.

1938   Japan begins active assimilation programme for colonised Koreans; practice of Korean customs – including language, worship, art and music – becomes illegal.

1939   Japan enforces mobilisation of Korean men and women for the war effort.

1941   Japan attacks Pearl Harbor. The Second Sino-Japanese War becomes part of the Pacific War and the Second World War.

1945   August: US drops atomic bombs on Hiroshima and Nagasaki.

Soviets declare war on Japan, invade Manchuria, and enter North Korea.

Japan surrenders unconditionally to the Allied forces.

Second World War ends.

As part of the Japanese surrender, Korea is split into the Soviet-controlled North and the US-controlled South along the Thirty-Eighth Parallel. US occupation forces arrive in South Korea.

December: The US, UK, Soviet Union and Republic of China establish a four-way trusteeship of Korea until it can put a single government in place. After this, plans for a unified national government falter as Cold War divisions between the Soviet Union and US increase.

1948   April: Jeju Uprising and Massacre (also known as the Jeju 4-3 or 4.3 Uprising).

August: After unsupervised, democratic election on 10 May, Republic of Korea formally established in the South with Syngman Rhee as its first president.

September: Democratic People's Republic of Korea established in the North, Kim Il-sung becomes premier.

October: Soviet Union declares Kim Il-sung's government sovereign over both North and South Korea.

December: UN declares Rhee's government the only lawful government; US refuses to offer military aid to the South but the Soviet Union heavily reinforces the North.

Soviet Union withdraws troops from Korea.

1949   January: Chinese Nationalist leader Chiang Kai-shek resigns as
        president.

        US withdraws troops from Korea, ending Allied occupation of
        Korea.

        October: Mao Zedong establishes the People's Republic of China.

1950   June: Korean War (also known as the 6-2-5 Upheaval, or 6.25
        War) begins when North Korea breaches the Thirty-Eighth
        Parallel, invading South Korea. North Korea is supported by
        the Soviet Union and China, South Korea is supported by the
        US and the rest of the UN. More than 1.2 million people will be
        killed in the conflict.

1953   Korean War ends, leaving the division between the Democratic
        People's Republic of Korea in the North and the Republic of
        Korea in the South intact. Since the peace treaty was never
        signed by South Korea, the two countries are still officially
        at war.

1991   Kim Hak-sun tells her story of being a victim of Japanese mili-
        tary sexual slavery at a press conference and files a lawsuit
        against the Japanese government.

1992   January: First Wednesday Demonstration in Seoul.

        December: Election of South Korea's first civilian president,
        Kim Young-sam.

1993   August: Kono Statement issued by Japanese government confirm-
        ing coercion used to entrap 'comfort women' against their will.

2007   Japanese government retracts the statement.

2011   December: 1,000th Wednesday Demonstration takes place in
        Seoul; unveiling of the *Statue of Peace*.

2015   Japanese and South Korean governments announce a 'landmark agreement' on the 'comfort women' issue – to remove the *Statue of Peace* and never speak of the 'comfort women' issue again.

Further Reading

If you're interested in learning more about Korea's history, Mongolia, the wars in Asia, or other subjects touched on in this novel, like the *haenyeo* divers, this reading list contains many of the books that helped me during my research, as well as a few* that inspired me to write it.

1. *A History of East Asia: From the Origins of Civilization to the Twenty-First Century* by Charles Holcombe
2. *A History of Korean Literature* by Peter H. Lee
3. *Deep: Freediving, Renegade Science, and What the Ocean Tells Us About Ourselves* by James Nestor
4. *Dictionary of Wars: Revised Edition* by George Childs Kohn
5. *Echoes from the Steppe: An Anthology of Contemporary Mongolian Women's Poetry*, edited by Ruth O'Callaghan
6. *Everlasting Flower: A History of Korea* by Keith Pratt
7. **Half the Sky: How to Change the World* by Nicholas D. Kristof and Sheryl Wudunn
8. *Hirohito's War: The Pacific War, 1941–1945* by Francis Pike

9. *Hunting with Eagles: In the Realm of the Mongolian Kazakhs* by Palani Mohan

10. *Inferno: The World at War, 1939–1945* by Max Hastings

11. *In Manchuria: A Village Called Wasteland and the Transformation of Rural China* by Michael Meyer

12. *Japan 1941* by Eri Hotta

13. *Journey to a War* by W. H. Auden and Christopher Isherwood

14. *Korea* by Simon Winchester

15. *Korea: A Historical and Cultural Dictionary* by Keith Pratt and Richard Rutt

16. *Legacies of the Comfort Women of World War II*, edited by Margaret Stetz and Bonnie B. C. Oh

17. *Lost Names* by Richard Kim

18. *Mongolia: Nomad Empire of Eternal Blue Sky* by Carl Robinson

19. *Moon Tides: Jeju Island Grannies of the Sea* by Brenda Paik Sunoo

20. *Moral Nation: Modern Japan and Narcotics in Global History* by Miriam Kingsberg

21. *Riding the Iron Rooster* by Paul Theroux

22. *The Cloud Dream of the Nine* by Kim ManChoong

23. *The Comfort Women: Japan's Brutal Regime of Enforced Prostitution in the Second World War* by George Hicks

24. *The Comfort Women: Sexual Violence and Postcolonial Memory in Korea and Japan* by C. Sarah Soh

25. *The Hidden History of the Korean War: America's First Vietnam* by I. F. Stone

26. *The Hundred Years' War: Modern War Poems*, edited by Neil Astley

27. *The Mongol Empire* by John Man

28. *The Other Nuremberg: The Untold Story of the Tokyo War Crimes Trials* by Arnold C. Brackman

29. **The Rape of Nanking: The Forgotten Holocaust of World War II* by Iris Chang

30. *The Second World War: A Complete History* by Martin Gilbert

31. *The Wars for Asia, 1911–1949* by S. C. M. Paine

32. *The Woman Warrior* by Maxine Hong Kingston
33. *Travels in Manchuria and Mongolia: A Feminist Poet from Japan Encounters Prewar China* by Yosano Akiko, translated by Joshua A. Fogel
34. **True Stories of the Korean Comfort Women*, edited by Keith Howard
35. *When My Name Was Keoko* by Linda Soon Park
36. *When Sorry Isn't Enough: The Controversies over Apologies and Reparations for Human Injustice*, edited by Roy L. Brooks
37. *World War II in Photographs* by Robin Cross
38. *1914: Goodbye to All That*, edited by Lavinia Greenlaw